MORE PRAISE FOR
The House of Tomorrow

"Unexpectedly pits the teachings of R. Buckminster Fuller, architect, philosopher, and futurist, against the misanthropy of punk. There's only going to be one winner, but it is a measure of Bognanni's empathy that his narrator's decision is never an easy one . . . Sebastian—part Candide, part Christopher Boone from *The Curious Incident of the Dog in the Night-Time*—has landed deep inside the world of Rick Moody's *Ice Storm*."
—*The New York Times Book Review*

"As an author from the *High Fidelity* and *Rock 'n' Roll High School* [school] of thought, Peter Bognanni has written a book that is as rife with confidence, hurt, friendship, and tender heartache as it is with teenage angst and balls-out punk rawk!"
—*Girl About Town*

"At its best, Peter Bognanni's *House of Tomorrow* is tight and quick enough to pull you into its rhythm. It draws its audience in the way a steady bass line does—to the waxing and waning of the story's tides . . . Bognanni's ability to recall the anger, fear, and yearnings of being sixteen as well as the rush of possibilities on the horizon is also what makes the book so engaging."
—*The Boston Globe*

"I adore this book, not only for its ability to love our ludicrous hearts but also for the way it makes dividing questions about whether good literature comes from the heart or the mind seem like nonsense."
—Rivka Galchen, author of *Atmospheric Disturbances*

"A character-driven, funny novel about loneliness and the attitudes we adopt—whether scientific detachment or teen sass—to mask our essential need for one another . . . a beguiling coming-of-age story whose particular, eccentric charm plays true."
—*The Kansas City Star*

continued . . .

"*The House of Tomorrow*, as its title and premise promise, marries the visionary with the everyday, the whiz-bang with the domestic, and does it with beauty, humor, and love for each one of its flawed characters. Peter Bognanni remembers all the romance and awkwardness of teen life and teen music. His first novel is headlong, hilarious, heartbreaking."

—Elizabeth McCracken

"A young man lives with his grandmother in a geodesic dome in Iowa. No surprise: He's a total oddball. Yes, surprise: His life makes for a sweet novel."

—*O, The Oprah Magazine*

"The mantra recited every morning by the main character in Peter Bognanni's novel *The House of Tomorrow*: 'I will use my mind, not just my regular brain lobes.' (I like that more every time I read it.)" —*New York*

"Under the screaming rage of a Misfits or Ramones song, you can hear a heart beating, and that's where Peter Bognanni gets to work—his wild and tender book reveals how much a couple of scared boys can say to each other with a little hateful noise." —Rob Sheffield, author of *Love Is a Mix Tape*

"In this winningly precocious debut novel, a teenager raised in a geodesic dome by an R. Buckminster Fuller–obsessed grandmother escapes from captivity, discovers the Misfits, and explores the mystical outside world of adolescent rebelling and crap punk rock." —*Details*

"Funny and unique . . . An honest, noisy, and raucous look at friendship and how loud music can make almost everything better."

—*Publishers Weekly* (starred review)

"It's sort of like the next *Gilbert Grape*." —*The Des Moines Register*

"This interesting array of characters and emphasis on a first introduction to music make this novel an enjoyable read. If you love music, have ever felt like an outcast, or live in Hobbit Hollow, I highly recommend you pick up this book."
—*Petoskey (MI) News*

"Explores the unlikely friendship of two social outcasts and their desperation to be heard . . . fun and lively."
—*Booklist*

"Peter Bognanni would probably not appreciate the word 'sweet' being used to describe his punk-rock-fueled debut novel, *The House of Tomorrow*, but parts of the story are decidedly so. *The House of Tomorrow* is a hard-edged but heartrending story of growing up strange in a small Midwestern town. Anyone who's been there is sure to relate to Sebastian and Jared—and to hope that The Rash lives on beyond its monumental and unforgettable debut."
—*BookPage*

"Refreshingly, he is not interested in street cred or the namedropping that can spoil a punk novel—Bognanni is interested in depicting adolescence as it really is . . . *The House of Tomorrow* isn't *London Calling* or *Pink Flag*—but it is a welcome addition to the recent collection of punk rock *bildungsromans* . . . as truly pleasurable an achievement as the Misfits' *Collection I*."
—*The Rumpus*

THE HOUSE OF
TOMORROW

PETER BOGNANNI

BERKLEY BOOKS, NEW YORK

A BERKLEY BOOK

Published by the Penguin Group

Penguin Group (USA) Inc.

375 Hudson Street, New York, New York 10014, USA

Penguin Group (Canada), 90 Eglinton Avenue East, Suite 700, Toronto, Ontario M4P 2Y3, Canada (a division of
Pearson Penguin Canada Inc.) · Penguin Books Ltd., 80 Strand, London WC2R 0RL, England · Penguin Group
Ireland, 25 St. Stephen's Green, Dublin 2, Ireland (a division of Penguin Books Ltd.) · Penguin Group (Australia),
250 Camberwell Road, Camberwell, Victoria 3124, Australia (a division of Pearson Australia Group Pty. Ltd.) ·
Penguin Books India Pvt. Ltd., 11 Community Centre, Panchsheel Park, New Delhi—110 017, India · Penguin
Group (NZ), 67 Apollo Drive, Rosedale, North Shore 0632, New Zealand (a division of Pearson New Zealand Ltd.) ·
Penguin Books (South Africa) (Pty.) Ltd., 24 Sturdee Avenue, Rosebank, Johannesburg 2196, South Africa
Penguin Books Ltd., Registered Offices: 80 Strand, London WC2R 0RL, England

This is a work of fiction. Names, characters, places, and incidents either are the product of the author's imagination or
are used fictitiously, and any resemblance to actual persons, living or dead, business establishments, events, or locales
is entirely coincidental.

While the author has made every effort to provide accurate telephone numbers and Internet addresses at the time of
publication, neither the publisher nor the author assumes any responsibility for errors or for changes that occur after
publication. Further, the publisher does not have any control over and does not assume any responsibility for author or
third-party websites or their content.

PRINTING HISTORY
Amy Einhorn hardcover edition / March 2010
Berkley trade paperback edition / March 2011

Berkley trade paperback ISBN: 978-0-425-23888-2

The Library of Congress has cataloged the Amy Einhorn hardcover edition as follows:

Bognanni, Peter.
    The house of tomorrow / Peter Bognanni.
        p.   cm.
    ISBN 978-0-399-15609-0
    1. Young men—Fiction.   2. Grandmothers—Fiction.   3. Fuller, R. Buckminster (Richard Buckminster).
1895–1983—Influence—Fiction.   4. Social isolation—Fiction.   5. Maturation (Psychology)—Fiction.   I. Title.
    PS3602.O428H68   2010   2009023542
    813'.6—dc22

PRINTED IN THE UNITED STATES OF AMERICA
10   9   8   7   6   5   4   3   2   1

For my family, and of course, Junita

Everyone is born a genius, but the process of living de-geniuses them.

—R. BUCKMINSTER FULLER

Gabba gabba. We accept you. We accept you as one of us!

—THE RAMONES

1. Welcome to the Future

EVERY SINGLE HUMAN BEING IS PART OF A GRAND universal plan. That's what my Nana always says. We're not alive just to lounge around and contemplate our umbilicus. We're metaphysical beings! Open us up, and there's more rattling around in there than just brain sacs and fatty tissue. We are full of imperceptible essences. Invisible spectrums. Patterns. Ideas. We're containers of awesome phenomena! Which is why it's important to live right. You have to be attuned to what's around you, and you have to keep from clogging your receptors with crap. According to my Nana, the universe is sending signals every day, and it's up to us whether or not we want to listen. We can either perk up our ears, or walk around like dead piles of dermis. I always preferred the former. Which is why I found myself up on top of the roof of our dome on that fall Sunday when everything began.

I couldn't tell you for certain that I'd ever heard messages from space up there, but at the very least I had a tremendous view. Hanging in the brisk October air, Anver heavy-duty suction cups on my hands, and a no-slip rubber guard harness around my chest, I could see the entire town of North Branch arranged with the uniformity of an architectural model. It stretched below me like a wide lake of split-level dwellings, flowing over the small hills and dips in the eastern Iowa landscape. And above the horizon was the endless ice-blue troposphere, nearly unobstructed save for the waving branches of our black walnut trees.

It was this towering group of trees that gave me my official reason for ascending to the top of the dome that Sunday. Every autumn they bombarded our translucent roof with pungent green-shelled nuts the size of tennis balls, and it was my job to climb the walls like a salamander and scrub away the stains. For this purpose, I kept a large squeegee strapped to my back along with a small bucket of orange-scented cleaning solution. And once attached to the glass, I scrubbed each insulated panel, and kept an eye on my Nana inside at the same time. Right beneath me, through a soapy triangle of glass, I could see her on her NordicTrack, grinding away. *Click-Clackita Click-Clackita Click-Clackita*. The sound was like a distant Zephyr train.

Just the day before, she had told me that most human beings only saw a hundred-thousandth of the world in their lifetime. Maybe a ten-thousandth if they traveled a lot. Only she called the world "Spaceship Earth," because that's what Buckminster Fuller called it, and she thought he was humanity's last real genius. Either way, I was sure I could see my entire portion from this spot. Up on top of the dome, my view was quite possibly someone's whole lifetime.

"Sebastian!" Nana called from below, her voice echoing off the glass. "Are you watching for visitors up there?"

She stood outside now, squinting up at me.

"Affirmative!" I yelled. "No sightings at present."

Nana called the weekend tourists to our home "visitors," as if they were alighting on our lawn from other galaxies in blinking mother ships. In reality, most of them made the trip in large automobiles, and it was my job to spot them from my perch. It was early yet for visitors, though. Every Saturday and Sunday we opened our home to the public at nine o'clock sharp, but it was usually ten or ten-thirty before anyone arrived. According to Nana, people in the Midwest had to finish with church before they could seek any leisure. They had to exalt and repent, and perhaps attend potlucks.

We had begun giving tours a few years back because our home was the first Geodesic Dome ever constructed in Iowa, and there seemed to be some interest in that fact. In truth, we were only a moderate-to-marginal tourist attraction, but most years we made enough to supplement Nana's modest pension, which is all we needed. No matter how much we brought in, though, I was supposed to behave as if we were overrun with business. Negative thinking sent out the wrong kind of messages to the higher powers, Nana said. Each negative thought was like a hemorrhoid to the controlling forces of the universe. It burned them endlessly.

"Make sure to get the northwest side, Sebastian!" Nana shouted now. "I spotted some bird waste over there. Then come down for breakfast. I need to speak with you."

"Will do," I said.

I took a deep inhalation of chill air and began pressing and releasing my suction cups, moving over the apex of the dome to tend to the bird stains. At the age of sixteen, I was already the same height my father had been when he passed away, and my lanky frame covered a surprising amount of space on the dome. When I adjusted myself perfectly on the top, every major landmark in town was visible with the naked eye.

If I looked to the east, for example, I could see the slanted water tower that read "North Branch Beavers" in rust-colored lettering. Farther north was the symmetrical row of small businesses in the town square. Then past the businesses, a little to the west, was the giant brick castle of James K. Polk High School, which I was not allowed to attend because Nana said their worldview was myopic and wrong. And finally, to the far west, I could see all four lanes of the expressway, including the exact exit that the tourists took to visit us. I couldn't see our garish billboards, but I knew they were there, facing the road, imploring every motorist to visit "The House of Tomorrow."

I scraped my squeegee slowly over the last of the stains, and then pressed and released all the way down to the brittle grass of our lawn. I had seen on the World Wide Web once that a man from France climbed the Empire State Building with just his hands and feet. No cups. No harness. He was arrested, but he claimed it was worth it to know he was really alive. It was a secret goal of mine to one day scale our dome in this fashion, but for now I played it safe. My sneakers touched the ground with a satisfying crunch, and I undid my harness and let it drop to the ground. I walked around to the front yard and turned the knob on our clear front door.

There sat Nana in our open dining room, imbibing one of her signature smoothies. Every day, she performed the morning ritual of dumping things in her Vita-Mix, a machine that pulverized her breakfast. Anything that could fit through the clear plastic shaft was fair game for one of these shakes. This morning, the concoction was the same color fuchsia as her tracksuit. She owned a rainbow of these sleek workout suits, and this particular one was made of pink, sweat-resistant fibers and had a matching headband for her shock of flour-white hair.

"Oh, Sebastian," she said, glancing up at me. "You look like a cave dweller, or one of those horrible men who collect all the lumber."

"A lumberjack?"

"Yes," she said. "Exactly. One of those."

I was wearing the same blue flannel shirt and jeans that I always wore. But my dirty-blond hair had gotten a tad shaggy around the ears. I pushed it off my forehead and sat down. Nana leaned over and kissed the top of my head.

"Is your room arranged to specification?" she asked, her mouth hovering back over her straw.

"Affirmative," I said.

"Have you performed your toilet?"

"With startling success," I said.

"A yes or no answer would be adequate," she said.

She sipped again on her smoothie, then frowned and let the straw rest against the lip of the glass. "Well, enough idle chatter," she said. "We need to have a conference."

I moved in closer and watched her face. It was inexplicably tight for a woman of her age. You had to stare at it closely before you could begin to find the thin wrinkles, like hairline cracks, in the firm skin around her mouth and eyes. And it was only when she glowered or furrowed her brow in the deepest of concentration that you could tell that she had lived nearly eighty years on this earth.

"I'll be direct with you, Sebastian," she said. "The heating bill is going up this month, and we need to maximize all sales efforts in the gift shop. Do you read me?"

"I think so."

She slurped at her shake.

"Additional capital must be raised. I need you to try to sell a photograph today. That's your quota," she said.

I sighed softly.

"What?" she said. "What is that dramatic breathing?"

"The photographs are costly," I said.

"The photographs are art objects," she snapped, "and they are priced accordingly."

I sighed again.

"Would it surprise you to know that your numbers are down since August?" she asked.

"I don't know."

"Well, they are. They're down."

I avoided her stare, but I could still feel it on me.

"An education means knowing how to do everything. Including things you don't have a predilection for. You should have seen the way Bucky made things salable. He could make men salivate over a new kind of winch. A winch!"

"Bucky" was R. Buckminster Fuller, Nana's onetime colleague and personal hero. He was the inventor of the Geodesic Dome, among other things, and, according to Nana, "the most unappreciated genius in all of human history." His life's work had been dedicated to futurist inventions and ideas, which he thought could eliminate all negative human behavior. Fuller dabbled in everything: architecture, physics, engineering, cosmology, design, and poetry. And he dreamed of creating a "Spaceship Earth" where every human could prosper and grow. Nana had worked with him at Southern Illinois University in her younger days. And by the time she was finished in his company, there wasn't a single one of his ideas she disagreed with.

This included his belief that Nana, aka Josephine Prendergast, was the most beautiful and vibrant woman he'd ever met. Nana claims to have been Bucky's mistress for two years, though it has never been mentioned in the biographies I've read. Whatever their relationship, though, I had been homeschooled almost exclusively according to his philosophy. And these were the guiding principles that were tacked directly above my bed:

1. Every day I will give myself wholly to futurist thinking. Not to useless past thinking, which will steer me very far off course.
2. I will learn all the organizing processes of the universe, so I may use them to accomplish startling feats of triumph.
3. I will use my mind, not just my regular brain lobes.
4. I will forge my journey alone to keep accepted and totally boneheaded notions from blinding me to truth.

I woke up every morning and read this credo. If Nana was in the room, I read it aloud. If she wasn't, I did not. Either way, it kept my focus sharp for the hours ahead.

Outside now, a teal minivan passed and we both turned to look west at the top of the hill. This was the place where the road from town passed our drive. The van didn't stop.

"I'd better change," said Nana. "Meeting dismissed."

But she didn't move. She just placed a hand on top of mine. Her palm was cold from gripping the smoothie. She stared at an indistinguishable spot outside. I looked, too, but I couldn't see anything. I felt her pulse ticking through her palm.

"Nana?" I said.

She snapped back and looked at me as if for the first time.

"You have your father's eyes," she said. "Have I informed you of that before?"

"You have," I said.

"They are very striking eyes. They haven't dulled a bit since your childhood."

"Are you all right?" I said.

She rose from her chair, using my thin shoulder for leverage. Then she walked off toward her bedroom, slower than usual. If I had really been attuned to her patterns that morning, I probably would have noticed something was amiss. She hadn't mentioned my father in over a year. He had died, along with my mother, in a Cessna crash more than ten years ago. We almost never spoke about it.

"Can't I talk about how handsome my boy is?" Nana said over her shoulder. "Is that some kind of unlawful act?"

She walked out of sight. I looked outside a second time and saw the teal minivan drifting past the dome again. This time it slowed down and idled for a moment in the street. The glass on the windshield was tinted, so I couldn't view any of the passengers inside. It lurched forward and docked in our semicircular drive.

I stood up and tucked in my shirt. I forced myself to start thinking about a sale in the gift shop. Nana was right; it would probably have to be a photo. But maybe a Bucky Ball would do. The Bucky Balls were glow-in-the-dark plastic dome balls that you could kick or throw or hang from a ceiling. They retailed at $29.95. But the framed photographs were fifty dollars even, and they featured our dome, lit up from the inside against a scene of night woods. Nana took this photo herself, and if you looked closely at it, you could see my tube-socked foot coming out of a bedroom closet. I had been hiding in there to stay out of the way, but my sock had lurked out at the exact moment of the flash. No customers ever saw it, though, unless I pointed it out.

I was not allowed to point it out.

I was not allowed to say much of anything to the visitors, really. Aside from the fragments of conversation I employed for my sales tactics, I was supposed to remain a silent operative. Most of the time this was painless enough; the people from town were often loud and very intent on telling me jokes I didn't understand. But every once in a while, I could hardly contain my impulse to speak up to a boy or girl my age. Someone like me who was also so very much not like me. Those were the moments I could feel my credo slipping to the back of my mind, and something else taking over.

Outside, the driver's-side door of the van opened and a short middle-aged woman stepped out in high-heeled shoes and brown kneesocks. She had flushed cheeks and large eyes, and she wore a long tan wool coat with a cyan scarf wrapped around her neck at least three times. Her black hair was tied in a braid. She peered up at the dome, a hand at her forehead like a scout's. Then, turning on a dime, she walked over to the back door of the van and slid it open. She leaned in and a pale hand took hers. Then she gave a quick tug and a ghostly teenager emerged from the van dressed completely in black.

He wore a leather jacket with straps, buckles, and snapped epaulets. And under the jacket there was a T-shirt made to resemble the front of a tuxedo. He had skinny black jeans and frayed canvas sneakers. He was even thinner than I was and wore squarish glasses. A thick lock of uncombed dark hair hung over the top of the frames like a dirty wave. Tiny headphones were buried in his ears.

He kneeled for a moment on the concrete of the driveway, retying a broken shoelace, a deep scowl on his face, then sprang up and followed the woman, who was already plodding toward our door. I walked outside to my station at the gift stand. The woman clacked up the drive and smiled at me through the little open window in my stand. She paused a moment, then stuck a pink hand right inside.

"Janice Whitcomb," she said.

I shook the hand.

"Sebastian," I said. "Welcome to the future."

Janice smiled politely. "That's my son, Jared," she said.

The boy stood behind her, adjusting the volume control on a music player of some kind. He looked even smaller and frailer up close. His jacket hung on him like a leather poncho.

"Don't bother speaking to him," she said quickly. "He's mad at me, so he's playing his music. He stays inside too much since he got out of the hospital, so I thought I'd get him outside in the elements today. I don't think he's pleased."

I nodded and smiled at Janice.

"I passed this place on the way to a conference once," she said, "and then this morning it just popped back into my head. I got up and I said, 'Jared, we're going to see that fascinating bubble on the hill today. And we're going to learn something from it.'"

I looked at Jared again. His magnified green eyes were like beacons.

"Here's admission for both of us," she said, and handed me a twenty. "Are you the tour guide, Sebastian?"

"Oh, no," I said, "my Nana will be happy to . . ."

I stopped at that point and realized that she wasn't there. Usually, Nana was outside in her special tour pantsuit at the slightest sound of a muffler. I gave Janice her change. "She'll be out in sixty seconds," I said. "Give or take."

She looked toward the dome then, studying it anew. I wanted to ask her more about Jared. But I sensed that he had turned down the volume on his music and was listening and observing now. His eyes were locked on the photograph of the dome, sitting in the display window. He seemed to consider it deeply. I watched his eyes scan every room, moving up from the living room.

Janice took a deep breath and shivered a little. "Probably the last of the real fall days," she said.

"Is that a fucking sock in there?" asked Jared.

His voice was grating, high-pitched. Janice and I both turned to look at him.

"What did you just say?" she asked.

"I see a sock in that picture," Jared said. "That's all I'm saying."

"Jared!" said his mother. "What's the matter with you? Don't you have any sense of . . ."

But Janice was not given time to finish her question. Because, at that moment, Nana burst out of the house dressed completely in her pantsuit, waving her arms over her head, as if signaling for a rescue.

"Welcome, visitors!" she said. "Greetings. Greetings."

Nana's hair was a bit out of place. But she carried two stickers on her fingertips. They were black-and-white, with a cartoon of Buckminster Fuller's bespectacled head in the center, a wry grin on his face. Nana fastened one on Janice's wool lapel. She pressed the other one on Jared's T-shirt, directly on his left nipple.

"We'll start inside right away," said Nana, immediately shepherding us over the lawn. "Welcome to the future."

"I already told them," I said.

"Oh," she said, and laughed a little too long.

"Nana," I said when she was finished, "maybe you should slow down a little, I . . ."

She interrupted me with a pinch on the side. Then she gave me a confident grin and tromped ahead of me. We proceeded right into the dome, past the NordicTrack, into the very center of the living room. There was something wrong with Nana's appearance that I couldn't put my finger on. As she cleared her throat to begin her speech, I looked down at her arch-supported dress shoes and discovered what it was.

They were on the wrong feet.

"In his famous book *Operating Manual for Spaceship Earth*," said Nana, looking up, "R. Buckminster Fuller, the greatest mind of our age, states that in order for mankind to progress, 'We must first discover where we are now; that is, what our present navigational position in the universal scheme of evolution is.'"

She paused a moment and caught me looking down. She glanced at her feet, and then her eyes met mine. It only took a second, but her face changed entirely. Her eyes unfocused. Her teeth found her bottom lip. The Whitcombs were still gazing skyward.

"And you see," she continued, a little slower, "when you stand in the very center of a Geodesic Dome, you have the sensation of being propelled right out into the cosmos. Like the universe is sucking you out. This, as Bucky said, is really one of the most intriguing of paradoxes: in order to expand outward, we must go . . . inward."

After "inward," Nana stopped speaking and stared up at the center point of the dome. We all looked up with her. The few clouds that hung above us were small and gauzy. The wind was blowing, whistling over the dome. A few feet in front of us were our kitchen cabinets, hovering over the counter, hung from the ceiling by tension wires. Nana coughed and tried to speak again. And that was when it happened.

My name was all that came out. Only she ran it all together so it sounded like "Sebas-yan." Then she took an uneasy step backward.

"I think I follow what you were saying," said Janice, still looking up. "Go on . . ."

I observed Nana's face closely. It was becoming partly splotched with red. And her mouth was tightening. Just as I noticed this, she reached out a hand to grab me. It seemed to happen in slow motion, but I couldn't tell what she was attempting. Her fingers didn't quite make it to my blue flannel. Before anyone could react, she let out a long breath and then tipped straight backward, crumpling to the thin carpet of the dome floor. The dull thump reverberated through the space.

"Oh!" said Mrs. Whitcomb, looking down immediately. "Oh my God! Are you all right?"

She bent over Nana. Nana said nothing. She seemed to be holding her breath. I stood completely frozen. Next to me, Jared very slowly removed his headphones.

"Oh God!" Mrs. Whitcomb yelled. "Is there a phone in this place? Where's the telephone?"

I pointed her toward the cordless phone, and she sprinted toward it in her heels. A bit of spit was forming at the corners of Nana's mouth. Suddenly, I felt a bony hand clap down on my shoulder. I turned around, and it was Jared. He had a grave expression on his face. "Hey," he said. "Hold her hand."

His voice was oddly calm. I didn't question him. I got down on my knees and grabbed Nana's palm. It was warm and I held it tightly. I was unable to think at all. I just looked over her anguished face, and massaged the hard nubs of the knuckles. I couldn't remember the last time I had even seen her resting. She was always up. Always in motion. Jared got down on the floor across from me. He picked up the other hand and pressed it tight. We looked at each other.

"Sebastian, right?" he said.

"Yes," I said.

"This is fucked," he said.

Behind us in the kitchen, Janice Whitcomb was starting to cry into the phone.

"We just came to tour the bubble!" she yelled. "I don't know anything about her condition."

Meanwhile Jared and I held tight to Nana's hands, and I thought for a moment that maybe, somehow, we were allowing life energy to course through her spindly frame. Like she was the middle link between our two life-energy links, and if we could just hold on, everything else would be fine. I listened intently for a signal from the universe. But all was quiet.

"Jared," I said.

"Yeah," he said.

"You were right."

"About what?"

His enormous fish eyes blinked twice.

"There's a sock in that picture."

2. A Metaphysical Connection

BUCKMINSTER FULLER ONCE SAID THAT THE BIGGEST problem with Spaceship Earth is that it came with no instruction booklet. No directions whatsoever. We have to figure it all out by ourselves and that is some incredibly grueling work. Where do we begin? What methods do we use? How do we know when we've arrived at the right answers? I thought about all this while I waited in the dome, looking frequently into the wide eyes of my barely conscious Nana. There was no manual for her, either, I realized. There was no manual for any of this. All I could do was wait and see how the forces would respond.

They took approximately fourteen minutes to arrive. They came in the form of a blaring ambulance. When it pulled up, I watched as the uniformed men fanned out and then stopped to look up at my home with stupefied expressions on their faces. They were hypnotized by standing so close to something they must have seen often from the highway. But they remembered their duties shortly and gathered in the dome, loading my grandmother onto a neon orange stretcher.

Nana was motionless for the duration, but her absent gaze remained steadily focused on me. I stayed as close as I could, and gripped her hand as long as possible. Eventually I was forced to let go. The men in jumpsuits gave her short pulls from an oxygen cylinder and rushed her across the lawn and toward the open jaws of the emergency transport. They ushered me inside to a padded bench. The Whitcombs, Janice shouted, would trail in their van.

I sat unmoving for the first moments of the ride, my palms slick on my denim-covered knees. I could only watch Nana's sallow face. Her closed eyes. Her slack mouth. But she was respiring. I watched her frail chest rise and fall. She sucked air through the clear mask and pushed it back out. Finally, I reached out and clutched her pointer finger in the grip of my left hand.

I was too shocked to cry. And I also knew it would not please Nana. Crying is nearly all I had done when I first moved into the dome after my parents' death. It pained Nana greatly, and she immediately took measures to make it cease. At first I wept all through the night, and wet my new bed too many times to count. Eventually, Nana stayed the night with me to keep me calm. She slept next to me on a single mattress for the entire first two months. And every night she told me a different reason why it was completely normal to live in our globe.

"The dome structure has been used since humans first began building homes," she'd say. "And there's a reason why, Sebastian. Sailors landing in foreign countries would turn their ships upside down and stay the night under there to be safe. They realized how much space it provided with such few materials. The people of Afghanistan have lived in circular tents called yurts for years. And of course, you know about igloos. But did you know the strongest shape in all of geometry is the triangle? Our house is made of equilateral triangles, Sebastian. We have the strongest house on earth."

These had been my bedtime stories, along with anecdotes from

Buckminster Fuller's life. And in time, I came to believe that the dome was a secure place. I even took a shine to it. The acoustics, for example, continually roused my childhood imagination. There were places in the dome where you could whisper, and someone else would hear you clearly on the opposite side. Nana and I knew all the echo spots, and we used this feature as our personal intercom system. Eventually, this new habitat, full of peculiarities (a misting "Fog Gun" shower! A toilet that packed waste for fertilizer!) became as ordinary to me as anything else. So when it came time to start school, Nana fashioned a small classroom upstairs, across from my bedroom. And that's the way things had operated since. Work, play, and school, all under one great pellucid roof.

After a short time riding, the ambulance hit a small bump, and Nana nearly toppled off her gurney onto the floor. I jumped from my seat, but a paramedic grabbed her roughly in order to keep her steady. I saw, though, that she was not able to secure herself. If the man hadn't steadied her, she would have flopped to the ground like a giant fish. It was at that moment that everything began to take hold. The veil of shock lifted and I wondered, plainly, if I would ever spend a night in the dome with Nana again.

We arrived at the hospital soon after and the men unloaded Nana with unbelievable deftness. They dragged the gurney toward the white double doors headfirst. Before she disappeared through, she opened her eyes for a moment and looked at me again. It seemed like she wanted to say something, but I had no clue what it was. Her lips moved. They formed no discernible words. I stared back, unsure what to do. But by the time I raised my hand to wave, it was too late. The soles of her dress shoes (still on the wrong feet) were receding into the well-lit passageway, and the doors were swinging shut.

————

IN THE LOBBY, THE WHITCOMBS WERE THERE AS promised. They were the only people in the room aside from a hunched security guard watching a TV bolted to the wall, and a tiny woman in a turtleneck murmuring into a telephone. The room was another world entirely from the white tiles of the hospital proper. Here, there was soft light, coral-colored carpeting, and a machine full of nonperishables.

Also, there was cola. Janice handed me one when I sat down between her and Jared, and I triggered the top. I had only drunk soda twice before. Once with my parents when I was young, and once on a hot summer errand by bicycle to pick up an allergy prescription for Nana in town. In the hospital lobby that Sunday, I had my third. A glacially cold can of Royal Crown. The first sip was so sweet I nearly gagged. My tongue burned from the carbonation, and my eyes leaked a few tears. Janice saw them and patted me on the back. After each pat, she rubbed.

Next to me on the other side, Jared sat staring at the bolted television. Sitting down, he looked even smaller and more emaciated. Like a malnourished nestling. There was barely the outline of a body under his voluminous jacket. And his skin was so white it was almost translucent. I could see the washed blue of the veins in his neck and just above his ears. Yet there was something older in his eyes, in his stare. It was difficult to discern his age.

For the first few moments, no one said anything. But eventually, Janice took my hand in hers. Her palms were warm and dry. "How are you holding up, Sebastian?" she asked. "Would it bother you if I said a short prayer for your grandmother?"

"Can it," said Jared.

Janice whipped her head around. "What was that?"

Jared continued watching television.

"Well?" said Janice. "You always have something to say about the ways I find comfort. So go ahead. What is it?"

"It's time for my pills," he said.

Janice sighed and let go of my hand. She opened her purse and withdrew a small airtight pill case. She reached across my lap and handed Jared a large pill. He held it up to the fluorescent light of the lobby.

"Cyclosporine," he said, "compliments of the chef."

He swallowed it dry. He was handed another. He swallowed that, then two more. Finally, he was handed the last one. A light orange tablet, smaller than the others.

"This one," he said, his eyes still on the TV, "this is the one that will give me diarrhea."

"Jared, please," said his mother, wincing.

"It's just a bodily function," he said. "God created it. God created loose stool. Take it up with him."

He looked over at me for the first time.

"Well, I can see what kind of mood you're in today," she said. Her voice was calm. She looked at me. "I'm going to ask about your grandmother. They must know something by now."

"Thank you," I said. "Thank you for your consideration."

She got up and marched up to the receptionist's desk. Jared gagged a little when she was gone, and coughed up a sour pill smell. He didn't look my way for the first few minutes. He just kept his eyes on the screen, watching a program about high school students with symmetrical haircuts. But when the program was replaced by an advertisement, he took off his glasses and rubbed the bridge of his nose until it began to redden. He shot me a sideways glance.

"You're not some kind of annoying asshole-genius, are you?" he asked.

"I don't think so," I said.

He wiped the lenses of his glasses with his tuxedo shirt and put them back on.

"Autistic?"

"No."

"Why do you talk like that then?"

"How do I talk?"

"Not the right way, I'll tell you that," he said.

He looked right at me.

"You talk like a jack-off."

"Well, I'm not . . . I don't really leave our home very often," I said. "Maybe that's what you're picking up on. I haven't been out much."

Jared seemed to take this in a moment. I took another harsh mouthful of RC and tried not to tear up. Jared examined me closely. He looked at my clothes, my worn gray tennis shoes, my blue flannel. I felt like a specimen under the magnifying lenses of those glasses. Somewhere in another part of the hospital, doctors were probably looking at Nana in the same way.

"Have you ever heard the Misfits' first album?" he asked.

I shook my head, and Jared immediately began searching one of the deep pockets of his jacket. "Janice keeps a close watch on me, too," he said, "but she has my sister to worry about. She doesn't open my mail."

He pulled out his music player, a thin rectangular box with a glowing screen and a circle of buttons. I had seen one advertised in a store window, but I could not remember its name. He began rapidly steering his thumb over the controls.

"I order my albums off the Internet," he said.

"The World Wide Web?"

He shushed me with a single finger and pressed a final button.

"I want you to hear something, Sebastian. But first you have to prepare yourself."

"For what?"

"To have your shit rocked," he said.

He looked at me, altogether serious.

"All right," I said. "How should I prepare?"

"I don't know," he said. "Just do it."

So I closed my eyes and took a few deep breaths. I thought of North Branch from a bird's-eye view. I pictured myself floating over the bare trees, the top branches scraping against the tips of my shoes. Then I opened my eyes again, and Jared seemed satisfied. He placed the headphones in my ears and turned the volume up.

"What is this?" I asked.

Jared pressed a button. There was a brief moment of white noise; then it sounded as if someone were running a chain saw inside my head. Only this chain saw made melodies. And a drumbeat pounded along with it. The singing began seconds later, and I tried hard to make it out over the crunch of what I assumed to be a guitar. But the words were too fast to understand. And the singing switched alternately into yelling and whining. Then a series of *whoa*s. Before I knew it, the song was ending and Jared was looking at me for my reaction.

"What was that about maggots?" I asked. It was the only word I'd been able to parse.

"The maggots in the iron lung won't copulate," said Jared. "Then later he changes it to . . . the maggots in the eye of love won't copulate."

"Oh."

"That's the Misfits. I'm learning how to play that song right now, but I don't really have the calluses yet," he said. "I started too late."

"Guitar?" I asked.

"Damn right," he said.

"It was . . . a very accomplished song," I said.

"Yeah."

He watched his mother for a moment. She was listening to the receptionist, nodding her head solemnly.

"Let's go outside," he said.

"Now?"

"Yeah, I hate this stupid place. I need some air."

He was already getting up, and when he began his journey toward the exit, I found myself following. It seemed like the right idea. I could already tell that objectionable things happened inside the building. People breathed into machines. Grandmothers were wheeled away to secret rooms.

So we stepped outside into the early afternoon air. The sun had vanished behind an opaque cloud cover, and a green neon cross above us cast an unearthly light on the pavement. Jared reached back into the tentlike folds of his leather coat and produced a pack of cigarettes. He tapped out a Lucky Strike.

"You tell Janice about this and I'll make sure you die in a drainage ditch someday," he said.

"Understood," I said.

He lit the cigarette and then smoked what looked like a fourth of it in one long inhalation. He pulled in the enormous drag, then coughed it out in a thick, green-tinted cloud.

"So you really live in that goddamned thing in the middle of the forest?" he asked me, in between puffs. "Is that what you're feeding me?"

"You mean the Geodesic Dome?"

"Yeah. That thing."

"I really live there."

"And you go to school there?"

"Nana instructs me," I said.

"So is she, like, your overlord?" he asked.

"She's my guardian," I said. "She says we have a bond stronger than the average parental one."

I watched him blow smoke through his tiny nostrils.

"What the hell does that mean?"

"We make up for the lack of direct mother-son connection with a greater communicative capability." I was talking too much, but I felt the words coming against my will. "A kind of telepathic bond," I added.

He stomped out his cigarette and immediately reached for another one.

"You can read each other's thoughts?"

"Not exactly," I said, "but there's a kind of hyperawareness present. She senses me."

Jared considered this. "Okay, then," he said. "If you can read her mind, then what's happening to your grandma now?"

"What do you mean?"

"I don't know," he said. "Is she going to die?"

I felt something inside me drop. I looked down just to concentrate on something. I looked at the flattened cigarette butt lying in front of me. It was still emitting smoke.

"I resist my powers," I said.

And before I could really think about it, I picked up the remains of the cigarette, appraised it, and took a small puff. My first ever. I got a little smoke, and almost immediately began to hack. I took a step backward and steadied myself against a metal bench. My throat and nostrils felt scorched.

"That's the filter," said Jared. "You're not supposed to smoke that part."

The taste in my mouth was horrible. Like the smell of burning plastic. I rested the back of my head on the top rail of the bench. I felt my nose starting to run. I wiped my forearm across my face, but it didn't stop.

"Are you crying?" asked Jared.

I didn't answer.

"Hey," he said. "Hey, man. I'm sorry. I'm sure she's going to be okay and everything."

Jared walked over and stood next to me. He reached in his coat for a wad of old Kleenex. He unwrapped it and handed it to me.

"People get sick, you know?" he said. "Bad stuff happens."

His voice was an octave lower now, and quiet. He sat down next to me, reeking of smoke. Then he glanced at the hospital sign.

"Believe me," he said. "This is the kind of shit I know about."

Jared looked away. He coughed a little. Suddenly a voice came from behind us.

"Sebastian!"

We turned around, and Janice was standing in the doorway, the institutional light of the hospital shining behind her. She walked up to us and pulled the unlit cigarette out of Jared's mouth. "Are you crazy?" she said. "Have you gone absolutely insane?"

She snapped the cigarette in half and tossed it in the bushes.

Then she shifted her gaze directly to me. Her face softened, and she attempted a comforting smile.

"I found a nurse," she said. "I found a nurse to take you to Josephine."

MY NURSE WAS A MUSCULAR WOMAN IN OLIVE HOS-pital clothing. And she spoke to me about brains while we traversed the spare hallways. She spoke about brains in general, but I could deduce that she was really talking about Nana's brain. She told me that they needed nutrients and oxygen, but that sometimes clots or clotlike things blocked the arteries and resulted in interruptions of blood flow. Some version of this interruption, she said, had happened to Nana. And it had caused a thrombotic stroke and some temporary aphasia. Nana was having some difficulties with her speech. Fortunately, they had been able to supply her with drugs in time to ward off too much permanent damage. Still, said the nurse, strokes killed brain cells; that was what they did.

When she finished, we were standing at the door to Nana's room. It was a sizable space, with a row of empty beds. It smelled like mothballs. Nana had the room to herself, and the second I stepped inside, her eyes fluttered open and followed me, just as they had when she was taken from her home. I walked to her bed where she sat, pierced by a few small tubes. Her skin was pale, and her lips were chapped. Her unwashed hair had been matted down against her head.

I hefted myself onto her bed and sat beside her. The nurse stood outside, scrawling on her papers. I rested my hand on Nana's shoulder. When I was five, the only way I could fall asleep was with her hand on my back. That weight had to be there. I needed something to pin me down. I worried that sleeping without an anchor would cause me to drift right through the domed ceiling and out into the night.

"Nana," I said now. "I understand you have aphasia. So I'm just going to speak slowly to you."

She coughed a single soft husky cough.

"You told me once," I said, "that physical bodies are just elements and energies. That they are always changing. That's what you said."

Nana did not look at me.

"I mean some of the things that are me today, were just proteins and water yesterday. There is no 'real' me. I am in a constant state of flux. Right?"

Nana closed her eyes and took a few deep breaths. Then her eyes opened again.

"Soba," she said.

"What?" I asked.

Nana contorted her mouth.

"You drank soba," she said quietly. "Coke cola."

I looked closely at her. "Janice gave me an RC," I said.

Nana winced and shook her head.

"You should," she said, "you should not consume . . . these things."

"Nana, you've had a stroke," I said.

This gave her pause. She looked around the room and down at her hospital gown. She seemed to see it all for the first time.

"I was worried," I said. "I've been out there worrying about you . . ."

I heard my voice shaking.

"Sebas-yan," she said. "You shouldn't drink these things."

She didn't seem to be listening anymore. I looked out into the hall and the olive-clad nurse was still there. She was watching me. "She's experiencing some disorientation," she said. "I wouldn't pay much attention to what she's saying at this point. Your grandmother is on some strong medication."

Suddenly Nana opened her eyes wide and gasped. I turned to her, startled.

"You are going away," said Nana.

She grabbed at my arm, but her body wasn't quite getting the messages.

"No, Nana, I'm right here," I said. "I'm right here with you."

She looked at me, but I couldn't tell if she was really seeing me.

"You are going away," she said. "I know this."

Her eyes fell closed. I wanted to reassure her, but she had already drifted from consciousness again. I watched her sleep for a moment. Then I got up and left her bed. I intuited my way back to the waiting room and found Janice reading from a glossy paperback and eating a bag of saltless pretzels. Jared was no longer beside her.

"Mrs. Whitcomb?" I said.

She looked up at me, chewing slowly.

"It looks like I'll be sleeping here tonight," I said, "but I want to offer thanks again for your help."

"Oh, of course," she said. She got up and threw her arms around me. "Is everything going to be all right?"

"I hope so," I said.

She let go and took another bite of a pretzel.

"I'm going to give you something," she said.

She rifled around in her overlarge handbag until she pulled out a receipt and a pen. She began scribbling something. "Jared wanted me to give you this information," she said. "If you ever want a day away from your . . . home, you should just call us up or e-mail

Jared. I know you kids get on your computers and talk that way sometimes. And Jared is . . . well, he's had some troubles. But he's a sweet boy at heart. He's in the car right now, thinking about his behavior."

She handed me a phone number and an e-mail address.

"Jared told you to give me this?" I asked. I gripped the paper hard in my fingers.

"Well, he didn't actually say it, but he doesn't say much of anything to me. I could just tell he wanted to hear from you again."

I stuck the receipt in my pocket, and Janice gave me another hug.

"Immanuel Methodist," she said.

"I beg your pardon?"

"That's where I teach the Youth Group. I'll bet you would like it, Sebastian. I really bet you would. There's singing and study groups, and we have outings from time to time."

"Nana and I don't attend church," I said. "We believe in synergy."

"Even so," she said, "maybe you'll consider it."

She handed me her bag of pretzels and smiled. Then she turned around and walked out of the hospital. Not far away in the parking lot, I could spot the teal minivan. It stuck out, half bathed in a dim parking light in the darkening evening. And directly under the light, coming out of the van's open sliding door, I could see a black pair of tennis shoes swinging against the side of the van in a steady beat. Jared's music player dangled at his side, illuminated, and there was something affixed to it. I narrowed my eyes.

It looked a lot like a Buckminster Fuller sticker.

3. The Domecoming

THREE DAYS WENT BY BEFORE NANA RECEIVED PER-
mission to leave the hospital. Three days of waiting. Three days of
consuming forkfuls of odd-smelling food and viewing inscrutable
daytime television programs full of people who laughed and cried
and fondled each other's bodies, all within a half hour. I had never
really watched much television before, and I was surprised to find so
many lives full of constant torment and indecision. The people in
the programs just endlessly *wanted*. They wanted things and other
people and they wanted other lives. Then some music played, and it
all began again somewhere else. And, in the midst of all this, I continued to wait for what I knew I wanted: to go back home.

When the moment of Nana's release finally came, the afternoon
was alive with the first snow flurries of the year. It was like the world
had suddenly been reanimated. The snow came down in wisps,
spun-out flakes, twirling toward the sidewalk. Some hit Nana and
blended seamlessly with her hair, making her white bouffant look
like a giant dew-wet dandelion spore. I watched this while I waited
for the cab we'd called. Nana stood, silently holding a twenty-dollar
bill in her fist. She'd hardly spoken in days.

The rules of her departure were as follows: Nana was only
allowed to go home if she promised to come back to the hospital

for regular checkups. And she had to call once a week so they could monitor her progress. These conditions were nonnegotiable. Her doctor was a compact man with thin brown hair and a nervous habit of licking his mustache. And before she could be discharged, Nana had to stutter her way through an argument with him about whether or not she could still take care of me. I was forced to leave the room, so I could hear nothing they said. But when he came out into the hall, the doctor's tongue was darting all over his upper lip, and I was going home with Nana.

I hadn't slept much the last three nights. The hospital was an unnerving place, and I couldn't get comfortable in the bed next to Nana's. The first night she was hooked up to two machines that blinked red and white and hummed like a refrigerator. The faint glow made Nana's features look spectral. She slept fitfully, and a few times I had to call the nurse because of her moaning. I assumed she was in pain, but she was always fine when awoken, with no memory of her dreams. Once, however, on the second night, she called to me after a long, low whine. My name came out crisp, in a voice seemingly unaffected by the stroke. Every syllable in line, "Se-bas-tian."

"Yes?" I said, startled awake. "It's me. I'm here."

She sat up in her bed and looked across the dark at me, her eyes wide again.

"You are mine," she said.

"I know," I said.

She looked at me for nearly a full minute without speaking. But I think she was still asleep. "It's already happening," she said.

Then she lay back in her bed and closed her eyes again.

"What?" I asked. "What is happening?"

I waited for her answer. But it didn't come. The hospital was entirely silent around me. I got up and pushed my wheelie-bed closer to Nana's. I tried to sync my breathing with her measured rasps. One . . . *wheeze*. Two . . . *wheeze*. I counted each breath until I got above a thousand. Then I started over.

Now, under the light snow, our taxi finally arrived in the hospital lot, and Nana presented the man with the twenty. She didn't say a word.

"Two-forty Hillsboro Drive," I said.

I sat up front with the driver.

"Where's that?" he asked.

His wipers squeaked back and forth in front of us. The lot was empty.

"We live in the glass dome," I said, "just off the highway and up the hill."

He nodded and turned on the meter.

"I've been meaning to take the tour," he said.

"Closed," said Nana, just a notch above a whisper.

We both turned around.

"What?" I asked.

"Closed," she said again.

She looked out the window. Her breath fogged the snow-specked glass beside her.

"Hmm," said the driver. "Then I guess I missed the boat."

SPRINKLED WITH A LIGHT DUSTING OF SNOW, THE dome resembled a puff pastry that day. And it appeared smaller than before. We entered and both of us looked around; everything was where it should be. The smell was a familiar one of Windex and Nana's Lavender Talcum. The light was soft and gray, dimmed from a slight tint to our dome panes. Nana exhaled deeply. Then she trekked directly to her bedroom and closed the door softly behind her. I barely heard from her the rest of the day.

As far as I could tell, she just lay in bed for the first few hours. She spent the evening, however, with her door ajar, examining photographs of architectural work she had done in the 1980s. For years she had been hired by dome manufacturers to invent new variations on the standard kit structure. She pored over her pictures now, even tacking a few to a bulletin board outside her bedroom. One picture showed a place she'd designed in Arizona with enormous triangular skylights, surrounded by hexagonal shingles. Another photo showed a compound on a peak above the Pacific Ocean in California. It was a series of three domes connected by underground walkways. Around eight, I came to ask Nana if she needed anything, and she dismissed me with a detached smile and a brush of her hand.

Upstairs in my room, I sat alone in front of our computer. I had spent the afternoon trafficking Web sites that Nana had previously sanctioned for me. Normally, she sat with me anytime I was on the computer, and then took away the modem every night. But now she was gone, and I could distinctly feel her absence. Earlier, I had been reading Web pages about design science, and I had tried to memorize and take notes. *The ultimate geometry-based creation is the sphere. All spheres are created from a point of singularity at their center. This center silences all waves, and opens the door to the life force.*

By dusk, I couldn't read another word about it. My mind was saturated. But before I got up from the computer I felt myself typing two last words into the Web. I typed them without thinking. I typed them with one finger. And when they appeared, I noticed my pointer finger was quivering.

I had typed "the misfits."

I pressed enter, and a list of sites popped up. I clicked on the very first. Right away, an image of a long-haired man loaded on the screen. He was glowering at the camera. A giant biceps flexed below his face, and on his arm was a tattoo of a bat creature with a skull head, and a tiger. Under his picture were the words "Punk rock icon."

I quickly shut down the browser.

But an hour later, I returned to the keyboard again. I typed "punk rock music." This time, I began to scan the articles. And I found right away that it was another language entirely. There were so many words I didn't recognize, and I couldn't distinguish between the band names and the songs. It all came at me in a jumble. Minor Threat. The Buzzcocks. Rudimentary Peni. Forward to Death. Warfare. I Don't Care AboutYouFuckArmageddonThisis-HellJohnWaynewasaNazi.

Yet I couldn't look away. After every few lines, I took to nervously shutting off the monitor and moving back to the other side of the room to read trigonometry. Sine. Cosine. Tangent. Sine. Cosine. Tangent. "Note the position of the terminal side. Do these angles have the same terminal side?" But gradually my eyes left the book again, and I made my way back to the screen. I did not sleep until three A.M.

The next day I continued my research in longer stretches. And eventually, bits of ideas started to filter through. It was still hard to make sense of the terms; I had never really listened to music. All I'd heard before were Nana's classical music albums, and the tape of beluga whale calls she listened to at night to aid her digestion. But I could begin to understand some snippets of what was written about the music. After every sentence, I looked over my shoulder. And each time I fully expected to see Nana there. In all our life together, I had never possessed this much continuous time alone. I felt untethered.

But still, I moved on from articles to songs. All I had to do was click on a title on the Web, and the song would begin playing from the tinny speakers in our monitor. I kept the volume low and pressed my ear to the plastic. I played a few songs over and over, trying to understand them. They didn't have an immediate effect. This was a new species of sound. Something entirely different. The shrill squawks from the guitars. The fuzzy bass guitar parts, and the caustic singing. It didn't make sense necessarily, but eventually I found the simple melodies sticking in my brain. The fast rhythms and thundering drums made my pulse jump. I could tell that something was happening.

I took a long walk that second evening, singing the choruses to myself as I passed the rows of white oaks and basswoods. *"Now I wanna sniff some glue! Now I wanna have somethin' to do!"* I had walked these woods, all the way to the edge of town, since I was a child. If you walked long enough, the brush turned directly into guardrail, and you faced the highway traffic into North Branch. Deafening cars speeding toward home. I walked along the road, in time to the drumbeats, playing the guitars in my head. I yelled into the cars' whizzing paths. *"All the kids want somethin' to do!"*

I began to feel that music like hot blood in my veins. I jumped up and down. I cupped my hands and shouted into the air. I felt all my synapses firing at once. And on the walk back home, I finally thought of the information Janice had given me. I searched my jeans pocket and found the paper right where I'd stuffed it. I unfolded it and looked down at Jared's e-mail address. It read:

jaredhatesyourface@yahoo.com

The writing was Janice's. Loopy. I had registered an e-mail account myself years ago in order to ask questions of the Buckminster Fuller Institute. I hadn't made use of it since I was twelve. But that night, I opened it up and typed in my secret password (even Nana didn't know what it was). I typed: orphan.

And then I composed this short message:

> Dear Jared,
>
> Sebastian Prendergast.
>
> Your mother handed me this Web address along with a bag of pretzels.
>
> You were in the car at the time, ruminating about your behavior. I don't believe you witnessed any of this.
>
> I wonder today, did you really want me to contact you?
>
> All best, Sebastian
>
> P.S. Why do all the kids want to sniff some glue?
>
> P.P.S. If you give me the coordinates of your house, I'll tell you what it looks like from hundreds of feet in the air.

It wasn't until the next morning that his response came back. I checked the computer every half hour after rising until I saw the reply. It sat among the strange advertisements I had compiled in my idle account: low-cost condominiums and pills for the male anatomy. Then there was Jared's response. I held my breath and opened it up.

> Sebastian,
>
> Your writing is worse than your talking. It makes me want to pound you.
>
> One thing to know about my mom: she is ignorant plus a liar.
>
> Call me tomorrow at six o'clock or something. Janice will be out.
>
> Jared
>
> Oh yeah, and your answer: all the kids want something to do! And I don't know coordinates. Don't be a retard.
>
> Can you really see from a hundred feet up?

I had just finished reading it for the fourth time when I turned around and saw Nana waiting in the doorway. I sprang up from the chair. It was late morning, and she was still in her burgundy bathrobe. I'd been too engrossed in my reading to notice the sound of her footfalls on the stairs. Now she was there, and her gaze jumped from the screen to me. In the last couple of days her eyes had regained a bit of their luster. They seemed to flash at me now like a cat's.

"Nana," I managed. "Is your health improved?"

"Your . . . homework," she said, and held out a flat palm.

She still sounded the words out slowly, but there was force behind them.

"Oh," I said. I clicked my tongue. "I didn't know if I was supposed to complete it without the accompanying lessons."

She shut her mouth tight and took a couple of steps into the room.

"What have you been . . . accomplishing?" she asked.

I looked at the screen. "Well," I said, "I've been investigating some things on the Web. The Fuller Institute has begun to archive some documents, which is really . . ."

Nana walked across the room and picked up my open math notebook. She began flipping through it, licking her finger each time she turned a page. I knew what was in there; it was not impressive. There were unfinished graphs. Unsolved problems. Triangles with no identified angles. At one point earlier in the day I had written the words "trigonometric identities" over and over again until an entire page was full. I was sure it was when Nana reached this page that she dropped the notebook onto the floor.

"You have used . . . my illness," she said, "for your own purposes."

"No," I said. "I just didn't know what I was supposed to do."

It took me a couple of moments to realize why I felt so anxious.

My muscles all seemed to tighten at once. I was lying to her. And she knew.

"You don't need me to tell you!" she said. "You never did. You just complete. You . . ." She stopped for a moment to think through her sentence. She looked around the room again, like she was searching for the word in the air. Her eyes returned to mine.

"By tomorrow," she muttered, "you finish."

Her voice was low, and she was breathing heavily. I suddenly became afraid she would collapse again. I walked toward her, but Nana turned around before I could reach her. She stepped out of the room and took the stairs slowly, one at a time.

"You are on a path!" she yelled from the staircase.

4. Guinea Pig S

IN THE BEGINNING, NANA SPOKE VERY GENERALLY about my path. I wasn't going to be like other boys, she said. There was the traditional way to live; then there was the dynamic and independent way. My life would resemble the latter. A life of experiment and higher ideals. A life of constant question and risk. This is the way Fuller had lived, so this is the way I would live. In fact, Bucky had once called himself Guinea Pig B, stating plainly that his life was an experiment. He wanted to see what an average man on earth with few resources could accomplish in a single lifetime. When I was just a boy, Nana had sometimes called me Guinea Pig S, and she told me I was a living experiment, too. My life, she said, would serve humanity just like Bucky's.

It wasn't until a couple of years ago that she began to get more specific. Until this time, I had never even heard any particulars about her relationship with Fuller. But one night just after my fourteenth birthday, she sat me down at the kitchen table and poured us both a small glass of Canadian ice wine. She told me she had been waiting to tell me some information for a very long time. And that night, she would finally reveal to me what we were working toward in the dome.

She started with a long sip of wine. Nana normally didn't drink, but she was so fascinated by the Canadian tradition of squeezing water crystals from frozen grapes that she made a few exceptions a year with ice wine. She asked me to join her in a drink. We sipped the sugary wine, and eventually Nana began to speak in a soft and reverent voice.

"We were in my small apartment in Edwardsville," she started.

I knew, by this time, exactly who she was speaking about.

"It was three-thirty in the morning and he was up preparing for a lecture. I remember waking to the sight of him perspiring and breathing heavily by an open window. He was sucking in full breaths of cool night air. There were big drops of sweat on his brow. The streetlight from the town square was reflecting in his glasses. It almost appeared that his eyes were emitting light.

"I asked him what was wrong. He immediately removed his glasses and grinned his sly Bucky grin. He took a long drink from a glass of water I kept by the bed. Then he told me that in our life-time there were going to be no more governments and no more corporations.

"'Once all my inventions are available,' he said, 'people will see that all these bureaucracies they are living under are no longer nec-essary. When people can meet their own fundamental needs, when individuals themselves can do it; that will be the judgment day for our rulers. The officials, the leaders, and power mongers will all be out of a job!'

"He told me that once his design science principles were put into effect on a world scale that we could start pouring all human-ity's resources into sustaining life. He talked all night. Everyone on Spaceship Earth was going to be able to survive without poverty, he said. Humanity would evolve. The species would thrive.

"'Eventually,' he said, 'the freedom of this revolution will be so intoxicating, humankind will have no choice but to take part. Because that's what I'm talking about here, Josie, freedom. An absolute personal freedom.'"

Nana stopped after that. She took a drink of wine and motioned for me to do the same. "He even imagined domes," she said, "that could be heated and made to levitate. He called them Cloud Nines. They would one day be joined to make full cities, hovering over the earth. They could migrate according to the weather. People could go anywhere, become true global citizens. If we chose, we could all live aboard these airships with no strings to base earthly phenomena. We could be completely free."

She raised her glass to mine. "Of course," she said, "he never got to see it all come together in his lifetime."

I could see her eyes starting to moisten.

"But geniuses are never appreciated in their own time. And after all, we are here, Sebastian. You and I. The revolution is not going to happen in my life, either. I have come to terms with that. But I think it will happen in yours."

Our glasses were still in the air.

"We've started small, showing people in town a new way to live with our tours. But gradually, once your education is complete, you can take our operation to the next level. Who better to do it? With no parents, you belong to the universe now. Just like Bucky. You can teach people to be free!"

She clinked her glass against mine. Her cheeks shone with tear lines. I drank quickly and felt a happy dizziness come over me. Nana came around to my side of the table to hold me in a long hug. I could feel the relief in her body at having told me these things. Her sinewy muscles were slack. Her chest heaved in great liberated breaths.

Nana poured us more wine, and I believe I became a little inebriated. We brainstormed the rest of the night, trading ideas about advertising the dome tours. Eventually, Nana fell asleep at the kitchen table, a tired smile on her face. I transferred a large Vellux blanket from our couch to her shoulders. I turned out the light and imagined the dome switching off like a giant lightbulb. I walked upstairs and my body felt weightless the way it did when I was a child. It was exhilarating. I had been chosen for something. I had a path. I fell immediately and heavily into dreamless sleep.

EVER SINCE THAT NIGHT, HOWEVER, NANA HAD pressured me even harder to excel in my studies. She had never repeated the things she told me, but I could tell I was supposed to have reached a new level of understanding. I wasn't just being raised by Nana; I was being groomed to lead a social revolution. Our dome was not just a house; it was a starting point. Centrally located even. How much more central could you get than Iowa?

But I began to think more and more about her plans, and whether or not I fully understood them. The telepathic bond I'd explained to Jared was, in actuality, a complete mystery to me. It was wholly possible that Nana could sense me and see me wherever I was, but thus far, I only saw Nana when she was in front of me. And I found myself wondering now if she could see me in her mind at all times.

If my father had still been alive, I would have asked him what it was like when he was a boy. Did Nana know he was going to scrape his knee before he scraped it? Did she appear in his doorway with all his secrets on her lips? And most important, was he originally on my path? Was he going to save the world, before he strayed and chose to study archaeology? He had eventually chosen to learn about the past instead of the future. Why? There were so many questions I wanted to ask him.

I had only seen one photograph of him at my age. He was in a house with right-angled walls, in a kitchen. He was looking at the camera, a sanguine smile on his face. His hair was long and he wore a thin T-shirt that frayed at the bottom. He was spreading peanut butter on bread. The flash of the camera reflected in his eye. He looked happy. But it seemed to me that everyone looked happy in faded photos. Family history was written by mothers and grandmothers, and the frowns were clipped away.

In every picture of me taken in the dome, I was laughing, smiling, staring at something in marvel. Surely, there had to be some photos from those first days, when my eyes were always red, and I was wandering around my new home in utter confusion. I wondered where those photos had gone.

5. The Lone Comprehensivist

THE NEXT DAY PASSED IN A STORM OF RECIPROCALS and inverse functions. I studied trigonometry all day long, and by evening my mind had reached a wall. I could progress no further, and I was thinking only of one thing: Jared had asked me to call him. Nana had always kept our phone line active in case of calls about dome tours. But that was all it was employed for. I had never once attempted a personal phone call, and I was fairly sure that now was not the ideal first time to try. As the clock neared six, I sat on the floor of my upstairs room, rubbing my temples, unable to move.

I thought back to the last line of Jared's e-mail. The first evidence of real curiosity I had heard from him, "Can you really see from a hundred feet up?" I wanted to call and tell him, "Yes. Yes, I can see from a hundred feet up! I can see your whole town. I've probably seen you walking around. You were a speck!" I looked back down at my textbook and tried to clear the thoughts from my head.

Then there was a knock at my door. I looked over and Nana peeked her head in. She looked pale, maybe even frightened. I instinctively held out my completed homework pages, offering them to her. Nana ignored them.

"Listen to me, Sebastian," she said.

"Okay."

"I'm taking . . . a cab to the hospital for a check," she said.

"You are?"

I could barely contain my shock.

"These people," she said, "they don't—they are truly the worst kind. One thing. That's all they know. They learn their thing and the world goes nowhere."

She looked over at the book open on my lap.

"You are progressing with your lessons?"

"I am," I said.

She nodded.

"It's all connected, you know," she said with perfect lucidity. "You learn these things, then you get closer."

"Closer to what?"

She opened the door all the way, and my question was lost in the creak. I could see she was already dressed to go out. She wore her long thermal raincoat over a pea green tracksuit, and she toted the small dark leather satchel she used in lieu of a purse.

"There is supper down on the . . ."

"Table." I said it a bit too quickly.

She repeated the word under her breath. She turned around again.

"I'll return," she said.

Then she left, and I listened with disbelief as she took each stair, one at a time. I watched from above as she ventured out onto our semicircular drive and met a yellow cab. Then I watched the cab depart. I closed my eyes and counted to one hundred. I opened them again. She was still gone. Rapidly, I made my way down the stairs and grabbed our old cordless telephone in my sweaty palm. The dial tone droned in my ear. I fished the receipt out of my pocket and entered the telephone number written above Jared's e-mail address. It rang four times. Then a voice answered. But it was not Jared's. It was a higher voice.

"What?" it asked me.

I held my breath for a moment.

"Hello," I said.

"I'm here, big guy," she said. "Talk to me."

"Mrs. Whitcomb?" I asked.

There was laughter at that. Not giggling, but a few real hearty laughs.

"Oh, my God," she said. "Who is this?"

"Sebastian Prendergast," I said.

"Sebastian who?" she said. "How did you get my number?"

"From Mrs. Whitcomb," I said.

"Are you a comedian, Sebastian?" she said. "Do your friends think you're the funny one?"

"No," I said. "I don't have any friends."

"Well, that's a relief," she said.

"I think there's been a misapprehension," I said.

"A what?"

"I'm calling . . ." I began.

"I know why you're calling," she said. "But it doesn't seem like you've got the balls to ask me anything."

At that point, there was some mumbling in the background, and I heard Jared's voice, low and loud. Then there was arguing, and I heard a bevy of strange words, which included "hoochie." After that, his caustic voice was alive on the line.

"Hello?" he said.

"Jared?"

"Uh-huh."

"Jared, who was that?"

"Oh, that was just Meredith," he said.

"Who?"

"My sister, Sebastian. This is her private line. My mom must have given you this number by mistake."

"Oh."

"I'm in her room now," he said. "It smells like fucking apricots or something."

He sniffed so loud I could hear it on the phone.

"Anyway," he said. "What did you want?"

"What do you mean?"

"Why did you call me? Did you want something?" he asked.

I felt for a moment the urge to start crying.

"No," I said.

"So you just wanted to chat like a couple of girls?"

"I suppose."

"Are you in the dome right now?" he added.

"I live here," I said. "I live in the dome."

"Wild," he said.

"Jared, I received your e-mail. You instructed me to call you . . ."

"You got me thinking about the Ramones," he said. "With your stupid glue question? I've been learning some of their songs. Do you know they stole all their equipment?"

I said nothing.

"Yeah, they just realized they wanted to start a band so they stole a bunch of equipment and taught themselves to play. I've been learning 'Beat on the Brat.' *Da-da-da-nuh-nuh-Nuh. Da-da-da-nuh-nuh-Nuh!* The bass part is so easy anyone could play it."

"I've been investigating music, too," I said.

"Say 'listening,'" said Jared. "Jesus. Say, 'I've been *listening* to some music.' I honestly want to scream in your fucking ear when you talk like that sometimes."

I was quiet.

"No offense," he said.

"I've been listening to some music," I said.

"All right!" he said. "Okay. Anything good?"

"I don't know what's good yet."

"Yeah," he said. "What's good, right? That's the point. That's the whole point. If I wanted to listen to *good* music like my sister, I'd just suck on a muffler. Who wants to listen to *good* music? Maybe we should all listen to the radio and buy everything on TV."

"An important point," I said.

Outside it was almost completely dark. Inside, I could see my dinner across the room on the table. Polenta with some kind of greens. I could tell just by looking that it was cold.

"Jared," I said.

"It's not apricots, actually," he said, "it's mango. I fucking hate mango."

"Jared," I repeated.

"What?"

"I want to come over to your house and listen to music."

I spoke so fast I was amazed he was able to comprehend it. But he was.

"Not right now," he said. "I can't right now."

"I meant at some date in the future," I said.

"The future," said Jared.

"Yes," I said. "The future."

"Maybe," he said.

"I'll let you know agreeable times," I said. "I can call you again and tell you some times."

Jared paused for a moment, and I heard him yelling out the doorway.

"Relax, you ho-bag!" he screamed.

Then his voice got so loud I couldn't tell what he said.

"Jared?"

"Sorry. That was Meredith," he said. "She wants her phone back."

"Do you have to terminate the conversation?"

"Yeah," he said. "In a minute."

His voice was much quieter now. I was standing in the murky light of the dome. I could see my reflection in the glass, looking back at me.

"Let me ask you something," he said. "What do you do for fun over there, Sebastian?"

"Fun?" I said.

"I mean, when you're not telepathically communicating with your grandma."

"Well . . ." I said.

"C'mon," he interrupted. "You can't always be doing weird shit in that globe. You have to have some free time. You have to have a day off."

"I climb sometimes," I said. "I climb up on the roof."

"Really?" he asked. "You scale that mother?"

"I have suction cups. It's my task to clean the surface of the glass. Nana says it attracts more tourists."

"Sebastian," he said, "that's pretty fucking wicked."

"I asked for the coordinates to your house, remember?"

"You can see my house from up there?"

"Maybe," I said. "I can see quite a vista."

There was another silence.

"But you never go anywhere."

"What do you mean?"

"You never go any of the places that you watch."

"Not very often, no," I said.

"Yeah," he said. He started to speak again, but then there was another shout from his end and I couldn't hear him. I could only hear Meredith, who said, "Get off my phone with that weirdo, already!"

Jared just sighed this time. "Okay, Sebastian," he said. "I guess I have to go."

"I'll call you with possible times," I said.

"Sure," he said. "You do that. You call me with possible times."

The line went dead right after he spoke, and I removed the hot phone from my ear. I deposited the device back in its cradle, then looked around the room. The sun was completely gone now, and the woods were dark all around me. All I could see when I pressed my face to the glass were the few boughs extending over the dome like giant skeletal fingers. I suddenly found myself ravenous, faint even. I walked over to my cold dinner and began forking it mechanically into my mouth, shoveling huge bites with my spoon, holding the food down with my thumb. The greens crunched, bitter and fibrous. The polenta was a bursting mouthful of mush. By the time I thought to sit down, everything had been consumed.

My chest ached. But it was not from the food. It had started bothering me soon after I put the phone down. I pressed a hand to my sternum and left it there a moment. I took a few deep breaths and let them out slowly. I walked a slow lap around the room. Improbably, it wasn't until Nana walked in the door a few minutes later that I realized what was bothering me: I'd forgotten what loneliness felt like. But now it had moved from the far reaches of my mind, where it usually sat, to a cramped place just beneath my ribs. I could feel it swelling in my chest.

"Are you okay?" asked Nana, stepping inside. "Why do you look like that?"

"Like what?" I said.

She brushed past me and picked up my plate from the sink.

"Nana?" I said.

I looked at her arm then. There was a puncture where they had drawn blood at the hospital. The skin around the small wound was yellow and purple.

"Yes?" she said.

She was sweating, and her hand shook almost imperceptibly while she ran water over my plate.

"I can do that," I said. "Why don't you sit down and rest."

"I'm fine," she said.

I walked up to her and held out my hand for the dish. She reluctantly handed it over. I began to cover it with our herbal dish soap, and Nana sat down at the table. It took her a moment to relax, but when she leaned back in her chair, I could see she was completely exhausted. In no time, her eyes were closed tight. I watched her closely. Even in repose, her face looked pained.

"Would it be so wrong?" I mumbled. "Just to have someone else . . ."

"What are you saying to me!" Nana said. "Speak up."

She pushed open her heavy lids to glance at me. I scrubbed at her dish.

"Nothing," I said. "Don't worry about it."

6. *The True Path of the Voyager*

NEXT WEEK ARRIVED AND NANA LOCKED HERSELF in her room to work on a secret project. I barely heard a noise for two days. And when she came out at sundown of the second, it was just to ask my help with something. I entered her room and only then did I see the fruits of her labor: an enormous banner made from a bedsheet. It read CLOSED TO PUBLIC in greasepaint. She needed me to climb a ladder outside and help her to drape it over the entrance of the dome. She was already gathering up the banner while I tried to make sense of everything.

"Are you sure about this, Nana?" I asked. "You want to close?"

She didn't answer. She just walked outside and began to set up the ladder for me. I followed and clambered up in a daze. Then I spent an hour in the cold, trying to get the banner to hang straight. When I went back inside, it still seemed crooked. But it was done. Ever since I had lived in the dome we'd given tours. It was simply a part of life there. Now there was a bedsheet rippling in the raw fall wind. A curtain had closed.

On the couch, I tried to thaw my hands with breath. Nana sat nearby, expressionless.

"When do you think we might reopen?" I asked.

Again, no answer. She got up and walked into her bedroom, and

I expected her to stay there for the rest of the day. I expected yet another day of silence. But instead she emerged minutes later with some money in her hand, a wad of bills.

"Take your bicycle to town," she said. "Purchase paint and alter our signs."

She dropped the money. It landed in my lap with a flutter.

"The highway signs?" I said.

I waited for her to address my question. She did not.

"Where do I buy the paint?" I asked.

"You can access that information in the . . ."

I waited again while she searched for the word.

"The phone book," I said, finally.

She was expecting me to get up right away, but I sat where I was. The money stayed in my lap, scattered across my thighs.

"What?" she said. "What is it?"

"Can I ask you something?" I said.

She did not respond.

"Can I ask why you don't just let me administer the tours? We could stay open. I could do it! Until you're properly . . . rejuvenated."

She shook her head slowly from side to side.

"I've seen you guide them a hundred times," I said. "I've even committed everything you say to memory. It would have been impossible not to. So I . . ."

"Sebastian, please," she said.

"It's my duty to operate the gift stand, Nana. I grasp that. And I know each part of our work is important. But the situation is different right now, isn't it? I'm sixteen years old. And since you've come back from the hospital . . ."

"It won't," she interrupted, toneless. "It won't occur."

"Why not?"

"I don't want to discuss."

"I want to, Nana. I want to *discuss* this."

She was quiet for a moment.

"Because you do not possess the necessary . . . aptitude!" she said.

"What?"

"It pains me to say this. You barely comprehend what I teach. How can you expect to teach . . . others?" Her strangled speech made the words even sharper. They seemed to puncture the air. I felt my stomach clench.

"I see," is all I could think to say.

She took a long breath. My face was starting to warm.

"Now go and do what I've asked you."

I got up on what felt like someone else's legs, and walked directly to the telephone stand. I pulled open the drawer and thumbed through the telephone book. In a moment, I had found Small World Paints in downtown North Branch. I turned around, at that point, to watch for Nana, but she was no longer in the living room. The door to her room was closed again, and presumably she was behind it. I exhaled and almost choked on my breath. I was holding it all in. I flipped to the pages of the residential section. I located the *W*'s. Whisler. Whitaker. Whitby. And finally . . .

WHITCOMB Janice & Ronald 3200 Ovid Ave

I copied the information onto a note card and walked briskly out of the dome into the nip of the afternoon. I marched across our property, moving toward a large storage shed about a hundred yards down the hill. This was the building that had once housed Nana's three-wheel eco-car. It was a curiously small auto, and we had used it to buy groceries in the winter. But now, in the wake of the car's irreparable breakdown, the storage shed housed my Schwinn Voyager bicycle. My only gift from Nana on my twelfth birthday. I often wondered if she'd only purchased it for me so I could run her errands. It had come equipped with large handlebar-mounted baskets for groceries, and a seat pocket for money. I brought it down from its hooks and checked the tires. I adjusted my seat and mirrors. Then I grabbed my mustard-colored helmet off its peg, and I opened the doors of the shed. I tried to hold back tears.

I launched myself out of the shed and was off, shooting over the dead leaves and clingy brush of the hill. My tires bounced over the uneven slope and my teeth clicked together. I pedaled harder, cranking the chain over its gear, and eventually I hopped the curb onto the sharp decline of Hillsboro Drive. I gripped the handlebars and pedaled away as fast as I possibly could. The wind burned my eyes, and I let them water. I felt the hot streams glance down my cheeks. I watched the blurry road disappear under my tires.

IT TOOK ME A HALF HOUR TO ARRIVE AT SMALL WORLD Paints. The store was packed with merchandise, but I was able to locate the fast-drying spray paint in white. I calmly selected two canisters and walked under the humming fluorescent lights of the store to the shiny counter. A squat balding man was awaiting me. I handed him the paint. He rolled it around in his palm. He looked at my face, raw from crying.

"You aren't planning on getting up to any kind of vandalism with this Krylon paint, are you?" he asked me.

"No," I said, "I just have to alter some road signs for my grand-mother."

He looked me over again before hesitantly ringing me up for the paint. He handed me my change, slowly. Then he watched me as I stepped outside and loaded the canisters into my handlebar-mounted basket. I looked around the small square of downtown North Branch. I'd been told it was supposed to be modeled after Dutch architecture. The buildings were brick, tall and narrow, with decorative awnings. It was a bit disorienting. Even the streets were cobbled instead of paved. I looked up and down the road, and even-tually my eyes landed on the corner shop across the way and came to an abrupt halt.

"The Record Collector," read a large sign.

From across the street, I could see the front glass covered in bright wall-sized posters of large men with gold teeth, and women clad in small neon shorts. The performers had one-word names and seri-ous faces. A T-shirt hanging up nearby showed a man in a goat mask brandishing a chain saw. I guided my bike up to the front and put my hand against glass. It throbbed under my palm. I opened the door.

I stood for a moment in the entryway, holding my breath, taking in the environs. It was ill-lit inside, and it smelled like the stinky incense Nana burned sometimes on the eve of Bucky's death. In front of me were waist-high shelves of compact discs, organized alphabetically. An obese man with a tight stocking cap sat behind a counter, looking at a magazine. He had large black glasses similar to Jared's. On the stereo, a man said:

I seen her on the street, a definite cutie
But my eyes were locked on that pirate's booty!

I looked up to find the origin of the sound and instead met the stocking-cap man's spectacled eyes. They were pink and narrow.

"You need something!" he screamed over the song.

He picked up a soggy sandwich of some kind and took an impressive bite.

"I'm on break technically," he chewed, "but I'm here to help you. Right on."

"What?" I asked.

"Right on!" he said.

I walked away from him and into the belly of the store, the music playing from tiny speakers all around me. I scanned the categories above the racks. Pop. R&B. Country. Classic. I was the sole patron in the place. It felt as if the store existed only for me. I picked up a few discs and examined them. They were glossy, covered in strange photographs. The beat still thundered through the store. I walked back up to the counter.

"Do you have any discs by the Misfits?" I asked.

The man chewed and swallowed. "Metal," he said.

"What?"

"They're in Metal!"

I looked up at him. He sighed and slapped his magazine down on the counter.

"It helps if you can read," he said, more to himself.

He grumbled as I followed him to the back of the store. He pointed a meaty finger at the words "Heavy Metal." Then he pointed at the discs housed under that label.

"I thought the Misfits played punk rock music," I said.

"Listen, man," he said, "I don't make up the retarded rules around here. I'm just a wage slave. If you want to take this to the Supreme Court, that's your decision."

He waddled away, and I went to the *M* section. I looked through the discs until I saw a picture of a yellow and black skull staring at me. I picked it up. On the opposite side, the song titles were listed. I scanned down the list. "Vampira." "I Turned into a Martian." "Green Hell." "Skulls." The disc cost seventeen dollars and sixty-eight cents with tax. I chewed a fingernail. That was a third of our weekly grocery bill at the cooperative.

I dug into my pocket, where I had placed the change from the paint. I felt around and pulled out some one-dollar bills, some change, and finally a crumpled twenty. I smoothed the bill on the leg of my blue jeans. I was rarely given any money at all. The cash I earned from the gift stand went right back into sustaining the dome. And, according to Nana, the money that my parents had left me only covered the expenses needed to raise me. Nana was usually very careful with her finances. Maybe this time she had just reached for the money without looking. Maybe she had meant to give it to me. Or maybe it was a test. I looked at the skull. I slowly walked the disc up to the counter.

"I've made a selection," I said.

"Amazing," he said. "Way to go."

He surveyed my choice. "Oh," he said, "you have to be eighteen to buy this one."

He handed the disc back to me.

"Eighteen years old?"

"Yeah," he said. "They measure age in years now, man."

I turned it over in my hands. There was a sticker on the front that warned about explicit content. The man ignored me now, pretending I wasn't there.

"It's my first one," I said.

The man broke his trance. "Your first what?"

"My first compact disc."

"You've never bought an album before?" he asked.

I shook my head. He looked like he was going to choke on his sandwich. And for a minute, he seemed unsure what to do. He looked around the store, his eyes shifting back and forth. Then he looked behind him at a door to the back room.

"Jesus," he said.

I watched him intently.

"Here!" He spastically waved his hand. "Gimme that damn thing back."

I handed the disc back to him and he punched a series of buttons on the register. I placed my bill on the counter and watched it disappear into the cash drawer. Twenty dollars. The man shook his head, uttering more profanity to himself. He ripped the explicit-content sticker off the cover and made my change as fast as he could.

"Now get out of here," he said. "You've seriously compromised my job, man."

I obliged him, walking a straight path out the door. The fact that I possessed no form of disc player did not even occur to me at that moment. I had just known, somehow, that I was supposed to purchase the album. It had been there to be found by me. I held tight to the brown wrapping all the way to my bike.

The disc fit safely beside the paint cans in my basket. I stood looking at it a moment. A small square inside a paper bag. I understood then why I wasn't concerned about my lack of a stereo. The answer just clicked into my head. I wasn't buying this album for myself. I never had been. I zipped up my basket cover and angled my bike away from the expressway. I dug my feet into the Dutch cobblestones of historic downtown North Branch, and fastened my helmet. I rode off in search of Whitcombs.

7. Tensional Forces

SOMETHING THAT IS EASY TO FORGET ABOUT THE universe when you live in isolation is just how full of motion it is. It's in a state of perpetual motion, technically. The whole entire thing: going, going, going. Never stopping. At least that's the way Fuller described it. He said the universe is always transforming. And since every human body is composed of the same elements that compose the physical universe, then people are actually miniature universes in and of themselves. We, too, are in a state of persistent motion. And if the universe has unlimited possibilities, we, too, have unlimited possibilities.

Nana was right when she said I hadn't retained everything I'd read under her tutelage, but I had retained that fact. And until that afternoon, I wasn't sure I had ever believed the part about unlimited human possibility. But now that I was pedaling forward, the scenery rushing past me, it seemed plausible. My feet were flying. My calves were burning. I didn't know where Jared's house was, but I was traveling there.

Had I been looking at the town from above, I believe I could have located the place in a matter of seconds. But now that I was on the ground, everything was different. It was all so immediate and near. I had to ride over the avenues in nearly all directions before

I happened to arrive randomly at Ovid Avenue. I stopped right below the sign, almost on the verge of giving up. But there it was. A green street sign with the letters perfectly placed. OVID AVENUE. I looked up and down the street. The address of the nearest house was only 440. How many blocks away was 3200? A thousand?

I briefly thought of leaving and coming back another day, but I found I was no longer concerned about painting the highway signs. There was nothing I could do but keep moving forward (like the universe). So I embarked down the street, getting my legs in a rhythm again. I watched as the wall of houses flashed past. White-White. Brick-Brick. White-White. I could see some people through their windows, the same way I was so often visible inside my glass dome. These people were on display, too: eating, viewing TV, conversing. I could see seconds of their lives happening.

I became so absorbed trying to see inside the North Branch houses, I nearly passed the Whitcombs' home twenty minutes later. I only came to a stop because Ovid Avenue had reached a dead end. And Jared's house was midway into the final circle of houses. I had to hop off my Voyager and walk closer to check the numbers, but I found it soon enough. 3200. Painted white on the curb. I leaned my bike against a large beech tree in the yard and stood on the sidewalk, staring at the Whitcomb residence.

It was not a dome.

I hadn't presumed that it would be. Nonetheless, that was my first thought. It was not a dome, and it shared no quality with domes. All geodesic domes, like ours, were based on a concept that Fuller called *tensegrity*. The word was one of his hybrids, in this case a combination of "tension" and "integrity." A tensegrity structure was one that had reached a perfect balance. Each part buttressed its neighbor part faultlessly to distribute pressure.

The Whitcombs' house had little to no tensegrity. If anything, it had *tengility*. There was nothing wrong with the home. It was a modest two-story structure, tan brick, with a pointed gable roof. The windows were all rectangular except the big one on the second story, which had a curved top. I had seen many houses like it from the dome. But, up close, the structure seemed tenuous to me. There was a barely perceptible sag to the awning of the porch. The roof had recently been reshingled, but the pattern was not even. And the downspout had been partially detached from the side of the house.

I grabbed my brown bag from the front basket and stepped onto the lawn. I looked up and saw a pair of purple athletic sneakers hanging from a branch in the tree. I heard the tinkle of a wind chime, and looked to the porch where a swarm of aluminum angels clanged into one another over the door. Below the chime was a thick welcome mat that said, "God Bless This House." The curtains were drawn on the bay windows, and the inside looked dark. I took another step toward the house, and when I did, I heard a voice.

"Sebastian?"

It came from behind me, slightly muffled. I whipped around and there was Janice Whitcomb, crossing the street. She was bundled in her beige coat and green-blue scarf. She carried a box of something rustling and rolling around.

"I thought that was you," she said. "I was just down the street at this ridiculous candle party and I said to myself, 'There's a prowler on our lawn.'"

"I didn't mean to prowl, Mrs. Whitcomb," I said.

"I know that, Sebastian. Don't look so nervous. I recognized you when I got closer."

She stopped and looked me over. Her dark hair was in a ponytail that day, and a few long wisps hung over her round cheeks. She looked oddly exhilarated.

"Jared will be pleased," she said.

"He's at home?"

"Oh, yes," she said. "Where else would he be?"

She walked over the porch and swung open the front door. Right away, a blast of warm air came out, stinging my eyes. Janice propped open the door with the box of candles. There were large thick tubes of wax inside, at least twenty, and it smelled like gingerbread. "Everyone is home but my husband," she continued. "He's always flying somewhere. Sales. I'm glad you took me up on my offer, though. How's your grandmother?"

"Nana is improved," I said.

"Good to hear."

I still stood outside. The door was open, but for some reason I hadn't yet stepped through. Janice watched me, confused. I clutched my small brown bag tightly.

"You can leave your shoes on, Sebastian," she said. "This is a shoes-on house. Just give them a wipe!"

I glanced down at the mat again, taking in each word individually. God. Bless. This. House. I wiped my feet, slowly. There were smells drifting from inside, the smells of another family. I inhaled sharply and stepped across the threshold. Janice kicked the box aside, and the door closed right behind me. Mrs. Whitcomb stood looking at me, and I realized I was still wearing my bicycling helmet.

"Jared's in his room," she said. "Upstairs and to the right."

I took off my helmet and looked around. The living room was to my left. It was an adequate-sized room, but it appeared so much smaller than any space in the dome. The ceiling was low, and there was a lot of furniture. Two immense brown sofas fit together at a right angle across the room, and two leather chairs sat near the front windows. On the wall opposite the windows was a gargantuan television with an elaborate sound system attached. Above the television was a small brass cross with Jesus splayed across it. I had never been to church, but I'd seen the image.

"Go ahead," said Janice. "Just go up and knock on his door. I'll make some grilled cheese sandwiches."

I walked to the end of the hall to a staircase. I was about to go up when I noticed a closed door with an enormous poster of a shirtless man covering it. The man was sitting on the hood of a shiny black car, and his hair was dripping wet. He seemed to be looking right at me. Across his broad hairless chest in thick black marker read the words "MEREDITH'S ROOM." Then, on his flat, sweaty stomach, it said, "STAY OUT!" I could hear a slight murmur from behind the door, then a laugh. I hurried past.

The stair steps were covered in worn red carpeting. I ascended all the way up to a narrow hall about the same width as the staircase. At the end of the hall, on the right, was a door. The only thing that was on the door was a short command scratched into the wood. "Rise Above!" it said. I stuffed my helmet under my arm and approached the door. I knocked four times. A few long seconds passed, then the knob turned and the door opened a crack. An enlarged eye looked out at me through a fogged lens.

"Hi," I said.

The door opened slightly wider, and Jared wiped the condensation from his glasses. He removed a mini white headphone from his ear.

"Hey," he said.

He was wearing black pants and a black shirt that had the chest and arm bones of a skeleton on them. The shirt was supposed to create the effect that Jared was a skeleton-man. Unfortunately, the bones were way too big to be realistic.

"I apologize for not telephoning," I said, "but Nana sent me on an errand nearby."

Jared nodded. "What kind of errand?"

He still hadn't opened his door all the way.

"Paint," I said.

"Paint," he repeated slowly.

He tapped his fingers on the door, then looked back into his room. I examined his hair. There were drops of moisture clinging to his individual scraggly black locks. He looked at my helmet.

"Did that come with a tampon?" he asked.

I didn't respond. Instead, I just held out the paper bag I had been carrying.

"What's this?" Jared inspected the bag.

"It's for you," I said.

I had been holding it so tightly that the paper was crinkled. It looked like a piece of trash now. Yet Jared's skeleton arm took the bag. His glasses were clouded over again, and he wiped them and peered inside. He pulled out the disc. Despite the wear and tear of the sack, the compact disc itself was still shiny, the plastic wrapping untouched.

"Where did you get this?" he asked, staring at the cover.

"At a disc shop."

"How did you buy it, I mean?"

"With a twenty-dollar bill."

Jared blinked twice behind his lenses. "Come in," he said.

He opened his door all the way and I followed him inside. The room had dark carpeting, and every inch of wall space was covered in photographs of musicians. Cutouts from magazines. Rail-thin men with bald heads or just a single row of hair down the middle. They were frozen midshriek, midleap. Guys with black guitars, spitting great arcs of water into the crowd. Across from his bed were two giant shelves of compact discs and record albums, some of them stacked on top of a computer (it must have been the one he used to contact me). There were also discs on the floor and on a bedside table next to some small plastic devices that looked medical. A humidifier huffed out dense clouds of mist in the corner. The temperature was balmy.

Jared picked at the wrapping on the disc. "I don't have this one," he said quietly.

"What's that smell?" I asked.

Soon after I entered the room, I had noticed a strong vinegary odor.

"Nothing," he said. "There's no smell."

He walked toward his stereo and placed the disc in its slot. While he fumbled with some knobs, I looked over at a bulletin board leaning against his wall. It was covered in "Get Well" cards. One of them was open and every inch of the card was covered in signatures. Jared pressed a few buttons on his stereo.

"This is a good one," he said.

I sat down on his bed, unmade, the sheets knotted. He sat down at the opposite end. Three sharp drumbeats exploded at full volume. Then a chomping angry guitar started. And finally, that same operatic voice I'd heard first in the hospital.

Well, we land in barren fields on the Arizona plains.
The insemination of little girls in the middle of wet dreams.

Jared nodded and played some drums in the air. But he seemed far away. He continued wiping at his glasses. The song moved to its chorus.

> *Teenagers from Mars*
> *And we don't care*
> *Teenagers from Mars*
> *And we don't care*
> *Teenagers from Mars*
> *And we don't caaaare*

The song ended after a minute or two, and Jared switched off the stereo. He stood there a moment, looking at the speakers. The only sound was the gurgle and hiss of the humidifier. I felt my hair dampening with sweat.

"It's very temperate in here," I said. "Warm."

"What do you want?" he asked, suddenly.

"What do you mean?"

"What do you want from me, Sebastian?"

Jared faced me. "I mean, I never really said you could come over here, did I? Maybe I said you could call me up with times and everything like you asked. Maybe. But I didn't say you could just pop over anytime you goddamned pleased. I didn't say you could just waltz your ass in here and start talking about smells and heat!"

He was huffing.

"Have I done something wrong?" I asked.

"Just because you do stuff in a weird-ass way," he said, "doesn't mean the whole world has to be weird-ass to fit you. Some people have normal lives to lead."

"You don't like the disc?"

"That's not the point," he said.

"What is the point?" I asked.

"The point is you annoy people," he said. "You fucking annoy people."

I still had my helmet under my arm. I picked it up now and placed it back on my head. The sour smell in the room stung my nostrils.

"I'll go now," I said. "Nana doesn't know where I am."

"Nana doesn't know where I am," Jared mocked.

I walked to the door and opened it. I stepped out into the hallway, trying not to cry. My throat was tightening. My eyes stung. And I was hoping I could just pad quietly down the stairs and out of the house. I could be back on my Voyager before Janice saw me. I wouldn't have to talk to anyone. I wouldn't bother anyone ever again. Please, please, just let me go. But at the end of the hallway, just coming up the stairs, was another human being. It was Janice Whitcomb. She spotted me immediately.

"Sebastian, you're not going?" she said.

I froze. "I have a lengthy bike ride," I said.

"But the sandwiches are ready."

She spoke with such gravity that her real words took a moment to sink in.

"Do you like grilled cheese?" she added.

I watched her face. She smiled, but it seemed to belie a kind of desperation.

"Sebastian has to go," Jared said from behind me.

"Oh, come eat your sandwiches," she said. "I'll take him home in the van."

I stood still between them.

"Are you feeling better?" Janice asked.

She was staring at Jared now.

"I guess," he said.

"How's your stomach?"

"Fine," he said. "Please drop it."

He met my eyes, then turned away. Mrs. Whitcomb looked at me again.

"So, what's the verdict?" she asked.

"Oh, c'mon!" said Jared. "Jesus Christ! Let's eat sandwiches."

8. How Little I Know

WE WERE SERVED OUR AFTERNOON SNACK ON BROWN
plates with a blob of deep-red tomato ketchup and some sliced
pickles stacked in a pile. To drink, there was grape-flavored punch,
bright purple. I watched as Jared picked up a diagonally cut half of
his sandwich, dipped it in the ketchup, and took a bite. I followed
the same process, and was pleased to find a rich cheesy, tomatoey
flavor bursting into my mouth. I hadn't realized how hungry I was
until I began chewing the golden-toasted white bread. It was but-
tery and made a loud crunch when you bit it. The cheese was salty
and melted down to a near-liquid state. The ketchup was a tangy
accent. The first half was gone in seconds.

We ate in mutual silence, both of us concentrating on our food.
Mrs. Whitcomb stood at the sink, washing out her skillet, listening
to talk radio. Every few minutes, she turned around to glance at
us. More than once, she winked at me. My plan had been to eat the
food as fast as possible and leave. But I actually started to relax at
the table. I took long gulps of grape drink. It was so sweet and cold.
It made my mouth tingle. By the time my food was finished, I had
almost forgotten about Jared altogether. He ate steadily at the other
side of the table, paying me no attention.

I looked around the kitchen, taking inventory of the bright-colored snack foods on the counter. Neon wafers and lurid orange chips cut in perfect triangles. Mrs. Whitcomb walked to the giant avocado-colored fridge and brought out the jug of grape drink. She refilled our glasses and then walked back. I caught a glimpse of the refrigerator door before she closed it, and saw what appeared to be a picture of Jared in the newspaper. It was clipped to the door. The headline said, "On the Mend." I only saw the picture for a moment, but Jared was lying in a bed. He looked even thinner than he was now.

"What are you staring at?" he said.

I looked over at him and found him glaring right at me.

"Jared," said Mrs. Whitcomb. "Have you played your electric guitar for Sebastian?"

"No, *Mommy*," he said, "I haven't."

He narrowed his eyes at me.

"I finally gave in and got it for him, Sebastian, after he promised he'd play it at Youth Group meetings. He's always been musical. He used to have a beautiful singing voice before the surgery."

"God," said Jared. "No one wants to hear about the shitty songs I used to sing. I sang like a girl. Mrs. Huron told you so."

Mrs. Whitcomb flinched at his profanity. "You sang beautifully," she said.

Then she turned to me. "He never sings anymore."

"A real travesty for the world," said Jared. "How will mankind ever recover?"

Then a familiar voice came from the doorway.

"Shut up, already," it said. "I can hear your whining from down the hall."

"Don't start with him, Meredith," Janice said.

I looked up and Meredith Whitcomb rushed into the room, moving in a beeline toward Jared. She was taller than he was. I noticed that first. And her hair was light yellow (almost white), the exact opposite of Jared's. It got darker when it reached her scalp. Her thin lips were covered in a sticky glistening gloss, and her cheeks looked so soft. Her nose was small, and her eyes were a severe grayish blue. She looked at me, and I felt my neck redden. She was magnificent.

"Who is this guy?" she asked, taking a pickle right from Jared's hand.

"This is Sebastian," said Mrs. Whitcomb. "Remember we told you about that dome and the unfortunate woman who had the stroke."

Meredith shrugged, tossing the pickle in her mouth.

"Kind of funny-looking," she said.

She sat down next to me and chomped noisily on the pickle. She looked from Jared to me. "You two make the perfect little pair, don't you?" she said. "Two little wieners."

"Meredith," said Jared, "could you please have your period somewhere else in the house where it won't bother anyone."

"Could you please stop stinking up your room," she said. "It smells like piss again. I can smell it through the floorboards."

Jared had been ready to say something else, but at that last comment he closed his mouth tight. His head sank a few inches. He was quiet for a moment, then scooted out his chair. "C'mon, Sebastian," he said. "I don't want to be infected by the PMS rays in this room."

"Please, just leave each other alone!" said Janice.

For a moment, she sounded on the verge of tears. She placed a frying pan on a rack, clanging some pots together in the process. Jared was already walking out of the room.

"Where are we going?" I asked.

Without looking back at Meredith, I stood and followed Jared's path out of the room. When I found him, he was already halfway up the stairs.

"I should really go, Jared," I said from below. "You told me to . . ."

He wasn't listening to me. He was mumbling something to himself. He paused and looked down the stairs at me. It looked like he wanted to tell me something.

"Have you ever played a guitar before?" he asked.

"No," I said.

"I can teach you a chord."

He looked at me intensely.

"You'll show me your guitar?" I asked.

"Do you want to learn a chord or not?" he asked.

"Yes," I said. "I do."

We walked back into his room and this time I didn't comment on the smell. I pretended not to notice it at all. This time Jared went to his closet and took out a hard black plastic case. He unbuckled it and pulled out a dark blue guitar shaped like an upside-down V. I had never seen anything resembling it. It gleamed. On the side of the strings were thin airbrushed lightning bolts. He set the guitar in my hands.

"Be careful," he said. "Don't drop it."

The plastic was cold in my hands. I gripped the neck and let the V sit across my legs. He went to the closet and pulled out a small amplifier and a cord.

"You are now holding probably the most badass ax ever," he said.

He plugged everything in and a small hum escaped the amplifier when he flicked it on. "It has dual-fucking-humbuckers," he continued, "a compound-radius fingerboard, and twenty-four jumbo frets. It will, if played right, melt your face off."

"Do you play it at church?" I asked.

"Hell no, I do not play it at church," he said. "It would probably piss off God so much, he'd have to blow up the chapel or something."

While he spoke he arranged the fingers of my left hand on the hard metal strings. He pressed my fingers down once they were in place, and a pain shot through my hand.

"Strum," he said.

"What do you mean?" I asked.

He sighed. Without replying, he ran his thumb fast over all the strings at once and a crunchy blast erupted from the speaker. It took a few seconds for the amplifier to return to its initial low fuzz.

"Ha!" said Jared. "Did you feel that one in your balls?"

"I don't know," I said.

He ran his thumb over them again, up and down this time, and out came another wave of music. That same push of noise and harmony. It was a powerful flush of sound.

"That's E!" he shouted. "It's the best chord!"

Again, his thumb and forefinger attacked the strings. I pressed my fingers down as hard as I could, and the sound bucked out of the speaker and into the room. I felt an odd pulse in my arms, spreading all the way to my chest. Over and over, he strummed. The sound was deafening. The strings poked into my fingertips. My ears buzzed. And when the sound reached its frenzied peak, Jared waited what felt like minutes before he calmed the strings with his flat palm. I hadn't been watching him during the last round of noises. I had closed my eyes in deep concentration, pretending I was solely responsible for the sounds. I looked at him now, and noticed his eyes growing red.

"Jared?" I asked.

"What?"

"Are you hurt?"

"No," he said.

The guitar was still screeching a little in my hands. I tried to settle it, but it kept going, shrieking.

"You were in the newspaper," I said. "I saw it on the fridge."

Jared blinked. "I pissed myself, earlier," he said.

I nearly dropped the guitar, but I caught myself.

"You urinated . . ."

"In my pants," he said. "That's what stinks in here. I lied when I said there was no smell. There's a smell. It's my pissed pants. They're in the closet."

Jared let escape a short laugh, then punctuated it with a sniffle.

"How did this occur?" I asked.

"Meds," he said. "It's this new med I'm on. It makes me go to the bathroom all the time. I got tired of it, so I tried to hold it in, you know. And . . . I fucking couldn't."

He sat down on the floor now in front of a box of compact discs. He lifted up a few and pulled out a package of cigarettes.

"Would you put a towel at the bottom of the door, Sebastian?" he asked.

I laid the humming guitar on the bed and found a towel, hanging on a hook near the closet. I covered the bottom of the door. Jared lit a cigarette.

"My mom wants me to try going back to school soon," he said. "How am I supposed to do that when I'm pissing in my pants? How is that going to work?"

He took a long inhalation and spit it back out.

"How old are you?" I asked.

"Sixteen."

"How did you learn to smoke?"

"A kid at the hospital showed me," he said. "This eighteen-year-old in for back surgery. He was really into the Dead Kennedys. Anyway, he taught me. Any other questions?"

The smoke crept up and gathered around the light.

"Why were you in the hospital?" I asked.

"Do you want to see?" he said.

"See what?"

"I can show you what I was in for."

"I want to see," I said.

Jared extinguished his cigarette in a nearby soda can. He rose to his feet and walked to the stereo. He fumbled with the switches again. I watched him push track number five again on his disc.

"Take a good look, okay?" he said. "I'm only going to do this once."

The opening drumbeats of "Teenagers from Mars" began again. Jared closed his eyes. I saw his eyeballs fluttering behind his lids. The humidifier was still going in the corner, and I noticed now how the room seemed to be alive with shiny droplets of moisture. It glistened on the front of his music posters. On his disc cases. On the frames of his black glasses. Jared pulled an arm inside his shirt. Then he pulled the other arm in. He wriggled for a moment and then lifted the skeleton shirt over his head.

He held onto his shirt, and I could see his hand shaking. On the stereo the song was in its rollicking chorus again.

Teenagers from Mars, and we don't care.
Teenagers from Mars and we don't . . .

Right in the middle of Jared's chest was a long thin scar. It was purplish and perfectly even. An entirely straight slice.

From downstairs came Mrs. Whitcomb's voice, scarcely audible over the music.

"Sebastian, I can take you home now if you're ready!"

I didn't answer. The stereo kept playing.

"I have someone else's heart," said Jared.

I stared at his hunched pale body, his ribs like metal struts. I tried to imagine the heart in there, an enlarged tangle of blue and purple valves. I thought of the scar opening up like an eyelid to show me.

"I've only had it for a couple of years," he said, looking down toward his chest.

I walked over to Jared. He didn't move. He just watched as I reached out a finger to touch the scar. At the last minute, though, he grabbed my hand. He gripped it for a moment then let it go.

"Jared!" shouted Mrs. Whitcomb. "Did you guys hear me?"

"He's leaving right now, Mom!" Jared yelled.

He moved away from me and started carefully pulling his shirt back on. I retrieved my helmet from the bed and stood watching Jared for a moment. He did not face me. I could tell he was waiting for me to exit the room. So I just walked out, and he did not follow. We didn't say good-bye. I made my way down the hallway and back downstairs. Mrs. Whitcomb was waiting by the front door with her van keys in hand. Meredith was nowhere to be seen.

"C'mon," said Janice. "Let's get you back home."

9. The Greater Intellect Speaks!

IT WAS DARK AND STARLESS BY THE TIME I GOT back to the dome that evening. The woods were profoundly still and the leaves on the ground were coated in a slick frost. There was only one light on in the dome, the hanging lamp in Nana's bedroom. I couldn't see the light itself, only its reflective glow on the tall trunks of the walnut trees. Nana was not waiting for me at the door. I had anticipated a serious face behind the glass. Possibly a vexed one. But she was not there. And she didn't make a sound when I stepped into our house, holding a thick cylinder of spray paint in each hand.

Moments ago, I had asked Janice Whitcomb to deposit me halfway up the hill with my bicycle so I could walk the rest of the way. She agreed, but when she pulled the van to a stop on the shoulder of the road, she hadn't unlocked my door. I'd yanked on the handle, but the door wouldn't slide. I had looked to Janice and found her just watching out her window, taking in the dark woods around her. I lifted the handle once more, and that's when she looked over at me and began speaking.

"He doesn't really socialize very well," she said. "I know that. How could I not know that? He's my child."

I tried to maintain a neutral expression.

"He has some challenges with maturity," she said. "I guess that's obvious. And then there's his father . . ."

She gripped the steering wheel hard and then opened her palms and rested them on top of it. "And we don't get along," she continued, quietly now. "So there's that. I don't know how to talk to him, Sebastian. I've read books. I've read a whole library of these silly books. But it doesn't . . . it won't take. He doesn't have anything to say to me."

Her last sentence was nearly a whisper.

"Mrs. Whitcomb?" I said.

She looked at me like she'd forgotten I was in the van.

"I'm sorry," she said, and laughed a little to herself. "I just wanted to tell you one thing. I didn't mean to go on."

"It's okay," I said.

"What I want to say is . . ."

She closed her eyes.

"I just want to say, I hope you'll come back."

"Come back?"

The windshield in front of us was beginning to fog.

"Come back to our house, sometime, to see him," she said.

After she said this, she reached her hand down and popped the latch to the back of the van. The cold evening air rushed through in an instant and cooled the interior. Janice got out of the car, but it took me a second or two to do the same. She helped me unload my Voyager, and set it gently against the back bumper. Then she wrapped me in another of her hugs. It took me by surprise, but it didn't bother me once it was occurring. I had only met Janice Whitcomb twice, and both times she had embraced me. It made me wonder how often most families touched.

"I really hope you'll come to a Youth Group meeting, Sebastian," she said. "I think you'd like it."

She released me, and I grabbed a hold of my handlebars. I steadied the bike against my side.

"I'll try," I said.

She nodded her head once and then got back into the van. She fastened her seat belt and pulled a great circling U-turn. She sped off, back the way she came, leaving me bewildered at the side of the empty road. I looked at the spot in the gravel where her tires had been. I could still feel the warmth of her coat. I turned and entered the woods.

My heart was beating quickly as I jogged with my bike. Without a second thought, I stopped and removed the spray cans from the basket and tore off the caps. I pressed the triggers and activated them until they were both half empty. In the process, I purposefully let a mist of ivory paint land on my wrists and the tips of my hair to make it appear that I had spent the day working.

And now, in the moonlit dome, the spray paint gleamed in my tiny blond arm hairs like ice crystals. I shook the cans again, knocking the ball bearing around, trying to alert Nana that I was home. She did not stir. The place was soundless. So I knocked on Nana's door with the end of a paint cylinder. Then I pushed it open without invitation and entered. "Hello, Nana," I said. "The signs have been altered as you asked."

Nana was sitting on the floor, a circle of books and papers around her. It took her a moment to realize where she was in the room. She looked outside first, and then spied my reflection in the glass and turned around.

"Sebastian," she said. "Oh. I'm so glad you've returned."

"You are?"

"Something has happened," she said.

I noticed now how vacant her eyes appeared. She was looking right past me.

"I have experienced a moment," she said, and stopped to think. "A moment of prescience."

"A vision?"

She nodded slowly. "I fell asleep this afternoon," she said, "and I slept for . . . so long. I thought I had slept for a day. Or a week! All the while I thought that I was dreaming. But, you see, I was not."

She paused, and I could see her moving her lips, trying to articulate the next part in her head. "I was not dreaming at all," she said. "I was attuned to the signals of a Greater Intellect."

She coughed then, and her poise temporarily faltered. "I'm so thirsty," she said. "Please . . . a glass of filtered water."

I set down the spray cans and walked, half conscious, out of her room and to the tap where we had long had a state-of-the-art filtration system installed. I rubbed a palm over my painted left wrist. My hairs were stuck together. I recalled the feeling of holding Jared's electric guitar and how my thin muscles had felt full of some kind of current. But the sensation withered in a moment, and I filled a glass with water. I walked back to Nana's room. She was lying in her bed now, looking out into the trees. I moved to the side of the bed and held the water out to her.

"Put it to my lips," she said. "Please. Dispense it."

I rested the glass on her thin lips and tipped it slightly.

"Nana, do you feel okay?" I asked.

She swallowed huge mouthfuls of water before stopping for a breath.

"From now on," she gasped, "I think the truth! The Greater Intellect told me that today, just like he told Bucky."

She drank the rest of the water and wiped her mouth with the back of her hand.

"I was in this room," she said, carefully selecting each word, "when the Greater Intellect spoke. It was a low voice. Very quiet. And it told me my life was drawing to a close. It said, 'Josephine, your time is fleeting, but you must devote the last moments to the highest advantage of others. You must act with great ambition!'"

"This happened here?" I asked.

I looked around the room.

"Then I saw an image," she continued. "Perfectly clear. It was our dome from a great height, Sebastian. I saw it. And it was not the home we live in now. It was not the present version, but . . . a future dome."

An odd smile formed on her lips.

"What did it look like?" I asked.

"It was a marvelous Geoscope," she said.

"I don't know what that is," I said.

"A globe. A world!"

She sat up and gripped my left shoulder with her long fingers.

"Every single country! Painted to scale on the side of our house. Spaceship Earth realized. And I knew what it meant!" she said.

She gripped harder, and her fingernails dug into my skin.

"It would be a way to remind the people. To remind them about the relationships between human beings and our planet. It would instill a comprehensive worldview in everyone who saw it. And of course, it would be the first location of my institute."

She spoke the last part quickly, and I almost didn't catch it.

"Your institute?" I said. "You haven't even been administering tours, Nana. You've barely been speaking until today."

She was not listening to me, though. She got up off the bed and removed her hand from my shoulder. She sat down in the middle of her papers.

"I've been drawing up plans," she said. "Of course some of our view will have to be . . . obstructed. But that can't be helped. This is for the highest advantage."

She picked up a pencil and flipped open her sketch pad. The page was covered in graphite-smeared drawings of our future planet-dome, nestled in the middle of a crosshatched section of woods. North America stretched over the living room. Canada blanketed my room. I sat down on the floor across from Nana. She continued drawing, forming the big toe of southern India over her bedroom.

"Nana," I said softly, "is it possible that your physician at the hospital might disapprove of this plan?"

Her eyes shot up and stared into mine. A lucidity returned to her gaze.

"Sebastian," she said, "I end this state of inertia today. Do you understand?"

She held a pencil aloft. It quivered.

"I must embrace the final act. This is the next stage on our paths. And for me, it will be the last. One last thing I can do before the Greater Intellect reclaims me. Do you see? This is everything we've been working toward."

Nana returned to her sketching. Her eyes scanned the thin gray lines of continents and islands. She moistened her dry lips.

"I hope you liked your trip to town today," she said, her head down. "You're going to take more of them now. It's going to be a big responsibility for you. That should make you happy."

She looked up at me one last time, a slight smile on her face.
"Yes," I said. "Very happy."

THAT NIGHT, I WAS NOT ABLE TO SLEEP.

I twisted myself around in my sheets, and by the predawn hours, it felt like my body had entirely disremembered how to slumber. At first, I thought only of Nana and everything she had told me. There was something extremely disquieting and familiar about her story the more I pondered it. Eventually my memory caught up with me, and I realized why her words had bothered me so much. An occurrence similar to hers had happened to Fuller long ago.

The year was 1927, and Bucky had just met with one of many business failures early in his career. Ordinarily, commercial failure was just a temporary setback in the life of a man half blind with curiosity and ambition. But this time he had a wife and a new daughter to support, and he had no income at all. He began avoiding his home, numbing himself with liquor. One evening he wandered down to the shore of Lake Michigan in a self-pitying state. He stopped by the water to deliberate about his future. He conjured up his history of failed plans. His wife's family had made known their dislike for him. They thought he was impractical, a joker. This last debacle would surely bring a new round of recriminations. Some of the family elders had even invested in his venture.

Bucky decided that the only way out was to end his life. He would simply swim until he could no longer see the land behind him. He would disappear. His insurance money would improve the lives of his family. They would be better off without him.

He made up his mind to go through with his plan and right when he was about to act, something happened that would profoundly shape the remainder of his years. All at once, Bucky felt himself rising off the ground and floating in what he called a "sparkling sphere of light." He looked around, and it seemed to him that time as he knew it had come to a complete halt. The earth was standing utterly still. All was quiet. Then a voice, confident and soft, began speaking to him. It seemed to come out of the air itself and find its way to his ear. This voice told him that he did not have the right to kill himself. He could not cease to live yet. This was because he was important to the universe. He would, in fact, be hurting others if he followed through with this grave action. "You think the truth," the voice told him. "Now go proclaim the truth."

Bucky was not told precisely what his role was that day, but at the very least, he knew that he had one. That simple knowledge was enough to change Fuller's course forever. He could now move forward into uncertainty with at least one small light to guide him.

Nana's story was not quite as harrowing. She had not mentioned a desire to eliminate herself, as far as I knew. But I wondered if her experience that afternoon had been similarly preceded by a very real dispirit of Bucky's kind. What exactly had she been thinking and feeling since the hospital? How serious was her anger and humility? I continued to tumble around in my bed.

I was finally able to drift to sleep by the early morning. But even in a dream state, my mind was filled with the most puzzling images. I watched, for instance, as Jared lay on the floor of his bedroom, trying to keep his beating heart from leaping out of his chest. His face was obscured by his hair, and I could only see his small struggling body, a human heart bouncing like a baby rabbit. In another dream, Janice Whitcomb sat across from me in a room, watching intently my every movement. It seemed like there was something she wanted to tell me, but I didn't know what it was.

Then there was the single image I could not shake loose. The most surprising one of all. It kept creeping back into my mind's eye, in spite of my anguished attempts to suppress it. Strangely enough, the picture was one of Meredith Whitcomb. More accurately, the image was one of Meredith Whitcomb snacking on a pickle, just the way she had been in her kitchen.

In all my early reading about Fuller, there were most definitely sections about women. But I did not come to realize this until my fourteenth year. This is because portions of his biographies were entirely redacted, crossed out by Nana with a thin black Magic Marker and one of her T squares for drafting. Thus, there were many times over the years when I came upon a paragraph that was stricken from the record. No identifiable words. Not even a participle. Most of these sections seemed to occur in his young adult years.

His childhood was blackout-free, right up to the teens. Then, at some point near the end of his prep schooling, I always reached a dead end, and my eyes were forced to skate over the black ice of redaction. The sentences were perfectly blocked out. Like so: ████
██
████████████████. As you can see, thick flawless lines of black. No stray dots above the *i*'s. No hovering umlauts. Nothing.

It wasn't until I was fourteen that I realized I could read the text under this marker just by holding the pages up to the brightest midday sunlight. Up to this point, I had suspected that Nana was simply removing the out-of-date information from the books. That assumption disappeared when the first rays of sun permeated her editorial smoke screen. The first sentence I read was the one above. It read: "Always searching for a party and a good time, Fuller also spent a great deal of his time in brothels."

I had to spend a large amount of time with a dictionary before I was able to grasp the significance of this detail. And when I understood it, on a surface level, it shed considerable light on other chapters that had also felt the wrath of Nana's darkening pen. On top of whole paragraphs, there were also images completely encased in a wall of black ink. Now imagine, if you can, the depth of alarm when I held the pages of an anatomy textbook up on a sunny afternoon and saw this:

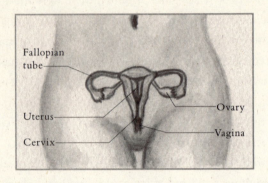

It took me days to recover.

But the fact is that I was already in possession of some facts about puberty and human development. I knew, for example, that the larynx enlarged during puberty and the voice got deeper. I knew that the shoulders broadened. I knew that hair sprouted in the underarms, and that the sebaceous glands produced sebum, which could cause acne. Finally, I was familiar with the fact that girls were likely to become especially stimulating to boys at this age.

Some of these things had happened to me, in a limited capacity. My voice, I found, occasionally switched timbre mid-word as if I'd suddenly swallowed a pebble and it had lodged in my throat. I had grown the intermittent blemish on my chin or near my hairline, but it always went away. And, I had noticed the cultivation of hair in surprising places. That being said, I had never been truly inconvenienced by the process of development until the night after my visit to the Whitcombs.

I had found out Jared's secret, a disclosure that left me with countless questions. And Nana had succumbed to one of her states of indeterminate wonder. I didn't know what to do about either of these matters. Yet I found my mind dominated by a single portrait of Meredith Whitcomb, her incisors so sharp, so white, tearing into a Gedney "Baby Dill" pickle. I had never been a tremendous fan of pickles, but the satisfaction of that crunching noise, combined with the way her eyes (that puzzling gray-blue) were squinting almost imperceptibly at the exact moment of the chomp, did something to me that I had not fully acknowledged at the time. That night, I couldn't seem to forget it. And not only did I see her face in my fleeting dreams, but I heard that crisp *crrrrr-unch*, played at high volume throughout. It was the sound track to my unconscious. *Crrr-runch! 'runch 'runch 'runch!*

I woke hourly in tizzies.

And when I woke up for good that morning, newly disoriented after a sleep-burst, my room was sun-filled. A sparse overnight snowfall was melting off the dome, and sunlight was reflecting directly into my eyes. It took me a few moments to remember the events of the day before, but it wasn't until I rose that I became entirely certain it hadn't all been a dream. My main evidence was the e-mail from Jared.

It read as follows:

> Sebastian,
>
> If you try to touch me again, I will beat your ass.
>
> I have an idea. Call me.
>
> J.

I read the message five or six times before wandering downstairs for breakfast. I went through the motions of preparing my meal with the muscle memory of an old man. My hands poured and dumped, independent of conscious thought. It took me a few minutes before I realized that Nana was not hovering around me. She was absent. I assumed, at first, as I sat munching my bland cereal, that she was still resting. I had heard her flipping sketchbook pages and generally rummaging around her bedroom until well past midnight. But I was shocked, when I finally got up to investigate, to find the door to her room standing wide open and absolutely no Nana inside.

"Hello?" I shouted.

I looked up, half expecting to find her atop the dome already transforming it into her Geoscope, but she was not there. I strode through the living room and right outside, still in my blue sateen pajamas. I walked around to the back side of the dome where I would have a fully unobstructed view of our property. I searched the trees as far as my tired eyes would let me. But no tuft of uncombed white hair poked over the hill. No neon tracksuit lay immobile in the light snow.

I waited an hour or so, unmoving on the couch, visualizing Nana's safe return. When she didn't materialize, I walked over to our old telephone and considered notifying the police. Instead, I picked up the phone book and turned to a rumpled page sticking out of the middle. There was the Whitcombs' address and number where I'd found it the day before. I dialed the number and Jared picked up on the second ring.

"What took you so long?"

"Jared?" I said.

"Yeah," he said, "I'm Jared."

"How did you know it was me?"

"Nobody calls my family," he said. "They're all a bunch of losers. Meredith's prostitution hotline is the only one that gets any action."

At the utterance of his sister's name, I pictured an amputated Baby Dill and my neck tingled. "I received your e-mail this morning," I said.

"I thought that might happen when I sent it to you," he said.

I could hear the quick puff of his breath. He was excited about something. I decided not to mention Nana's disappearance.

"So Janice said you scampered into the woods like a goddamn squirrel last night. Do you secretly live out there, and crap in the dirt?"

"No."

"Were you camping in a pup tent?"

"Is this what you wanted to speak to me about?" I asked.

"We'll get to that, Mr. McFeely," he said. "You're lucky I'm even speaking to you today."

"Mr. Mc . . . ?"

"Actually, you're lucky you're alive. If your stupid fingertip had even grazed my chest, I would have bitten it off."

"Jared," I said. "Why do you have to talk to me like this?"

"I think we should start a band," he said.

"What?"

As usual, he had slipped the most important words into a tiny space.

"Okay," he said, "okay. I know I'm taking a giant fucking risk here. I'm going to have to teach you everything, and you're obviously going to do it all wrong. But I'm not looking for a Sid Vicious, you know. I just need somebody to do what I say. Not somebody with a real personality. I get to have the ideas. Don't argue."

I tried to wade through his babble, but it was that first question that lingered.

"I don't know how to be in a band," I said.

"You don't know anything. You probably can't pee by yourself. But I'm going to mold you. That's the whole idea. I'm the front man. You'll play bass."

"Bass guitar," I said.

"Don't call it that," he said.

"But Nana won't . . ."

"Sebastian, don't start with all that," he interrupted. "C'mon and just listen to me for a second. I'm not done with my pitch."

"Jared."

"Do you know who Napoleon was?" he asked.

"The emperor of France," I said.

"Wrong," said Jared. "He was the first punk rocker."

"He was the emperor of France," I said.

" 'Death is nothing, but to live defeated and inglorious is to die daily,' " said Jared. "You know who said that?"

"Napoleon?"

"Yes. And do you know what, Sebastian?"

"What?"

"We are dying daily."

I could hear him breathing in short gasps. I imagined humidified air pouring into his lungs, swirling around in there.

"We are dying," he said, "and we are defeated and we are motherfucking inglorious. And Sebastian, Napoleon was right!"

I heard the flint of a lighter, and the sound of Jared's inhalation. I didn't know what to say, and Jared seemed content to enjoy the silence after his speech. I watched out the front for any sign of Nana.

"Where am I going to obtain a bass?" I asked.

"Church," said Jared. "We'll borrow it and tell Janice that we're practicing for a Youth Group performance or something. Jesus songs."

"Jared," I said, slowly and carefully. "Nana doesn't allow me to absent myself from the dome whenever I want. And she has just come up with a new project for me. She needs my aid. She needs me. It might be the next stage in my life."

Jared exhaled deeply, and I braced myself for his next tirade.

"Then I guess it's your choice," he said instead.

"It's not that I don't want to form a band," I said.

"One time," said Jared.

This time I just waited for him to explain.

"One time," he said. "I'm asking you one time. I understand your situation is effed up. My situation is effed up, too. But this is the one thing that doesn't make me want to puke. And that seems like a good enough reason to me. So think about it, and figure it out. Get back to me."

His dramatic pause was hard to miss.

"But don't plan on being my friend if you say no."

And again, I was listening to a dial tone.

10. *Once I Was Not Such a Fibber*

IN THE END, NANA DID RETURN THAT DAY, BUT NOT until the early afternoon. By the time she came back, the night's thin layer of flurries had melted completely and the day felt unseasonably warm. But I was inside, on the verge of nervous collapse, when the yellow taxicab pulled up and opened its door. Nana leaped out, very much alive and with a brand of energy I hadn't seen in some time. She handed a few crumpled bills to her driver, then plowed across the soggy brown yard in her pull-on duck boots, talking to herself, as the mud squished beneath her. Under her arm, she carried a small globe and a thin sleeve of papers. She walked into the dome, kicked off her boots, slick with sludge, and brushed right by me.

"Nana," I said, watching her march away from me. "Where have you been?"

She turned around and grinned. "Risking action," she said.

She wandered into the kitchen and immediately began peeling and coring things from a nearby basket. I watched as she eviscerated a quince and shoved it into the Vita-Mix without looking.

"I was worried," I said. "What kind of action?"

She continued preparing her smoothie without looking at me.

"I spoke to the . . . the newspaper people. The *North Branch*

Courier. I spoke about our new endeavor. They're going to cover our progress. A photographer will arrive in a few days."

"A photographer?" I said. "You went to the *Courier* this morning? I don't understand. I thought you said the *Courier* was a daily record of glorified navel-gazing."

"They provide exposure. Exposure is what we seek."

I could only watch her newly dexterous hands with incredulity.

"This is moving very quickly," I said. "We haven't even fully discussed how it will work."

She took a deep breath and closed her eyes.

"Everyone discusses," she spouted. "Everyone has ideas and they discuss and discuss and emit giant amounts of hot gas. The visionaries are the ones with the courage to act. To risk action. How is humanity supposed to improve if no one ever does anything? Can you please enlighten me, Sebastian? The time has passed for gas! It is time for solids. Manifestations. It is time for us to be visionaries."

It was the longest continuous speech I'd heard her utter since the hospital. I stood dumbfounded while she turned on the Vita-Mix and poured a pint of soy milk into its churning depths. The digestive sound of sluicing and gurgling filled the kitchen.

She stopped it again.

"Action," she said. "You see?"

I WAS STARTING TO SEE. ALL AROUND ME THERE WAS action. And I was standing in the midst of the tempest, trying my very best to dodge flying projectiles. I walked upstairs and looked out of my invisible walls at the town below. Chimney smoke from the houses mixed with the low clouds. Miniature cars propelled and whooshed down the expressway. Specks greeted one another.

I tried to imagine a scale painting of Saskatchewan blocking my view of all this. The Yukon over my bed, keeping me from the sky. I imagined living inside a miniature Earth. Could this really be the next stage?

I sat down at my computer and stared at the blinking cursor. I began to tap out a word with my pointer finger. The word was "Sid." I tapped another word: "Vicious." Sid Vicious, the bass player that Jared had mentioned. It took me very little time to find information and work out a brief biography.

Mr. Vicious had played for a band called the Sex Pistols. He was an illegal-substance abuser. He assaulted people and things. He may have stabbed his true love. And he died at the age of twenty-one just after being released from prison. I studied the black-and-white pictures that accompanied the articles. Sid was rail-thin like me, but he had tall bristly hair and a dirty smudge of a mustache. His eyes were slivers, and his thin brows arched over them fiendishly. Also, he seemed to be wearing the same pants in every photo. He looked not dissimilar to a picture of a feral child I'd seen in one of Nana's books about scientific curiosities. I read on for the better part of an hour before I came across the first nugget of information that actually meant something to me.

Sid Vicious did not know how to play the bass.

I had to read the sentence twice just to make sure it was true. But it was. He barely understood how to make the instrument work. Most of his parts on the Sex Pistols' albums were performed by other musicians. And, in concert, his amplifier was rarely plugged in. He could play a few notes, but his addiction to needle narcotics normally kept him from performing them in the right order. Yet here was his picture on every Web site devoted to punk music. There were posters and mugs and figurines with his sneering face on them. He was a hero. A quote of Bucky's immediately came to mind, one that Nana had been repeating to me since I was young: "Dare to be naive."

An improbable truth occurred to me, something I should have known all along. You didn't have to know how to play the bass to be a bassist. At least, not if you were a practitioner of punk. Artlessness was, perhaps, the main idea. Jared had hinted that this was so. If you dared to be naive, and dove in without guile and accepted notions, you could still be successful. Thus, it was possible that with enough practice I could learn how not-to-play-the-bass, in just the right way. In the spirit of this new endeavor, I decided not to think about it all too much. I simply composed an e-mail. I risked action.

> Dear Jared,
> I accept the offer to play music in your band. When is the next meeting of the "Youth's Group?"
> I have a plan. It is a naive plan.
> Sincerely,
> Sebastian
> P.S. Did Sid impale Nancy or not? Theories?

What I did not tell Jared, and what I admitted to myself only later, was that there was another part of Sid's story that had affected me. It wasn't so much in the text of the dramatic odes composed to him on the Web. And it certainly wasn't his later attempts at singing, which I heard in snippets on poorly recorded files. It was the fact that in every other photograph of Vicious, he was standing side by side with a brooding, mysterious blond girl, who appeared entirely devoted to him.

Granted, her hair was curly, not brushed into straight sheets, and she wore so much dark goo on her eyes it was hard to tell if they were really there. But from the right angle, Nancy Spungen of the infamous Sid and Nancy slightly resembled Meredith Whitcomb. At least the sneer was identical. And the hunched posture. And this man who was skinny and strange and a tad weasel-like had managed to capture her affections. Of course, things had ended very poorly, but just the fact that they had been romantic at all was nothing short of inspiring.

I didn't let my imagination wander any further than that. I just took note of the fact that at some point in history, an odd skeletal teen had entranced a beautiful angry woman. Such things were possible. And if this was possible, other things were possible. Like being in a band, for example. I checked my e-mail, to see if Jared had responded. His message was short and to the point.

> Sunday 5:00.
> Come to my house. Wear slacks.
> P.S. Sid was framed.

I went back downstairs and found Nana in her room, sketching again. She was lying down with her head facing the sky, holding the drawing pad above her. The sounds of male orca whale calls emanated from the small stereo on her dresser. I smelled the aroma of a recently lit scented candle. Sage. Egyptian musk, perhaps. She paid little attention to me when I stepped into her room. Nana had entered these obsessive fugue states before, but this one was the most all-consuming I had seen. I walked slowly up next to her until my shadow was blocking her drawing light.

"He's been dead for twenty-five years," she said. "Did you know that?"

I thought immediately of my father, but that had been only ten years.

"Bucky," she said, anticipating my question. "I . . . somehow. The day passed and I did not remember. It was the twenty-fifth anniversary of his death."

She looked up at me, puzzled.

"He would have been one hundred and thirteen." Her mouth stretched into a sad smile. "How could I forget? I never forget."

"If he were here," I said, "I'm sure he would have forgiven you already."

Nana took a long drink of water from a smudged glass next to her. She closed her eyes and breathed in through her nose. The squawk of a whale brought her back.

"If he were here," she said, "I wouldn't have to remember his death."

"Did you go to the funeral?" I asked.

She shook her head.

"Not invited."

"Why not?"

"His children never knew me," she said. "No one close to him really did. But it was better that way. I never had to compete, you see. My time was my time only. And otherwise, I kept him in my thoughts. Like I do now."

The flames of the candles shivered as Nana stood up and stretched. She coughed a little, and stood facing me. "Did you need something, Sebastian?"

"Yes," I said, "but I can come back if you're . . ."

"I'm perfectly fine," she said. "What is it?"

"I wondered," I said, a quaver in my voice, "how much paint will we need to begin with?"

Nana sat down on her bed. She shucked off a pair of slippers, exposing her small white feet. She cracked her toes. "A practical question," she said.

Her eyelids dropped closed.

"I'm imagining a few gallons. Something green. We'll want to start with Antarctica, the South Pole. It's always blue or white on maps. But I just don't envision that. On our Geoscope, it will be verdant."

I took a deep breath and then looked down into Nana's spacey gaze.

"When I purchased the spray paint, the owner of the shop told me about a sale . . . this upcoming Sunday. I think it would be to our economical advantage to buy the paint then. Is that satisfactory?"

Nana adjusted herself so she was recumbent with her back leaning against the wall. She picked up a drawing pencil and chewed on the end.

"Sebastian, Sebastian," she said.

I waited silently for her rebuke. From the stereo came another honking shriek of an orca, and I flinched.

"Of course," she said. "I'm proud of your business sense. Very shrewd. Bucky would be proud. It took him such a long time to . . . cultivate that talent."

"Sunday, then," I said. "I'll go for you Sunday."

Nana didn't respond. She just picked up her sketch pad from the floor and began to draw again. As I was leaving, I heard her talking to herself again. "Twenty-five years," she mumbled. I watched from the doorway as her pencil floated across the pad, her thin hand as steady and guided as always. When I was out of her sight, one last whale scream emerged from the distant stereo as if joining me in a private celebration.

11. In the Supply Closet of the Lord

"GOD IS A VERB, NOT A NOUN."

That is arguably the most famous of Fuller's comments about religion. It is also the closest he ever came to clarity on the subject. He made many other comments, but they weren't as direct. He said, for example, that he feared the use of faith for ulterior motives. He said he believed most in the individual's power to form ideas, not the group's. And when asked about his personal beliefs, he exclaimed things like "God is the everywhere and everywhen evolving omnireality." Or: "God is the eternal integrity of the omniregenerative universe!" Usually, at that point, an interviewer moved on to the next question.

Nana had always spoken about religion in much this same way. The result was that I had very little idea what to expect of the evening ahead of me as I pedaled my Voyager on the newly familiar route to the Whitcombs'. Much like God, I was also a verb that afternoon. I was a verb in slacks. My only pair of creased pants was from a few years ago when Nana briefly considered the idea of dressing me up in a suit to greet our dome visitors. The pants were too short, and left small patches of skin vulnerable to gales from the expressway. Fortunately, I had managed to find a scarf, earmuffs, and my puffy winter jacket from the year before. So I was not in serious danger of frostbite and amputation.

I had actually purchased Nana's paint the day before, during her afternoon nap, and I had ferreted it away in the shed where I kept the Voyager. So all I had to concentrate on was the mission at hand. My plan was a simple one. Before the meeting of the youths, Jared would show me where the bass guitar was stored. I would remember this location. Then, at some point during the course of the meeting, Jared would provide a distraction and I would slip away. At that point, I would stash the bass guitar somewhere outside where I could pick it up later. I had e-mailed this plan to Jared the day before, and he had seemed satisfied, replying only, "That's not completely asinine." Now the plot just had to be implemented correctly.

I arrived at the Whitcomb house at four-fifty P.M. and parked my bicycle alongside the house. The wind blew a tremendous gust right when I hopped off the seat, and I heard the angel chime on the front porch, tinkling away. I walked past the windows of the house. Evening was approaching, and all the shades were pulled. In the orange light of Meredith's room, I saw a shadow moving back and forth. I watched a moment, trying to distinguish her features. But I couldn't quite make them out. Her silhouette was moving too quickly. I realized she was dancing, her shadow playing over the shade. She swayed her hips and shook her head wildly.

I pulled myself away and wandered around to the front of the house. I knocked loudly. Nearly a minute passed before I heard her voice. "Fine, if everybody else is paralyzed or something!" The door flew open and there was Meredith, standing before me in a close-fitting green sweater and a dark skirt with tights. Her hair was down and a lock hung over her left eye. Her face was slightly moist. She smelled like peach lotion.

"Oh," she said. "You."

She didn't tell me to come in. She just left the door swinging open and stepped away. I noticed as she moved into the hallway that she had a thin silver phone pressed to her ear. Had she been dancing and speaking at the same time?

"No," she mumbled into the phone. "Just this little weirdo that my brother's in love with or something."

I watched her walk away, her tights swooshing as her thighs rubbed together. In front of me, Jared walked in from the kitchen. He wore a diminutive black suit jacket over a black T-shirt that read "WWJD."

"What Would Jared Do," he said.

"I don't know," I said.

"It's not a question, asshole," he said. "That's what the shirt stands for."

He pointed to the thick letters on his T-shirt. Then he looked at me.

"Your pants are small," he said.

"I know," I said. "Where's your mother?"

He pointed toward her bedroom.

"Still in communion with the Lord or something," he said. "She always spends time by herself before we leave. Who knows what she's doing."

He sat down on the floor and pressed a few buttons on his music player, scrolling through a list of songs.

"She seems like a very . . . devout person," I said.

Jared chuckled without looking up from the tiny screen.

"These days, yeah," he said. "She didn't use to go to church at all. When I was younger, all we did on Sundays was dick off and eat pancakes. But the last couple of years she's suddenly Saint Janice of North Branch. And of course she has to parade us around everywhere like her mini colony of lepers. The tiny cripple and the whore."

Mrs. Whitcomb walked into the room in a hurry, holding a tote bag of supplies.

"What did you say, Jared?" she asked.

"Nothing."

"Good evening, Sebastian," she said.

She looked at my ill-fitting pants and smiled. Then she looked around the living room and shouted Meredith's name down the hallway. Meredith sauntered back into the room, holding the phone at her side.

"I'm ready," she said. "God!"

"Please don't blaspheme on group night," said Janice. "Is that so much to ask you? To not be profane, one night a week?"

"Busted," said Jared. "Busted by God."

"And none of your cursing tonight," Janice snapped at Jared.

"What cursing?" he said.

"The kind that comes flying out of your mouth whenever you open it," she said.

Jared shrugged his shoulders. I looked over at Meredith, but she only met my eyes for a second. Then everyone was looking at me. Meredith turned to her mother.

"Is Sebastian going to take off his stupid helmet?" she asked.

I reached my hand up and felt the hard plastic of protective gear.

IMMANUEL METHODIST LOOKED MORE LIKE A MIN-iature of a church than a real one. I had seen a few churches previously, but this was the first time I had ever entered one. I was surprised to discover that it was only two stories high, and in most ways resembled an ordinary living space. There was worn tan carpet in most rooms, mint green tile in the halls, and the smell of old coffee in the air. Yet the windows were painted with splendid artistry, complete with robed and bearded men who gathered and wept and bled and bled. And above us (I had noted outside) an ornate cross-topped spire stuck into the darkening evening sky like a finger pointing up toward the cosmos.

Janice left us in the "Recreation Room" while she went down the hall to set something up in another location. Jared and I sat down on a threadbare couch. Meredith leaned against a Ping-Pong table and began typing on the buttons of her phone. The walls were bare save a few photos of sunsets and streams.

"We're going to the bathroom," said Jared. "Tell Mom not to freak out if she comes back."

"You guys going in there to bang your wangs together?" Meredith said, still typing on her device.

"Yeah," said Jared. "A round of wang-banging."

"Thought so," she said.

We walked out into the hallway and made our way past a series of classrooms with children's drawings on the walls. Our foot-scuffs echoed in the empty space.

"What a worthless hooch," said Jared.

"I don't know," I said.

All around us there hung crayoned portraits of Jesus. "Keep Him with You Every Day," read a banner over the drawings.

"You don't know *what*?"

"I don't know," I repeated.

I followed Jared down the dim hallway. It smelled like dust and the citrus-scented cleaner I used on the dome. The light of dusk shone through a glass door at the end of the corridor, turning the space into a pink tunnel. Jared stopped in front of an unassuming closet and pulled a single bronze-colored key from his sock. We both stared at the door. He held out the key.

"This is it," he said. "This is the spot."

I reached for the key. But he tugged it away.

"Do you even understand how important this is?" he asked.

"Yes," I said. "I understand. Napoleon."

"Is this some kind of joke to you?"

"No," I said. "No, I promise you it's not."

"This is a defining moment for our band," he said.

He pressed the bronze key into my palm. It was warm from his grip. We said nothing else. There was, I suppose, nothing left to say. Either I went through with it now, and we had a band, or I didn't, and Jared's dream was crushed. It was all remarkably simple. We returned to the room and found a few more group members lounging around. No one appeared to be friends. They just sat in isolation, listening to headphones or picking at the frayed cuffs of their khakis. Two large kids tried to hit each other with a Ping-Pong ball.

"One thing to know about Youth Group," Jared whispered. "It's filled to the brim with dickweeds."

Just then Janice reentered the room carrying a stack of note cards and a small tin can filled with pens. She beamed at the hang-dog gathering around her.

"Hello, all," she said. "So good to see everyone here."

The room went quiet at the sound of her voice.

"If I could, I want to start by doing something a little different this evening. So if you'd all follow me, I'd like us to go upstairs to the reading room."

There was a general hesitation, and then the group rose to its feet like sedated zoo animals. Jared and I were at the front of the room already, so we stood right next to Janice. Meredith brought up the back of the line, still typing away on her phone. We all walked out and headed single file up a narrow staircase. If anyone noticed me as an unfamiliar face, they didn't say a word. We reached the top and convened in a room full of old books and stacks of programs. At the far end of the room there was a small fire burning in a fireplace. Janice walked through the group and handed us all note cards and pens. Then she stopped and closed her eyes.

"Life is full of distractions," she began softly. "Problems, too. Some we can't help. But there are so many distractions these days that we often forget to concentrate on what is really important. And I'm not just talking about your spirituality here, folks. I'm talking about personal growth. Being a better you."

She opened her eyes. Her voice had sounded different than I'd ever heard it before. It was more even, assured. The group hung on her every word.

"What I want you to do tonight," she continued, "is to write down something that is holding you back. Something that is keeping you from committing entirely to God and to yourself. We'll call it an idol. I want you to write down this idol, or draw a picture of it, and then we're going to cast these idols into the flames. Does everyone understand?"

There were a few nods, but nobody began writing.

"This is how Mom thinks you communicate with God," said Jared. "You burn stuff and God reads the smoke."

"No talking please, Jared," said Janice. "Time for idol drawing."

Jared sighed and began halfheartedly scribbling on his card. I couldn't make out what he was drawing, but it looked like the beginning of a family portrait. I stared down at mine. What was keeping me from God? Or from myself? I didn't think it was a bad question necessarily. It was surprisingly valid. I noticed everyone else was connecting pen to paper. They appeared locked in unbroken concentration. I looked for Meredith, but she was no longer at the back of the room. She was gone. I began to perspire.

Soon, the first few teens began walking up to the fireplace. They smiled at Janice for permission, and when she nodded, they flicked their little folded papers into the shuddering flames. A big kid with a hat that read "Broncos" had constructed a paper airplane, and he dive-bombed it right into the heart of the fire.

"Praise Jesus!" he said, and high-fived Janice.

Everyone laughed. I looked at my empty card again, and then turned to Jared. I needed to ask him a few more questions about this supposed communication process. But he had his eyes closed, and his card was wadded up in his fist.

"This isn't going to be pretty," he said. "Just so you know."

"What isn't?" I said.

In front of me, the idol burning picked up momentum. A line of girls dropped their papers into the hearth, and then moved on to Janice Whitcomb for a big hug. Jared opened his eyes and adjusted his glasses. Then I watched him put his pointer finger directly down his throat. There was a loud gag, and then a second delay, before a staccatoed burst of vomit shot out of his mouth.

"Aww, God!" shouted Jared, "I'm having a reaction!"

Janice froze mid-hug and her eyes leaped immediately to her son.

"Jared!" she yelled.

Jared faked a terrific fall to his backside, deftly missing the small pools of his own vomit. The crowd backed away and looked down at him with contorted, deeply confused faces. Jared only glanced at me once, but the message was clear enough: it was time for me to go. I stuck my card in my pocket and headed straight toward the exit.

"I'll collect some towels!" I said, but I don't think anybody heard me.

They were all huddling around Jared. Janice was already kneeling, stroking his forehead. I managed to duck out in seconds, and found myself in the complete quiet of the stairwell. I took the stairs two at a time. My heart seemed to be beating in my forehead. My palms were slick on the railing. But I made it down without toppling over, and continued toward my destination.

I walked past the empty Recreation Room and back down the dim hallway of classrooms. The eerie portraits of saviors watched me from the walls. "God is a verb," I said to myself, "not a noun. Not a picture." I repeated the sentences like a mantra. Godisaverb. Godisaverb. The light from the end of the hall was now just a muted shade of rose. I was so focused on my task that I didn't detect another human presence in the halls until I had reached the closet. It wasn't until I had extracted Jared's key from my pocket that I heard the first muffled moan. I whipped around and squinted into the tenebrous light of the doorway at the hall's end.

At the far right side of the entry was Meredith Whitcomb in the embrace of a boy. He was pressing himself firmly against her tight-sweatered torso, and one of his hands was actually inside her shirt, cupped over a breast. I started to feel sick to my stomach. I watched raptly while he massaged her body and kissed her thin neck up to her hairline. She made a series of soft whimpers, and the boy laughed and covered her mouth. It was while the boy's hand was covering her lips that she happened to turn and notice me. Her eyelids flickered a moment as she met my stare. Then she closed them again. When the boy's hand left her mouth, her lips had formed a tight smirk.

As quietly as I could, I fit the key into the lock and submerged myself in the total darkness of the closet. I stood there huffing the musty air for a minute, attempting to get a full breath. In the pitch black, all I could see was that smirk. Meredith's eyes closed. Her chin tilted upward in pleasure. I nearly gagged. Finally, I gained the wherewithal to feel for the light switch, and the room exploded in a flash of fluorescence. Along the back wall was a row of old instruments. A nicked-up acoustic guitar. A long keyboard. A set of handbells in a felt-lined case. And in the corner, like a neglected child, there was a dark-wood bass guitar. The strings hummed when I picked it up.

It took me a moment to regain the will to leave. But then I thought of Jared, who had just induced vomiting for the sake of our endeavor, and I rushed out of the closet, sprinting down the hallway without looking back at Meredith. I ran away from her doorway, the one I had planned to use, and instead burst through the double doors of the front entrance. Night had arrived, and brought a deeper cold with it. I stuffed the bass under the lip of a hedge and then collapsed down in the grass.

I stuck my hands in my pockets for warmth, catching my breath. And I watched as a nearby streetlight flashed twice and popped on. My hand grasped onto something, and I knew before I took it out that I was holding Janice's note card. I looked it over. It was just a yellow piece of paper with pink lines separating it, but it seemed like more. It was a vessel for communication with a higher power. It was like an e-mail to the Greater Intellect. I looked down at it. I still had my pen in my pocket and I took it out and wrote a single question. I wrote: "Please, what is my path?" Then I folded it in even fourths and tucked it in my breast pocket, where it hovered over my wildly beating heart.

12. Transmissions

THAT NIGHT, I RODE HOME WITH A FENDER BASS guitar fastened to my back with a single leather strap. I had no carrying case so the body of the guitar banged against my back as I rode up the hill to the dome. The strings made sounds like the whales on Nana's tape each time my tire hit a bump. But when I arrived at the bicycle storage shed, the bass was still in one piece. I quickly hid it under a mesh tarp and exchanged it for two cans of Derbyshire Green paint. I had asked the ill-tempered man at the paint store for something "verdant and cheap," and this is what he had given me. The brand was not on sale, but it was well within Nana's budget. My business sense, I hoped, would still be celebrated.

It was disquieting to think about all the lies I had told Nana in the past few days. It was new territory, and like anything un-explored, it conjured both fear and excitement. I tried not to let myself dwell on it as I walked through the moon blue woods. The dome was dark this time, and I couldn't stop myself from speculat-ing about the goings-on at the Whitcombs', where I was sure the lights were still on.

The van ride home had been one long argument between Jared and Janice about the severity of his episode, and whether or not a visit to the emergency room was necessary. Meredith sat in the very back of the van, utterly quiet. I could sense her back there, watching my head, perhaps noticing the yellowed collar of my only white dress shirt. As of yet, no one had mentioned her absence from the idol burning, and I'm sure she was pleased that Jared's flop had overshadowed any other problems at the Group that evening.

"It was your meat loaf!" Jared screamed. "How many goddamned times do I have to tell you, I don't like green peppers in the meat. I can't digest them. But every time we have meat loaf, there they are! Then I spend the whole night on the toilet."

"Jared, you know the doctors treat any symptoms as a possible rejection until proven otherwise," said Janice. "I'm supposed to worry."

There was still that calm in her voice from the meeting, but it sounded on the verge of disintegrating any minute.

"I knew those peppers had a return ticket, man," he said. "They were just vacationing in my stomach."

I finally settled my gaze on the scenery passing by the window. I tried to keep quiet and avoid looking guilty. The neighborhoods of North Branch had always interested me. I was beginning to find some calm when I felt Meredith's hot breath on my ear.

"Don't turn around," she whispered.

Her short exhalation echoed around in the acoustic meatus of my ear. A shiver started in my neck and coursed through my body. I did as she said.

"Jared, it's been a long time since your last rejection occurrence," said Janice up front. "Don't you see where I'm coming from here?"

Jared belched in reply.

"I know what you did," Meredith breathed. "I know you saw me. But I saw what you did. And I'll tell if you tell. Is that clear, you perv?"

I nodded slowly. Upon uttering her last word, her lips had almost grazed my ear. I was paralyzed by the warmth of the almost-contact.

"Why does this always happen?" asked Janice to herself.

"Because I'm damaged goods," said Jared.

"Don't say that," she said. "Don't you ever say that about your-self."

Promptly, Janice turned her eyes to me in the rearview mirror. She looked like she might break down at any moment. "I'm sorry you had to experience this, Sebastian," she said. "I was so hoping you'd enjoy yourself and want to come back. Nothing ever turns out right around here."

Her gaze returned to the road. The passing headlights flashed over her eyes.

"Does Mr. Whitcomb go to church?" I asked.

I'm not sure what impelled me to ask the question. Most likely, I just felt I should say something to cover the silence. But there was a long pause after I spoke. I looked at Jared. His lips were pursed and he violently shook his head.

"Mr. Whitcomb does things his own way," Janice said. And that was all.

The rest of the van ride was a continuation of this uncomfort-able quiet. Jared refused to look at me. Meredith stayed far away from my tingling ear. I waited patiently for it to end, adding up what I now knew about Jared and Meredith's father. (1) He worked in sales. (2) He did things his own way. (3) I had never seen him.

Later, when I was biking back to the church to recover the bass guitar, my thoughts returned to the neighborhoods of North Branch and their sense of proximity that I found so perplexing. Even though there was ample space for building in the hilly landscape of eastern Iowa, residents chose to construct and live in neat rows of houses, connected by sidewalks like links in a chain.

Yet Bucky had envisioned a world where people could be more autonomous than this. A world where they would elect to live in remote areas and take care of all their own needs. But here was a spacious rural area, and the citizenry had not chosen isolation and privacy. They had chosen community. Nana had always extolled the virtues of Bucky's plan, which is why we lived in Iowa away from the town proper in our own "autonomous dwelling unit." To her, it was a more elevated stage of freedom.

But I had always had a sneaking suspicion that our tours were not just administered for financial and educational purposes. Before she had experienced her brain-blood interruptions, I often saw a real delight in Nana's eyes when people came to visit our home. She was never more spirited and dynamic than when she was leading a tour of nodding visitors. And there were days when she stayed around talking to a curious architect, or a child with a school report, for hours. This was not the behavior of someone with no use for community. Her acts were not those of a loner.

I hiked up the hill toward the dome, looking up at the basswoods that marked the exit from the heart of the woods. They were completely bare now and they contrasted greatly against a sky that looked white with clouds even in the dark. It was probably going to snow. If there was one thing I understood, it was the portent of night weather.

Everything was murky inside the dome, but not quite dark. It was only eight-thirty, yet it seemed Nana was already in bed. I checked on her after setting the paint on the kitchen table. For once, she was just where I expected her to be, curled up in her bedroom, one leg dangling off the bed. I delicately picked up her leg and arranged it next to the other one. It was so lightweight. It had never occurred to me until the stroke just how slight of build Nana was. I was watching her thin chest move up and down, trying to see if her breathing was regular, when she opened her lips and mumbled something like:

"Churrrp."

I leaned closer. "Nana," I said. "Are you awake?"

"Sebasyan," she said, plain as day. I took a step back. "Don't go in the church."

My heart seized.

"What?" I said.

Nana's eyes flipped open. But she did not look at me. Her eyes were white, the eyeballs rolled up in her head. "No one is your family," she said. "No one is your family but me."

Her words were slow and punctuated with long sighs. She was still asleep.

"Nana," I whispered. "I'm trying my best."

She did not say anything for a long time. And I thought she had fallen back into a deep sleep. But then she rolled over, and her leg dropped off the side of the bed again.

"This cannot last," she said.

I lingered in her bedroom after her last words, waiting for something else. Something that might allow me to fully understand what had just happened. Nothing came. Even her breathing quieted. I sat down on the floor and closed my eyes. I searched my memory for what I'd learned about this kind of thing. Bucky had explained it in terms of waves. Much like the way radio and satellites used invisible wave patterns, he thought the human mind was also capable of emitting and receiving these "ultrahigh frequency" waves. This phenomenon was typically referred to as telepathy. Nana had always claimed this was possible, but I had never been given cause to believe her until now.

Yet it appeared that I was emitting signals. Waves were streaming from my guilty conscience and crashing on the shores of Nana's perception. What's more, Nana was actively seeking them. She was waiting for them when I wasn't there. I sat cross-legged facing her bed, trying to shut off my brain, trying to erase every thought before it became swollen and frothy. It was impossible. I had always had a lively internal life, perhaps because of my solitude. All I had to do was shut my eyes and there were images and events, like a reel of film. I had no idea how much she knew, but it was clear she knew something. Wholly overcome, I walked back out into the night, and out to the shed. I uncovered the bass guitar.

It was still speckled with dust, even after miles of rubbing against my back. I found a stiff rag and some mineral oil, and I rubbed it down until it gleamed in the light of the white sky. I ran my fingertips over the body. The varnish was black at the edges and got gradually lighter on the way to the strings. The center was the color of parched summer grass. Under the strings was a caramel-colored stretch of tortoiseshell to protect the wood. The knobs were silver. The strings were corrugated, and I could feel the tiny grooves against my fingers.

I knew it had to be plugged in in order to really work, but I strapped it on anyway and stepped out into the woods. I didn't know where to put my fingers, so I just pressed down one string with my pointer finger. I plunked the string, and a quiet buzz filled the air around me. It wasn't the same feeling I'd had playing Jared's guitar. But I still felt the subtle vibrations from the string working their way up my forearm. I prowled around the dark woods in the cold, banging on the top string with my right thumb and moving the fingers of my left hand incrementally up and down the neck. Jared called each of these stations "frets." I let my fingertips linger at each one, and tried to take note of the sound. I looked up at the sky while I played, and eventually, true to my prediction, a light snow started to fall. *Thud. Thud. Thud-thud-thud.* I pulled harder on the top string and roamed deeper into the woods.

Picking up speed, I began jogging through the forest, slapping wildly at the bass. The snowflakes were few, but they were thick, and I could feel them on my face and neck. They bit my cheeks when the wind picked up. I zigzagged through the trees. Brittle oak leaves crunched under my shoes. Night animals heard me coming and scooted from their perches and hovels. *Bam. Bam. Thud-thud-thud.* My fingers continued attacking the strings. I stopped and leaned against a walnut tree. *Bam. Thud-thud. Bam.* I closed my eyes and let the snowflakes gather on my eyelashes. This bass guitar belonged to a God. Maybe, I thought, if I asked for his forgiveness, he would teach me how to play it.

I couldn't do it right away, though. First, I had to let him see that I intended to use it for good. To make my friend happy again. I tried to ignore all the potential repercussions of my theft, both earthly and for my exiled soul. It was possible in the snow, with my breath escaping in white blasts, to just appreciate the moment. A taste of that first exhilaration in Jared's room had returned. And I knew what I had to do to end the night.

I stowed away the stolen bass and crept back inside. I located the slip of paper Janice had given me the evening after Nana's stroke, and there was Jared's e-mail address. Underneath it was the wrong phone number. Meredith's private number. I picked up the cordless receiver. It was cool against my ear. I dialed the number and listened to it ring in short pulses on the other end. Then her voice came on the line.

"What?" she said.

"Meredith?"

I spoke almost in a whisper.

"Uh-huh," she said. "Who is this?"

I had intended to apologize for watching her at the church. I had intended to tell her that I would never inform another living being about what I had seen. I had maybe even intended on asking her what I could do to stop being a weirdo. What I actually said into the phone, in a coarse kind of whisper, was:

"You don't know me."

There was a slight pause on the other end.

"I don't, huh?" she said. "Then who gave you my number, Mr. Mysterious?"

"Is that of consequence?" I said.

"What?"

I quickly cleared my throat. "Does that matter?" I asked.

"I don't know," she said. "It depends on a few things, I guess."

I could hear an impish grin in her voice. And I realized that the way she spoke on the phone was much different from the way she spoke any other time.

"What does it depend on?" I asked.

"Why you're calling me, and what you look like."

"I'm pretty tall," I said.

"Okay."

"And I'm calling to . . . listen to your voice."

"Yeah?" she said. "Tell me more."

"I like you," I said.

She was quiet.

"I like the way you look. And I like your . . . scowls."

"My scowls?"

"You're beguiling," I said quickly. "Especially when you look mad."

"I see," she said. "So are you calling to set up an appointment?" she said.

"An appointment?"

"Jesus," she said, "I thought you guys talked about everything. You don't know how this works?"

"No," I said. "I'm not sure what you mean."

She sighed. "Tell me what night you want the window open," she said, plainly.

I couldn't speak for a moment.

"The window. I don't . . ."

"Let me make this perfectly clear . . ." she said.

"I think I have to go," I whispered. "I apologize."

"No, wait," she said. "Just tell me which night."

"I apologize," I said again.

I thrust the phone onto the charger and listened to it beep. I watched it, rigid with fear. The armpits of my flannel were soaked. From her bedroom, I could hear Nana lightly snoring. Outside the dome, the snow was still coming down in sparse swollen flakes. It looked like pieces of the white sky were flitting toward the ground all around me.

When I was young, Nana had said once that we lived inside a snow globe, only our weather was on the outside. Looking out now, her words came back to me. It was meant to be a comforting portrayal of our home, but on this night, as I felt my body relaxing and dream logic beginning to take over, all I could think about was a giant hand picking up the dome and giving it a healthy shake. In my mind, I watched all our furniture toppling over, the plates crashing, the NordicTrack spinning like an asteroid, Nana and I tumbling like two small animals caught in a dryer.

13. A Model World

THE FIRST GEOSCOPE WAS CONSTRUCTED IN 1951 AT Cornell University. It was completed under the supervision of distinguished guest lecturer R. Buckminster Fuller, and it was built by his students of architecture and engineering. The main idea was to create a "lifeboat" version of the larger Spaceship Earth. This lifeboat would enable a viewer to step inside and see things that they could never see from looking up at the sky from the real Earth. The Geoscope was, in essence, both a flawless model and a portal. And once you climbed inside, you would (Fuller hoped) be completely overwhelmed by a sense of world harmony.

I woke early the next morning from a nervous stomachache, and I used the hours before Nana rose to brush up on my knowledge of our project. I sat in my clothes from the night before, looking through a stack of architecture books. It was surprising to find that a Geoscope relied on a very simple design strategy. With the aid of a special kind of map, divided into triangles, one could simply transfer what was on the map to the corresponding triangle on the dome. The work, it seemed, was going to be more acrobatic than mentally taxing. I could already tell it was going to involve long-term dome-scaling on my part.

Nana began to stir around nine, and before I saw her, I heard her listening to her whale calls and humming to herself. Then I heard the susurration of the misting Fog shower in her bathroom. It used only a pint of water to send a fine high-powered mist across the entire body at once (I usually took baths). Finally, she walked into the dome with a yellow bandanna on her head, and a pair of overalls that must have been forty years old. She spotted me near the telephone in the kitchen area, not far from where I had slept. She looked at the cans of Derbyshire paint, and then she looked back at me.

"Good morning, Sebastian," she said.

"Hello, Nana," I said, looking at a book.

She opened the fridge and nosed around, pulling out half-empty jugs of juice and tubs of yogurt. After removing a few items and placing them on the counter, she stopped and walked over to my spot on the floor. She peered down at me.

"You'll forgive me for . . . drifting off so early last night," she said. "I wanted to recharge before our work commenced this morning."

"I understand," I said.

She kept staring at me. She reached down and pulled something from my hair. It was a small twig from the woods. She held it up to the light.

"I experienced the most peculiar and disturbing dreams last night," she said.

I swallowed hard. "What did you dream about?"

"I've lost it," she said. "For now, at least . . ."

Her face froze. "I can't recall."

She adjusted her bandanna, tucking some white locks underneath. Her eyes flashed. "It will come back. These visions, they always come back. They return when they want. I wish I could say I conquered the metaphysical in my life, Sebastian. But perceptions, you see, they operate on their own schedule."

She looked at me one last time, then moved back to the kitchen table. She slowly read the words on the side of the paint can, then she cracked open the lid with the small metal key that had been provided.

"I saw you," she said.

I held my breath a moment. "You saw me?"

"Just for a moment."

"In your dream?"

I waited, watching her eyes.

"No. I saw you outside last night. You were in the woods with a large branch in your hands. I woke for a moment and only saw you, your . . . silhouette. It was dark."

"Yes," I said.

"Where were you going?"

"Just walking," I said. "The winter air was so fresh."

She was still looking into the paint can.

"You relish moments without your Nana," she said.

"That's not it."

"You have made your feelings clear about this project," she said.

She stuck a wooden stirrer into the thick paint and began to swirl it around.

"This is what he was planning when we first met. Did you know that?" she asked.

"You and Bucky?"

She tapped the stirrer on the can and laid it down.

"He was building a fifty-foot-diameter Geoscope in Edwardsville the year I was there," she said. "It served as the university's auditorium. But he wanted to build a bigger one within eyeshot of the United Nations in New York. Blackwell's Island it was called at the time. I was going to go with him."

"But you've never lived in New York," I said.

Nana ignored my comment. She seemed to be speaking straight from memory. Like the exact words had been memorized along with the images. "It was going to be so big that all the delegates would have to do was look out the window, and there would be our planet, suspended by clear cables. And not only that, but Bucky was going to rig it with thousands of tiny computer-controlled lights. And anywhere in the world where there was armed conflict, the lights would flash red. So all the world's leaders could see the problems they caused right in front of their eyes. Every day on the job, they'd see their mistakes blinking in red."

"You were going to go with him?"

Nana nodded. "He met with the secretary-general and gave a stunning presentation. We were already making plans. There was an apartment rented. A real brownstone, Bucky said. A rooftop garden, and an old man in the next building who taught pigeons to fly in patterns."

"What happened?"

"No one could raise the money. He wanted ten million dollars to do it his way. He could have done it for much less, but everything had to be perfect. If it wasn't done to complete perfection, it wasn't worth doing at all. That's the way it worked with Bucky. Many great things were left behind."

Nana looked at me again. "We're going to create a . . . stunning Geoscope here. For less than a thousand dollars! And somewhere, somewhere, wherever he is, Bucky is going to look down and see it!" She paused and took a breath. "He's going to see it and he's going to see his mistake. But I need your help, Sebastian. I can't do it without your healthy frame, and your . . . acquired skills."

She walked into her bedroom and returned a moment later with a large map she had been working on. It was a combination of all her sketches, divided up into triangles and ready for transfer. She held it up before me, but she wouldn't look me in the eye.

"Now, are you going to assist me . . . or not?"

She spread the map out on the table and smoothed it.

"We'll finish it together," I said.

A shaky hand moved off the map and pointed to the South Pole.

"Good," she said. "Let's begin here."

WE WORKED ALL OF THE MORNING, AND MOST OF THE afternoon, wiping down the glass triangles with warm solvent-soaked rags then transferring the detail of the coastlines into the Atlantic, Pacific, and Indian oceans. We followed the intricate lines of the ice shelves, and dipped into the cavities of the Ross and Weddell seas. After two coats, the Derbyshire sparkled with an emerald sheen. We worked in complete silence, huddling over the map and transplanting the twists and turns of the land as best we could.

It was odd to obscure the surface of something that had been clear for so long, but Nana didn't give me much time to brood. She worked inhumanly fast, and I tried my best to keep pace. For the most part, I was able to keep my mind on my work. But I also found myself looking over my shoulder after every few brushstrokes, focusing on the roof of the storage shed where I kept my contraband bass guitar. I wanted to hold it again. I wanted to figure out how to operate it and make it rumble out those low melodies that I had listened to on the cheap scratchy computer speakers. What had Jared said about that Ramones song? The bass part was so easy anyone could play it. How did it go again? *Duh-nuh-nuh-nuh-Nuh*

Duh. Duh-nuh-nuh-nuh-Nuh Duh. Beat on the brat. Beat on the brat. Beat on the brat with a baseball bat, oh, yeah! OH, YEAH!

"Sebastian, what are you doing?"

Startled, I looked at Nana.

"What are you making those horrible sounds for?"

"I don't know," I said.

"Someone is here. A woman. Tell her to leave."

I turned around in an instant, and there was Janice Whitcomb standing in front of her van in the driveway. I dropped my paintbrush to the ground. Janice waved.

"Nana," I said. "You know who that is . . ."

Nana glanced at me with such hostile confusion that I knew immediately she didn't remember. She didn't remember any of the day of her stroke.

"Never mind," I said. "I'll inform her."

"Explain about the project," Nana shouted. "Tell her to come back and visit when the institute opens!"

Without wasting a second, she set to work on the shoreline of the Amundsen Sea. I trekked rapidly across the snow-spotted yard, past the closed-down gift stand, and directly up to the teal minivan where Janice was standing.

"Good morning, Mrs. Whitcomb," I said. "Is there a problem?"

I tried not to look toward the shed again, where the stolen bass was sitting, waiting to be discovered. Janice watched Nana for a moment.

"She didn't wave to me," said Janice. "I waved to her twice."

"She gets very wrapped up in her projects," I said. "It's really something. Try not to take it as an affront."

Janice frowned. Then she looked toward the long tinted window of the van.

"He wants to apologize," she said.

"Who?"

"Jared," she said. "He insisted I drive him over here to apologize to you for ruining your experience at Youth Group. He feels so bad about it. I've never seen him like this. It's really quite strange, to be honest with you."

I stared at the dark window. I couldn't see anything inside.

"Is he going to come out?" I asked.

"It's too cold for him, Sebastian," she said. "He'd like you to step inside."

I snuck a glance back at Nana. She was absorbed in her painting. Janice slid open the door for me. Jared was inside, bundled in two hooded sweatshirts under his leather jacket. He wore a stocking cap with a patch on it that read "Discharge." He was watching out the opposite window. Janice closed the door behind me.

"You don't check your e-mail now?" he said.

Inside, the van was warm and sticky like his room.

"I check it when I'm able," I said.

He turned and faced me. There was a light bruise under his left eye.

"What happened to your face?" I asked.

"Fight with Meredith," he said. "Forget it. We have more important things to chat about."

"Does anybody know about the bass guitar?"

"No," he said. "But we need to practice soon. So we need to move quickly."

Jared shivered and pulled one of his hoods up over his stocking cap. The top of the hood rested on his glasses. He licked his dry lips.

"Janice is watching my every move after my little puke-tastic diversion. The house is in total fucking lockdown. I had to pretend to cry just to get over here. It was humiliating."

"Nana might be onto me, too. I think she had a psychic episode."

Jared just nodded at this information. It didn't seem to register.

"I had to tell her you were my best friend," he said.

"Who?"

"Are you even listening to me?" he yelled. "Janice! I told Janice you were my best fucking pal and that I had to talk to you."

"Oh."

"Don't get your hopes up, though," he added quickly. "I don't really know anyone else right now. You can't be my best friend unless I have more than one friend and then I choose you to be the best. That's how it works."

He looked out the window and fogged the glass with a sigh.

"But you are *a* friend, I guess," he said.

"I know," I said.

"You don't know anything," he said.

A digital watch beeped on his wrist, and he pulled out a container of pills from inside his jacket. He unscrewed the cap. I stared at the bottle.

"I want you to teach me how to play the bass," I said.

"I'll try," he said. "I'm not a damn miracle worker, though. If you suck ass, you suck ass. End of story."

"I won't suck an ass," I said.

Jared looked at me, surprised. Then he started laughing. He dry-swallowed a pill.

"It's just *suck ass*," he said, "but that's the first time I've ever heard you swear."

"Bucky believed that curse words were sullying the English language," I said.

Jared downed another pill. Then he reached down and pulled out a piece of paper. He handed it to me. It was a sheet of bass guitar notes and chords, printed off the Web. There were no musical notes. The paper just showed each string of the bass, and where to put your fingers to make different notes.

"This is a tablature," he said. "It's the fastest way to learn. Practice these notes, and we'll set up a time this week. Learn them, okay? Practice every night when the old crone goes to bed."

"Nana is not . . ."

"Just practice!" he said.

I folded the paper up and stuck it in my pocket.

"Thank you," I said.

"Go fuck yourself," he said.

He smiled. "Say it back," he said.

"Why?"

"If we're going to be in a band, you need to start learning these things."

"But, I just told you—"

"Say it!"

We stared at each other.

"Go . . . fuck yourself," I said, quietly.

"Good," he said. "Now don't ever say that to me again. Get out of my van!"

When I slid open the door, he yelled out to Janice, "Problem solved. Let's go! Now!"

I got out and slammed the door closed. Janice was waiting patiently, watching Nana paint. She grabbed a hold of my hand when I walked by and pressed it.

"Your grandmother doesn't know about us, does she?" she said.

"What do you mean?" I asked.

Janice just looked at me.

"No," I said. "She doesn't like me going into North Branch very often. And I don't think she recalls the day of her accident."

"I don't like lying," said Janice.

"I'm sorry," I said.

She pressed my hand again and let it go. I waited for her to march across the yard to Nana and tell her about everything. My visits. That first drive to the hospital. But she didn't. She kept her eyes on the dome, a glazed expression on her face.

"I can't get over this," she said, finally.

I watched a slight grin form on her lips.

"Over what?" I asked.

"The way you live out here."

"Oh," I said.

She brought a fist up to her mouth and blew into it.

"You know, I actually thought about studying architecture in college," she said. "Just for a little while. I never did it, but I was interested. I took this great appreciation class, slides and slides of beautiful buildings. In the end, I didn't have the math skills."

Janice's face remained locked in concentration, like she was seeing the dome again for the first time. "But the artistic part appealed to me. Your grandmother designed this, right?"

"She did," I said.

We both watched my grandmother, who was now wiping off a smudge of paint with her index finger. Her fingertip skated slowly along the edge of a triangle.

"Amazing," she said. "She must be really proud of everything she's done."

"She is."

Jared's hands pounded against the glass. Janice glanced at his window. Her smile disappeared. "I guess that's my cue," she said, and laughed nervously. She took a step toward the door and grabbed the handle.

"What did you end up studying?" I asked.

"Studying?"

"In college."

"Oh," she said. "I wanted to be a teacher of some kind. But I never finished."

She opened the door to the van. I thought she was going to get in, but she turned around again. "I took . . . an indefinite break," she said.

She looked down at the ground, then she entered the van. Jared shouted something at her, but I couldn't make out the words. She closed the door behind her. I could just barely distinguish her features through the tinting, but she seemed pensive. She put the car in drive, but before she drove away, she rolled down the window.

"We hope to see you soon, Sebastian," she said.

She didn't smile this time. She just rolled the window back up and pulled out of the driveway. Then the teal van was coasting down the hill, sending up a cloud of bright white exhaust, like a long winter breath. I watched it wind through the switchbacks toward town. When it was out of sight, I went back and rejoined Nana.

"What was the delay?" she asked.

"They were interested in the new project," I said. "I gave them all the details I could supply."

"Are they going to return?" she asked.

"I think so."

"The word continues to spread!" she said. "All we need is a . . . point of entry into the collective consciousness! You'll see. You'll see how it works."

"I believe you," I said.

I picked up my paintbrush from the cold ground and started work on the intricate crescent of the South Shetland Islands. Painted green, the South Pole didn't look at all cold and forbidding. Maybe that's what Nana liked about it. This version was not Shackleton's country of frostbite and starvation. It looked like a nice place for a picnic, actually. Or some camping. Somewhere you could just stroll the verdurous hills for days, jumping from island to island. Swimming in three oceans in the same day. It looked, above all else, like a good place to be alone.

14. Experiments in Rocking

AS IT TURNED OUT, I WAS NOT A NATURAL AT THE bass guitar. I wish I could say that I awakened a secret talent in the echo chamber of our storage shed. I wish I could say I was even good at not-playing-it in a memorably deficient way (like the framed Mr. Vicious, perhaps). But these statements would both be untruths. The fact was I had long maladroit fingers that tripped over one another on the way to a chord. I seemed to have no sense of internal rhythm. And my fingertips felt like they were on fire after minutes of playing. Yet every night for the next three days, I practiced like Jared requested. I worked on the Geoscope with Nana by day; I snuck out to practice bass by night. I had no earthly idea what I was doing.

The whole ritual was made worse, perhaps, by the fact that I tried to listen to and comprehend a new punk composition each night before I went to the shed. After an e-mail to Jared requesting songs that had particularly agreeable bass lines, I received a flurry of suggestions. And so I pressed my ear to the circle of holes on the computer monitor that functioned as speakers, and listened carefully to the tunes I found on the Web. I hoped I might learn them by rote, humming and internalizing night after night. But oftentimes the bass parts started the songs, and then disappeared under a blanket of guitar and screaming. Then I was left to puzzle over the words.

We're gonna steal your mail on a Friday night.
We're gonna steal your mail by the pale moonlight.

Bitchin' Camaro, Bitchin' Camaro!
I ran over my neighbors.

All the girls are in love with me.
I'm a teenage lobotomy!

Despite the baffling lyrics, I was continually amazed by the musicianship. The bassists played so fast and the screams were exceptionally well-timed. By the time I got out to the storage shed, sitting on the cold seat of my Voyager, I felt my hands freeze up entirely. I heard the pounding bass parts in my head, deep notes that filled my whole body with hum. But all that came out of my bass were anemic clunks and clonks. I went to bed each night, trying not to think about how deficient I was at Punk Rocking. It was all I could do not to weep.

On my fourth night of practicing, though, I had my first small triumph. I had been thumping around for nearly an hour when I finally managed to produce a perfect-sounding A minor chord. One finger on the ninth fret of the D string. One on the twelfth fret of the A. One on the twelfth fret of the E. And then out it came: a long and sustained sound that seemed to fill the entire shed with harmony. I just listened until it faded completely from the air. I looked down at my fingers. They were in perfect position. Each of the three fingertips pressing the strings without touching and dulling the sound of another. I strummed again and again and the chord rang through the air, echoing off the metal slats in the shed. I saw it as a sign to stop for the night. I carefully wrapped the bass up tight in the mesh to keep it warm, and went directly inside.

In the dome, everything was cozy and tea-smelling. Geodesic domes are efficient structures to heat. They are also adept at imprisoning smells. And the more time I spent away from the dome, the more I was starting to notice the strange odor of our home. Steamed vegetables. Aromatic candles. The pungent paint fumes. I kept hearing the chord in my head, as I cut through the fog of scents. A chord on any instrument, it occurred to me, was a prime example of the concept of synergy. Synergy is the cooperation of two different agents to produce an effect greater than their individual parts—i.e., two notes played together to form a pleasing sound. Synergistic music!

I gravitated toward the cordless phone and picked it up. I dialed Meredith's private number with my blistered fingertips. It rang only once this time before her perfectly apathetic "What?" shot through the phone like a threat.

"Hello," I said, modulating my voice back to the same half whisper I had used before.

"You," she said. "You again."

"How does it work?" I asked. "What you told me before."

"Why would I tell you now?" she asked. "Why would I tell some chump who hung up on me? Somebody I don't even know."

In the past I would have believed she was angry, but I knew her telephone voice better now. I could actually hear the smile spreading on her lips.

"I don't know. Maybe I'm shy."

"I don't have time for that," she said.

"Maybe I made a mistake."

"Hell yes, you did. You made a huge mistake. Nobody hangs up on me. I decide when the conversation is over."

My mind whirred, trying to find the right thing to say. But Meredith moved on without me. "Tell me more things you like about me," she demanded.

"What?"

"Tell me more things you like about me. There have to be more."

"How many should I say?"

"Five," she said. "Tell me five, and I'll stay on the phone."

"I can do that," I said.

I closed my eyes and tried to concentrate on her. The images leaped in and out of my head. It was hard to pin one down. I finally landed on the flash of her stomach I had seen that night in the church. The little bit of white between her pants and the shirt that was being lifted up. "I like your pale skin," I said. "And your nose. It bends a little. I wonder if you hurt it once. But I like looking at it. I think it's terrific."

I tried hard to speak in these short sentences, and in a way that I'd heard the boys talking at Youth Group. It was like translating. "I like your lips, when you paint them pink. I like it when you call me names. And I like it . . . when you dance."

Her voice shot through immediately. "I don't dance," she said. "When have you seen me dance?"

I tried to think of something plausible. A school party? A Youth Group event?

"Your window," I said.

"You spied on me through my window?"

"Not really," I said.

"That is the creepiest thing I've ever heard."

"It wasn't entirely creepy."

"You looked in at me when I didn't know you were there. You were probably jerking it, too. Oh, God. You were probably, like, saying nasty things and jerking it furiously in the yard."

"That's not true," I said. "I was coming to see you. I . . . got scared. I saw you dance by accident."

There were a few seconds of silence.

"You weren't whacking?"

"No," I said.

I was about fifty percent sure I knew what she was talking about.

"I don't know," she said.

"No lie," I said.

Another pause. She hadn't hung up, though. I could hear her breathing.

"You're right about my nose. My brother broke it." She paused. "We have problems from time to time."

"Your brother punched your nose and broke it?"

"No," she said. "No punching."

"He kicked you?"

"It was actually kind of an accident. But I don't want to talk about my brother, okay? I'm not really interested in telling you all about my *personal life*. I don't want to cry or tell you how nobody understands me. So just stop with all of that."

"Okay."

"It works like this," she said. "I tell you when the window is open. I open it at that time. You come in without waking up my mom. You can use your imagination after that, genius."

"That's all?"

"That's all."

"I'm sorry I watched you," I said.

"It's okay," she said. "Why don't you come inside next time? How about Saturday? Or maybe you could just keep pissing me off until I stop talking to you."

And before I could respond, she hung up. She had decided, apparently, that the call was over. It was a trait she shared with her brother. I felt a sharp sense of excitement along with an undercurrent of dread. I wasn't sure what I had gotten myself into. The idea that Meredith was expecting me was thrilling no matter the context. But then there was that unavoidable clarification: she wasn't expecting *me*. She was expecting Secret Phone Person. I was decidedly not Secret Phone Person. I was Sebastian, the "little weirdo" that her brother was "in love with or something." I was a "perv," which I was pretty sure was short for pervert. And a pervert, according to my dictionary, was "a person whose sexual behavior is regarded as abnormal and unacceptable." If I showed up at her window, even if I could muster the courage to do it, everything would very clearly be ruined. What would she say exactly if she saw me there, just below her sill, looking up at her? I couldn't imagine anything kind.

I GOT UP THE NEXT MORNING, STILL RUNNING THE situation in my head. I dressed and went out to see if Nana was at work. But instead of seeing her, I found a photographer from the *North Branch Courier* on our front lawn. Behind him was a small car with the newspaper's name stenciled across the door. Nana was at work on the side of the dome, and she didn't notice him until a flash went off. Nana blinked. The photographer raised his hand in a salute. He had a red beard and a pair of flip-up sunglasses. There were two cameras around his neck, hanging over a parka. He carried a crisp yellow notebook.

Without saying much, he began shooting pictures of our house. Nana rubbed her eyes for a moment, then followed. She slowly began to spout facts into his ear. "Good morning," she said. "Greetings. Did you know Bucky was obsessed with the word 'weaponry'? Yes, he was determined to create things that only made life better. This Geoscope was one of them. It was part of what he dubbed 'livingry.'"

"Uh-huh," said the photographer.

He turned the camera around and started taking quick shots of Nana. They seemed to happen ten at a time. She just looked into the lens like a curious bird at first. Then she regained composure and began to pose, staring at the dome with awe, smiling and pointing at our work. The man gave no instructions. His face registered no satisfaction or disappointment. "Anything else?" he asked. His pen hovered over the notebook.

"We haven't set admission prices yet for the institute," she said, "but there might be a slight increase. When something is completely remodeled, and the experience is so thoroughly changed, you can't expect us to . . ."

"Okay, great," he said. He shut the book, took one last rapid-fire shot, then walked back to his car.

"Should I come down to the office to provide . . . more information?" Nana tried. "I could author a caption or two, I'm sure!"

The man loaded his cameras into his trunk. Then he turned and saluted again. In minutes, his car was gone, and it was hard to remember if he had ever been there at all. Nana watched the space where his car had been for some time.

"Well . . ." she said, eventually.

I stepped close to her, our bodies side by side. I tried to think of something uplifting to say.

"What color will New Zealand be?" is what I said.

Nana still focused on the empty driveway.

"Yellow," said Nana. "Perhaps lemon."

"Tasmania?" I asked.

"Umber," she said.

"What about Australia?" I asked.

"I don't know yet!" she yelled. "It has to come to me!"

She opened the door and walked inside without saying another word. I followed her in and watched as she slammed the door to her bedroom. On the bulletin board by her door, one of her architectural photos fell from its tack and looped lazily to the ground. Nana had been so quiet the last few days; it was alarming to hear her yell. I swept past her room, listening for her, but she didn't make a sound. So I proceeded upstairs and found myself slumped down in front of the computer. Waiting for me on the Web was an e-mail from Jared. The subject read "The Time Is Nigh, Dickless!" Somehow, I knew before I even opened it what it was going to say.

S,

Janice is going out this Saturday night to do something churchy and gay. Now is our chance!!!!!!!!!!! Come at seven with your instrument.

No excuses or you're totally out of the band.

Which reminds me, we need a band name. I'll think of one. Try not to come up with any suggestions. They probably won't be helpful.

Later,

J

P.S. I hope you've been practicing. And I hope you've somehow become cooler. That would also help the band.

I read the e-mail over a couple of times to make sure I understood all that it was asking. But everything important was in the first line. Saturday night. Janice would be out. Of course that was why Meredith had selected that night. And that's why Jared chose it, too. It was either perfect or a nightmare. I couldn't decide. But I knew I would have to go to North Branch. We needed new paint, after all. There was New Zealand to think about, and Tasmania. Two small countries were depending on me. Not to mention, two small people in North Branch. I sat watching out of the glass, facing the boundless slanted rooftops of the town. Eventually, I heard the NordicTrack spring to life, clacking its familiar rhythm, and I went downstairs to ask for paint money.

15. Practice

MY ORIGINAL PLAN FOR SATURDAY WAS TO RETRIEVE Nana's next batch of paint sometime in the morning, the way I had the first time. But the day arrived and then seemed to disappear out from under me. And as it progressed, I realized I was not going to receive my opportunity. Nana was restless from the moment she woke that morning, walking in and out of her room, alternately making unanswered calls to the newspaper and deciding on the color scheme for South America. She left the dome only once, but it was just to pick weeds and beat the dust out of our rippling CLOSED banner. I knew by the time the afternoon was fading that I would have to get the paint and go to Jared's all in the same outing. I was getting ready to set out on this errand when Nana emerged from her room and looked at me from across the dome. Neither of us moved. The sun was almost gone behind her, and she looked more silhouette than human.

"Sebastian," she said. Her voice was hoarse.

"Yes?"

"Have you ever visited a chapel?"

Her question was surprisingly timid. Almost embarrassed.

"You mean . . . in a place of worship?" I asked.

"I suppose," she said.

I took a moment, pretending to think deeply. Really, I was trying desperately to clear my head of all relevant thoughts. She might be reading them as we spoke.

"No," I said. "I don't think I understand what a chapel is really."

Nana shook her head and closed her eyes.

"Of course not," she said. "How would you know?"

I smiled, nervously.

"Lemon," she said.

"Lemon?"

I tried to steady my quivering hands.

"Lemon yellow. For our next country," she said. "And umber. Remember?"

"I remember."

She closed her eyes again and inhaled a deep breath.

"How long will it take?" I asked.

"To complete the Geoscope?" she asked.

Nana looked at me strangely.

"To complete my path," I said.

She shook her head. "It's impossible to say," she said. "You'll know when you've accomplished something great."

"Oh," I said. I was about to ask her more, but she interrupted me.

"That's enough," she said. "Go and complete your outing."

I nodded and hiked resolutely out of the dome. I left the yard as quickly as I could. Nana stayed standing in the doorway to her bedroom. She was there until I was too far away to see her. And minutes later, I was on my bicycle, the bass slumped across my back again. I had intentionally waited until the light would be too dim for Nana to spy it, but my heart drummed in my chest until I had reached the bottom of the hill. Then my body took over, and I was able to forget all my anxieties for a few miles along the expressway. I focused on the feeling of my legs tightening and pushing, the pedals orbiting through the air.

WHEN I ARRIVED AT THE WHITCOMBS', I STASHED my bicycle in the usual location and paused to make sure I had removed my helmet. I had almost left it sitting on the counter of the paint store moments ago. The store had been minutes from closing and I'd had to rush to make my selections. Daisy for New Zealand. Butternut for Tasmania. Now, I left the helmet hanging from a handlebar. As I moved toward the front of the house, I looked at Meredith's window for a second. But the shade was not open. And there was no sign of her shadow inside.

"What are you looking for?" came a voice from nearby.

I surveyed the yard, but there was no one there.

"Up here," said Jared.

I looked up and found him sitting on the lowest branch of the beech tree in his front yard. He was kicking at one of the dangling purple tennis shoes, smoking a cigarette. "What were you looking at?" he asked. "That's Meredith's room."

"Why are you in a tree?" I said.

"I asked you first."

"I was looking up at your room," I said. "Not hers. Why are you in a tree?"

Jared sighed. "I like to climb this tree, okay? And Janice doesn't let me do it anymore because she happens to be a Nazi. So when she's gone, I climb it."

I nodded. Jared exhaled a puff of smoke.

"What's the story with the shoes?" I asked.

"These stupid things?" he said, kicking again at one of them. "Meredith keeps them up here on this branch. For good luck, she says, but I think they're a signal for guys to come over and feel her boobs."

"But they're up there all the time," I said.

"Exactly."

I walked over just below the tree and looked straight up at him. His undersized legs hung over the branch like a small child's. He tapped his cigarette and the gray ashes floated past me to the ground. I still had the guitar on my back and it was getting heavy. "I thought we were having band practice," I said.

"We are," he said, "in a minute. I've been inside all day. Just let me get a breath of air for once." He took a deep drag on his cigarette.

I took down the bass and sat on the frigid ground beneath the tree. I rested the instrument on my lap and ran my fingers thoughtlessly over the strings.

"Needs to be tuned," said Jared.

Another flick of ashes fluttered down around me like dirty snow. Some of it landed on my shoulders. "Let me ask you something?" Jared said.

"What?"

"Do you think girls will want to get it on with me when we're famous?"

I paused for a moment to let him know I was really giving it some thought.

"I think so," I said. "I've done some research about this."

Jared kicked at the shoes. "Yeah," he said, "famous people have to have bodyguards to punch out crazy fans and screaming girls. It doesn't matter if you're small or whatever. People just want your booty if you're an artist."

"It appears that way," I said.

"Fame's not going to change me, though," he said. "I'm not going to sell out or act like some powerful douche bag. I'm going to be the same Jared. I'm going to just rock and get it on with my groupies. That's it. And maybe make a horror movie later in my career about brain-eating werewolves. Something cool like that."

"Good idea," I said.

I looked up and saw he was watching me. It was hard to see his eyes; his glasses were reflecting the porch light from the house. But his jaw was tense.

"What's wrong?" I asked.

He took one last drag on his cigarette.

"Janice wants me to start school again by the end of the month."

He was quiet a moment. Then he dropped his cigarette butt from the tree like a guided missile. It landed in a splash of orange sparks on a patch of dirt.

"I've never been to real school before," I said.

"I know," said Jared. "I used to think you were a homeschooled moron. Now I think you might be the luckiest person I know."

He started moving toward the base of the tree, shifting his thighs over and holding tight to the branch. "High school is worse than you can even believe," he said. "The guys are all a bunch of chuckling assholes. The girls are all versions of my sister. Everybody likes sports. And the classrooms smell like armpit."

Jared began sliding down the trunk of the tree, dirtying his black pants.

"It's hell on earth, Sebastian. Plain and simple," he said, grunting.

He let go of the tree and fell to the ground, landing hard on his sneakers.

"Ow," he said. "Shit."

He walked around his yard a minute, shaking his ankles. His leather jacket hung down like a cape, and in the dark he could have been mistaken for a broken-winged vampire. Finally he loped back around and stood above me. He took his glasses off and rubbed his eyes. "What the hell am I going to do?"

"Are you scared?" I asked.

Jared didn't say anything. He pressed his glasses back on his nose.

"We should probably go inside," he said. "My free days are numbered and we have some serious goddamn work to do."

"Yeah," I said.

"Yeah," he said.

We walked over the yard and up the steps. We wiped our feet on the mat and I couldn't help looking down. *God Bless This House.* I looked back up quickly, making sure not to hit the bass on the door frame.

BEFORE WE COULD PRACTICE, WE NEEDED SUPPLIES. So we stopped in the kitchen and filled two large tumblers full of grape drink and big blocky ice cubes. Then we stopped at the pantry for some kind of bright orange crackers with peanut butter in the middle. It looked like food from another planet, but it tasted incredible. Salty. Sweet. Orange. I washed it down with a long drink of the grape stuff and closed my eyes to fully enjoy the taste. It was so cold and sweet. This drink certainly did not come from a co-op. It was certainly not organic. It was delicious poison.

Loaded down with our provisions, we headed down the hall toward the stairwell. Jared paused for a second in front of Meredith's door, and I wondered momentarily if he was somehow aware of the phone calls I'd been making. The door was shut tight, and a strain of despairing music was barely muffled by the door.

"Lucky for us, she's been acting like a suicide case all day," said Jared. "Usually when Janice is gone she goes into ultrabitch mode. But I knocked on her door earlier and she was just lying on her bed looking out the window like some abused puppy. It was pathetic."

"Maybe she's in love," I said, and instantly regretted it.

"Yeah," said Jared, "and maybe I have a fifteen-inch wiener."

We both looked at her door. Then we walked up the stairs and into Jared's room. Once we were settled, Jared made multiple trips to the closet for tangled cords and little boxes he called "Effects Pedals." He produced his amplifier and then another small one for me. The humidifier puffed and burbled in the corner, but the room smelled better this time. He worked quietly, plugging things in, flipping switches, tuning his guitar, and then tuning my bass. When he was finished, we both sat on his unmade bed, our instruments buzzing like enormous cicadas.

"What do we do now?" I asked.

"Give me a minute to think," said Jared. "Why do you always have to ask things?"

Jared coughed. We were close enough to touch elbows.

"How did you begin practices with your other bands?" I asked.

"What other bands?"

"I thought you had performed in other bands."

"When the hell did I ever say that?"

"I assumed," I said.

"Don't ever assume things," he said. "You don't know anything."

Jared looked at his guitar. I looked at my bass. We met eyes again.

"I can play an A minor chord," I said.

Jared seemed to think about this a minute.

"Okay," he said. "Let's hear your A minor chord."

I took some time to carefully adjust my fingers into the correct positions. D string. A string. E string. I strummed with my thumb, and there it was again, that perfect deep dulcet tone. It poured from the baby amplifier. I felt it in my toes. And as if answering an alarm, Jared immediately stomped on one of his pedals and put his fingers in position. Before the sound of my chord disappeared, he answered it with a growling riff from his guitar. The two sounds met and clapped together like waves. Then they blended and left the air of the room altogether. Synergy.

"Do that again," said Jared.

I slammed my hand onto the strings and the sound blasted back at me. Jared played his chord again, breaking it up into three choppy down strums. He looked at me again and nodded his head. I hit the strings. He strummed three times.

"Do it twice," he barked. "Play that twice in a row before I play."

I complied the best I could. My fingers were slipping a little from position but the note was almost right. I pounded. *Boom. Boom.* Jared came back. *Duh, duh, duhhhhh.*

"Keep doing it!" he yelled.

I looked closely at my fingers. I held the strings down as tight as I could.

Boom. Boom. Duh, duh, duhhhhh. Boom. Boom. Duh, duh, duh-hhhh. Boom. Boommmm. Duh. Duh. Duhhhhhhhhh.

We stopped at the same time and listened as the sound died out. Jared looked at me. "That was almost cool," he said. "Kind of like Gang of Four or something."

"What's Gang of Four?" I asked.

"Just do it again," he said. "I'll educate you later."

We spent the next half hour or so playing those two chords. Over and over. We tried to get the timing right. My part remained the same, but Jared added some flourishes to his until it nearly sounded like the beginning of a song. We were both sweating from the humidity of the room. And by the time we could play it how Jared wanted it, his face was pale and dripping. He tossed his guitar down on the bed and sat down against the wall on the other side of the room. He ran his hands through his knotty black hair.

"I'm actually supposed to do a warm-up before any physical activity," he said. "That was probably too fast."

I listened to him breathe. He put his hand over his chest.

"That's the only chord you know," he said, panting, "isn't it?"

"It is."

He took a deep breath. "That's okay," he said. "We gotta start somewhere."

It took about ten minutes of rest before Jared looked normal again. I was worried for a while that he may have overtaxed himself. I had a series of quick visions of myself in the back of an ambulance again looking at a respirator. But when he opened his eyes again, he seemed somewhat refreshed. Like all he required was a brief recharge.

"You ever catch a buzz?" he asked, still leaning against the wall.

I looked back at him, expressionless.

"You ever drink a beer or some schnapps or something?"

"I inebriated myself once on some Canadian ice wine," I said.

"Right on," said Jared.

He got to his feet and pulled a small box off the shelf above his stereo. He opened it up, and inside were stacks of guitar magazines. He tossed them aside and revealed a small collection of miniature alcohol bottles. "My dad steals these from hotels," he said. "He has a whole briefcase full in his closet."

He carefully selected two clear ones and then he lined up our grape drinks on his window ledge. Poised over our tumblers, his hair hung over his glasses and his lips were curled in a grimace. He unscrewed the caps of the bottles and dumped one in each of our drinks. Then he stuck a finger in both glasses and swirled them around.

"What did you put in there?" I asked.

Jared picked up one of the bottles and squinted.

"Bombay Sapphire," he said.

He held out my tumbler. I set the bass guitar on the bed and joined him at the window. When I took the glass, he clinked his against mine.

"Drink it fast and you won't even taste it," he said.

He tipped his up and started guzzling. I watched him for a few gulps, then did the same with mine. I angled the glass skyward and felt the drink flowing down my throat in long swigs. Jared was right; I could barely taste a thing. Just cold. Until I stopped and belched at the end. Then there was a piney taste in my mouth.

"Gone," I said.

Jared looked at me and laughed. His lips were bright purple.

"Gone," he said back.

He pressed play on his stereo and the Ramones burst through the speakers. "*I don't wanna go down to the basement.*" Jared started doing a little dance where he shook his fist in the air. I laughed and sat down on the floor. I was already getting a touch light-headed.

"How do you feel?" he yelled in my face.

He put his hands on my shoulders.

"I have to urinate!" I yelled over the song.

"Downstairs!" he said. "Unless you just want to go in your pants."

"I'll go downstairs," I said.

"Hey, don't knock it till you've tried it," he said.

He let go of me and kept singing with his eyes closed. I got up, walked out of the room, and wandered through the hallway and down the stairs. I was feeling warm from my chest up to my cheeks. My head felt light, too. I hummed the tune Jared and I had just played as I walked by Meredith's room. The door was still shut tight. I kept moving and found the bathroom just off the kitchen by the back door.

"Wha, wha, wha," I mouthed while I urinated in the cinnamon-smelling room. "We are in . . . a punk rock baaand!"

The toilet water was blue for some reason, and it swirled around and around when I flushed. Above the bowl, on the tank, was a row of tiny soaps shaped like seashells. I picked one up and sniffed it. Strawberry. I examined the shower, too, before I left. It seemed to pour out infinite amounts of water, as if there was a never-ending supply. And inside the curtain was a wealth of bathing accessories. All of them foreign to me.

On my way back, I got all the way to the third step before I noticed the crack of light coming from Meredith's door. It was open. I turned around and stepped up to the door. I was nearly face-to-face with the soaking wet muscleman on the poster. I could see the individual sprouts of his chest hairs. I peeked inside the bedroom. Just as Jared had described, Meredith was lying on the bed with her eyes open, looking at nothing in particular. Her feet were hanging off the end of the bed and I could see her toenails were freshly painted pink. The music had been shut off.

"Get the hell out of here, Jared," she said. "I'm fine."

"It's not Jared," I said.

I made sure to speak as much like myself as possible. Meredith craned her neck up from the pillow and looked into the doorway.

"Here on Earth," she said, "people knock on doors."

She laid her head back down and looked up at the ceiling. She did not tell me to enter. She did not tell me to go away.

"What are you doing in here?" I said.

"Masturbating," she said. "Can't you see?"

"I can't see much," I said, peering through the opening in the door.

"Too bad. You're missing quite a show."

I stood there, my head almost in the opening.

"Okay, Jesus," she said. "Come in for a minute if you're just going to stand around out there all pitiful."

I stepped into the room. The floor was covered in thick white carpeting. Hanging from the ceiling was a string of lights shaped like chili peppers. And the walls were every bit as crowded as Jared's only instead of tattooed musicians there were pictures of men in various states of undress. One lean guy seemed to be pouring a bucket of milk on himself. I felt a chilly breeze over my sweaty arms and looked at the window by the bed. It was open a foot or so. The shade rippled in the wind.

"Did you ever get in trouble with Janice after that night at the church?" I asked.

"Nope," she said in a monotone. "Did you?"

"No."

"I guess it's the fires of hell for us," she said.

She sat up in bed and looked me over.

"What's the deal with you, anyway?" she said.

"What do you mean?"

"I don't know. Why are you so weird? Why do you look like that? Do you ever wear anything else?"

She pointed at my flannel.

"I suppose I have a lot of similar shirts," I said.

She pulled up the shade of the window and looked outside. The neighborhood was quiet as usual. Only the sound of traffic a few streets over came into the room. I could feel the warmth from the alcohol pulsing through me.

"Are you waiting for someone?" I asked.

She flipped right around and stared at me.

"Who told you that?"

"Nobody."

"Why would you say that, then?"

"I don't know, you were just looking like . . ."

"God!" she interrupted. "The word 'privacy' means exactly dick around here. I know Jared's listening to my calls somehow. He probably has some kind of spy kit to ruin my life with."

She gave one more glance out the window and then shut the shade again.

"Why are you so mean to your brother?" I asked.

"What did you just ask me?"

"Why are you so mean to him? He's your family. And he's . . . sick. Don't you understand that?"

I could tell the piney alcohol was loosening my tongue. The words were coming before I properly thought them through. Meredith sprang off the bed and walked slowly across the carpet to me. Then she got so close to me that I could smell her vanilla perfume. She gave me a shove. I wasn't expecting it, and I almost toppled over.

"Listen, you chode," she said. "Maybe if you knew anything about anything you wouldn't have to ask such stupid questions."

"I see the way you treat him," I said.

I braced myself for another push, but it didn't come. Meredith just looked me right in the eyes. "I know you think you're king of the universe because you have this oddball life and my brother thinks you're funny, but I've lived with him for sixteen years and you've known him for weeks."

"What are you saying?"

"I piss him off because that's what he likes," she said.

I watched her closely.

"I piss him off because that's how it's always been and if I started being his best friend he'd know it was because of the operation, and he would hate me even more. You get it? I play my part and it makes him think that something is still normal around here."

"He likes to be angry?"

"Have you ever spent time with him?" she asked.

"Okay," I conceded, "maybe sometimes."

"So don't tell me," she said, "don't come in here and tell me that I'm making things worse for him because it's not true. My mom treats him like a five-year-old, and I know that's not right. My dad is never home, and I know that's not right. So I'm trying something different. I'm treating him like the irritating little shit that he is."

Her face was flushed now, and I could see her eyes were watering a little.

"I'm sorry," I said.

She was still right in front of me. It was the closest we'd ever been, not counting when her mouth was by my ear in the van.

"It's okay . . ." she said.

Then she leaned in closer and my heart suddenly felt like it might explode. But she was only smelling my breath. "Have you been . . . drinking?" she asked, perplexed. "What's wrong with your lips?"

"Bombay Sapphire and grape drink," I said.

She looked at me in disbelief.

"Do strangers really come through your window . . . to have *experiences* with you?" I asked.

Meredith didn't speak. She just stood transfixed in front of me. Then we heard Jared clear his throat right behind us.

"What in the hell is going on here?" he asked.

I turned around and saw him leaning against the door. His glance bounced back and forth from Meredith to me.

"Nothing," I said.

"Your friend came in here to bother me," said Meredith.

Jared walked out of the room before I had a chance to speak again. Meredith and I both watched out the door as he disappeared from sight. From up the stairs we could barely hear his voice. "Janice is home," he said.

There was a short pause.

"And she doesn't want you biking home this late. She says you're staying over."

16. The Complexities of Physical Reality

EVERY LOCATION ON THE PLANET MAKES ONE REV-olution a day, no matter where you live. Nana taught me that when I was barely old enough to understand it. Whether you reside in Antarctica, North Branch, or somewhere outside town in a dome, the same process applies. One day per revolution. Twenty-three hours, fifty-six minutes, and four seconds, to be exact. Most people talk about this in terms of "sunrise" and "sunset," but Fuller hated these words. The idea of the sun rising and setting was one left over from a time when we thought the earth was flat. Modern humans, he thought, should recognize that there is no rise and set, no up and down, only the earth revolving in and out of the sun's light.

I knew these to be facts. And I knew the days passed the same way everywhere. But I also knew that time seemed to take on different properties at the Whitcombs' house. It appeared to slow down and speed up at will. It could even stop entirely if Meredith entered a room. And when I finally found myself in Jared's room that night, I could almost feel the earth slow on its axis.

The whole room was ink black with only the thinnest lines of moonlight shining through the blinds. I was on a rickety cot across the room from Jared. It smelled of detergent and sweat and it creaked whenever I moved. Jared was in his bed, breathing heavily in the darkness. We didn't speak at first, but I could tell he was awake. He hadn't said a word to me since he found Meredith and me together.

"If Nana is waiting up for me," I spoke, finally, "this whole thing is over."

Jared said nothing for a few seconds. Then I heard his disembodied voice, quiet. "Do you want to know why our band has to be awesome?" he asked.

I looked into the dark, trying to distinguish his facial features. I couldn't.

"I'll tell you," he said. "It has to be awesome because I'm alive and talking to you right now."

"Because you're alive . . ." I said.

"Because I'm alive and another kid is dead. He died so I could live," he said. "You get it now?"

"I'm not entirely sure."

Jared sighed.

"It's like this," he said. "Once they decided I needed the transplant, we got a beeper. Then we had to wait around for them to beep us when they found a heart. I was on a list. They said it would probably be sixty days or so. But it could be as long as a year."

My eyes were starting to adjust and I could almost make out his face now. His voice seemed to be coming from all around me.

"It took me a couple of weeks to realize that they were going to call when some other kid croaked. Then I could be saved. That's the only way it could work. That's the only way they could get a heart that was the same size. I was waiting for somebody just like me to die."

"When did they contact you?" I asked.

"It only took a month. They flew the heart in on a plane and drove it to the hospital. It can only be preserved for so many hours."

"Was it someone your age?"

"Almost exactly," he said.

"How did he . . . pass away?"

"An accident. Got hit by a car near his school. It was icy, I think. He died that night, and by the morning, my surgery was over. That's how fast it all happened."

"Do you know anything about him?"

"A little. He was from Minnesota. And he played soccer. His mom wrote me a letter, but I've only read it once."

He paused.

"The thing is, I didn't think about it much at the time. I was just happy the way it turned out. Some kids wait so long they end up on machines, fighting to live every day until something comes through. I was lucky. But lately, I've been thinking about that kid all the time. His name was Matthew. What do I really deserve to have his heart for?"

"You deserve it as much as anyone else."

"Really?" he said. "What do I do with it? I complain all day and ruin it with cigarettes. And I'm not sure I've really ever been happy, even before all this."

"You used to sing like a girl."

He laughed. "You're right. I did that."

"Maybe you just don't remember how you felt before."

"Maybe."

"I think memory is strange," I said. "I don't really remember my parents. I was five. I should have better memories of them, but I don't."

"What happened to them?" Jared asked.

"They were commercial archaeologists, flying into Florida. They were on a small plane that went down in a mangrove swamp. Nana never gave me a real explanation about what went wrong with the plane. It just fell out of the sky."

"And you don't remember the way they look?"

"Not very clearly. Nana has photographs. We look at them every few years, but she discourages it generally. She doesn't want us to dwell. She doesn't want us to get stuck in the past. Her philosophy is a futurist one."

"That sounds shitty," he said.

"No," I said, "Nana wants . . ."

"It's shitty, Sebastian," he said, "just trust me on this. Those are pictures of your dead parents. You should be able to look at them whenever you want."

I thought about the photo album with the red cover. I wasn't even sure where Nana kept it anymore. It mostly held pictures of my father. My mother was in there, but it had taken Nana a long time to warm to her. So she only came in near the end.

"You're right," I said. "I don't fully understand it."

My eyes had grown accustomed to the light, and I could see Jared facing my cot.

"But Nana has a plan for me," I said. "I'm not supposed to question her."

"What's the plan?"

"It sounds a bit grandiose," I said.

"For fuck's sake, Sebastian, just tell me."

I held my breath a moment.

"I'm going to save humanity," I said.

Jared didn't laugh. He just raised his head up and yawned into the dark.

"From what?" he said in a monotone.

"I'm not entirely sure," I said. "But every human is put here for a purpose. That's supposed to be mine."

"Hmm," he said. "Let me know how that turns out."

He slumped back down on his pillow, and I could hear him grinding his teeth.

"Listen," he said. "Let's get something straight. You're *my* friend, Sebastian. Not Meredith's."

"I understand that."

"She isn't friends with guys," he said. "She uses them or they use her. Or both. I don't know. And then she never talks to them again. She's crazy, and I don't want you talking to her."

"We were talking about you."

"I don't care," he said. "You don't have time to chitty-chat with loose women. We have work to do. And you have to save humanity. That's a lot of shit to get done."

His voice was shaking slightly. I kept quiet.

"I got the beep, Sebastian," he said. He rested a palm against his chest. "I got to live and have a band. Matthew from Minnesota didn't get shit. So it's got to be a good band, okay? And nobody is going to mess it up or stop it before we get there."

"All right," I said.

I looked up at the ceiling. I counted the slivers of moonlight, but didn't finish.

"What are we going to be called?" I asked.

"I don't know," said Jared. His voice was muffled. When I looked over, he was facing the wall. "I've been trying like hell to come up with it. But it has to be something you can feel right away, you know? Something that tells people, 'Watch out, 'cause these guys are coming and when they're gone, you won't ever be the same. Your life will be turned on its head!'"

"Like the Sex Pistols," I said.

"Yeah," he said, "exactly."

The room grew quiet again. But I wasn't tired. I sat up on the cot. It creaked.

"What about the Dangerous Knives?" I said.

"Is that a real suggestion?" asked Jared.

"Sure."

"No cutlery," he said.

He was silent a few seconds, but I could almost hear the gears starting to turn in his head. "How about The Total A-holes?" he said.

"Too much," I said.

"You're right," he said, "Janice probably wouldn't buy me any more guitar stuff with a name like that."

"What about the Church Bandits?" I said.

"We're not cowboys."

He paused. "How about the Exploding Faces?"

"How does a face explode?" I asked.

"I don't know," he said. "Like from a missile. There are no wrong answers in brainstorming, asshole."

"Okay," I said. "The Pervs?"

"No," said Jared. "What about the Pissy Cargo Pants?"

"The Sins?"

"The Projectile Vomits?"

"The Slacks?"

"No. The Stool Samples?"

"The Crash?"

"The Clap?"

"What's the Clap?" I asked.

"I don't know. My dad got it in the army."

"Oh. The Trash?"

"No."

"The Gas?"

"No."

"The Rash?"

"No."

But then I heard his hand slap against the wall.

"Wait, what did you say?" he asked.

He turned around.

"The Rash," I said.

"The Rash," he said, slowly.

"The Rash," I repeated.

"Wait a minute now," he said.

"What?"

"Actually, that's sort of badass."

"Really?"

"Maybe."

"Why?"

"It's gross, but not too gross. You can almost feel it. The Rash. You can almost feel your skin start to itch. Like our sound is spreading like a rash or something."

"Is that a good thing?" I asked.

"Yeah. You break out when you hear us. Your body won't be able to handle it. Because we're The Rash, fuckers!"

We sat in silence for nearly a minute. Jared was whispering to himself, but I couldn't make out what he was saying.

"It's settled," he said eventually. "Yeah, it's totally settled. We're The Rash."

He chuckled.

"Pretty good, Sebastian," he said. "I mean I was the one who realized it was good. But you said it. You said it fair and fucking square. Pretty good."

I waited for him to tell me he was joking, that I hadn't really come up with the right name. But he didn't say another word. He just lay back and was quiet. I listened to his heavy breathing until he fell asleep. I could see him now in the dark. He was facing my side of the room, his mouth wide open. Then I felt my own eyes closing. And sometime, presumably while we were sleeping soundly, the earth started revolving again. It fell back into pace and found its way toward the sun once again.

IN THE MORNING, I LEFT WITHOUT WAKING JARED. I crept through the house, holding my breath, the bass guitar strapped on again. I walked down the hard carpeted stairs, past Meredith's closed door, and into the soft blue light of the kitchen. No one was up. The house was filled only with the ticking of a tall clock in the living room. I stopped at the closet for my coat and hat; then I slipped out the front door and into the piercing cold of the morning. I wiped a film of frost off my bike seat with the palm of a glove, and sent the pedals spinning to make sure they weren't frozen. I walked the Voyager toward the street.

I don't know why I happened to look back; I think it was because I wanted to make sure Janice hadn't seen me. But when I turned my neck, my glance went immediately to Meredith's window. She was standing in front of her bedside lamp, wearing only a tank top and a pair of bright blue underwear. She was right up against the window. Her blond hair was pulled back in a ponytail. She wore no makeup. She didn't smile or wave or make any acknowledgment that she saw me looking back. She just watched me for a couple seconds. Then she reached up a thin arm and yanked the shade down over the glass. And she was gone.

The ride home was a haze. There was frost on the trees and the beige lawns of North Branch. The sky was a dark purple. But I didn't look up much from the road and my basket. I wanted to make sure the cans of paint didn't go crashing to the street. And as I embarked on the last leg of my journey, up the hill of Hillsboro Drive, I saw myself only as Nana would see me, pedaling in a vision, cutting through a winter fog after a night of betraying her trust entirely. I imagined myself gradually making my way out of a vision in her mind and riding back into her temporal reality.

My heart seemed to be beating in every part of my body as I stowed my bicycle in the shed and shrouded the bass in its tarp. I closed the shed doors behind me and began jogging through the woods with a can of paint in each hand. *I should have left Jared's in the night.* This was the only thought in my head as I launched into a full run toward the dome. I could see it clearly now, even the deep green pastures of Antarctica. *Why did I fall asleep? I should have left in the night. Everything would be fine if I'd only . . .*

The paint cans swayed back and forth with each of my strides. The frigid air poured into my lungs and came right back out warm and white. And I would have continued right up the path and inside the dome if a flash had not caught my eye. Just as my gloved hand rested on the door handle, I saw a glint of something nearby. Sunlight was just starting to pour over our hill. A minute sooner and there would have been no light for a reflection. But there it was. I took a step into the yard and saw that it was a bottle of ice wine.

It was half empty, and it sat in a burgundy puddle. I set the paint down on the stoop. I picked up the bottle and sloshed it around. The contents were still tepid.

"Nana!" I yelled.

I gripped the bottle tighter.

"Nana, where are you?"

Her name echoed off the wall of the dome. I looked around frantically and noticed slight indentations in the frosty grass. Footprints. They led away from the dome and to the small copse of pines at the beginning of our hill's incline.

"Nana!" I shouted one last time.

No response. But I did hear a faint shuffle of clothing. I followed the sound as best I could toward the slope on the other side of the hill. The light was better now, but still too faint to see much. I continued and soon heard another rustle followed by a small groan. The noises were close, and when I looked to my right I saw a figure hunched against a tree. It was hard to make out Nana's frame at first because she was wrapped in a blanket from head to toe. But her hazel eyes shone as I made my approach, and her bouffant bobbed in the wind. When I reached her, I set the bottle of ice wine at her feet.

"Nana," I said. "What are you doing? How long have you been out here?"

She looked up at me, and her gaze seemed out of focus.

"What does it matter?" she said.

"It matters because you're going to have hypothermia. You're going to freeze to death," I said.

"I don't care. We've been . . . disgraced."

"Who's been disgraced? What do you mean?"

"Don't pretend with me, Sebastian," she said. "I know you fore-saw this. That's why you ran away. You didn't have the decency to face your Nana."

"I didn't run away from anything," I said.

Nana's face strained and then she coughed loudly.

"I've tried with you!" she said. "But you still exhibit weak-ness at every turn. You take flight when things get taxing, just like Buckminster."

She leaned back against the tree and shut her eyes.

"I've failed with you," she said, "just like I failed with every-thing else."

From out of the depths of her blanket, a frail hand emerged. In the hand was a crumpled newspaper. She flung the pages at my feet. I gathered the paper up as best I could and flipped to the front page. There, on the cover of the Sunday *North Branch Courier*, was Nana's face, frozen in the rictus of a forced smile. Her neck was bent at an odd angle. And there was a small bubble of spit on her lower lip. She looked like a maniac. And behind her, comically small in the dis-tance, was our dome with spatters of green paint near the bottom. The headline read: "Local Woman Wants to Live in Earth of Her Making." Underneath in small type, it said, "When this planet's too normal for you, why not move to your own! Area eccentric Jose-phine Prendergast is doing just that."

I glanced back down at Nana, huddled under the tree. Her eyes were wet, but it may have been the cold. "This is not what you told the reporter," I said.

"Fiction," she said. "A hack job. Every word. Libel. My life's work reduced to a joke."

I began skimming the article and stopped when I got to the words "New Age." This was one of Nana's least favorite phrases.

"This is the first I've seen of this," I said. "It wasn't the reason I was gone."

She shrugged her shoulders and burped again. "Where did you venture off to, then? Another brisk morning walk to get away from me?"

"I was at a friend's house," I said.

It took me a moment to realize that I had really just spoken the words.

"You're lying. You don't have friends."

"I do," I said. "They live in North Branch."

She was speechless for a time after that. And I thought for the first ten seconds or so that we were going to discuss the situation civilly. I should have known better. She rose to her feet and began walking back to the dome, her blanket dragging behind her like a soiled cloak. I followed her, the paper still clenched in my hand.

"Where are you going?" I shouted. "We need to have a conference about this!"

She kept trudging across the lawn. I didn't notice at first that she had reclaimed the bottle of ice wine. But I saw it all too well when she stopped to take a long drink. She wiped her mouth with the back of her hand and then dropped the bottle on the sidewalk. It smashed to pieces.

"Nana," I said. "You're inebriated."

She turned around just long enough to look me in the eyes and mouth one sentence: "And you're a liar."

Then she was inside the dome, laboring up the stairs to my bedroom. I watched her from the outside as she quickly crested the Antarctic Circle. I entered the dome and stood at the foot of the stairs. I heard the sound of objects being moved and overturned, and I thanked the Greater Intellect that my bass guitar was in the shed.

"Nana," I said. "Listen. I should have spoken to you sooner. I should have told you. I was afraid to tell you. You have to know that. I'm sorry."

I don't know if she heard me over the racket she was making. Either way, she didn't answer. I walked up the stairs, but I was met halfway by Nana, stooped over like a hunchback with something heavy in her arms. The blanket was still draped over her, and it was hard at first to tell what she was holding. But it became clear soon enough. It was our computer monitor.

"Please," I said. "Nana."

Her old body buckled under the weight of the screen as she toddled down the steps, coming right at me. I reached out as she passed and grabbed onto one of the cords. She grunted and gave the monitor a tug, and the cord was wrenched from my grip.

"Out of my way!" she barked.

She hobbled down to the landing and kept going toward the front door. She knocked the door open and headed back to the crest of the hill. All I could do now was stay back and watch as she retraced her steps all the way to the top of the slope. It was here she released the monitor. I watched as it left her hands and rolled down the wooded declivity. It gathered moisture and frost as it tumbled, and whipped off drops into the air. The sound of upset brush was loud in the still morning air. And when the monitor finally crashed into a rocklike trunk of a walnut tree, the sound sent a covey of birds flying from the bare branches.

Nana took a step backward and slipped. She fell hard to the ground and I immediately ran to her. I grabbed her shaking body and pulled it up, but she fought me at every turn, mumbling something I couldn't hear. I leaned closer to her.

"What are you saying?" I asked.

I barely saw her hand before the palm caught me square on my cheek.

"Leave!" she said.

I held my face where Nana had struck it. I could feel it warming.

"You have done nothing but lie to me since I fell ill. You were waiting for this to happen," she said. "You were waiting until I was weak. So you could . . . tear down everything we've been working toward."

"That's not true," I said.

"I promised your father after he died. I promised him I would help you, but what can I do? It's clear to me that you called the paper to sabotage this project. You called them, didn't you?"

"I didn't."

"You . . . don't have the right," she said. "You don't have the right to ruin this!"

Nana was up and panting now. In between her sentences she closed her eyes, her jaw trembling. Her arms hung at her sides. They looked too heavy for her to lift.

"Get out of here, Sebastian," she said. "Leave me alone."

She was walking away from me before I could speak.

"Nana," I shouted, "please. Why won't you listen to me? You have everything wrong."

I was watching her through tears now. Her Vellux blanket was covered in mud. She didn't notice. She gathered it and slung it over her shoulder.

"I was lonely," I yelled at her back. "Aren't you?"

She did not turn around. She kept moving at the same pace until she reached the dome. She noticed the paint for the first time and kicked the cans over. I looked behind me at the woods that surrounded our property. Down the hill sat the ground-scuffed plastic computer monitor, my first form of communication with Jared. The screen was cracked and shattered. Wires hung out its back like overlarge nerve endings.

I thought about trying to take it with me, but there was no way I could carry it on the bike. So I left it behind. I took one more look at the dome and started walking back to the shed. I watched for Nana when I passed by the walls, but she was nowhere in sight. In case she was watching me in her mind, though, I waved good-bye. And though she must have known by then, I apologized for being a less-than-average visionary.

17. Elements in Motion

THE COLD HARD WORLD. THESE WERE THE WORDS
implanted in my brain as I returned to North Branch proper with
nothing but my instrument and a few dollars in my pocket. I had
first read the phrase in a biographical work about Fuller when I
was a boy. The "Cold Hard World" was what his family had said he
needed a taste of when he was thrown out of Harvard in his forma-
tive years. Technically, Bucky was expelled from college for missing
too many classes, but the real reason was much more scandalous.

The truth was he had become infatuated with a showgirl. And
when her performances moved from Boston to New York, Bucky
tagged along. He withdrew his savings and took an entire chorus
line of girls out to dinner at one of the city's most exorbitant restaurants. He came home broke, and his parents promptly shipped him
off to be an apprentice in a textiles factory in rural Quebec. It was a
freezing little village. The work was miserable. It was one of the saddest parts of his biography.

I had to believe North Branch was better than the frozen plains
of Quebec, but it was just as empty on that Sunday afternoon.
Everything was closed and the streets were completely bereft of
humans. I walked my bike over the cobblestones looking for HELP
WANTED signs in the shopwindows. My nose had been running

for the last hour, and my eyes were sore from crying. I tried hard to ignore my numbed feet and my hunger, and imagine a bright new life for myself instead.

The diversion only lasted so long. Hope dissolves quickly in the cold. I passed the dark windows of The Record Collector and Small World Paints. Neither advertised the need for an unskilled teen. I passed a drugstore and a jeweler's. Finally, I rounded a corner and immediately spied what I thought was a mirage. A neon pink OPEN sign in the window of a hole-in-the-wall cafeteria. The Canteen, it was called. I counted the odd two dollars and coins in my pocket. $3.63. I locked my bike to a drainpipe and brought my guitar in with me. The warm breath of the café's interior almost made me cry all over again, but I held myself together and sat down on a stool at the counter.

Within seconds, a plastic menu slapped down in front of me and an overfull glass of water came after it. I looked up to see a tall middle-aged woman nudging at a pair of glasses. She wore thick bifocals. Her face was tired but friendly.

"A traveling musician," she said. "Isn't it a little chilly to be out on the road?"

"Yes," I said, "it is."

I looked down at the menu, and when I glanced up moments later, she was gone. There were only a few other patrons in the place. An old man filling out a crossword. A young family in church clothes eating hamburgers. Everything on the menu was too much money. Six dollars for the "baskets," sandwiches and french fries. I looked up again and the woman was walking by.

"Can you prepare a grilled cheese sandwich?" I asked.

"Impossible," she said. Then she smiled. "It's cheese and bread. I think we can handle it."

"How much does that cost?"

"Four-fifty for the basket."

"What about . . . with no basket?"

"Three even without fries," she said.

I nodded my assent. She scribbled on a light green ticket and strode away on her tall legs. I watched as she glided into a small open kitchen. She stuck my ticket up on a metal wheel, and an older man promptly grabbed some buttered bread, and tossed it on a large grill. The smell of the cooking butter spilled out into the cafeteria and I shut my eyes. I was alone. Ordering food at a restaurant for the first time.

It wasn't long before I started to remember my first grilled cheese. Two perfect halves, dipped in ketchup. An ice-cold grape drink on the side. The next time the waitress appeared I asked her politely where the pay telephone was. The truth was I had only one real option left. I watched the church family carefully on my way to the phone. In the old days they might have come for a tour of the dome after their meal. I might have sold them a magnet or a Bucky Ball. That was all over now.

I paged through the phone book for the Whitcombs' home number just to make sure I had it right. I deposited my change and dialed. Janice answered on the third ring.

"Whitcomb residence," she said.

"Mrs. Whitcomb."

"Sebastian? Is that you?"

"It is," I said.

"Did you want to speak with Jared? He's changing out of his church garb right now, I'm afraid. Actually, I can't really tell the difference between his church clothes and the regular ones . . ."

"I called to talk to you," I said.

There was a pause on the line.

"Oh," she said.

"Mrs. Whitcomb," I said. "It appears I've become homeless."

I tried to laugh, but nothing came out.

"What are you talking about?" she said.

"Nana asked me to leave this morning. I've been temporarily displaced. And I'm not sure what my next course of action should be. I . . ."

"Where are you?" she interrupted.

"The Canteen cafeteria," I said. "I think maybe if I could find employment . . . but I'm not sure that's possible. There are some factors that don't seem to be in my favor."

"Don't move," was all she said.

"Okay," I said. "But I just need some advice."

Janice hung up. I removed the greasy phone slowly from my ear. I placed it on its holder and turned back to the cramped dining room. The young family was watching me. They were no longer eating. I realized I might have spoken too loudly on the telephone. I felt their eyes on me as I made my way back to the counter, but I looked straight ahead. When I sat down, I found my sandwich steaming in front of me. It sat, like the original, in two triangular halves in the exact center of a red plate. The waitress bolted past.

"Your mom coming to rescue you?" she asked over her shoulder.

"Yes," I said. "My mom."

She kept moving without comment. I placed my three dollars on the counter and took a bite of the crisp grilled cheese. I looked out at the Cold Hard World on the other side of the glass. Nana had told me once that everything we looked at, our roads, trees, buildings, flowers, were all just groups of moving energies and elements. And they were all seeking the path of least resistance. Humans, she said, were no different. Change was the only constant for people. I tried to find some reassurance in this fact, but instead, the only thing I could think about was my old classroom in the dome. Before Nana's interruption, there had been days where we spent the whole afternoon in discussion about these things. Life. Energies. Time and space. Everything.

TWENTY MINUTES LATER, JANICE WHITCOMB WALKED through the door. I was still at the counter, drinking my fifth or sixth refill of ice water when I saw her. She wiped her boots on a dirty wool mat. Her eyes and cold-reddened nose peeked out of the space between an orange hat and scarf. She took a seat on the stool next to me and lowered her scarf.

"Have you paid for that?" she asked.

She pointed at my grilled cheese.

"I have," I said. "But I don't have enough for service. I didn't . . . know."

Janice reached into a deep pocket of her coat and pulled out a narrow billfold. She removed two dollar bills and set them on the counter. We both stared at them.

"Are you ready to go?" she asked.

"Where?"

I honestly meant it. I wasn't sure where she was going to take me. She didn't answer. She just motioned down at the bass guitar at my feet. I picked it up and she led me out to the parked van. I tightened against the cold, and lowered my neck into my coat. Exhaust swirled around the back bumper of the van. I unlocked my bike and watched while Janice loaded it in the back. I slid open the passenger door and climbed inside.

As soon as I leaned back in the seat, I realized how fatigued I was. I tried to keep my eyes open, but they kept dropping closed. Janice put the van in gear and drove slowly down the brick street. When she started speaking, I was already near sleep. But her words, calm and measured, cut through the murk somehow.

"My husband doesn't live with us anymore," she said.

Her voice nearly broke on the word "husband."

"If you're going to be staying with us, there's no reason I should keep lying to you about that. I don't know why I do it. But I shouldn't. He's gone. He won't be around."

"Okay," I said. It was all I could think of to say.

"It's still a new thing, though," she said. "Even a few months ago, he'd drop by. The kids aren't used to it yet."

She flipped on the defroster, and I felt a burst of warm air from the front.

"Did he leave because of Jared?" I asked. "I mean . . . because of . . ."

"I don't know," she sighed. "That was part of it. But there were other reasons, too. Problems between us."

She watched me in the rearview mirror.

"We got married young," she said. "For one thing. And I think that when you do that, it's hard to tell if you're really going to be compatible down the line. Sometimes you are. And sometimes it just takes one big problem to prove that you aren't."

She took a deep breath. "It also helps if you don't marry a giant selfish baby."

I tried to keep my eyes open.

"I shouldn't say that," she said. "It's not that simple."

I waited for her to tell me more. But instead she changed gears.

"I need to ask you a couple of questions," she said. "Can you answer some questions for me, Sebastian?"

"I can," I said.

I tried to straighten up in my seat.

"I'm going to be blunt," she said, "because as much as I want to help you, my family has enough complications. Do you understand?"

"I do."

"Good," she said. "Then we have an understanding."

She took a long breath. "First, I want to hear honestly: Did you really get thrown out of your house, or did you just run away after an argument? Are the police going to show up at my door?"

"Nana instructed me to leave," I said. "She was clear about it."

She nodded.

"Are your parents really dead?" she said.

"They are."

She flipped on her turn signal. She turned off the main thoroughfare onto the backstreets. A light sleet was falling from the sky now, and Janice switched on her wipers.

"Do you believe in God, Sebastian?" she asked.

"I don't know," I said.

She winced a little.

"I might," I added, "I'm just . . ."

"Your first answer was fine," she said.

She turned the wipers to a higher speed.

"And you understand about Jared's condition?"

"I think so," I said.

"It's very possible that Jared could die," she said. "Do you understand that?"

Her voice strained a little with the words, but she got them out.

"His body will never stop trying to reject that new heart, and that takes a toll on the health of an organ. We don't know exactly how many years he has. Every case is different. But he'll probably need to be back on the list for another one someday. Fifteen to twenty years is the longest they last. That's the best-case scenario. Then he has to survive another transplant."

"I see," I said. It was hardly a whisper.

"Jared hasn't told you all this?"

"No."

"Well, he knows. He insists on hearing everything the doctors tell me."

I was beginning to feel faint.

"It's better to know the facts about these things in the end."

She continued to drive steadily ahead.

"This last question may be hard to answer. And I would mind my own business if I wasn't taking you in for the time being. But here we are."

I closed my eyes, focusing only on the sound of her voice.

"Sebastian," she said. "Do you think your grandmother is of *sound mind*? Do you know what that means?"

"I know what you mean," I said.

Instantly, I pictured Nana being hauled away somewhere. Back to the hospital. I saw her strapped down again to a gurney, a confused and defeated look on her face.

"I think she'll be okay," I said. "She's confused. I'm sure it will pass eventually."

We were coming up to the Whitcomb residence now, and Janice stopped talking long enough to concentrate on pulling into her garage. I watched the electric door wind up. I was starting to feel a real dizziness now. Maybe it was the information about Jared.

Or just plain weariness. But my mouth was dry, and my neck was so hot. We docked in the unlit garage. Janice turned around and examined me.

"Hey," she said, "are you okay?"

"I'm sure it will pass," I said.

"What will pass?"

I slid down the bench seat of the van and laid my head down on the cushion.

"I'm sorry," I said. "I'm sure if I can only keep from emitting the wrong waves then everything will be . . ."

I couldn't think of a way to finish the sentence so I just let out a long breath. No words were coming. I closed my eyes again and this time when I tried to open them they would not comply. After that, I remember only the sound of the driver's-side door opening, and then Janice's cool hand on my forehead. And as I fell into a deep sleep, I heard her voice.

"Okay," she said, over and over. "It's going to be okay."

18. Divide and Conquer

WHEN MY EYES DECIDED TO OPEN AGAIN, I WAS LYING on my back on a sofa. I was buried under a musty blanket, and there was a teeming glass of juice next to me on an end table. Also, Meredith Whitcomb was standing over me. I didn't see her at first, all the way at the end of the couch, but my sleep-blurred vision instantly cleared when she came into view. I didn't speak. I wasn't sure what to say. I felt feverish, and everything came at me at once: the sound of loud music upstairs, the clamber of pots and pans in the kitchen, the warmth of the room. I took a sip of juice. Meredith sat down on the arm of the couch.

"You're not in a coma," she said. "I guess that's a good thing."

She looked sagely out the front window.

"How long was I sleeping?" I asked.

She held up five fingers.

"Five hours?"

She nodded.

"I can't believe it."

"My mom thinks you're suffering from malnutrition or something. She's cooking all the vegetables in the house. I can smell the onions in my room."

"How did I get in here?"

"I wasn't finished," she said.

"Okay."

She cleared her throat. "I was going to say that you've only been here an afternoon and you're already screwing everything up and ruining our lives. All right, now I'm done."

"How did I get in here?" I said again.

"We carried you. You weigh more than I thought you did. I would watch the carbs. You might be getting fat."

I felt my neck reddening.

"I'm just kidding. You weigh like five pounds."

She laughed. "You have a temperature, but not a high one."

"Have the police come to look for me?" I asked.

She didn't answer, and when I looked over, her smirk was gone.

"It was you, wasn't it, you asshole?"

"It was me, what?"

She sighed. "You made those calls to my private line."

"I don't know what you're talking about."

"Don't try it. I figured it out after you left last night." "You kept looking at the window when we were in my room. How else would you know about that?"

The music upstairs suddenly stopped and we both looked up at the ceiling. Jared was stomping around, shouting something.

"I don't think it's okay," she said. "I want you to know that."

Her voice was quieter now.

"Which part . . . specifically?"

"I don't think it's okay to invade someone's privacy. And lie to people and say things you don't mean!" she said.

"I meant what I said."

"You don't know what you mean," she said right away. "You've probably never met another girl. You don't know me. And you can't just go around saying things like that to people. It's not some dumb joke."

Meredith got up and started toward the kitchen.

"Wait," I said.

"No," she said. "I've said what I want to."

I sat up, and the quick motion made me feel faint again.

"Why were you watching me in your underwear?" I asked.

She stopped in the doorway. "Look," she said. "I'm sorry you got tossed out on your ass. Just don't talk to me. It would be better if you didn't."

She walked out of the room and into the kitchen.

"Are we having a real dinner?" she asked her mother. "Or is it greens and mutant potatoes?"

"You like sweet potatoes," said Janice.

"I like real dinners," she said.

Every hint of emotion was gone from her voice. It was as if our conversation hadn't occurred at all. I closed my eyes again. The smells coming from the kitchen were not much different from those I would have smelled at home, but they made me feel nauseous. I wondered if Nana would cook without me there. What would she have for dinner and what would she do with the hours that followed? Janice's words leaped back into my head. *Sound. Mind.* I had never seen Nana react to scrutiny the way she had that morning. Maybe she needed someone to watch out for her now. I knew she needed company, but I also knew that person couldn't be me. She had asked me to leave. She had struck me for the first time in the history of our time together. I couldn't go back now.

"Jared!" called Janice from the kitchen. "Dinner is ready!"

Jared yelled something down the stairs I couldn't quite make

THE HOUSE OF TOMORROW   183

out. But I could tell by the pitch in his voice he was excited about something.

"Go wake Sebastian," Janice said to Meredith.

"Why can't you do it?" I heard her say.

I got up off the couch.

"I'm up!" I said. "It's okay. I'm awake. I'm ready for vegetables."

I DIDN'T KNOW ENTIRELY WHAT I HAD EXPECTED FROM dinner, but what I received was not a hero's welcome. Meredith absconded to her room with her plate of vegetables shortly after sitting down, claiming the conflict of a television program. Janice spoke (more to herself than to Jared and me) about the next Youth Group meeting, and new ways of making people test their faith. She also kept a roving eye on my plate to make sure I was eating. Jared stuffed big hunks of potato in his mouth and complained about the lack of a main course. But all the while, he threw conspiratorial looks my way, and I felt like I had forgotten something important. I ate just enough to be polite, and not enough to induce vomiting. When the meal was over I followed Jared upstairs, and it wasn't until the door was closed safely behind us that he finally told me what was going on.

"Big news for The Rash," he said. "Giant news, actually. Are you ready?"

It took me a moment to remember the name of our band.

"Jared," I said. "This hasn't been the best day for me."

Jared looked at me blankly. "What the hell are you talking about?"

"I don't feel well, and I'm confused," I said. "So I don't know if I really want to discuss the band at this moment."

He took this in. Then he violently pushed his glasses up his nose.

"I'm trying to distract you, you ungrateful ass," he said. "I'm trying to get you to concentrate on brighter things. Do you really want to wallow about how bad and messed up your life is right now and act like some giant vagina?"

"Not really," I said.

"Well then, there you go."

I said nothing.

"Fine," he said. "I acknowledge that your life sucks, and your grandma is batshit and that's sad. But I have good news about The Rash, and I've been waiting to tell you. So, nut up, Johnny! Think about the band for a minute and not just yourself."

"Okay," I said. "What's the news?"

"Are you ready?"

"I'm ready, Jared."

"Are you really ready?"

I just looked at him.

"We have a gig."

After he said the last word, he punched me in the shoulder and shook my arms.

"And if we rock our asses off, we might even get paid," he said.

"What's a . . ."

"A gig is a show," said Jared. "We're going to perform. It's going to be so fucking awesome I can't even think about it without getting a humongous boner."

"Where are we going to perform?"

"It's perfect," said Jared.

"Where?"

"It's so perfect," he said. "We're rocking the site of our crime."

"Immanuel Methodist?"

"The Youth Group hosts a talent contest every year. And it's coming up in a couple of weeks. Bam! We're going to win. We are going to conquer their asses like Napoleon!"

"Weeks?" I said.

Jared punched me again.

"Please stop punching me," I said. "We don't know how to perform any songs."

"*Yet*," said Jared. "But that's the best part about you being all abandoned and everything. We'll finally have enough time to practice!"

He jumped up on his bed and began playing an invisible guitar.

"I admit it's a pretty exciting idea," I said.

I sat down on an amplifier.

"I wonder if Christian girls will throw their panties onstage?" he asked, jumping on the bed. "Do you think any of them wear thongs?"

I didn't say anything, and eventually he looked up at me.

"Goddamn, you're impossible today."

"I don't know what to do," I said. "I think my grandmother might need serious help."

Jared collapsed on the bed and ran his palm over the sheets.

"Well, when you put it that way, it sounds pretty shitty," he said.

He looked up at the ceiling, seemingly lost in thought.

"I won't let my mom give you the boot," he said quietly. "You have a home here, man."

"Yeah," I said.

"I mean it," he said.

"I understand," I said.

But I couldn't feign excitement anymore. My words fell from my mouth like chewed bread. Jared watched me closely. He got up off the bed and walked over to the closet where he had once hidden his soaked cargo pants. I couldn't see what he was doing, but I heard the contents of various boxes being spilled onto the floor.

"Dammit," said Jared. "I swear there are little gnomes that come in here and move my shit around."

"What are you looking for?" I asked.

No answer. Just more shuffling.

"Ha!" he said, moments later. "Gold mine."

He emerged from the closet with two metal handles in his hands. They were painted white, but the silver showed up in thin nicks and scrapes. He tossed the handles on the bed.

"What are those?" I asked.

"Pegs," he said.

He walked to the bed and grabbed one. He pointed to a hole at its end.

"You fasten these little bastards onto the screws that hold your back wheel in place. Then someone else can ride on the back of your bike."

He handed a peg to me.

"That's great," I said.

"Don't humor me, Sebastian. They aren't that fuckin' great, okay? But I thought we could put them on your bike. Then we could go check on your crazy-ass grandma at night."

"You mean sneak out?" I said.

"Do you think in a million son-of-a-bitching years my mom would send me out in the cold on the back of a bike?" he asked.

"No," I said.

"Then we shall sneak!" he said.

He handed me the pegs and I rolled them around in the palm of my hand. They were surprisingly heavy.

"I'll make you a deal," said Jared.

"What?"

"Tonight we work on songwriting and tomorrow we check on . . . Nana."

I stuffed the pegs in my pocket. "Okay," I said. "But it has to be tomorrow."

"It will be."

"All right then."

"So we have a deal?" he asked.

"We do," I said.

"Great," said Jared, "Then take off your shirt."

I looked at his face to see if he was joking. His hair hung over the frames of his glasses, and underneath, his eyes were perfectly calm.

"Why?" I said. "I don't feel well."

Jared reached over and started unbuttoning my flannel.

"I have a fever," I said.

"I liked you better when you did everything I told you to," he said.

I smacked his hand away. "I'll do it myself," I said, "if it's so important."

"Whoa, killer," he said. "Save that rage for the band."

I finished unbuttoning my shirt and sat only in my ragged T-shirt.

"That goes off, too," he said.

I was too tired to argue. I pulled my shirt over my head, exposing my pale white chest. I felt goose bumps rising. Jared returned to his closet and pulled a fresh white folded T-shirt off the shelf. He let the fabric drape open and I could see that he had decorated it with Magic Marker. The front had our band name spelled in crude lettering. "tHe rAsh," it said. He turned the shirt around and there was a picture of a stick figure with long hair and headphones on. It said, "JESUS DIGS THE RASH!"

"I made one for myself, too," he said. "We have to start promoting ourselves. I want our name on people's minds before they even hear us."

He tossed me the T-shirt, and I stretched it over my head. I had been sweating out my fever and it felt pleasurable to be wearing a clean, dry shirt. It fit tight around my thin arms, and hugged my chest. Jared pulled out a shirt that almost matched. The drawings weren't exact because he'd done them by hand. He turned around and put on the shirt. He looked from my shirt to his. Then back to mine.

"Oh, man," he said. "Now we just need some songs."

19. The Architecture of Noise

EVEN THE SMARTEST PEOPLE ON EARTH CAN'T CON-
trol the human thought process. That's what Fuller believed. There
are simply too many spontaneous ideas and perceptions that move
through our brains at any time. Trying to corral them would be too
difficult. Yet Bucky did believe we could methodize our thinking
to a small degree. He called this practice "sorting." The basic idea
is that if we didn't "sort" on a daily basis, we would be so overwhelmed by thoughts that we could never make any decisions. But
something tells us to order the grilled cheese when we are hungry.
Thinking about global starvation is too big. Thinking about our
digestive system is too small. Getting food in a timely manner is the
result of sorting. Thus, the sooner we recognize the way our brain
files away relevant experiences, the sooner we can harness our own
mind power.

I attempted to explain all of this to Jared when we sat down to
write our first song that night. My fever had not subsided, so my
explanations may have lacked coherence. But as we sat side by
side on his bed, our instruments humming again, I began to see a
glimmer of recognition in his eyes. My proposal was that we had
to rid ourselves of all thoughts irrelevant to composing a punk
anthem. If there was a large garbage bag, say, full of all our song

ideas, we had to start letting some out, and retaining the best, most precise ones.

"Why is it a garbage bag?" asked Jared. "Are you saying our ideas are a bunch of nasty trash or something?"

"The receptacle is irrelevant," I said.

"Your testicles are irrelevant," he said, "but I think I see what you mean."

"So what stays in?" I asked.

"The best ideas. I get it."

"So what are our best ideas?" I asked.

"We'll start with that beginning we wrote like a hundred years ago. Do you remember that?"

"A minor," I said.

"Yeah," he said. "But after you play that chord, just play the root note of what I'm playing on the top string, like this."

He showed me where to put my finger and I kept it there.

"Just play it over and over like this," he said, and played his E string repeatedly at a steady rhythm.

"Okay," I said.

I mimicked what he had done to the best of my ability. The rhythm wasn't as good, but it wasn't awful.

"Punk bassists don't really need to learn chords. Those are for bands that try too hard."

I kept playing the droning repetitive bass part.

"Now this is the part of the song where I'm going to sing," said Jared. "As soon as we write some goddamn lyrics."

Next to him on the bed was a spiral notebook. He'd written the word "Songs" at the top in sloppy cursive. Then he'd drawn a picture of a skull and a pentagram. But there was nothing written beneath the drawings. He took up the pen and looked at me.

"What are we pissed off about?" he asked.

"I don't know," I said. "I'm not sure I am pissed off."

"Yes you are!" he said. "You don't have a house. Your grandma dogged you."

"I know, but I'm more hurt by that," I said. "I'm hurt and befuddled, not angry."

"Well," said Jared. "Punk songs are not about hurt, okay? That's country. Punk is about anger and not taking any shit, and living how you want to, and catching an awesome buzz from some beers, and being a shit-head, but a great shit-head."

"So what are you so angry about?" I asked. "Specifically?"

"That's the problem," he said. "I'm furious about everything. It's hard to narrow it down."

"Relevant thoughts," I said. "You have to get to the precise ideas. What about that school your mom wants you to go to?"

"What about it? It sucks hard."

"So why don't we inform people about why it sucks . . . exactly."

"I don't know," he said. "Who cares?"

"That's it," I said. "Who cares. That's the whole idea, right?"

Jared looked at me.

"I don't like your mind games," he said, but underneath the word "Songs" in his book he wrote the word "Topics." Underneath that, he wrote the words "Stupid School."

"That's the title."

"What is?" he said.

" 'Stupid School.' That's the perfect title."

"How do you know what a good title is?"

"Before I left home, I was studying," I said. "It's similar to that song by the Replacements. 'Fuck School.' But we can't . . . we can't utter that word at your church."

Jared looked down at the title again.

"I love the Replacements," he said.

"They laughed in the middle of his speech," I said, "that's what the song was about, right? Getting back at all those fellow students who mocked the singer."

"Yeah."

"That's small. That's precise."

Jared took a deep breath.

"Okay," he said. " 'Stupid School.' Let's try it. Play that root note again."

I clamped down the string with my middle finger and used the thumb on my other hand to play. The low-pitched thunder of the bass buzzed out of the tiny amplifier. Jared just listened for a while. Then he came in at the same rhythm I was playing with a fuller, crisper version of my note. After a few seconds, he just opened his mouth and sang.

"Mom's taking me to stuuuupid school!"

I nearly stopped playing when it happened. I skipped a note, but when Jared looked at me, I got back in time right away. I tried not to look at him, afraid I would reveal something with just a glance. Afraid I would reveal the truth:

His voice was incredible.

It didn't sound like his speaking voice at all. It was lower and cleaner. But not too clean. It sounded like it came from someone at least twice his age. And it appeared to emerge out of him effortlessly. I couldn't believe it. I stopped watching my fingers on the bass and watched him play instead.

"Mom's taking me to stuuuupid school, and I want to diiiiiiiie."

He switched chords to something different. Something higher. I tried frantically to find a corresponding note on the bass, and when

I reached a note that matched, I saw his brow relax. He listened to the mix of our parts and somehow when he switched back to the original chord, I was right with him, back on the same fret of my E string. Jared played harder, and out came the voice again:

"*Teacher, teacher, teacher, and I want to die! Teacher, teacher, teacher, and she teaches lies! Why, teacher, why!*"

Jared stopped playing a moment, but he motioned for me to keep going.

"You should sing that part," he said. "In the final version you'll shout out that last part in, like, a scream. Okay? Backup vocals."

"Sure," I said.

He was in charge now, I could see. Something had been switched on. He didn't play again for a while. He just let me keep going. But he wasn't stopping. He was singing softly to himself, hashing things out. As he sang, he tried variations on his part. He made it even choppier. It sounded like the notes had been sliced with sharp knives. I was waiting to hear him sing again. And eventually he did. But he switched chords again first. Then he took a breath and belted out what he would tell me later was the chorus.

"*Everybody goes to stupid school, then the stupid rule the world. No. No. No!*"

He played a couple of shrill notes, faster than I'd ever seen him do anything. Then sang again.

"*Everybody goes to stupid school, and the stupid rule the worrrrld. Yeah. Yeah. Yeah!*"

At the end of the last line, he stopped playing abruptly. I had already stopped when he started in on the chorus. Not because I thought that was what he wanted me to do. But because I just wanted to see where he would go next. After he stopped, he looked at me, and his lip was curled funny. He looked sheepish.

"I don't believe it," I said.

Without saying anything, Jared walked to his bedroom door and kicked a wadded-up towel underneath it. Then he took a pack of cigarettes from a sweatshirt pocket and lit one. He cracked his bedroom window and aimed the smoke toward the small patch of screen. The wind stole the smoke right from his mouth when he exhaled. A frigid breeze blew back in. It gave me the chills, and reminded me that I was still sick.

"You actually know how to do this," I said. "You know how to compose songs."

I walked over, fighting a little dizziness, and punched him in the shoulder.

"I was in church choir," he said, still facing the window. "And elementary band."

"I thought your mom was exaggerating," I said.

I punched him again.

"Don't punch me," he said. "It's not a song yet."

"It's something resembling a song, though."

He took a drag. "Yeah, but it's not a real song. I'll figure it out."

Mrs. Whitcomb's voice came suddenly up the stairwell and interrupted us.

"Jared!" she said. "Guitar practice is over. It's time for lights-out!"

"Okay!" he yelled. "One minute!"

"And Sebastian has to come down here!" she said. "You shouldn't be sleeping in a room with someone sick."

We waited in silence and heard her footsteps retreat from the stairs. I watched the slivers of streetlight cut across Jared's sweaty hair. He took another drag.

"I would always watch for my dad through this window," he

said. "It's the one right above the driveway, so I could see the car come in when he was home from trips."

He exhaled, and the smoke gathered by the screen before being sucked out by the night.

"When he came home, I would flick my lights twice. Then he would flick his headlights twice. It was our secret signal."

He took one more drag, then stamped out his cigarette in a little metal jar.

"My mom was waiting downstairs, too. I wonder what she thought of those flickering headlights? I wonder if she ever asked him about it."

He coughed out a laugh.

"When he stopped coming home, it was just the two of us awake, actually. Me and Janice. On separate floors. Two idiots waiting around for something we both knew wasn't going to happen. Really pathetic when you think about it. I thought about going down there a few different times, just to let her know I was awake, too. But I never did."

"Why didn't you?"

"I don't know," he said. "Because I was pissed. She was driving him away with all her yelling and holy-rolling bullshit. The day after we found out I needed the surgery, she just woke up and didn't laugh anymore. Maybe it didn't happen that fast, but it felt like it. Everything became so fucking serious all of a sudden. And everything my dad did was wrong. He couldn't keep all the details straight. We missed an appointment once and Janice kicked him out of the house for the night. And the longer I went without a transplant, the longer the trips he took. Then one day, he just didn't come home."

Jared turned his head around and looked at me.

"He's come back after the surgery, but only now and then. He sticks around for a few days, sometimes as long as a week. Then the fighting starts again, and he's gone."

Jared slammed closed the window, and the walls vibrated.

"Now I don't even hear from him," he said. "She doesn't allow him near the house."

"Yeah, but . . ."

"I'm not trying to be a whiny bastard here!" he interrupted. "This is how things are, Sebastian. And it's her damn fault!"

He walked over to his bed and sat down. He took off his glasses and his eyes looked so small and beady.

"She's worried about you," I said.

"So what," he said. "Great. She wins the worry award."

He wiped his lenses with his band T-shirt. Then he slapped his glasses back on his face, and I watched his eyes enlarge in front of me.

"I didn't go downstairs to talk to her," he said, "because she didn't deserve it. She doesn't deserve to be my friend."

He made a nasal breathing noise.

"You got anything else to say about it?" he asked.

"No."

He lay down on his bed, one arm hanging off the side.

"Good," he said.

He swung his skinny arm, his fingertips just grazing the dark carpet.

"I keep my promises," he said. "Tomorrow we'll go make sure your grandma's okay. But you should head downstairs now. I bet you're infecting me with some kind of foul dome-scabies as we speak."

I turned and started walking out of the room. Then I stopped.

"Jared," I said.

"What?"

"You have an immense musical talent."

He was quiet as I walked outside his door. But eventually, I heard him answer so softly I couldn't tell if he wanted me to hear it.

"Thank you," he said.

The light snapped off in his room.

I SLEPT ON THE COUCH THAT NIGHT, COVERED IN THE same old blanket. In the same strange living room. I slumbered in short bursts, never longer than an hour. And each time I woke up again, it was harder to get back to sleep. Finally, around four in the morning, I got off the couch and made my way into the Whitcombs' kitchen. There was a telephone hanging on the wall, and I picked it up and listened to the soft whine of the dial tone. Then I punched in the numbers to our home telephone number at the dome. It rang easily seven or eight times. We had no answering service, so I could let it ring all night if I wanted to. But on the tenth ring, Nana picked up. If she'd just said hello, I might have poured my heart out to her. I might have broken down and begged her to allow me back.

Instead she rasped, "Leave me alone, you bloodsuckers! Stop calling here. You understand nothing of my project!"

Then she hung up. I set the phone delicately back in its cradle. I opened the fridge and searched around, half blind, for grape drink, but there was none to be found. I settled on something orange and sat down at the kitchen table. It had never occurred to me that there would be so much fallout from one insignificant article in the newspaper. But the more I reflected on it, the more it made sense. People had always thought we were strange. Maybe they were just waiting for permission to laugh at us. Now they had it. The paper told them they could mock. I felt a rush of anger, the exact kind Jared had been speaking about earlier. Only hours ago, the dome had still been my home, too. Those harassing phone calls were meant for me as much as Nana.

At least I was sure she was alive. That was the only thing that calmed me. It was no small revelation. Part of me had been convinced she would walk into the woods hours after I was gone and drink herself into a comatose state. I didn't know what she was capable of anymore. And the sound of defeat in her voice was the scariest part of it all.

There had been a time when she would have fired back at any potential attackers without the slightest injury to her confidence. I remembered one instance vividly. A Halloween night, years ago, when a group of high schoolers from town thought it would be funny to shine their industrial-strength hunting spotlight onto our dome from a strategic spot in the woods. I was eight years old. Maybe seven. But I remember each moment in great detail.

First the beam cut through our home, refracting in the triangles into hundreds of mini-beams. It was quite a sight in retrospect, all those points of light shooting through the rooms like lasers. But it also frightened me to the point of bed-wetting. Yet only seconds after the light came in, I heard Nana's voice. "Stay where you are!" she called up to me.

Then I heard our front door slam, and I watched out my wall while she sprinted through our backyard, a slight figure in pajamas. The silhouette of her hair was wild, and she carried a crowbar I didn't even know she owned. As she got closer to the source of the light, I heard the laughter of the high school boys. But their guffaws died in a collective gasp when the crowbar connected with the searchlight. The sound of the impact, that hollow pop and shatter, rang over the hill like a gunshot. I saw a flare of sparks, some running boys, and then the woods were left in total darkness again. The only sounds that followed were high-pitched screams and the churning of jeep wheels in the mud. I also heard Nana's voice over the din.

"It is my right to kill anyone on my property in self-defense! And by the power of the Greater Intellect, I will use that right! I will return you to your fundamental elements!"

After she came back into the house, we stayed up laughing about how frightened they were of a little old lady. We drank chamomile tea with lots of honey and Nana retold the story until I got sleepy. She put me back to bed. Then she made her own bed of blankets on the floor next to mine. She kept her crowbar in her palm, and told me not to worry. Everything was under control. Nobody was going to hurt me. I heard her say it in between long breaths. Nobody was ever going to hurt me as long as she was around.

20. The Mission

THE DAY AFTER OUR FIRST SONGWRITING SESSION
was a Monday, and everyone in the house got up early. Janice was
up at six A.M. to get to her part-time job at the church. I lay on the
couch while she got ready, pretending to be asleep. I watched her
whisk by, and I wondered what she used to be like before Jared's illness. Did she look different? She was pretty now, but it was easy to
see the worry lines when she grimaced. And it was easy to see in her
eyes that she didn't sleep much. I tried to think if I had ever heard
her laugh. I pictured her, rearing back her head and opening her
mouth, but no sound escaped.

She walked up to me before she left and rested a palm on my
forehead. I held my eyes closed tight. She moved my tousled hair
out of the way and touched my brow in different places, feeling for
a fever. I didn't open my eyes until the hand was gone and I heard
the click of the front door lock. A light perfume hung in the air
around me.

An hour later Meredith rose, and I got up from the couch and
watched in fascination while she prepared herself for school. For
nearly an hour, she meandered in and out of the bathroom near the
kitchen, glossing her lips, blow-drying her hair, trying on three or
four different combinations of clothing. She knew I was watching,

but she didn't say anything. She just went about her regimen, talking on the phone at times, listening to headphones at others. Finally
she grabbed some kind of pastry from the toaster and breezed right
by me and out the front door.

"Have a pleasant day at school," I said.

She closed the door hard, and I went to the front window to
watch her. She ducked into a car full of girls who looked identical to
her in hairstyle and dress. But none of them was as beguiling. None
of them had that mystery, that fiery look in their eyes. Meredith
could try to blend in, but it was impossible. Her intensity and her
beauty betrayed her. Right before I turned away, I saw her look up at
the window. She met my eyes and smirked so quickly it was almost
imperceptible. But I saw it. She was looking for me, hoping I'd be
there to torment one last time before the official start of her day.

I woke up Jared soon after she left, and then looked on while he
cooked us "Scrambled Eggs Whitcomb." He made room for me by
the stove and turned the gas on underneath the pan. Then he took
me through the secret process. First, he added cream to whisked
eggs. Then pepper, sea salt, and a splash of green Tabasco. He
whisked again and poured them into the pan (he showed me right
where to scrape with a half-melted plastic spatula). When they had
been properly executed, Jared and I took them upstairs and ate
steaming forkfuls while he worked on finessing our song from the
night before.

I practiced my bass part, stopping only for intermittent bites of
spicy eggs. I was feeling better in the light of day, and I found I had
a gluttonous appetite. We finished all the eggs and moved on to the
toaster pastries. They were frosted and filled with syrupy apples
and spices. I ate two, but I could have consumed the entire box.

"Jeez," said Jared, "didn't the old bat feed you?"

We practiced our song easily ten times that morning before Jared stopped to rest. I ventured out of the room and down into the front yard to attach his "pegs" to my Voyager. The procedure didn't take long. Just some unscrewing and tightening of a few nuts and bolts with a socket wrench from his father's old toolbox. I fastened the white footrests to the center of the wheel so tight that my palms were raw when I was finished. But the pegs were on securely, and the bicycle was ready for a passenger.

When I was done, I stopped in the front yard and watched the purple tennis shoes twisting around a bare tree branch. I remembered what Jared had said about them being a signal for Meredith's parade of amorous visitors. The laces were begrimed now from hanging up so long, and the lining was frayed. The color had faded to brownish lavender. I walked directly over to the tree and grabbed on to a low limb. I brought the other hand up and pulled myself up and into a prime climbing spot. The bark scraped across my stomach. I sat down on the long branch, just as I'd seen Jared do, and shifted my way down. When I got far enough, I plucked the sneakers from their place and held them up by the laces. They were smaller up close. Meredith had delicate feet. I kept them aloft and surveyed the neighborhood. It felt good to be up high again. I stayed up there a minute or two, shivering in the wind, before I dropped back down to civilization.

Inside, I tried the handle to Meredith's room. I don't know why I expected it to be locked, but the door opened. It smelled like her all over the room. Or at least, it smelled like the row of cuisine-themed beauty products on her dresser. Moisturizing Almond Body Butter. Nutrient-Enriched Apple Face Lotion. Pomegranate Power Scrub. Was the idea to slather yourself in sweet sauces and fruity relishes? To prepare yourself for consumption? There were clothes all over the floor and I was afraid she wouldn't even notice the shoes, so I set them on her bed, neatly, side by side. I thought about leaving a note, but I decided she would understand my message without one. "Meredith," I hoped the shoes would shout, "why are you doing this with the shoes? You don't need to do this with the shoes. Put them away and choose me!"

EVENING CAME AND WE ALL SAT DOWN AT THE TABLE again. A "real" dinner this time, complete with some kind of roasted beef that dissolved in my mouth, and a dessert of peach cobbler that was even better than the morning pastries. Conversation at the table was minimal, but not entirely unpleasant. Janice asked Meredith about her day, and Meredith responded with mostly single-word answers. Fine. Yes. No. Okay. Lame. Whatever. She didn't look at me once. Janice made sure we were all attending the Youth Group meeting that week. We were. Then Jared cleared his throat.

"Mom," he said, and stopped for dramatic pause. "I need you to sign Sebastian and me up for the talent contest at Immanuel. We've formed a . . . group."

Janice's tired eyes brightened noticeably. "Oh, Jared, that's great," she said. "I've been trying to get you to sing at that thing for years."

"Well, your dream has come true, Mother," he said. "At long last."

"What are you going to sing?" she asked, transporting more food onto my plate.

" 'Stupid School,' " I blurted.

"What?" said Mrs. Whitcomb.

Jared laughed in a short high-pitched burst. "Sebastian's just kidding," he said. "We're probably doing a hard rock version of 'Awesome God.'"

Meredith smiled smugly at Jared, her mouth full of cobbler.

"Oh," said Janice. "That sounds like your style."

She looked over at me, and I thought I saw a pinch of admiration in her expression. "Is Sebastian comfortable playing a religious song?"

"Of course," said Jared.

"I like the tune," I said quietly.

"Me too," said Janice.

We continued eating our dessert. Meredith excused herself. I expected a sarcastic comment, but she left quietly and proceeded to barricade herself in her room again. I watched her disappear with longing.

"I think this is a good idea," said Janice.

She beamed at me. Then she walked over and put a hand on Jared's shoulder.

"I do, too," said Jared.

She left her hand there a moment. Something seemed odd about it, and I soon realized that it was the first time I had seen her touch him (when he wasn't fake-collapsed on the floor). It was only a second, then it was over, and she walked to the sink to begin the dishes. She flipped on the radio. Jared shook his head violently at me. He mouthed something at me that looked like "What were you thinking?" I shrugged. Then Janice looked out the kitchen window and turned around. "Does anyone know why Meredith took her track shoes down?" she asked.

WE WAITED UNTIL MIDNIGHT TO COMMENCE OUR mission. We spent the evening hours listening to record albums at a reasonable volume. As soon as one ended, Jared sent another one spinning. MC5, The Stooges, The New York Dolls, Television. The theme of his audio lecture was the birth of punk. We listened, then went to bed at eleven without being asked. We lay in the dark, across the room from each other, just like the first night I stayed over. Only this time we didn't speak.

At twelve o'clock exactly, Jared tapped me twice on the shoulder, which was the agreed-upon sign, and we padded softly across his carpeting to our clothes. Jared dressed in three jackets, with his leather coat on the top. He pulled his hat tight over his head and put on a pair of thermal fingerless gloves. "So I can still smoke," he said, wiggling his pink fingertips. He pulled his hat down, and I saw that it was a face mask with eyeholes. He put his glasses on over the mask. I stared.

"You got a problem with my ninja mask?" he said.

I shook my head and fastened myself inside my bubble coat. I put a stocking hat on under my bicycle helmet. We crept to the foot of the stairs and started down. There was no sound behind Meredith's door, and the light was out under the crack. We advanced through the kitchen and into the living room. Then we were outside and the whole neighborhood was dark around us. Even the streetlights looked dim.

My bike was kept in the garage now, so we had to take it out a side door. In the driveway, I hopped on and held it steady for Jared's ascension. Using my back to balance himself, he stepped onto the pegs and then grabbed onto the back of my seat. I turned around and looked down at his worn black sneakers, sitting perfectly on the rests.

"Onward," he said, cracking an imaginary whip. "Onward, manchild!"

I began pedaling. It was hard at first with the extra weight, but once I got going it wasn't so bad. Soon I fell into a rhythm and our speed increased. Jared had been worried we might be spotted by the North Branch "pigs" (which he explained to me were officers of the law), but there wasn't a car on any of the roads. After a while, he moved his hands from the seat and grabbed on to my sides.

"I'm not trying to touch your wiener," he said. "But it's just easier this way."

"It's all right," I said.

I manned the bicycle through the night air, going as fast as I could. And when I looked back at Jared on occasion, his lenses were fogged, but his eyes were open wide. Whenever we went down even the smallest hill, he tightened his grip on me. I pretended not to notice. We didn't start talking until we had successfully made it out of North Branch without problems. Then Jared shouted at me, through the wind.

"So do you really think your grandmother has supernatural powers?" he yelled.

He seemed to be completely serious.

"She knows certain things," I said. "That's all I can say."

"If she sees us, will she, like . . . do things to us with her brain?" he asked. "I saw this movie once where a little girl could start fires with mind power. She burned a barn."

"She can't do anything like that," I said. "She's just very attuned. She cultivates the metaphysical."

"I don't want to be brainwashed," he said. "That would be fucked up. I want to think my own thoughts, not someone else's."

"Jared, are you afraid of Nana?" I asked.

"No," he said, a bit too quickly.

"We won't stay long," I said. "I just need to see that she's well."

"Great," said Jared. "We're walking right into her firetrap."

I got a second wind on the path near the freeway and picked up the pace. There were only a few automobiles zooming by, and they either didn't notice us or didn't care to slam on their brakes and ask what we were doing out so late. I didn't stop pedaling until I got to the bottom of Hillsboro Drive.

"We'll walk from here," I said.

Jared hopped off the pegs and we began to work our way up the hill until the dome was in our sights. The top glass panels cast back a powder blue moonlight, but inside the lights were all off. I guided Jared past the storage shed and up around to the back of the dome. The darkness inside could mean so many things. Most likely Nana was asleep, but it could also mean that she wasn't there at all.

"How did you live out here in the woods like this?" whispered Jared. "This is spooky as hell."

"You get accustomed to it," I said.

"But aren't there bears and lynxes that prowl around looking to maul your ass?"

He looked over his shoulder, his eyes darting madly through his mask holes.

"Just deer and raccoons," I said. "The occasional fox."

"What about rattlers?" he asked, studying the dry shrubbery.

We approached the dome on the side of Nana's bedroom, and I squinted, trying to make out her form on the bed. But something was obscuring my vision. It looked like Nana had hung another curtain of some kind. I walked closer, right out in the yard. Jared stayed back. "What are you doing, dipshit?" he said. "You're in plain sight."

I kept walking. There was definitely something on the dome. I stepped right up to the glass. I followed its contours with my eyes. It was Africa.

"Is she in there?" Jared asked.

I looked up higher. There was Saudi Arabia. Iraq. Turkey. The Ukraine. The entire back side of the Geoscope had been completed. I couldn't make out the color scheme exactly, but it looked like blues and purples. It was expertly done. The contours of each country were precise and captured with artistry. Africa alone must have taken hours.

"What the hell is wrong with you, Sebastian?"

I heard him traipse across the hard lawn.

"Have you gone . . . holy shit!" he said. "Is that the post-Soviet bloc?"

I turned around to face him.

"It's a Geoscope," I said. "It was our project before I left."

His eyes traveled the mural from north to south.

"It's kind of awesome," he said.

He ran his hand over Angola, then pointed toward Russia.

"How did she get way up there with that bony little body?"

"I don't know," I said. "She must have used my climbing gear."

"Your old granny shot up there like Spider-Man?"

I couldn't believe she had accomplished so much in a couple of days. Where had she gotten all the supplies? Where had the energy come from? I found my way to a clear spot just southeast of Tanzania and looked inside. Nana was not in her bed. I started walking around to the front.

"Wait," said Jared. "Where are you going? You came to see if she was okay. And she is. She's been painting her elderly ass off. She's fine."

I continued walking along the side of my home. I glanced up at Indonesia, perfectly rendered in some shade of navy. I made it around to the front door and slipped my old key in the lock. It still fit. I turned the handle slowly and stepped back into the dome. I took in a long breath full of paint fumes. The first thing I noticed was the mess. There was plastic sheeting in a tangle on the living room floor, held down by half-full cans of paint, rollers, and a step-ladder. There were brushes soaking in Nana's stockpot, and a new, more elaborate map lay near the NordicTrack. Here were all her supplies, but where was Nana? I reached the staircase to the second floor and peered up, uneasily.

The moon provided only enough light to see the landing. I took a step. Then another. I crept as silently as I could until I made it to the top. I looked into my old schoolroom. It was empty, and the furnishings were still disheveled from Nana's drunken monitor-napping. I turned next into my bedroom. I set one foot in, and right away I stepped down on a large book and nearly tripped. I hopped back a step and looked closely at it. It was my parents' photo album, and it was right next to Nana's feet.

She was there on the floor next to my bed, amid a makeshift pallet of blankets. She was still fully dressed from the day, and her amber tracksuit was covered in pointillist freckles of paint. I had to listen really closely to hear her breathing. She was procumbent, face to pillow, and she seemed to be pulling in air from the very corner of her mouth. Just the faintest whistle. What I could see of her face was anxious in sleep. Her one visible eye seemed to be searching for something under the lid. I leaned down to wake her, but before my hand got all the way to her arm, I stopped it.

She was completing her project without me.

The realization was not a pleasant one. It was true that the Geo-scope had never been my ambition, but I couldn't believe she had moved forward by herself. And so soon. Despite what she'd said, it seemed she didn't need me at all. With scarcely a day's passing, she had resigned herself to my absence. It took all my willpower not to fall to the floor and embrace her, begging for answers. But I couldn't do that. She was leaving me behind. I had betrayed her trust, and she had made it known to me early on that trust and communication were the truly evolved states of humankind.

Bucky believed that, though scientifically immeasurable, an understanding between two people is one of the strongest bonds that can exist. It is metaphysical synergy. Two minds reaching a point of acceptance and harmony with each other. No physical act can match it. And trust is at the heart of it. A false understanding is tantamount to false love. In short: I had hurt Nana. And now she was hurting me back.

Using every bit of grace and quiet left in my body, I reached into the folds of the photo album and thumbed out a few pictures at random. I chose from the back of the book, hoping Nana wouldn't remember the very last images as clearly as the others. I slid the glossy prints into my back pocket and nudged the album back exactly where I found it. I looked down at Nana one last time. She was fast asleep, wholly static. I turned and left the room, taking the stairs with care.

"Good night, Nana," I whispered into an echo spot in the dome.

I listened closely for her voice, but nothing came.

21. The Sublime Wonder of Human Physicality

WE MADE IT BACK TO JARED'S HOUSE BY TWO IN THE morning. The ride passed quickly, and we didn't linger or pay particular attention to the quiet mystery of the night. We were both weary, ready to be back amid the balmy puffs of the humidifier. I hadn't said anything since I left the dome, and Jared had only posed one question. "Is she still kicking?" He asked it when I came around to the back of the dome. He was peeking out from behind a black walnut tree, his mask pulled up onto his forehead. I nodded once. Then we'd walked wordlessly back to our transport and gone soaring down Hillsboro Drive.

The only task left to us now was to reenter the Whitcomb house without being caught. Early conditions were promising: the whole house was still dark and silent. No one seemed to be waiting up for us. And there were no "pigs" parked in the driveway to nab us upon arrival. We stowed the bike away, closed up the garage, and got all the way to the front porch before Jared discovered an oversight.

"Balls!" he said, as soon as his hand was in his pants pocket.

He felt his other pocket, then frantically patted every pocket of his jackets.

"Horse balls," he said.

"You've forgotten the key," I said.

"This is an unbelievable load of balls," he said.

"But we didn't lock the door," I said.

"It locks when you pull it shut!"

We stood looking at each other. The cold was feeling colder already.

"We can't wake Janice," I said. "She'll send me away. This was all my idea."

"We'll stay in the garage," said Jared. "Tomorrow we'll say we got up early and locked ourselves out."

We both looked at the garage. "It wasn't considerably warmer in there."

"I'm just thinking out loud," said Jared. "Just give me a damn minute here."

He sat down on the porch and took off his glasses. He covered his mask holes with his hands. I hopped in place for warmth and breathed giant steaming breaths into my hands. After a while, I looked up to the tree branch where Meredith's shoes used to twirl in the wind. It was odd to see them gone. Jared looked up and saw me watching.

"It's really the only way," he said.

"What is?" I said.

"You know exactly what I'm talking about," he said.

And after we started walking around to the side of the house, I did. My heartbeat accelerated riotously as we drew nearer to Meredith's window. I had looked at it in passing when we went by the house, and it had appeared completely dark. But up closer, it was clear that there was a light on. It was just being muted by a dark window shade.

"Thank God she's still awake," said Jared. "All we need is some harpy shriek when we knock on the glass to wake up . . ."

He stopped talking when he reached the window. The shade was pulled down almost all the way, but there was an inch or so of exposed glass. Jared was looking through this opening.

"What is it?" I said.

He turned away from the window. "There's a dude in there with her," he said.

I took an icy breath and joined him at the opening. Through our sliver of unobstructed glass, I could see Meredith's lower body on the bed. She wore a pair of men's boxer shorts and her smooth legs were crossed at the knee. Her foot was lolling in the air. I couldn't see a male in the room, but I knew Jared wouldn't have lied. I waited a little longer, and sure enough, a boy's hand came down and his fingers splayed across her thigh. I felt myself flinching. Jared turned around from the glass.

"Jesus Christ," he whispered. "What is it with her? It's like this is her only hobby."

I kept watching. The hand just sat there, then started inching farther up.

"It figures the one time I need her help, she's letting some mouth-breather feel her up. Now we're going to freeze to death."

When the hand got to the hem of the boxer shorts, Meredith pushed it off. The hand retreated for a moment. Then it landed back even higher up the shorts. Again Meredith shoved it off.

"Sebastian," said Jared. "Knock it off! That's my sister you're peeping at."

"She doesn't want him in there," I said.

Meredith was holding his hand now, and I could hear her through the glass, shouting something at him.

"Of course she wants him in there," said Jared. "She's not going to stop until she jerks off the whole town."

Suddenly, the guy stood up, blocking my view. He took a slow step toward Meredith. That's when I threw open the window.

"What the hell are you doing?" yelled Jared.

The pane went up with surprising ease, and I was up and through the window in two solid motions. First I hoisted myself to window level, then pushed myself through headfirst. I crumpled onto the floor, and when I opened my eyes, I was looking up at a shirtless guy with red hair and what appeared to be shaving stubble on his chin. He looked down at me, puzzled. I scrambled to my feet. Meredith was speechless.

"Out!" I said.

"Wait," he said to Meredith. "Who is this guy?"

"Sebastian," said Meredith quietly, "I think it would be best if you left."

"Hold up," said the guy. "Is this your little punk rock brother? The sick one?"

He looked at me and laughed for some reason.

"Don't be an ass," said Meredith.

He leaned down toward me. "You know about what your sister does?" he asked. "You know what she does in here?"

I glanced over at Meredith before I acted. Her face was bright red, and she was looking straight down at the carpeting. I walked up to the guy with my arms cocked, and let loose. I shoved him as hard as I could, and his chest sprang right off my hands. He fell hard, just missing a crack on the cranium from the window frame. I could almost hear the anger hissing in him after he hit the ground. And I knew when he got up he was going to cause me as much harm as he possibly could. But when he tried to rise from the ground, two small arms came through the window and grabbed onto his neck.

"Gotcha!" said Jared.

"*Ahhhh,*" he screamed in an oddly high voice. "Get off me!"

But Jared didn't let go. He was hanging off the ground, holding tight to the guy's neck. He was wearing his face mask down with his glasses. He resembled a bookish criminal. Meredith stood up on her bed.

"Jared!" she said. "What are you doing? You're going to hurt yourself!"

"Die, meathead!" yelled Jared.

The kid started swinging wildly, trying to knock Jared off. And he likely would have succeeded if I hadn't jumped on top of him. I used all my weight to pin him against the wall in a sitting position. We had him now. He was nearly immobile. I dug a knee into his thigh and he sputtered a small yelp.

"*Gah!*" he said. "Let me up, you bastards."

"No chance," said Jared.

"You're . . . choking me," he grunted.

Then we saw a faint light go on under the door, and heard the creak of the house.

"Meredith!" yelled Janice in a froggy voice. "What's going on in there?"

At the sound of her voice, Jared dropped off the guy's neck and hit the ground below. With Jared's weight gone, the guy pushed me off him and then stood above me, jaw clenched. He looked down at me like he wanted to stomp the life from me. But Janice's voice came from her room again and sent him running to the window. He stopped right before he jumped out and looked like he wanted to utter something devastating. But instead all he did was breathe a burst of air out his nose and say, "Outrageous." He may have even said it twice.

He ducked out the window and hit the yard running. Jared

waited a moment, then poked his head up, but Meredith closed the shade. She looked at me and pointed under her bed. I dove to the ground and crawled under just as Janice opened the door.

"What do you want?" said Meredith with irritation. "I was just watching TV."

I could only see Janice's slippered feet, but I could sense that she was looking around the room. "What was with all the banging around?" she asked.

"I got up to use the bathroom. I tripped."

Again there was quiet I could only interpret as further surveying.

"Well, what are you doing watching television at two in the morning on a school night? Get to bed and turn it off! Do you think I can sleep through all that noise?"

"Fine," said Meredith.

I was sweating profusely in my down coat. There were cobwebs and dust puffs brushing against my face.

"Fine is right," said Janice. "You know your brother needs his sleep. Waking him up for no reason is just idiotic. It's just asking for trouble. I'm trying to get him back in school. He needs to be on a regular sleeping schedule."

"I'm sorry," she said, finally. "I couldn't sleep."

"Well, read a book. Meditate."

"I was thinking about Dad, okay?" she said.

I could tell by her emotionless tone that it was a calculated move, and it seemed to work. Janice sighed. She shuffled over and sat on the bed. The springs gave, and the extra weight nearly crushed me. "All right," she said. She adjusted a bare foot in her slipper. "But he's not coming back anytime soon; I take it you know that. He's had his chances."

"Jared misses him," said Meredith.

"How does it help to say that?" asked Janice, raising her voice. "Tell me, please. Do you think I don't know that?"

"Okay. I'm sorry."

Janice took a deep breath and her voice softened.

"You don't have to be sorry," she said. "I understand. But Jared doesn't know the way things really were. He has a selective memory when it comes to his dad. You know that. He doesn't remember the way he was abandoned during the . . . whole process. He doesn't remember how hurt he was. It's not going to help him get better to have that man in his life. That's the hard truth."

"So, you're making that decision for him?"

"I don't have to make it," sighed Janice. "I never hear from him anymore."

The room was so quiet, and I wondered if they would hear my breathing.

"Are you doing okay?" she said finally. "I know I should probably ask that more often."

"I'm getting by, Mom," she said. "Are *you*?"

"Well," she faltered. "To be honest, I don't have too much time to think about it. I'm working on getting another job. I'm trying to keep us afloat."

Meredith didn't speak, but there was some shifting on the bed.

"Hopefully," said Janice, "Sebastian will patch things up with his grandmother soon. He can't stay here forever."

"Yeah," said Meredith.

Her voice could have betrayed my presence if Janice had thought for a minute I might be there. Instead, she rose from the bed. The mattress let up again.

"He's never going to have a completely normal life, Meredith," Janice said.

"Who? Sebastian? That's for sure."

"I'm talking about your brother. He's always going to have to think about all of this. And so are we. But it doesn't help things to put him in avoidable situations. You need to learn to live with this and step up. So keep the noise down, okay?"

Janice sounded so tired. I had never heard her more tired.

"All right," she said. "I know."

I heard a kiss being bestowed somewhere, then Janice walked slowly out of the room, closing the door behind her. I stayed where I was, trying not to breathe in any spiderwebs. Just to my left was a wadded-up pair of lime green panties that I hadn't noticed before. I reached out and ran my finger over the waistband. Meredith walked over to the window and opened it back up. She didn't say a word. Jared pulled himself in.

"Sweet merciful balls," he said. "It is cold out there."

"Are you okay?" she asked.

"Yeah," he said. "As soon as they amputate, I'll be fine."

He paused. I watched his canvas shoes. "Where's weirdo?" he said.

I was about to call out to Jared.

"He went upstairs already," said Meredith.

"What a traitor. I might have to draw on him in his sleep tonight."

"Listen." She stopped him before he left. "I won't ask what you were doing tonight if you don't ask about . . . my situation, either."

"That smells like a deal," said Jared. "Now please remove your hand from my shoulder. I'm not sure where, or on *what*, it's been."

He snuck out the door, and when I heard it close I shimmied my way out from under the bed. I stood up right away and tossed off the down coat that had been smothering me for the last fifteen minutes. Then I wiped my face and hair with my hands, trying to get all the phantom spiders off of me. When I looked back at Meredith, she was back on her bed. She still wore only her boxers and a tank top (with no bra underneath, I observed now). Her beautiful legs were stretched out on the bed. Her lean neck was at a bit of an angle. She was watching me.

"I didn't need that tonight," she said.

"I'm sorry," I said.

She rolled her eyes and smoothed her boxers over her legs.

"So, how many times have you spied on me now?" she asked. "Is it ten? Twenty?"

"Three," I said. "This was number three."

"What's the allure?" she said. "Don't you know how to leave people alone?"

I shook my head.

"I see that," she said.

Suddenly, she reached down and pulled her tank top over her head. She did it so quickly I nearly fainted from the unexpected stimulus. A moment ago, I understood some things about the world; now everything needed restructuring. There were Meredith Whitcomb's breasts, drooping slightly off her chest. They were ivory and amazing, with a small mole just at the very bottom of the right one. I wanted to press that little spot with my fingertip. Just once. She was still looking at me with no change of expression.

"Is this enough?" she said. "Is this what you want to see?"

"Jared's going to come back down for me, any minute," I said.

"Do you want me to put my shirt back on?"

"No," I said. "I do not."

I looked down her chest to her flat stomach, and down farther to her boxers.

"I don't think so," she said.

She got up off the bed and walked up close to me. I could smell her now. Sweat and fruit and sleep and sheets and shampooed hair. Everything all at once. She reached out and grabbed my hand. She pressed it to her right breast. It was cool and warm at the same time. The smoothest thing I had ever touched. The bump of her nipple stuck in the middle of my palm. I didn't squeeze. I just held my hand right where she had placed it.

"The shoes were in the tree for my brother," she said.

I could hardly listen. My whole hand was tingling, and so was everything below my waist.

"It was an old track team superstition. For good luck. They have nothing to do with . . . all this. I want him to get better."

"I want to kiss you," I said.

"I know," she said.

She opened her door and looked out into the pall of the night kitchen.

"Go to bed," she said.

"Who was that guy in here?" I asked.

"Go to bed," she said again.

I stole one last look at topless Meredith before the door clicked shut and I was stuck watching the chiseled features of a half-naked man on a poster. I stood in the hall, not yet ready to go upstairs, trying to catch my breath. According to Bucky, our bodies are just repositories for the metaphysical phenomena inside. Much like a telephone is an agent for transporting our voices, our physical selves are just agents for our ideas. He found them practically irrelevant. I, on the other hand, was beginning to find them more and more relevant each day.

I looked from the body on the poster back to mine. We could have been two different species of human, this hulking man and I. But when I got to his face, his eyes, I grinned at him. He might have been the male ideal, but he had never seen what I had. His poster was stuck on the outside.

22. Tests of the Will

NOW THAT I KNEW NANA WAS SAFE, I ENDEAVORED for the first time to unfasten her from my consciousness. This was no easy feat. Nana was, in many ways, all I had ever known. Her thin-lipped smile, her moist eyes, her crescent of milk-colored hair continued to find me in my dreams at night, along with her voice, set to a constant burble of Bucky facts. I could tell by the feeling in my chest when I woke each morning that our synergy had been severed. Yet I knew I could not return to the dome. I knew this because along with my morning pangs came some very different feelings altogether. Sensations that had only begun since my stay at the Whitcombs'. The manic energy of playing bass guitar, for one. Or the feeling of a long feverish shower, with water enveloping every part of me at once. And then, of course, there was the sight of Meredith Whitcomb's ponytail bouncing up and down in the front seat of a minivan.

It was the evening of my second Youth Group meeting, and Jared and I were huddled in the backseat. Meredith was in front with Janice, typing on her phone. For the duration of the ride so far, Jared had been trying to explain to me why we were not musicians, but he could tell I wasn't paying much attention. This only made him louder.

"Yes," he shouted, "we play music! Sort of. But that word 'musician' suggests that we have talent. And talent happens to be for boners. It's the last thing we want!"

I couldn't keep my eyes off the back of Meredith's head. The tips of her hair swished each time the van hit a bump. Occasionally, she turned slightly, and I caught a look at her eyes, staring down into the screen of her telephone.

"So when they ask us questions about our act tonight," Jared continued, "we just tell them it's called The Rash. Let them wonder about what it is. Just don't tell them we're musicians, or I think I'll puke up. Are you even listening to me?"

I opened my mouth to respond, but just then Meredith turned around and glared back at us. "What are you plotting back there?" she asked, "the Bed Wetters' Revolt?"

"Actually, we were talking about teen pregnancy," said Jared.

I waited for Janice to chime in, but she ignored the situation entirely. She was already lost in concentration, whispering something to herself. I moved my gaze to Meredith's neck, and the almost imperceptible curls at her hairline. The only contact I'd had with her that day was a moment before we left. Jared had given me one of his Black Flag T-shirts to wear, and he had put some kind of gelatinous substance in my hair to push it up. We needed to work on our image, he said. Uniformity between bandmates was key.

"So, he's dressing you now?" Meredith had said, standing in the doorway.

"I'm just experimenting with something different," I said.

She studied me. "The hair looks all right," she said, "could be worse."

Ever since my sacred moment in her room on Monday, she'd only spoken to me a handful of times. It was always like that. Two or three sentences and a disappearance. She had yet to acknowledge what had happened.

Now, on the way to the Youth Group, I was being ignored again. Jared had put his headphones on after the mini-spat with his sister. I pulled one out of his ear.

"Why don't you handle all the preparations," I said.

"That's all you had to say," he grumbled.

He plugged his ear back up, and I could just make out the guitar part from "California über Alles," a song Jared tried to listen to at least once a day. He closed his eyes and nodded to the beat. Soon enough, the van arrived at Immanuel, and we rode gradually over the sanded parking lot. I watched the older boys, indistinguishable from their shadows, slouch and idle toward the church. They kicked at one another's shoes from behind. One of them turned and gave a half wave to Meredith. I felt my entire chest freeze and shatter.

"What's with you?" asked Jared, too loudly. "You're acting like a moody girl."

AN HOUR LATER WE WERE IN THE CHURCH RECREATION Room, preparing to walk blindfolded across a balance beam. The activity was about community this time, Janice explained. We gathered around the beam to listen. The idea was that while we walked across, our group mates were supposed to shout encouraging platitudes to help us achieve our goal and conquer our fear. If we toppled off, kids lined the side of the beam to catch us. Because of our diminutive size, Jared and I were placed at the very beginning where nobody would fall.

"Just tell me!" Jared said.

"I don't want to discuss it," I said.

"I don't want to *discuss* anything, either," he said. "I just want you to tell me what's wrong so I can knock some sense into your ass."

One of the larger guys from the group made his way across the beam. He engaged in some dramatics while he walked, holding his arms out in a perfect T from his body.

"You can do it, DJ!" came a low voice from the crowd. "You're the man!"

"Jesus," said Jared. "These are my future classmates. I might as well slit my wrists in the bathroom."

"Meredith," came Janice's voice from the end. "Your turn on the beam."

Meredith sulked to the edge of the balance beam. She pulled at a short skirt and stepped up onto the small foot-space. It was only ten inches or so off the ground (as far as I could tell the activity was more symbolic than a test of athletic ability). Meredith closed her eyes and a short blond girl tiptoed up to fasten the blindfold. Meredith took a hesitant step forward. The group immediately started in with the motivation. "C'mon. Feel it!" "Show that beam who's boss!"

She took another step, moving past Jared. I watched her delicate hands form nervous fists. She adjusted her blindfold.

"Hey, no peeking," yelled the guy in the Broncos hat.

Meredith sighed and put her hands back at her sides. She took another step. And then somehow I saw what would happen next before it even transpired. It was a rare moment of prescience. I could tell by her hesitation that her right foot would land off the center of the beam when she took her next step. I could tell she would teeter.

Then it occurred.

She put her right foot forward and lost her balance completely, falling sideways. Falling right at me. I didn't have time to be afraid. All I saw was a body plummeting rapidly toward me. So I put out my arms and caught it before it hit the carpeted floor. Meredith landed in my arms, her head knocking into my skinny chest. My arm was around her warm stomach. I held her for a moment, just to make sure she was steady on her feet. The room broke out in mild applause. Someone whistled.

"Well done, Sebastian," said Janice. "Strength in numbers. You see? We're strong enough to deal with any challenge if we stand by one another."

At the sound of my name, Meredith inched up her blindfold over one eye and blinked. She calmly stepped out of my embrace.

"Way to go, pervert," she said, just loud enough for me to hear.

She stood back on the beam and took a deep breath. I watched her move lithely across the rest of the way with absolutely no problems. When she got to the end, she took the blindfold off and gave a little bow. I felt myself grinning like a fool.

"Oh, my God," said Jared.

I had almost forgotten he was next to me.

"What?" I said.

"Oh, my holy God, no!" he said.

"Jared, be quiet," I said.

"You have a chubby for my sister. I knew it! I knew it the whole time, you rotten son of a bitch!"

People were starting to turn to look at us.

"Jared," I said. "You have to stop talking right now."

He was getting louder and louder with each burst.

"What did I tell you!" he said. "What did I tell you about her! Not *good* things."

More people were watching.

"Jared, what are you going on about up there?" asked Janice.

She was walking down the row of youth-groupers to us. But Jared didn't seem affected. It was too late to turn him off now.

"I don't believe this. What a betrayal. What a supreme fucking betrayal. I'm the one who saved you, Sebastian," he said, "if you don't remember. Not her."

Everyone in the room was listening now.

"I'm the reason you're in an awesome band. I'm the reason you have a home right now. You were just some freak from a dome! And now you choose Meredith. What were you doing the other night when you were supposed to be upstairs, huh? I trusted you, you Judas!"

Jared was walking away now. His mother tried to stop him, but he shrugged off her hand and walked right out of the Recreation Room. He turned around one last time before leaving. "Oh," he said. "And you're completely out of the band."

He slammed the door behind him. Once he disappeared, every pair of eyes in the room turned toward me at once. Janice stood, flabbergasted. Meredith looked surprisingly calm. Finally, the small girl who had fastened the blindfold to Meredith spoke up.

"What band?" she asked me.

The whole Youth Group waited for an answer.

"Jared and I are in a band," I said.

"You mean you *were* in a band," said the first beam-walker.

"Correct," I said.

"I didn't know you were musicians," said the girl.

I watched the doorway where Jared had stood only seconds ago.

"We're not," I said. "We're The Rash."

––––––––––

THE MEETING ENDED EARLY. JUST LIKE THE PREVIOUS one. Another Youth Group spoiled. A team of helpers dismantled the beam, and everyone left without a post-activity discussion. A tin of oatmeal-raisin cookies sat on a table unopened.

"Any idea where he went?"

I turned around to find Janice behind me.

"Mrs. Whitcomb," I said. "I'm sorry. I didn't intend for any of this to happen."

She closed her eyes and didn't respond for a moment. Then she sat down on the gray folding table. She tore open the plastic band around the tin of cookies and set it aside. "Of course," she said, selecting a cookie. "Just like you didn't intend to steal an instrument from this church. It's interesting what we intend to happen and what actually happens."

I opened my mouth to speak, but I didn't know what to say.

"I've worked here for four years," she said. "I have every church possession memorized. You thought I wouldn't notice?"

"Why didn't you mention anything?"

She took a bite of her cookie and wiped some crumbs from her lips.

"I'm considering it a loan," she said, mouth full.

"A loan."

"Sebastian," she said, "it is a mother's destiny to be lied to. Do you realize that? People lie to their mothers. That's the way the world works."

I couldn't bring myself to look at her.

"I lied to my mother. Jared lies to me at least once a day. I don't know what he lies about, but I can see it in his face."

She grabbed another cookie from the tin. "Here," she said, holding it out.

I took it, and watched the crumbs fall to the carpet.

"He's all I think about," she said. "It's not healthy. I know that. I try to turn it off, but it's impossible. From the time when I wake up in the morning to when I go to bed, I think about everything that's going on with him. I scan him for symptoms. I try to judge his mood, his social progress. Everything. I know it's unfair to Meredith."

"And to yourself," I said.

She took another bite and raised her eyebrows.

"And that," she said.

She looked down at the disassembled balance beam.

"It was so much easier when they were babies. I could handle that. It was so simple. There's this little person, and you just have to hold it, and feed it, and change its diapers. And you can even do other things when it goes to bed."

"It?" I asked.

She smiled. "That's the way I used to think of Meredith and Jared when they were babies. Just tiny things. Its. I was terrified of being a mother both times. I felt like I was too young. Now I see how easy I had it. I still had room to think about other things back then. I still thought about myself."

I took a bite of my cookie. It was hard as a rock.

"Now," said Janice. She waved her arm over the room. "Now I have this."

She hopped off the table like a child, and pushed her hair over her ears.

"I hate to break it to you, but it's not what I dreamed of."

"Then why are you here?"

"I don't know," she said. "It just felt good to be a part of something after Jared's illness. And I can teach here. I know it's not the same as being a real teacher but . . . you know. It's something."

She looked out into the hall. "You can borrow the guitar, Sebastian," she said. "Just keep an eye on him for me. Can you do that?"

I chewed another bite of cookie, swallowing what felt like sand.

"Now go look around the church," she said. "I'll check outside."

She waited for me to catch up to her and we walked side by side for a few steps. She put her arm around me, for only a split second really. Then she removed it and we split paths. I headed into the hallways of Immanuel and Janice walked outside without her coat, a half-eaten cookie still in her hand.

Around the children's classrooms, I felt that inexplicable sense of trepidation creep back into my body. God was in every church. That's what Janice had said at Youth Group. I couldn't stop wondering: if he's here, where is he hiding? I looked in the small window of each classroom door, half expecting to see the Holy Spirit, floating around over a bulletin board. But all I could see was darkness.

I thought about the band while I wandered the short hallways. I wanted to tell Jared that he couldn't make decisions for both of us. But I knew better. It was his band. He needed me, but he could find someone else if he ever dared to make another friend. I started singing "Stupid School" to myself as I wandered, but I couldn't get the tune right.

"*Why, teacher, why,*" I sang out.

My voice was still soft and unsteady.

"*Why, teacher, why!*" I tried, louder.

"Not here," said Meredith.

I looked behind me in the hall. There was nobody there.

"Hello," I yelled. "Meredith?"

Next to me was the boys' bathroom. I heard Meredith's voice again, quieter this time. "I said you can't do this here," she said.

She was in the bathroom. With a guy. My whole body sank. I took two steps to the door. I inched it open just enough to look through. I saw her standing up over somebody. She met my eyes and took a step to the side. It was Jared. He was breathing heavily, taking a drink out of a small wax cup.

"You need to get up," said Meredith. "I'll help you to the van."

"Give me a minute, okay?"

"Okay," she said.

Her voice was soft and composed. I'd never heard her speak that way to Jared before. She reached down and pushed the hair out of his eyes. He didn't protest.

"Jared . . ." I said. I walked inside.

"Not now, Judas," he said. He sipped loudly.

"I've cleared up our little misunderstanding," said Meredith. "We need you to go get Mom."

"Mom?" I said.

"Janice," said Meredith.

"Meredith doesn't want your bod, Sebastian," said Jared. "It's the sad truth. You're too skinny. Not her type. There will be no"—he burped—"romancing in the near future."

He took a deep breath and let it out slowly. Meredith looked at me severely, making any possible argument on my part irrelevant.

"I don't see you moving," she said. "Someone needs to get Janice."

Jared looked up at me for the first time.

"I think I'm having a rejection," he said.

I stared dumbstruck.

"Fine," said Meredith. "I'm going. You stay here, Sebastian. Just sit with him. Get him anything he needs!"

She cruised by me and started into a run by the time she reached the door. She swung it open and was gone in seconds. Jared handed me his empty cup and I filled it with cold water from the tap. The fluorescent lights above reflected off the laminate floor.

"What happens when you have a rejection?" I asked.

"Your body goes after the new organ. It involves the immune response. Now just sit down and shut up," he said.

He was shivering a little now, breaking out in a cold sweat. He removed his glasses and stuck them in his pocket. His eyes looked much smaller.

"Actually," he said, "I changed my mind. Talk to me."

"What do you want to talk about?"

"Anything," he said.

"Everything I know about is boring," I said.

"It's okay. You're a boring person. Just talk."

He smiled with his jaw clenched. And I suddenly remembered something and stuck my hand in my back pocket. I was wearing the same pants from the night in the dome, and right where I left them were the photographs I had removed from Nana's album. There were three in total, each one discolored and faded.

"Look," I said. "I found some pictures in the dome."

I handed him one of the photos.

"Who are those people?" he said. "Nineteen eighties porno stars?"

I snatched it back immediately.

"Okay," he said, trembling. "I didn't mean it. Let me see. Give it back."

He took the picture again and looked closely at it.

"These are your parents, aren't they?" he said.

He held up the first shot. It was a picture that had been taken outside in the backyard of our old ranch home in a small town east of North Branch. My parents were standing beside a tree. It was the only tree in the front yard. My dad wore a shirt with a V-neck and his chest hair came out in dark tufts. He had a long mustache and a pair of caramel-tinted sunglasses on. My mother stood next to him in a strapless dress, looking caught by surprise. Her eyes seemed to sparkle, even in the weathered picture.

"My mom used to lift me up to the little perch in the tree," I said. "She'd hold me up there long enough to get a look, then I'd scream and she'd put me back down."

"Did your grandmother tell you that?" asked Jared.

"No," I said. "I remember."

I flipped to the next shot. They were sitting on the lawn, on a red-and-blue-checked blanket. "My dad mowed the lawn with a pair of gardening shears. It was so small he could accomplish the entire task by hand. In the summer, there were fireworks in the park down the street. We could see them from our patch of yard."

I moved to the third shot. My parents were lying on a double bed and a baby was curled up asleep between them. The baby was me.

"What's that thing?" said Jared.

He laughed. Then he stood up and ducked quickly into a stall. He heaved and I heard his vomit land in the toilet bowl.

"Are you okay?" I asked.

"Man," he said. "There's something about Youth Group. It just has this effect on me every damn time."

He chuckled to himself and then threw up again. I looked down at the picture of myself as an infant while I waited for Jared.

My father's hand was holding on to my bare foot. His thumb was pressed against my big toe. He was kissing the back of my shirt.

"Hey," said Jared.

"Yeah?" I said.

"Your mom was pretty," he said.

I looked at her, lying next to me in the photo. She was smiling. Her eyes were closed this time. "Thanks," I said.

"Can I tell you something," Jared said. "A secret."

I didn't answer him. My eyes were locked on the picture.

"I haven't been taking my medicine," he said.

My eyes leaped up.

"What?" I yelled.

I felt my mouth go dry. He heaved again.

"What do you mean, Jared? Today?"

I stood up and rushed to the door of the stall. And that was the moment Janice and Meredith returned. They burst through the door, Meredith first. Both of them looked at me like I'd done something to Jared. I just pointed toward the toilet and stepped out of their way. My face must have said everything. They rushed past me, straight to the stall door. On the way, Janice knocked the photos from my hand with her elbow, and they whisked into the air. I tried for one moment to catch them, but they all went in different directions, and I was left standing, looking at my parents on the floor.

"Jared," said Meredith. "Keep your eyes open!"

On my knees, I peered through the stall door and saw Meredith holding him like a doll. Her inky eye makeup was running down the side of her face. She kissed Jared's wet hair.

"Pick him up," said Janice.

She turned around. "Sebastian," she said." Please. We need you!"

I managed to grab only the photo of myself as a baby. Then I ran to the bathroom stall and picked up Jared's legs. The soles of his canvas sneakers brushed across my chest. He was unconscious, humming something to himself. What was he humming? His laces were untied. I thought his shoes might fall off. I watched them carefully. We all started running. I recognized the tune he was mumbling just as we made it to the van: "Teenagers from Mars."

And we don't care.

23. Applied Synergetics

IT WAS IN THIS WAY I FOUND MYSELF BACK IN THE
hospital. Waiting in the same room, with the same cola machine
buzzing in the corner. This time the television was off. There were
no other lives, just Meredith and me sitting for two hours in total
silence. During that time, Nana's incident returned to my memory.
As did her frightened face, and her nighttime assurances that I was
leaving her. How could she have known even then? I thought now.
True, it was Nana who eventually implored me to leave, but maybe
she'd been right when she said it was already happening. I looked
back to the hallway, almost expecting to see her being wheeled out.
Instead, I saw Janice.

It was time to go, she said. There was nothing more we could do.
She would stay in Jared's room, but there was no place for us. She
would call with updates. That's the best she could do. As she related
this information, her voice sounded like it was coming from someone else entirely, some half-alive person now residing in her body.
And when she reached into her pocket for the van keys, I saw that
her hand was shaking.

The ride home was uncomfortably silent, except for Janice's
quick mention of canned spaghetti for our dinner. I didn't dare
speak. When we arrived at the house, Janice just motioned for us to

get out of the van. So we did. Then we stood rigid in the yard watching her back out of the drive. Her taillights receded into the ill-lit streets ahead. She did not wave good-bye.

"I've never seen her like that," said Meredith.

The night was foggy, and the porch suddenly seemed like a refuge. We both turned and stared at the yellow bulb, the angels beneath.

"Well," she said. "I guess we should eat some canned spaghetti."

"Okay," I said.

We shuffled into the house, dropping our coats and hats on the floor. There was already a light on in the kitchen and we followed it like a star. I sat down at the table while Meredith opened up a tin can from the pantry. She slopped the contents into a small pot and turned on the burner. "It's actually ravioli," she said. "Is that all right?"

I shrugged.

"It's not bad," she said. "Jared eats it cold out of the can. But I wouldn't recommend that. My dad used to tell him that's how they ate things in the army."

We didn't talk while she stirred the simmering pot. When it started to heat up, a heady odor filled the room. Sweet and strange. Meredith pushed a wooden spoon around in lazy circles. It didn't take long to cook, and in minutes she dished it out in mismatched bowls. She slapped a spoon in my hand.

"I don't get it," she said, sitting down. "Why the hell wasn't he taking his meds? It doesn't make any sense to me."

I blew on a spoonful of pasta to cool it down. It was dark orange, plastic-looking. It bubbled in the pool of my spoon.

"He didn't tell you anything?" she asked.

"Not really."

I blew again, then glanced up and found Meredith's eyes still on me. Her eyebrows were arched just slightly.

"I have a theory," I said.

"Well."

"Okay," I said, "I think it might have had something to do with side effects, and beginning school again. He was ashamed."

Meredith took this in. Then she let her spoon clatter to the table.

"That's bullshit!" she said. "Jared's smarter than that! And he knows better than to care about the other morons in his school and what they'll think!"

"But it's impossible not to care," I said.

"It's possible," she said.

I took a bite of the pasta. It tasted good at first, but the aftertaste was acidic. It burned in my mouth. For the first time, I felt I could actually taste the additives. I had a sudden and irrational craving for Nana's whole wheat spaghetti with tomatoes. I let the head of my spoon sink down under the orange surface.

"You care," I said.

"What?" she said.

"I've watched you with your friends. I hear you on the telephone. You seem to care a lot about what people think."

"Shut up," she said. "I do things the way I want."

"Sometimes, perhaps. But you speak differently on the phone. Not like you're speaking now. And you laugh in a certain way when you get into the car with your friends. I see it. I watch you."

"I don't have to listen to this from you," she said.

"I see the boys you admire," I continued. "You care. You care what people think of you. And so does Jared."

She got up and walked to the sink. She tossed her full bowl of

ravioli into the basin and the glass broke, sending shards skat-
ing over the stainless steel. She said something over the noise I
couldn't hear.

"What?" I asked.

"Jared is better than that!" she yelled.

Her face was red.

"Better than what?"

"He's better than me. It's that simple, okay?"

I stood up. "That's not what I intended to say," I said.

She stayed standing by the counter, facing away from me.

"Don't come over here," she said. "Just stay where you are."

I stood near my chair.

"If he wasn't my brother," she said, "I probably wouldn't even be
his friend."

She dipped her finger in a spot of sauce on the counter and
smeared it around.

"But he is your brother and you love him. So it's okay."

"No, it's not okay," she said.

She looked into the sink. "Things haven't been okay with me for
a while."

Jared's words came back to me all of a sudden. They formed in
my mouth.

"People get sick, you know?" I said. "Bad stuff happens. We can't
help it."

Meredith looked at me skeptically.

"Jesus," she said. "What a mess. All of this."

I got up and brought my bowl to the counter. I picked up the
chips of white glass, pinching them between my fingertips, and
placed them in the trash under the sink. They clinked into the bag.
I washed the tiniest fragments down the roaring garbage disposal.

By the time I was done with Meredith's wreckage, she was gone. The door to her room was closed and something told me not to open it. I turned off the lights in the kitchen and walked upstairs, completely enshrouded in darkness, feeling the wall for a light switch.

THE KNOCK CAME AROUND ONE-THIRTY IN THE MORN-ing. At first, I thought I had invented it. I was asleep in Jared's bed, but in my dream I was sitting in a hospital room between two beds. They were both obscured by thick white sheets. I was waiting for someone to tell me who was in which bed. A doctor maybe. Someone who could help. In my groggy semiwakened state, I expected a hospital worker at the door of Jared's room. When I opened the door though, there was a pale girl in a tank top and underwear. She didn't speak for a few minutes, and when she did, it was in a whisper.

"Nothing sexual, okay?" she said.

Her words sounded crisp. I could hear every syllable.

"Meredith?"

I was still trying to wake up. My eyes were so heavy.

"I just need to . . ." she began.

She didn't finish her sentence. I stepped out of the way. I could barely distinguish her form as she walked by me and fell onto the bed. She rolled herself into the wadded sheets and pulled the covers up around her. We'd forgotten to turn on the heat and the room was cold. The humidifier was silent in the corner.

"I need to be with someone," she said.

I watched her from the doorway. "Do you want me to get in the bed?" I asked.

The words sounded strange coming from my mouth.

"I think so," she said.

My feet were soundless on the carpeting. I could just barely make out the small piles of CDs on the floor to avoid them.

"What about the things Jared said?" I asked. "About me and you?"

I hesitantly slipped under the covers, adjusting the sheet over me.

"Let's not talk about that," she said. "Let's not talk at all, for a minute."

She backed up and I felt the heat from her body. It radiated off her back. I held my hand out, close to her skin, and I could feel the change in temperature. I moved closer until my chest was barely touching the back of her shirt. She grabbed my arm and slung it around her waist. I left it there, my wrist half balancing on the point of her hip.

"Don't go to sleep," she said.

"I won't."

Her stomach rose and fell with her breathing, taking my arm with it. She spoke again, so quietly. "I don't sleep with them," she said.

"Who?"

"The guys who come to my room."

"You don't . . ."

"We don't screw. I don't screw them."

"Oh."

"We do other things."

"I see."

My whole body felt like a bass string, humming. She moved her head on the pillow and her hair brushed against my chin. It tickled, but I didn't want to move.

"I'm going to talk about myself for a minute," she said.

"Okay."

"I'm just warning you because people are always talking about themselves. It feels good, though. That's why they do it."

She paused.

"Except you. You're a listener, Sebastian. You're the only real listener I've ever met. You take it all in. I don't know if I like you yet, but I like that part."

She rolled onto her back and looked up at the ceiling.

"I'm still afraid of the dark at the age of seventeen," she said. "There. It feels good to say that out loud. *I'm afraid of the damn dark.* God, it's true. But it's not the dark itself, I guess. It's just that the dark leaves me alone with these thoughts that I don't like. And they pop back up. The daytime keeps them down pretty well. So does talking, I guess."

She grabbed on to my hand.

"It's part of the reason for the . . . boys, too, I guess. They're so boring most of the time. Just so, so dull. But it's nice to be touched. That's another thing that keeps me distracted. Being touched. Like right now. It helps. I don't know why. But it does."

She rolled over toward me and then she was in my arms. I could feel her small breasts against my chest. Her forehead was touching mine.

"That's all I want to say."

There was a long pause.

"Now I'm starting to fall asleep," she said.

"Go ahead."

She kept her eyes closed. Her body relaxed. She stayed that way for nearly a minute before she spoke again.

"Did you actually mean those things you said to me on the phone?"

"I did," I said.

"I'll choose to believe you tonight . . ."

She yawned and her voice drifted off. She was moving farther into my arms. I leaned down and gave her a kiss on the forehead. Her eyes opened and she was awake again. "I can't," she said.

She whipped the covers off and put a foot on the carpet.

"I can't sleep here," she said. "Janice will be back in the morning."

She put the other foot down and walked right to the door. She stopped in the doorway. I sat up, my back against the wall.

"Just don't say anything else," she said. "Just don't."

"I want to ask about Jared," I said.

"What about him?"

"How often does this kind of thing occur? This thing that's happening."

"Only once before," she said.

"And he was treated?"

"He was. They'll give him a biopsy and then probably he'll be on an IV all night. Normally that takes care of it. Normally."

"Okay," I said. "Thanks."

"Is that all?"

"It is," I lied. I wanted to say half a million things. I wanted to scream into the quiet neighborhood cul-de-sac.

"Good night," I said.

She didn't answer. Without even a look back, she crept out the door and slowly closed it behind her. I waited in the dark for it to open again. But it didn't, and after a minute or two, I got up and activated Jared's stereo. I'd seen him operate it enough now to know how to turn it on. I placed a record on the turntable in the dark and started it spinning around. At the last moment, though, I was scared to damage his needle. It was enough just to hear the static as the record revolved around. I lay down next to the speaker and listened to the hisses and pops. It sounded like the air around me had come alive.

24. Familiar Ghosts

EVER SINCE MY FIRST NIGHT AT THE CHURCH, LONG ago, when Nana seemed to know where I'd been, I had been trying to avoid the subject of her metaphysical powers. I didn't want to consider the real possibility of her telepathic abilities. It was paralyzing. But I realized, after what had happened with Jared, that I needed to start facing the facts more often. I needed to consider the difficult things in life before they snuck up on me.

So, the next morning I sat in the kitchen making toaster pastries and contemplating brain waves. Nonverbal communication. Patterns and signals. In the brief quietude of the early morning, I thought of Nana again, alone in the dome, and I wondered if she was trying to communicate with me. If she was right, and it was my destiny to take her place, shouldn't I be capable of this kind of communication? Bucky believed he was able to telepathically connect with his infant daughter only days after her birth. So there must be some hereditary component.

I tried, in the Whitcombs' kitchen, to empty my head of everything that made me resist my powers. I tried to calibrate the rhythms of my thoughts to those beyond the realm of the senses. I didn't know how to do this necessarily, so I just tried to concentrate on something blank. The color white. I saw it as an empty space in my head, and kept it there, waiting for it to be filled. I held my head in my hands and sat tight. I whispered Nana's name to the table. "Nana," I said, "talk to me. I am attuned."

There was a long stretch of silence. Everything in the house seemed too quiet for me. I thought of absolutely nothing, and gradually unrefined images started to form. There was no direct communication—only mental pictures, some moving, some still. *Image,* Bucky had said, was the root word of imagination. And chances were good that I was simply imagining the scenes that began to form like developing photographs in my consciousness. But there they were all the same. And there was Nana.

She was on top of the dome. I saw her from far away, but as I waited, she moved closer to me. She was wearing my harness. Suction cups were fastened to her hands and knees. A delicate paintbrush hung in her fingers. Despite the great cold, her face was sunburned pink. Her hair blew wildly in the places it escaped from her hat. She ran the paintbrush in small careful strokes over the farthest reaches of Greenland, where the land met the Arctic Ocean. Then she stopped. She held the brush aloft, and she turned her head slightly, looking up. It felt like she was staring right at me. Another moment and she would start speaking.

I opened my eyes, and the phone began ringing on the kitchen wall. I jumped up and staggered forward a step or two. I was sure it was her. She had felt my presence and intuited the Whitcombs' phone number somehow. Nana was calling me home. I grabbed the phone and pressed the plastic to my ear. "Hello?"

"I'm calling from beyond the graaaave," said the caller.

"What!"

"Just kidding. I didn't croak yet, man. I'm alive as hell."

"Jared?"

"Yes, for God's sake, man, relax. Do you think I'd call you if I was really a ghost. No way, I'd haunt you while you were on the toilet or something. I'd fly away with the TP."

I realized I was clutching the phone white-knuckled with my right hand. I loosened my grip. "I thought you were Nana," I said.

"Well, I'm not. Get over it." ·

I breathed a little easier. "Are you . . . better?"

"Kind of," he said. "I don't know. They've been giving me atomic bombs of immunosuppressives. I feel like a big fat water balloon full of meds right now. I could probably pee out of my eyes if I tried hard enough."

It was pleasing to hear his voice, but I didn't know what to say to him. I could already feel the irritation growing in spite of my best efforts to quell it. Part of me had never expected to hear from him again.

"Meredith is pissed, I bet," he said.

"She is," I said, passively.

"Yeah, Janice is in a fury, too. She's not really speaking to me, except to make sure I'm still breathing. She brought me a milkshake from McDonald's this morning and almost threw it at me."

He laughed longer than usual at his own joke. Then he cleared his throat just to fill the silence. "What?" he said. "What is it with you? I still haven't forgotten about your betrayal, okay, so don't start with me. You don't have a leg to stand on."

"I don't care," I said. "You're a major asshole."

He exhaled. "Wow," he said. "Did you really just say that?"

"What did you think you were trying to accomplish? Why did you stop listening to your doctors?"

He sighed. "Look," he said. "I don't know, entirely. I've been talking to a counselor they brought in for me. He asked me if I was trying to off myself."

"Were you?"

"No."

"But you knew what would happen if you stopped taking the medication."

"I hoped it might be different. I was feeling better. I thought maybe they were dosing me up too much, trying to keep me weak."

"Why would they do that?"

"Tons of reasons."

"Like what?"

He let out a quick breath. "They don't want me to take any risks! They just want me to be this bedridden clone all my life."

I didn't speak.

"That's how they keep you down," he said. "This whole country's on pills. That's how they turn us into zombies."

"You're being dramatic," I said. "And foolish."

"I was experimenting," he said.

I just waited for him to speak again.

"The experiment failed."

Meredith walked into the kitchen without looking at me. Her bare feet squeaked on the linoleum. She wore pajama pants and a T-shirt. Her unwashed hair touched her neck in wisps. I felt a swell of guilt replacing my anger. I had been in a bed with Jared's sister last night.

"Hello?" he said. "I just humbled myself. Did you hear it?"

"I don't know what to say, Jared, except that today is Friday."

"Is it supposed to mean something to me? Because it doesn't mean something to me."

"The talent show is less than one week away. It's next Thursday."

"Oh," he said. "That thing."

"We need practice," I said. "And we need an additional song. Don't we? We need two songs. This was all your idea."

I tried to gauge Meredith's reaction. She was standing over the toaster, grabbing a pastry with a paper towel.

"The band is broken up right now," Jared mumbled. "In case you forgot."

"I didn't forget," I said.

"So," he said.

"So what?"

"So before we can practice, I have to decide whether or not I want to reunite the band. It's a hard decision. I just can't make it on the fly. Also, I have to get the hell out of here."

"How long are they going to keep you?"

"I don't know," he said. "Not too much longer. Janice made it clear we don't have any money. I'm sure they'll kick us out soon."

I heard the sound of voices in his room.

"Listen," he said, "I have to go. They're here to pump me full of zombie drugs again."

"Jared," I said.

"I have to go."

"I'm sorry this is your life," I said. "I wish I could help you."

He was quiet. I heard the phone shuffling against his ear.

"All right," he said. "I have to go."

"I mean that," I said.

"I know," he said.

I hung up the phone and walked right by Meredith. I didn't even give her time to ignore me. I just took the other pastry and walked back upstairs to Jared's room. I excavated some equipment from the closet and grabbed my bass. I plugged into the amplifier and started practicing the only song I knew. The same notes at a steady rhythm. I played loud, hoping the sound would seep through the floorboards. I wanted the whole house to thrum and vibrate. I turned the volume up until I was sure it was damaging my ears. Then I turned it up further.

JARED WAS RELEASED LATE THAT AFTERNOON. AROUND three o'clock he was allowed to depart with Janice. I had been upstairs making noise when Meredith received the call. And soon after, she appeared in the doorway, squinting into the room. I stopped playing and Meredith entered. She switched off the amplifier, and all the noise disappeared in an instant, sucked out of the air.

"He's on his way," she said.

"I see," I said.

"He's still a little out of it," she said. "So we're supposed to leave him alone. He has to rest. They barely agreed to let him go."

"I'll begin cleaning up," I said.

She moved over to the bed and tossed off the blanket. She peeled off the sheets and wadded them up. She chucked them into the hallway.

"What are you doing?" I asked.

"He'll smell my body spray," she said. "He'll know."

She didn't look at me; she just grabbed the sheets and took them downstairs. She came back a minute later with a new set. I helped her stretch them over the mattress. We worked at different ends tugging them tight. Then we replaced the pillowcases and flipped on the humidifier. I turned down the blanket so it looked like the bed was waiting for him. I put away the instruments and arranged his albums in neat piles. The room looked somewhat welcoming.

"This is good," she said.

I assumed she meant the cleaning we had done, but I held out hope that she meant the night before, too. I didn't ask for clarification. I just walked out behind her and closed the door to Jared's room. Then we both waited in the living room. Meredith turned on the giant television and sat, unblinking, for the extent of a program about trying to have sexual relations with a stranger. I watched as a line of nude-torsoed men licked whipped cream off a woman's neck. The woman chirped out the same laugh each time like some kind of stimulated machine. Then she disparaged the men for being "naughty." She smacked one of them on the buttocks. I tried to gauge if Meredith was entertained by this, or if this was perhaps what she wanted. A line of men by a brilliant turquoise pool. Something sweet sprayed on her neck. Endless human contact.

She turned off the TV when the front doorknob turned. The screen went black and Jared ambled in, gripping Janice's arm for balance. They walked in front of the TV, and the contrast was jarring. Where there had just been attractive tan people, now stood Jared. He was pale and drowsy. His skin looked almost gray in the harsh daylight of the living room. He needed help getting his sneakers off, and I watched while Janice undid his laces. Jared sat down and seemed to notice us for the first time. He pushed the hair out of the way of his glasses. I saw he was still wearing a hospital bracelet on his wrist.

"Hey, guys," he said slowly. "There's a real party atmosphere in here."

Janice frowned at him.

"We sent the magician home," said Meredith.

"Don't get him started," said Janice. "He needs sleep."

"Yeah," said Jared. "Don't get me started. It's bed rest for me. Maybe a stay in the country to hearten my constitution. The sound of the birds. The fresh manure . . ."

"He's on a little morphine," added Janice.

She stood him up and walked him through the living room and into the kitchen. I watched him hold Janice's hand as he gradually climbed the staircase to his room. More than ever before, he looked like a child to me. It was hard to remember sometimes that he was my age. When he was at his most overbearing, he seemed like the ruler of his own small country. The reality was that he was scared sometimes. And he still needed his mother. After he was gone, I sat there on the couch, thinking about all of this. Meredith was quiet, too. She rested cross-legged on a nearby chair. I looked over at her and she snapped out of her brief trance.

"What do you think I should do?" I asked.

"About what exactly?"

She looked uncomfortable for a moment.

"The band," I said.

"Oh," she said, "that."

"Speak honestly," I said.

"Honestly," she said, "I think you're going to embarrass your-selves. Terribly. And I'd like to be there when it happens."

"That's not what I meant."

"But Jared doesn't care about that," she added quickly. "Not when it comes to music. He thinks it's everyone else's fault if they don't get it. He's always been like that. You should hear what he says about the music I like. He never changes his mind."

"Janice knows about the stolen bass," I said. "I imagine she'll only let me keep it for so long. I think the band is dying."

Upstairs we heard the sound of Janice walking around the room, speaking in a sharp tone to Jared. Her voice sounded desperate.

"And I think Jared needs it," I said.

Meredith looked down at the carpet a moment.

"Well, then it's simple," she said. "You have to save your stupid band. What's the matter? Don't you have any balls?"

The smirk was back.

"Stay right here," I said.

"You can't order me around," she said. "I'm not your dog."

"Just . . . please," I said.

"I'll sit here because I want to," she said. "Not because you told me to."

I walked into the kitchen and turned into Meredith's room. I was looking for a piece of paper, a certain size. I checked on her dresser and on the floor. I looked in her schoolbag but only found notebook paper. Finally I reached up and detached a small poster from above her bed. It was a picture of a well-built man standing on a sandy beach, with a small set of trunks on. His hands were on his hips. He looked like he could have stepped right out of the television program. I turned the photo over and found white space on the back. I grabbed a marker from Meredith's bag. I came back into the living room and set the picture on the coffee table, facedown.

"Where did you get that?" she asked right away. "Let me see that."

She grabbed for the paper. I grabbed back. We both held on to separate ends.

"Listen, Meredith," I said. "I understand if you're not in love with me. It's okay if you want to forget last night. But if you're really my friend, then I need you to help me with something."

Janice was coming back down the stairs now. We both heard her. I felt Meredith's fingers slowly release the paper. I uncapped the marker.

25. Calculations

BACK WHEN I STILL HAD A COMPUTER, BEFORE IT
went rolling down the hill like a boulder, I had come across something of interest in my research. One of the first groups to use the
word "punk" was not a band. It was a magazine. *Punk Magazine.*
They composed articles about the music in New York City in the
1970s. And once they decided to form this publication they knew
they needed to inform people about it. So they walked all over
New York City putting up posters that said, "WATCH OUT! PUNK IS
COMING!" Nobody knew if it was a band or what exactly Punk was.
But people began talking. And before these writers had composed
a word, there was already forward momentum. Their words were
already lodged in the minds of curious passersby.

That afternoon, when Janice lay down for a much-needed nap,
Meredith and I traveled to the copy store in downtown North
Branch and produced one hundred photocopies of a homemade
poster. She loaned me the money for the paper and a large stapler
that resembled a firearm. It all cost over forty dollars total, and if
I didn't pay her back in a week, she said it was going up to fifty.
Along with the money, though, I also received her help. And as the
big red sun started to descend, she held each poster in place while
I blasted a staple right through the top and bottom. We fastened

them to splintery telephone poles mainly, but also to community bulletin boards and weathered park benches. Each poster said the same thing.

WATCH OUT! THE RASH IS HERE!

We avoided people, and when someone snuck up and asked us what The Rash was, Meredith told them she didn't know. She said we'd been paid to put up the signs. I couldn't believe how casually she was able to handle these situations. She actually seemed to take pleasure in confusing strangers. I could tell, even more than with Jared, anything secretive charged her with a new energy. She'd begun the afternoon dragging her feet, but on the way home, she was more enlivened about our handiwork than I was.

"This place is totally littered with signs," she said, walking a step ahead of me. "All these boring townies aren't going to know what the hell is going on. They're going to be checking their bodies for hives!"

Around us, orange lights were coming on in the front windows of houses. Chimneys were spouting smoke, chalk white against a blue-black sky. Our shoes scraped over the tiny jagged crystals of the salted sidewalks.

"Do you think we should have included the date of the performance at least?" I asked.

"No way!" she said. "That's the whole point. Once you have everyone talking, then you put up the next batch of signs that tells everyone where to go. They'll follow like cattle. It was actually a good idea. Don't second-guess it."

It was hard not to be infected by Meredith's spirit. Her cheeks were flushed from the cold and her eyes were watery. She hadn't had time to apply her makeup before we went out that day, and her face looked friendlier somehow. Less severe. She slowed down to let me catch up, and then reached a hand over and pushed up my hair.

"You have to put fresh hair spray in this," she said. "It won't just stay up. You know that, right?"

"I'm still deciding if I like it," I said.

I was wearing Jared's clothes for the second day in a row. A pair of jeans too tight and short for me, and a T-shirt under my coat that said "Minor Threat."

"Well," she said, "you have to decide one way or the other. Or you just look like you don't shower."

We were getting closer to home now, which is how I was starting to think about it. Home. Our bodies were near one another. And I felt a little of that mysterious quality returning from the night before. I suppressed a quick guilt-flash. Jared was just going to have to understand that it was possible to have two friends. Before the last month, there hadn't been anyone. Now there were two people who cared enough to speak to me. I felt Meredith reach out for my hand. It was ice-cold when I took it.

I knew better than to try to make any overtures as the numbers on Ovid drew closer to the Whitcombs'. I was learning how to be quiet at the right time. It was so easy to spoil a moment. All it took was a wrong word or gesture and that tender quality vanished in a blink. You cleared your throat too loudly. You actually said what was on your mind. Or a tall redheaded kid rounded a corner when you least expected him and said: "Hey, Meredith."

I saw him first, but Meredith was first to let her hand drop to her side.

"Hey," she said.

I hadn't noticed right away, but he was trailing an old dog, a rust-brown canine on a leash. It nosed at the base of a bare tree.

"I've been trying to call you," said the guy. "I keep getting your message." I looked at him closely and saw he was trying to grow a beard of some kind. The patches of wiry orange hair waved to one another from opposite sides of his chin.

"I haven't really been taking phone calls," she said.

"What? Did you find Jesus or something?"

He grinned, exposing a dental apparatus I hadn't remembered. I took a step toward him, but before I could say anything, his dog raced around and started barking at me. Its mouth clapped open and shut wildly, sending deafening bursts of noise right into my face. The guy tugged his choke collar.

"Dude," he said, laughing. "You should have seen your face just now."

I looked at Meredith. Her hands were thrust in her pockets.

"We need to go," I said.

"Whoa, hey!" said the guy. "Is this the same guy from that night? Hey, man. No hard feelings. I hope you were okay. No bruises, right, bro?"

He punched me in the shoulder. I looked down at his dog. It was still eyeing me, probably biding its time for a second attack. I walked around the canine, keeping a wide berth. I hoped Meredith would follow. She did not.

"You go ahead," she said. "I'll see you in a minute."

She reached down to pet the guy's dog, ruffling the fur on its neck. I could only watch for a couple of seconds before I had to turn away. It was just another block to the house, but I suddenly wished I could transport myself there somehow. I'd just close my eyes and when I opened them again I'd be in the kitchen, sitting back at the table. Then the day could start over again. When Meredith came down from our night together, I'd say, "Enough, Meredith. You can't confuse people the way you do. I won't take it! I won't!" I was talking out loud to myself. Behind me it was already too dark to tell what was happening between her and the redhead. I reached a palm up and tried to flatten my hair. It wouldn't go down all the way. I could feel stray pieces sticking up in the wind. I had one flyer left and I felt it, folded in four, in my pocket. I entered the dark house.

I thought, at first, that mother and son were still resting, but then I heard a faint murmur from the kitchen. I walked through the living room and up to the doorway where the carpet met the tile. I saw Janice with her back to me. She had the telephone pressed to her ear, and she was pulling at a long strand of her hair. Her index finger looked like a corkscrew with those dark locks wrapped around it.

"I just told you, they said he didn't show up in the database," she said. "I talked to the woman for over an hour."

I assumed, at first, that she was in a conference with the hospital.

"Well then, don't," she said. "But you said he was still on your insurance and I didn't have any reason to . . ."

She tugged at her hair and began pacing. I ducked back a step, trying to stay out of sight. Her fingers squeezed the top of a chair. Suddenly, she pushed it hard against the table. It crashed into the scuffed protruding lip.

"Maybe if you'd seen him, you'd be more worried. Okay? But don't tell me how worried I should be! You don't get to say anything because you don't know a thing about this!"

Her voice cracked; it sounded like she was about to cry. I knew now who she was speaking to. "Yeah, that's great. I'll see if the church can swing it."

She yanked at her hair.

"Or maybe I'll just find a new husband. I'll go to one of those . . . those speed-dating things. Two minutes, let's see. What can I tell you? I have two children that hate me. One of them is . . . just be quiet! One of them almost died the other night. And I'm a part-time Youth Group director who has insomnia."

She was breathing hard now. "No, you can't."

I heard a distant grumble through the receiver.

"Because he's resting!"

She turned around suddenly and seemed to look right at me. My heart stopped. But she didn't acknowledge me at all. It was as if I didn't exist.

"Yes," she said, quieter now. "*Really.* This isn't a conspiracy."

I saw her mouth open, ready to speak again.

"Well, he sleeps a lot. The kid is tired. But I'll tell him you called. Just don't keep promising to visit because you know I won't allow it and you're just breaking his heart."

I wondered if she was even aware of what she had just said.

"Uh-huh," she said.

I took a step toward her.

"Sure," she said. "All right. Send the forms. That sounds just perfect. Okay. Yep. Good-bye."

She looked at the phone like she was surprised to still find it in her hand. Then she slammed it down. I thought for sure it was going to fall off the wall, but it stayed on somehow, and Janice didn't move. She closed her eyes and took a few long slow breaths. Gradually her hands unclenched. She let them drop to her sides. Then she walked over to the counter, where the Whitcombs kept their mysterious snack foods. She tore open a big bag of potato chips and stuck her hand in the bag. But she didn't remove a chip. She didn't do anything at all. She just stayed completely still with her hand deep inside a package of chips.

I walked into the kitchen, trying to be silent. I moved right behind her toward the stairs. I thought she hadn't even noticed me, but then the chip bag crinkled.

"Don't say anything to him," I heard.

She didn't look at me.

"I won't."

I moved past her, and I heard her slowly crunch a potato chip as I climbed the staircase to Jared's room. I wanted to wake him up and tell him everything, swear him to secrecy. But I couldn't. Maybe it was the expression on Janice's face. Or the way her voice had sounded on the phone. But I knew it would be a betrayal. Instead, I stopped in front of his door and pulled my last poster out. I unfolded the paper and spread it over the pale wood. Then I took my new staple gun out of a coat pocket. *Ka-thunk!* It wasn't quite centered, but there it was on his door. THE RASH IS HERE! I sat down and leaned against the opposite wall, trying to steady myself. I felt like I'd been holding my breath for the last fifteen minutes. Now, I finally let it out.

THE RASH REUNITED THAT NIGHT AROUND TEN P.M. I was sitting at the foot of Jared's bed and we sealed the deal by spitting into our palms and shaking. We didn't tell anyone. It was best to keep it secret for the time being, Jared said. Janice had told him earlier that the talent contest was off. If he couldn't take care of himself, then he couldn't make his own decisions about activities. She said he was deliberately sabotaging her efforts to get him back in school. Jared didn't want to talk about any of that, though. He wanted to talk about the band.

"Of course I think it was kind of a dick move to take promotional action without me," he said, lying back on his pillow. "But I'm also in the tricky position of admiring your balls."

"Thank you," I said.

I tried to sound upbeat, but I couldn't shake Janice's voice from my head.

"From now on, you consult me before any marketing campaigns," he said. "Remember, I made the T-shirts. I have the ideas. I know how I want to brand us."

"I know."

"Good. So don't get cocky. This isn't a pissing contest."

There was a knock at the door and we both turned around. Mrs. Whitcomb opened the door. She looked surprisingly put together since the last time I'd seen her, but her eyes were slightly red. She glanced from me to Jared. She was holding an armload of books.

"Sebastian, time to go downstairs," she said. "Jared needs to start his study hour."

"Study hour?" said Jared. "What the hell is that?"

I got up from the bed and wandered toward the doorway.

"I contacted the principal at your school last week. There are some big things you need to catch up on."

She made right for the bed and deposited the books where I had just been sitting.

"We didn't talk about this," said Jared.

"We're talking about it now," she said. She stood right over him. "Do you want to fall back a grade after everything you've been through? I'm not going to let that happen. You need to take some responsibility and start thinking about the future, Jared!"

She was yelling now, her eyes wide. "This thing is not going to ruin your life! And it's not going to define your life! Not while I'm around."

I wanted to leave, but I was afraid I'd draw more attention to myself if I moved. Instead, I stayed glued to the black carpet.

"I get it," said Jared. "But I just got home from the hospital."

"I've been babying you," Janice said, softer now. "And now I see what the consequences are. You act like a baby and almost get your-self . . . killed. Well, things are going to change. Starting tonight. One hour of study. Next week it goes up to two. We can't just sit around waiting for bad things to happen anymore!"

Jared was speechless. He seemed to have been driven farther into bed by his mother's words. He reached over and pulled up a book.

"Geometry," he said.

"That's right."

"I don't know how to do this."

"That's what the book is for."

Jared nudged up his glasses. "Yeah, but when you're in school you have teachers. I can't figure this out with just a book. It's not possible."

"Well . . ." said Janice.

Her nerve was faltering already. There was a long silence in the room. Jared stared at the cover of the book. He turned it upside down. Then he turned it around, and I saw the cover. A neon pink tetrahedron sat on a cobalt background. I immediately recognized the book. I had read it easily three times over, by the age of ten.

"I can teach him," I said.

I was nearly in the hall, and they were surprised to hear my voice. They turned and stared at me.

"I can do it," I said. "Nana's specialty as an architect was spherical geometry. Geodesic domes are actually wonders of geometry. They're based on a shape called the icosahedron. It's a twenty-sided polyhedron, and each side is an equilateral triangle."

I wondered how much longer I should keep going. I decided on one more statement. The closer. "I've solved every problem in that book," I said.

It wasn't quite true. Nana had aided me with many of them. But it was true enough.

"Damn!" said Jared. "I told you he was some kind of fucking genius, Mom. I told you he was king dork."

Janice was still watching me. "Language," she said.

I looked Janice Whitcomb in the eyes. "I'd like to do something for you," I said. "I've just been additional trouble so far. I understand that. But I can make sure Jared understands this book."

"Yeah," said Jared. "Let him do one thing, Mom. God! Just give him this!"

"Jared, be quiet," she said.

She looked back at me. "You can't do the work for him. I want him to be caught up. You teach. He solves the problems."

"He will," I said.

"And you have to stay focused during study time. You need to work quickly. There's a lot to get through before Christmas break. That's when I want him back in class."

I saw Jared shift uncomfortably in his bedsheets. I could tell he was nearly ready to raise an argument. I jumped in to cut him off.

"We'll get through it," I said. "But we need something from you."

Janice looked surprised.

"Isn't it a little early to be making demands?" she asked.

"We need time to play music," I said. "Jared has a talent. And I don't think it's fair to keep people from pursuing what they're interested in. That's what my grandmother does. Anything that isn't part of my 'comprehensive education' is useless. I don't think you want to be that kind of parent, Mrs. Whitcomb. I really don't."

I glanced at Jared. His mouth was agape. Janice was biting her bottom lip.

"Studying first," is all she said.

Two words. Then she left the room and headed down the stairs. We understood the deal. Geometry. Then music. Jared didn't say anything. Decisions had been made without him, and it was not his manner to sit back and watch that happen. But eventually, he picked up the math book and opened it up to the first page. He scooted over in bed.

"Well," he said. "Get in here and teach me about these goddamn shapes, Professor Brain-lobes."

I sat down next to him and he handed me the book. I checked the clock. It was getting close to eleven and Meredith still wasn't home. I opened the book and flipped to the first chapter. The first night our band was back together, we would spend talking about points, lines, planes, and spaces.

"You see this?" I said. I put my finger below a dot in the book. "This is a point. It has no dimensions. It has no length, breadth, depth at all."

Jared listened without complaint.

"I don't know about you," I said, "but I feel very similar to a point lately."

"Fuckin' A," he said.

26. Return of The Rash

THERE WERE THREE DAYS LEFT UNTIL THE TALENT show when we composed our second anthem. We didn't know if Janice would allow us to perform, but we had official practice hours now, so we put them to use. The schedule broke down thus: daytime was study time; the evening was music time. First: the coordinate system. Second: punk rocking. That was the deal I had engineered. And if we adhered to it, our lives would be manageable. We took most of the weekend to get a jump start on the geometry, but by Monday, The Rash was back. Jared was not at full strength by any means, but he was able to play sitting down on the bed with his V-shaped guitar on his lap. I sat across the room on top of my amplifier. We both wore our T-shirts.

"Your backup vocals need work," said Jared. "I just have to be honest with you at this stage. You sound like a big limp wang every time you open your mouth."

We had been practicing "Stupid School" for a half hour. My bass playing had improved slightly, but Jared was right, I was still self-conscious about my singing voice.

"It's not singing so much as just letting it rip," he said. "Scream like a banshee. Howl like a horny dog."

"What's a banshee?"

"I don't know," said Jared. "Just act like you have a pair. That's the point I'm making."

"I'll try to improve," I said.

"Good," he said. "But let's take a break first. I'm getting the spins."

He flipped off his guitar and set it on the bed. He motioned me over, and then reached under his pillow and extracted his song-writing notebook. The two single mattresses had been his home base since he returned from the hospital, and you could tell by their smell. He flipped through pages of doodles and flame-engulfed versions of our band name until he got to a page covered in scrawl.

"I started something in the hospital," he said.

"A new song?"

"Maybe. Just let me finish."

"Fine."

He pressed his finger to the page.

"I was thinking this one could be different," he said.

"Different how?"

"Well, not really different. But I was just brainstorming, and I thought that even though we're mostly about hating everything and wanting things to be destroyed and mutilated, I think we might need to write a little something for the ladies."

I noticed a drawing of a pair of breasts in the upper right-hand corner of the page.

"A song about feminine subjects?"

"What's wrong with you?" he said. "No. A song about hot chicks."

"Oh."

"I mean even the Ramones have that one on their first album. 'I Wanna Be Your Boyfriend.'"

I shook my head.

"Hey little gir-irl, I wanna be your boyee-friend," Jared sang. *"Swe-eet little gir-irl . . .* Come on! You know it."

"I don't think I know it."

"Anyway, it's totally for the ladies. No matter how angry you are, you have to get girls involved or you're not really a band. That's a rule. You don't want your concerts to be big sausage parties."

I decided not to ask any more clarifying questions. These early sessions were the most delicate times for Jared's self-confidence. He could wilt in minutes.

"Is there a title?" I asked.

"A working title," he said.

"What is it?"

" 'I Wanna Fondle Your Chests,' " he said.

I didn't say anything.

"I was going to just say 'breasts' or 'hooters' or something regular. But we might get kicked off the stage for foul language at Immanuel. 'Chests' could mean anything. It could mean that part below the neck that's not really the boobs yet. The pre-boob region."

I looked at the notebook. I could see now that the word "ta-tas" was crossed out.

"I don't know, Jared."

"Oh, God, what?"

"I think it's a bit disrespectful."

"To who?" he yelled.

"Women."

He cocked his head to the side. "Well, yeah," he said.

"So you don't care about that?"

"Listen," he said. "Guys in bands are supposed to be disrespectful to women. That's part of our charm. If the ladies wanted someone respectful they'd go see the ballet or something. Instead they come see us to rock and take off their shirts."

"I don't like it."

"Fine," he said. "Then we don't have a second song. Way to go, you spoiled everything."

"Don't you have a tune?" I asked. "Didn't you write some music?"

"Maybe."

"Play it, Jared. It's only the title I'm questioning."

"You've already taken a steaming dump all over my dream."

"Just play it. We're a songwriting team."

"Don't call us that."

He sat back and closed his eyes a minute. He removed his glasses and rubbed the bridge of his nose. He released a dramatic sigh. He opened his eyes and examined the open notebook in front of him. The pen tip circled the words of the title. He drew a line under it and wrote a question mark at the end. "I wasn't sure about the word 'fondle' anyway," he said. "It's kind of a sissy word."

He clicked the toggle switch at the base of his guitar and the sound of his tuning filled the room. He barely touched a string with his fingertip, and a shrill harmonic escaped. "Do me a favor," he said. "Turn up the distortion and reverb."

I leaned down and adjusted the knobs on his amplifier. A slight growl of distortion came out of the speaker. He took a breath, then began playing a high-pitched pealing guitar part. The notes were hacked apart in a style similar to that of our first song, but there was a more agreeable rhythm this time. I could already hear the beginning of a bass line in my head. Something simple. Just a descending scale. I wanted to pick up my bass and give it a try, but I decided to give Jared time to play the song through.

"*Saw you on the sidewalk . . . lookin' pretty cute,*" he started.

His voice spilled out again, grimy but perfectly clear. His hand worked feverishly over the frets of his guitar. He didn't look down at his hands once.

"How I wish you were . . . in your birthday suit!"

He picked up the pace and played a fuller-sounding version of the guitar part. His lyrics were so fast: *"If I had a machine that zapped off clothes. I would use it on you from head to toes! Oh yes I would. I would. I would. I'd zap off your shirt. Oh. I'd zap off your skirt!"*

He stopped a moment. "This is the chorus right here," he said. The guitar slowed down a little and the tune changed to something slightly more melodious. The strumming was less palsied.

"Oh, it would be cooler if you were naked. Yes indeed. It would be cooler if you were naked. Here with me. 'Cause I'm going mad up in my room!"

He added a flourish or two with his guitar then repeated himself.

"'Cause I'm going mad. I'm going madddd. I'm going madddd up in my room!"

He stopped and held the guitar for a minute. He closed his eyes and let the last note slowly fade away. Then he turned down the volume and looked at me.

"So," he said. "What do you say?"

"What does the title have to do with that?" I asked.

"It's the same girl on the sidewalk. I want to fondle her chests. After I've zapped her clothes off. The title is a flash-forward at things to come. I'm experimenting with time."

"Hmm."

"Stop with the suspense. Just tell me if it's a horrid piece of crap and we'll move on."

"I think . . ."

He rolled his eyes.

"I think I like the song," I said. "It's sad actually."

"What do you mean it's sad? It's about forcibly removing someone's clothes. It's awesome."

"Well," I said, "I guess I'm thinking of that part at the end about going crazy up here in your room. That's the entire point of the song, isn't it? You're up here just imagining things because you can't really go out and accomplish them. It's the same thing I used to do in the dome."

"You imagined girls without their bras on up there?"

"Not really, but I imagined conversing with people who walked by. Girls, too, I guess. I felt like I had no real experiences. I was just frustrated in my room."

"Great," said Jared.

"What?"

"I try to write a song about hooters and it turns out sad. I might as well grow a ponytail."

"It's a good song," I said. "But we're changing the title."

"To what?"

" 'Up in My Room,' " I said.

" 'Up in My Room,' " he repeated. "It's too obvious."

"Trust me this time," I said.

"What about 'I Wanna Massage Your Buttocks'?"

I walked back to my seat on the amplifier and picked up my bass. I adjusted the strap on my back.

"All right, fine," he said. "But we're losing our edge. I hope you realize that."

We spent the rest of our allotted time practicing the new song. It took me longer than I thought to come up with an adequate bass line. Jared made everything appear much easier than it actually was. And this time, his chord changes were harder to follow. By the end of the hour, though, I was starting to get it down: a simple back and forth between the A string and the E string. *Dum-Dum-Dum-mmm-Bah-Bah-Bah.* But the part was faster than anything I'd ever played. I knew I was going to have to practice intensely in order to have it down by Thursday night.

At eleven-fifteen, we called it a night and I went downstairs to brush my teeth and wash my face. Jared had to have a check-in with Janice about his condition. The hospital had given them a list of questions to discuss, and a nightly conference was required now. So I headed downstairs, thinking about the song. It felt like it still needed something, and I wondered if the problem was mine, if my bass playing wasn't holding up, even in a punk song. I wished I had started learning earlier.

I was in the bathroom with my shirt off, and soap all over my face, when Meredith showed up in the doorway. I had just splashed the first handful of water over my face when I opened my eyes and saw her reflection in the bathroom mirror. I squinted to keep the trickles of soapy water out of my eyes. Meredith was wearing pants this time, and a baggy sweatshirt. Her hair was down and just touching her thin shoulders.

"I have an idea for your next poster," she said.

I finished rinsing my face and dried it off with a plush wash-cloth.

"I don't have the money for the first ones yet."

"I know," she said. "How would you? You don't do anything."

I turned around and covered my skinny chest with crossed arms.

"I think Jared wants to come up with the next idea. He was upset I did the last one by myself. But thanks."

I faced the mirror again and started squeezing toothpaste on my brush. In the dome, I had used natural paste made of herbal oils and extracts. The Whitcombs' brand was tricolored and it always surprised me when it came out of the tube. Bright green, white, and blue. Like a pureed flag.

"I see," said Meredith.

I started brushing, making little circles around my gums the way Nana had taught me. I wondered now if this was the way everyone else cleaned their teeth.

"Well, maybe we could brainstorm some ideas, and then you could let Jared make some additions. You have to learn how to manipulate him. If he thinks something is his idea, he'll go with it."

She laughed a little and continued to watch me. I wanted so badly to smile when she did, but I knew I couldn't do it. I couldn't let her think everything was fine. The sting of the night before was still there.

"Okay then," she said. "If you don't want to chat."

Her reflection drew closer in the glass until she was standing beside me. She took a bright pink toothbrush from the metal holder. She coated the bristles and started to brush the same way I did. Little circles. The swish of our combined brushing hit different timbres. It was like a conversation. *Scritch. Scritch. Scratch. Scratch. Scratch.* Finally I got to the point where I needed to spit. But I didn't want to perform this action in front of her. I tried to hold it in. Meredith didn't pay any attention. I tentatively swallowed a little bit of paste, but the overpowering mint burned my throat.

"Are you okay?" Meredith stopped brushing.

I was choking now, and I had no choice left. I expectorated into the sink, spraying the whole basin with aquamarine spittle. There was toothpaste on the fixture and the hot and cold handles. We both looked down. Meredith started laughing. I couldn't help it this time; I laughed, too. I tried to disguise it by turning on the water, but I was still chuckling as the paste washed away. Meredith kept giggling as she finished with her own teeth.

"Well," she said when she was finished, "it's been a pleasure watching you do disgusting things with your mouth, Sebastian."

She made a move toward the door.

"Wait," I said.

"Yes?"

"Have you actually drawn out the poster?"

She nodded.

"Okay," I said.

"Okay what?"

"I'd like to see it."

We walked together across the kitchen to her room. Sitting on the bed was a full-color poster with our band name in bright red, with Band-Aids stuck to it. The letters were shaded so they looked like they were coming right off the page. And the Band-Aids looked like they'd been covering a bleeding wound. Underneath the name was the time and location of the show in simple black letters. I took in the whole thing. It looked professional, like the album posters in the window of The Record Collector.

"I didn't know you could really draw," I said.

"Just lettering and stuff. I can't do faces or anything."

"This is incredible," I said.

"Tell Jared you did it."

I looked her in the eyes.

"I can't take the credit for this," I said.

"He'll never use it if he thinks it's mine," she said.

She handed me the poster. "Jared has some money up there

somewhere," she said. "I've seen him counting it. This time he foots the bill."

I held the poster delicately between my thumb and forefinger. She had drawn it on thick paper, but I didn't want it to wrinkle or tear. I held it at my side as I left the room.

"Hey," she said when I was out in the kitchen. "I'm sorry about last night, okay? But if you're going to be mad at me forever, then just shove it up your ass."

She shut her door before I could accept or unaccept what I guessed to be an apology. She left me in the kitchen with her artwork. So I walked back upstairs and waited until Janice was finished with her meeting. Then I slipped in and made my petition to Jared. He seemed skeptical at first, but I knew there was no way he could veto the poster. It was too good. I had seen his drawings in his songwriting notebook and they were crude childish things. This one made us appear like a real band. It suggested what we wanted most: professional credibility.

In the end he only had one addition. And he didn't even tell me what it was ahead of time. He just went to his small desk, grabbed a marker, and wrote something else at the bottom of the poster.

"There," he said. "Now it's a good poster."

Jared smiled and dropped it on his bed. There were two new words written under the talent show information. Block letters. All caps. They read:

FREE BEER!

27. *Weightless on the Ground*

EACH ONE OF US IS THE CENTER OF OUR OWN UNI-
verse. That's the only way it can be. From our point of view, we are
stationary and everything else is swirling around us, dropping into
our lives just for our reaction. This isn't true in a scientific sense, but
Fuller said it was how things really feel when we're alive every day.
That's why it's easy to forget about things that don't directly revolve
around us. War. Famine. Everything else we're too self-absorbed
to ponder. For me, the major element that had escaped my orbit
recently was Nana. Sure, she existed somewhere back in the abandoned wings of my memory, but I was trying my best to keep her
locked there during my stay with the Whitcombs. To think about
her daily, and about what I had done, was too painful.

I had been successful at blocking her out, of recent, but that
didn't mean she would disappear completely. And it didn't mean
that everyone else was keeping Nana shut away, too. I realized these
things fully the next evening after dinner. There were two days left
before the contest, and as I cleared the table, I was already thinking
about band practice. Meredith was rinsing plates for the dishwasher,
and each time I brought a new load from the table, she greeted me
with a small closed-lip smile. I piled the dishes in the sink beneath
her, and tried not to catch any mist from the spray head.

My orbit was very small that night. Nearly everything was happening in my head. I wasn't much aware of the external, so when Janice touched me on the shoulder, I was brought back to reality in a rush. I dropped a bowl of green beans and the stray leftovers bounced off the carpet like grasshoppers. The bowl stayed in one piece.

"I'm sorry," she said. "I didn't mean to startle you."

"That's okay."

I bent down to scoop up my mess, one bean at a time. She hesitated for a second, watching me, but I could tell she had something else to say. She came out with it when all the beans were back in their bowl.

"I'd like to go for a walk if that's okay with you."

I looked up at her from below. Her smile slackened.

"Of course," I said.

"You can leave the rest for Meredith," she said.

She took the bowl gently from my hands and rested it back on the table. Only minutes ago we had all been joking at the table over a story Meredith told about dissecting cows' eyes in her biology class. That levity was completely gone now.

"Jared's waiting upstairs for his lesson," I said.

"He can keep waiting," she said.

I followed her to the closet by the front door and donned my coat. I was wearing Jared's pants again, so I pulled my socks up this time before stepping out into the cold. I stuffed my hands in my pockets. It was getting dark early now, and even though I had noticed this before, I was surprised anew when Janice and I stood on the porch.

"Oh," she said, just after stepping out, "look at that."

I looked where she was pointing and saw a small metal angel lying on the smooth concrete of the porch. We both glanced up. The angel had come unclasped from the wind chime. Janice scooped it up with a mittened hand and held it up to try to reattach it, but it was broken. She eventually surrendered the metal silhouette to her jacket pocket. The other angels held still on their rungs. They did not clang. Janice stepped off the porch and hiked toward the sidewalk. I caught up to her and walked by her side.

We didn't speak for the first couple of blocks. She took faster strides than I did, walking with a contagious sense of purpose, and I felt myself scrambling to keep up. The air was misty. Not enough to really affect my vision, but just enough to make the streets I'd only recently walked with Meredith seem a touch unfamiliar. The trees disappeared into a gray broth of sky at the top, so it was hard to tell how high they went up. It could have been miles. I was looking up when Mrs. Whitcomb finally started talking.

"I've been asking myself a lot of questions lately, Sebastian," she said.

She kept walking, just a step ahead of me.

"What kind of questions?" I asked.

"Questions about a lot of things. But mostly about you."

I started to feel a little anxious. And I had the irrational thought that I wouldn't be returning to the Whitcombs' house after this walk. I was sure of it suddenly, and I felt the urge to turn around and sprint back.

"I've been asking myself what my intentions are. And if . . . I'm really helping you at all."

I felt my feet clapping the sidewalk. I was starting to speed up.

"Well, you shouldn't have . . . doubts about that, Mrs. Whitcomb," I said, faster than I wanted to. "You've done so much. I can't even tell you."

She listened to me, but I could tell she was not going to be pushed from her intended path. She waited for me to cease talking, and picked up where she had left off.

"I had always thought I could do something for you. I wanted to reunite you with your grandmother, and help you find a way to work through your difficulties. I thought I could do it. But I forgot all about that for a while. I was distracted. I've been so distracted lately. And it was good to see you and Jared so close."

She was quiet a moment, possibly imagining Jared and me together.

"But I need to wake up," she said. "I've been in this kind of *trance* the past few years, just letting everything happen to me. I need to trust myself to make some decisions, even if they're hard ones. Maybe I'm not explaining this very well, but it's what I've been thinking about."

I started to formulate a response to all this in my head. But before I could utter something out loud, she leveled me.

"I met with your grandmother," she said.

I waited for the information to set in. But it didn't really. I found myself unable to imagine the circumstances in which this would have happened.

"You went to my house?" I said.

"I did," she said. "I've been trying to call for the last week, but she never picks up. The one time she did, she called me some unpleasant names without even listening to me. So I drove over and knocked on her door. *Your* door."

I still couldn't picture it. I couldn't see Nana springing to life from her bed and coming to answer. I couldn't see her inviting Janice in.

"Your house is a map of the world now, Sebastian. Did you know that?"

"The Geoscope," I said. "Is it completed?"

"I think so," she said. "She told me she was planning a second coat on a few countries, but that was basically it. It looked like a real globe. It was breathtaking in its own way, really. An accomplishment."

We were a good five blocks from the Whitcomb house now. Everything behind us was encased in brume. The mist felt cold on my exposed skin.

"She misses you," said Janice. "She wants you to come home."

"She said that?"

Janice touched me again. This time on the back. I felt a lump rising in my throat. Suddenly, it dawned on me why Nana would have let her in the dome. Me. She was hoping for some information about me. She had gotten to the point where she would welcome strangers into our house to see if they knew anything.

"She never really intended for you to leave," said Janice. "Maybe for an afternoon. She told me that her moods have been uncontrollable. And she told me about the newspaper article. It hurt her more than you could believe, Sebastian. She felt like her whole life had been called fraudulent. Like all her ambitions had been trampled in that moment."

I thought back to that day. Her exhausted eyes. Her crumpled body under the blanket, sitting on the dirty ground. I tried to shake the image free.

"I'll be going back to a world of isolation," I said. "You know that, right? That's where she's asking me to return. That's what . . . you're asking."

Janice stopped walking. We were all alone in the street, between two sidewalks. When she looked at me, I could see that her eyes were moistening.

"I can talk to her about that," she said. "She just . . . doesn't remember what it's like to have a teenager. I'm sure if we just talk all of this over . . ."

"It's okay," I said. "I know I can't stay with you. I understand that."

She sighed, and backtracked a couple of steps. She pulled her hat down tighter over her braid. "She's your guardian," she said. "She has great plans for you."

She was sniffling now. That resolute quality I had heard in her voice in the last day was disappearing again.

"Does Jared know?" I asked.

She shook her head and paused a moment. "Just Meredith," she said.

"Meredith knows?"

"She wanted to see the dome. She was curious. She waited in the car while I went in to meet with your . . . Nana. She wanted to see where you lived."

"How long has she known?"

"We went yesterday after school."

I thought about the poster. Her apology. Her smile. It was all pity. She knew I was being taken from her world. Sent back to my "eccentric" life on the town's fringe. For now I couldn't bring myself to think about everything I would be going back to. And everything I was going to miss. It was too overwhelming. Instead I had to buy some time, hold off the inevitable just a little longer.

"I'll go back next week," I said. "Give me the rest of this one."

Janice breathed into her mittens to warm them.

"I'm not sure your grandmother is going to agree with that."

"Please," I said. "Give me time . . . to tell Jared. I can't just leave him like this."

I knew I was being manipulative now, but I couldn't help it.

"I don't want him to think I'm just walking out on him."

She seemed to consider this deeply. I didn't know if she was thinking about her husband, but the pained expression was back on her face. She breathed again into her mittens. They smoked with frozen air.

"Friday," she said.

I watched her closely.

"Friday, I'll take you back. That gives you two days to tell Jared. I'll talk to him when you're done. I'll tell him there was nothing else we could do."

"All right," I said. "Friday."

She came up to me then and gave me a hug. She hadn't hugged me since I had moved in. Only those few times before, when she was trying to save my soul. I let myself be enveloped in her tan wool coat. It scratched against my cheek. It felt good. And I realized I couldn't blame her for any of this. She had already done much more than I expected. She had a host of her own difficulties. This was my problem alone.

"She thinks you're going to save the world," said Janice.

"I know," I said.

She let go, and the warmth of her coat left me.

"I wish someone had thought that about me," she said.

We fell into stride and were silent the rest of the walk back. When I looked at Janice, I got a sad smile, so I stopped looking. I just concentrated on my feet, laying down one shoe after another. My orbit had opened and spanned the globe, or at least all of North Branch.

When I finally made it inside and up the stairs, Jared was waiting with his math book open and his headphones on. He was studying by himself, sitting cross-legged, muttering words too loudly. He couldn't hear himself over the music pounding in his ears. I listened to him read: "Octagon. Nonagon. Decagon."

He didn't notice as I entered the room.

"A triangle is the only polygon that is coplanar . . . coplanar. What the hell is coplanar?"

"It means lying in the same plane," I said.

Jared looked up, startled. He plucked a white headphone out of his ear.

"Man," he said, "you scared me. I thought God was finally answering a question of mine. All this time and he finally decides to give me a geometry answer."

"It's just me," I said.

He squinted behind his glasses.

"Your nose is red," he said. "It looks like the end of a dick."

"I went for a walk."

"That's great. Some people have to pass math placement tests so they don't end up in Special Ed. But, you know, walking is great exercise."

I lay back on the bed and looked up at the ceiling. There were only a precious few nights left before my view would be the Arctic Circle, with trees and stars above it. I had just been getting used to the white paint of Jared's ceiling.

"Have you asked your mom if we can play in the talent contest yet?"

"I'm waiting for the right time," he said.

He closed the book and took the other headphone from his ear.

"I was wondering today," he said.

"Everyone seems to be wondering," I said.

"Don't interrupt me."

He closed his eyes a moment.

"I was wondering why you aren't going back to school along with me."

"Impossible," I said.

"Why! You're not being homeschooled anymore, so you should go to school when I do. What are you going to be, some kind of creepy-ass vagrant who wanders around and bothers people?"

"No, but . . ."

"Listen," he interrupted. "At least then we'd each have a god-damn ally. That's all you need really to survive in high school, I think, is one other person. Someone you can talk to while you walk down the hall. Without an ally, you're a target."

"Jared, I'm not sure that can work."

"Why the hell not?"

I froze. We still had to practice for the show. That was the only thing left that I cared about. If I said something now, the whole night would be shot.

"I think only a guardian can register me for school," I said hesitantly.

He adjusted his glasses. "Well, I'll go get Janice to take care of it, then. I'll do it right now if it's such a big damn deal."

He got up from the bed and started toward the door.

"Wait," I said.

He turned around.

"Talk to her about the talent show first. You don't want to over-whelm her. Don't request everything at once."

He looked out and down the hallway.

"Maybe you're right. I don't want her brain to explode."

"Let's just practice tonight," I said. "Talk to her tomorrow."

"What about geometry?" asked Jared. "We've got one more chapter."

I followed his eyes to the bright blue book, sitting in the middle of the bed. I knew I didn't have another lesson in me. It was all too cold and meaningless. I needed more than ever to play some loud music and not think of anything else. If I had possessed the power to do it, I would have wiped geometry off the planet. Poof! No more angles. No more vertices. No universal patterns for all mankind. Instead, I just shrugged and said, "Fuck geometry."

Jared looked at me, his brow raised. He eventually smiled.

"Too bad we don't need another song," he said. "That would be a killer title."

"Jared," I said.

"What?"

"I'd like to go to school with you. Don't think I wouldn't. That's not . . . what I meant to convey."

"I know," he said. "I get it. Nothing ever goes the way I want it to. I know how life works by now."

He set about plugging in his guitar, letting the hair hang over his glasses as he twiddled knobs on the amplifier. I watched his fingers move deftly over the controls, putting everything back in a perfect balance.

28. On the Verge of Something

BY MIDAFTERNOON THE NEXT DAY, NOTHING HAD been determined. The issue of the performance had not been raised. Our songs still needed improvement. And Jared's condition was tenuous. We had a little over twenty-four hours until our hypothetical performance, and we were mired in confusion and doubt. But that didn't stop us from piloting the Voyager into downtown North Branch that Wednesday to replace our old posters with the new ones that Meredith had created. Despite the uncertainty of everything else, at least our branding strategy could stay on track. Hype, said Jared, was everything.

The idea was to wallpaper the town. No post unposted. We were using full color this time, maximizing all our efforts. Meredith was right about Jared's undisclosed stash of money. He explained it all to me from the back of my bike. Every time he was in the hospital, his relatives on his dad's side sent cards laden with cash. They knew about his father's behavior, and they felt guilty. They assuaged this guilt by parting with crisp twenty-dollar bills. Jared had been saving the money for an escort service. But if our performance was a success, he decided, he might be able to grope some girls who didn't charge. It was an investment of sorts.

His hands were steady on my back as I pedaled through a rare mild winter afternoon. The weather seemed to be tempering itself in response to Jared's health. It must have been in the midforties, but Jared still wore a sweatshirt hood pulled snug over his head. The fabric covered half the lenses of his glasses, but there was a perfect space for his cigarette, which dangled on his lip, the breeze inflaming its embers. He had been trying to cut back on his smoking since the hospital visit, and this was his first cigarette in days. I could tell he was savoring it because every few puffs he actually moaned with pleasure.

"Ohhh," he said, after expelling one cloud that made it all the way to my handlebars before whipping past my face. "Tar."

We chose to poster parked cars first. Perfecting a quick set of three movements, we lifted the wiper blade with a gloved hand, inserted the overlarge poster, and slapped the blade back with a loud *whap*! The design faced down so that once you entered your car you'd be greeted with our artwork. Next we set our sights on the small stretches of quaint white fencing that the city had erected around the small public park. On one particular section, we made a continuous row of posters, twenty-five sheets long. Looking over the fencing from across the street, our name seemed to form a chant.

THE RASH THE RASH THE RASH THE RASH THE RASH.

After an hour or so, we had less than twenty left, and they needed to be placed in the most strategic of locales. We thought: fast-food restaurants, bar windows, grocery stores. Anything that people utilized daily and in large numbers. We were scouting and discussing when I spotted The Record Collector across the street. Specifically, I spotted the row of posters that lined the tall glass display window.

"We need one right there," I said.

I pointed and Jared nudged the hood up over his glasses.

"Hell no," he said. "The guy who runs that place is a complete ass-hat. He wouldn't let me buy a Black Flag album once unless I came back with my mom."

I looked in and saw the same overweight man with the stocking cap.

"We need our poster up with those other famous bands, side by side," I said. "It's the ideal last spot. You know it's true."

"We don't want to be next to those bands," said Jared. "They're all corporate shills who write songs about missionary sex with their ladies."

"What are you talking about?"

"The guy's a total ass-hat," Jared said, turning away from me.

"Well, I'm going in to ask," I said.

I began my trek across the street, pushing my bike next to me.

"Dammit, Sebastian," Jared said.

I didn't turn around but I could already hear his sneakers scuffing behind me. I walked directly to the shop without breaking stride, leaving my bike by the window. Inside, the air was choked with the same flavor of incense as last time. The music was earsplitting dissonant guitar sounds. The guy who had sold me my first CD was pressing price labels on discs by hand, and each neon orange sticker was crooked and misshapen. When I sidled up to the counter, he was trying to peel one off of his middle finger.

"Hey," he said. "I'm on break right now."

He looked down at me and then back to his thick finger.

"Well, I'm just inquiring about possibly hanging up our band's poster in the window. We have a performance coming up, and we're trying to draw a bit of a crowd."

The man finally got the sticker off his finger and onto the plastic. He adjusted his stocking cap. "Listen up," he said, "because I'll say this one time: the display window is for labels that pay for advertising. Not for any poseur with a garage band. Okay? So sorry about that and everything."

I was about to speak again, when Jared cut me off.

"It's not for *our* band," he said. "We just told the band we'd try to get their posters up around town. They're a hard-core act from D.C. Maybe you heard of them. The Rash."

"No," he said, "I haven't."

He chuckled to himself.

"Oh, you haven't?" Jared said. It was the most condescending voice I'd ever heard him use. "Wow, what is this? A music store for retirees? Is there anyone actually following the scene in here? Or are you into contemporary Christian mainly?"

"Hey," he said. "Listen, you little gnome, I saw Fugazi play for a crowd of twenty people before your parents even did it. So give it a rest, and take a hike."

"Okay, fine," said Jared. "You were cool in 1991. But maybe you should try listening to new music once in a while. Music didn't die when you turned thirty. This show is the coolest thing that ever happened to North Branch and you're not going to put up a poster? Maybe you should work at a Wal-Mart."

He was giving Jared his full attention now.

"I never even heard of their album," he said. "It's not in any of our catalogs."

"Limited release seven-inch," said Jared.

I knew enough to stay out of the way now. I had no idea what he was talking about. The guy pulled another neon sticker off his sheet and placed it on a CD. The sticker folded over itself, into a useless blob. Suddenly, he threw the sheet of stickers across the store. It fluttered to the ground somewhere in the Folk section.

"I keep telling the owner that we need to carry vinyl," he said.

"But the idiot won't listen! Maybe if he had any taste we could actually do something cool with this place . . . It pisses me off to no end! I'm tired of it."

"A real shame," said Jared.

The guy looked down at us again. I turned my head so he wouldn't recognize me.

"Gimme that stupid poster!" he said.

Jared handed him one. He held it up, reading it slowly from top to bottom.

"They're playing a Methodist church?" he asked.

"Pure irony," said Jared.

The guy nodded.

"Save some cred," said Jared. "Support real music for once."

The song on the stereo ended, leaving the small shop in silence. The large man stared at his window, full of professional banners and 3-D cardboard displays. There was a wistful look in his eyes. I wondered for a moment if he was going to cry.

"Dammit," he said finally. "Fine. Put it up. What do I care? I got to get out of here anyway. I need to move to Des Moines or something."

"Great decision," said Jared. "You're right back in the fold, man."

We walked to the window and took down a poster of a half-naked woman on a beach. We put ours up in its place. Then we left our man grumbling to himself at the counter. Outside, we stood by my bike, just looking at our poster in the window. Our breath fogged the glass. Jared lit another cigarette. In spite of his initial protest I could tell he was pleased. Validated in some way. The poster looked not dissimilar to the others hanging up. As far as anyone else knew, we had an album for sale inside. Jared nodded his head to the record store clerk. The guy nodded back and mouthed something that looked like "right on."

"Total ass-hat," said Jared.

WE MADE SURE MY BIKE WAS SAFELY STOWED BACK in the garage a good hour before Janice came home from work that afternoon. We required at least a half hour for the next item on the agenda: a full dress rehearsal of our act. It would be complete with hairstyles, attire, and a run-through of the songs just as we would perform them at the talent show. But first, Jared sent me downstairs with a bottle of hair gel and a pair of scissors I was supposed to use to cut up my band shirt. I had pressed for a full explanation, but Jared only said, "Not now, Sebastian," and then belched.

In the bathroom, I sat down on the toilet and jabbed the dull blade of the scissors into the fabric of my T-shirt until it tore and frayed. I cut a hole over my heart and one under my armpit to be used as an air vent. Then I poked one more at random that turned out to be directly over my right nipple. Next I squirted a handful of pink coagulated ooze into the cup of my palm and shaped my hair into a ridiculous tower that leaned to the left no matter how much I tried to straighten it. It wasn't exactly the Mohawk that Jared had asked for; I didn't know how to classify it, exactly. But I exited the bathroom and tried not to move my head as I took the stairs one at a time.

Back in Jared's bedroom, I found my front man asleep in the fetal position at the end of his bed. He was drooling, and his ears were still red from the cold. His glasses had dropped off the side of the bed and onto the dark carpet below. I picked them up. Then I flipped on the humidifier on the other side of the room. I sat down on the bed and felt my hair shift to the side. I put a hand on Jared's shoe. He looked so peaceful in repose. Not at all like the dour insult-spitting kid from a half hour ago.

"Jared," I whispered.

His left eyelid quivered.

"Jared, I'm leaving in two days."

I listened to his breath, coming in like a gasp, going out like a sigh. Gaassp. Sighhhh. Gaassp. Sighhhh. I ran my fingers through my hair and came out with a handful of slime. I wiped it on my pants and sighed. "I don't know what to do," I said. "I wish I did. But I've reached an impasse."

I got up and left the room, turning off the light on the way out. I needed to wash my hair. That was the only thing I was completely sure of. It was hard to feel properly melancholy when you looked as ludicrous as I did. And when you were confused, the last thing to do was dress up in costume. It was time to find my old clothes, wherever they'd gone. I gripped the banister and dragged my feet down the stairs.

"Very nice," I heard, the second my foot hit the kitchen tile.

Meredith was drinking a glass of milk. Her schoolbag lay on the floor. Her shoes looked like they'd walked off her feet and died halfway to the fridge.

"All you need now is some eyeliner," she said.

I tried to make it out of the kitchen without turning around, but I couldn't. And when I did, I nearly buckled. In all my days at the Whitcomb house, I had never seen her look so pretty. Her hair was up, gathered behind her head in some kind of bun. Her eyes were glistening from the warmth of the kitchen. There was just a smudge of pink lipstick left at the center of her bottom lip. She had a pencil-thin milk mustache.

I wanted to fall at her feet.

"You knew I was leaving," I managed. "Why didn't you tell me?"

I must have looked like a fool with my debilitated hairdo. But Meredith didn't laugh at me. She slowly wiped her mouth with the back of her hand.

"Why would I tell you sooner than you needed to know?"

"I don't need your pity," I said.

"I didn't say you did."

I eyed her. "I see through the act," I said.

"What act?"

"Your poster-making act. Your dish-washing smiley act. Maybe it's good I'm leaving."

She set her milk down on the table with a bang.

"Why would you say that?"

"This hasn't exactly been the most dignified experience for me."

Now she looked up at my hair, at my torn shirt. "I see what you mean," she said.

"I'm getting in the shower," I said.

"Wait," she said, "I was just kidding."

I walked out of the room, but right away I heard her chair slide back on the kitchen floor. My eyes were burning. I stopped at the bathroom door, then went inside and closed it. I took off my shirt and pants. I slipped off a pair of Jared's boxers and wrapped a towel around my waist.

"Fine," she said from outside the door. "It might be true, but it's not because of me. I don't have to act any certain way for you. I don't have to be what you expect."

"Consistency!" I yelled. "Can't you just ignore me all the time?"

"Maybe I'm a fickle woman. Have you ever thought about that?"

She was right outside the door now. I pushed the shower curtain aside and started the water. It screeched through the pipes and erupted onto the floor of the tub. It was so completely different from the misting shower in the dome. I still couldn't get over it.

"Maybe I can't be consistent about anything," she said. "Don't take everything so personally. Don't you know our whole family is completely screwed up? Are you blind or something?"

I held my hand out to test the water and felt it growing warmer. The air directly above the tub was already starting to steam. I took the few steps back to the door and opened it a crack. Meredith was still standing there.

"I don't think you're screwed up," I said. "I like it here."

"I can't begin to understand why."

"I can't help it," I said. "And I like you."

"Another mystery."

"It shouldn't be."

She frowned.

"Why do I always have to say the right thing?" I asked. "I haven't learned how to do that yet."

She pushed the door open wider and I took a shocked step backward. She stepped into the bathroom. The room was hot, but the air from the hall was cool. Meredith leaned forward in a blur and pressed her lips to mine. I made an involuntary noise that I can't really describe, except to say that it was not a flattering one. But her lips held. They were wet and they stayed glued there for the longest three seconds of my life. One. Mississippi. Two. Mississippi . . . She pulled them off with a small smack, and then came back for one more. Her mouth opened and so did mine, and I felt her tongue come in and lazily circle once around my mouth. Her breath had no taste. But it was hotter than the steam from the shower. I saw her pink cheeks and the dark blue makeup over her eyelids. Her eyebrows were blond and thin. She smiled shyly and stepped back into the hall.

"You really live out there in that dome?"

"I did," I said. "I will again."

"Are you from another planet, Sebastian?"

"Maybe."

I pulled the door slowly closed and I could just barely hear her socks on the wood floor as she walked away. I stood next to the pouring shower. Gradually, I found myself regaining feeling in my fingertips. It spread down my arms and through the rest of my body. I threw the curtains aside and jumped inside. And for the next ten minutes or so while I washed the gel out of my hair, and pushed my face into the torrents of hot water, I forgot all about everything else that was happening in my life. I just stood in the water, watching my skin turn pink, thinking about her.

29. The World's Forgotten Boys

LATER THAT NIGHT, LYING TEN FEET AWAY FROM A sleeping Jared, I was not so clear-minded. The reality of the deal I had made with Janice was beginning to set in. I had trouble visualizing my return to the dome, even after such a short time away. It was obscured now. One of the original advantages of living in a geodesic dome was the "invisible barrier" it provided between the inside and outside worlds. Of any shelter out there, it allowed the most immediate connection with our environment and firmament. Its creation was even inspired by terrestrial and celestial spheres.

However, I remembered that as Buckminster Fuller's career had progressed, he'd begun dreaming of grander and grander domes. And his original idea of environmental connection seemed to be replaced by one of control. In 1952, for example, Ford Motor Company hired Bucky to design a ninety-three-foot geodesic dome over its headquarters in Michigan. In 1959, he was commissioned to create a two-hundred-foot dome for a U.S. trade fair in Moscow. The domes kept growing. And flush with the success of his ever-towering space-age creations, Fuller became drunk with his own hubris.

He dreamed someday of encasing all of mid-Manhattan under an enormous "skybreak bubble," so New Yorkers could live in a virtual year-round garden. Energy costs would plummet. Tinted

panels would fight skin cancer. In this way, man's entire environment would be under complete command. Nana had never spoken much about these later ideas of Bucky's. Whether this was for
personal or professional reasons, I did not know. It was as if after
they parted ways, he (and his inventions) had ceased to exist. And I
wondered now how she had been able to sustain her devotion after
he was gone. What was it that had kept the connection alive?

I noticed after a while that Jared had become restless, his breathing troubled. He rolled over to the edge of his bed and coughed.

"Jared?" I whispered into the darkness. "Are you suffering from
insomnia?"

"I'm suffering from your presence," he returned. "You're mumbling to yourself."

"Sorry."

He rolled toward me, winding himself up in the sheets.

"I've been thinking of some things to do onstage," he said, and
cleared his throat. "So far I have crowd diving, playing a solo with
my teeth, and spitting on the crowd."

"I don't know about that last one," I said.

"Why? What's wrong with my sputum?"

I noticed he wasn't speaking in his usual sarcastic way. There
was something gone from his speech, some vibrancy.

"You know the next thing for us to do," I said, "is produce some
tapes. I think you convinced that record store worker that we were a
legitimate band. He would probably sell some homemade compact
discs in there."

"I asked for a four-track recorder for Christmas last year," Jared
said. "I didn't get it."

"Oh."

"Maybe my dad will pony up the dough if I write him a weepy

letter," he added. "But I doubt it. He doesn't really write much anymore."

I thought again of Janice's conversation with her husband. If he couldn't handle Jared's health insurance, it seemed unlikely that he would buy his son any expensive recording equipment.

"Ooh," he said, "but maybe I could write the Make-A-Wish Foundation. They're overdue to throw me a bone. If they send kids to Disneyland they could probably spare a couple hundred bucks for a four-track. I think you have to be a happy person to be considered, though. That might be a hurdle."

Jared lay quiet for a long time after that. And I thought, after a while, that he might have gone to sleep. It wasn't necessarily an unwelcome development. But eventually he shifted around in bed again.

"I'm not sure we should play tomorrow," he said.

I turned over on my side.

"What are you talking about?" I said. "The whole town is covered in our posters."

"Yeah, I know," he said. "But maybe it's not such a hot idea."

"What's wrong? Are you feeling ill?"

"I feel fine, doctor."

"Okay. Then we just require more practice," I said. "We can practice right now even, with no amps."

Jared sighed and then crawled out of bed. I could barely make out his scrawny form as it lurked over to the window. Then I heard the flint of his lighter and saw his puckered mouth in the yellow light. His eyes always looked so small without his glasses. He lit a cigarette and opened the window. The air had grown chillier, and the wind through the screen raised the hairs on my arms.

"Has it ever occurred to you, Sebastian, that I might be a tremendous fucking fraud?" he said.

I watched him blow a mouthful of smoke into the street-lit night.

"No," I said, "it has not occurred to me. Because you're not."

He didn't appear to be listening to me.

"What I've always loved about punk is that you can totally redefine yourself, right?" he said. "You are whatever your songs say you are. Like Iggy Pop. He can wear a white leotard and roll around on broken glass and that's who he is that night. He's broken-glass-leotard guy. But it's all just onstage. Do you know Iggy Pop's real name?"

"No."

"It's James Osterberg," he said.

"So what?"

"So you can use all of this as a way to blow immense amounts of smoke up your own ass."

"I don't understand."

He wasn't looking at me now. "My mom's right about one thing," he said. "I can't let my condition define me. She has a point there, for once. But that doesn't mean I have to pretend to be someone else entirely. I can't hide behind all of this band stuff forever. It's such . . . such an obvious load of bullshit sometimes."

He stopped talking and just looked out the window into the yard. I wanted to hear more of what he had to say, but I didn't encourage him to go on. Mainly because I understood some of what he was speaking about. It was extremely easy to get lost in the reverie of creating music and making a new image for yourself. It was even easier to forget about all the real problems you faced, the things that actually made up your days. It could, sometimes, feel like a giant lie.

"But no one knows him by that name," I said.

"Who?"

"James Osterberg."

"That's his name, though."

"It doesn't matter. Reality is boring," I said, "and mean. And he defeated it. Is that so wrong?"

"I don't know," said Jared.

I was losing him. I could hear it in his voice. And I wasn't sure I believed my own argument. I threw the covers down to my feet and I got out of my cot. I found my way over to his spot by the window, and I hunched down right by him.

"I saw my sister kiss you today," he said. "I was walking by. Are you guys doing the nasty now?"

I perked up and immediately looked away from him.

"No," I said softly. "It was just that one kiss."

"Relax," he said. "There's obviously nothing I can do about it. And I don't know if I really care anymore. In a couple of weeks, I'll be gone all day. Who knows what's going to happen?"

I held my tongue. When I looked down, Jared was holding something out to me. It was his cigarette. I took it from his fingers, careful not to burn myself.

"She treats you like crap," he said.

"I'm aware of that," I said.

I brought the cigarette up to my mouth.

"Don't smoke the filter this time," he said.

"I won't."

I took in a small bit of smoke, and it came right back out of my lungs in a single husky cough. Jared laughed. He patted me on the back too hard. I brought my head down close to the cold screen, trying for a breath of fresh air. Suddenly, I noticed something outside, up on the largest branch. Two objects, knocking together. Meredith's track shoes. They were back out there, swaying back and forth. For good luck, if she could be believed. And I decided to believe her that night. Because I needed to. In my mind, they were up there for both Jared and me. I didn't point them out, though, and I wasn't sure if Jared noticed. He finished his smoke and closed the window without making a sound.

"Don't listen to me tonight," he said. "I'm in a mood."

He extinguished the cigarette in the bottom of a soda can. Then he turned to me one last time. "I just want something real to happen," he said. "Can you understand that?"

"Yes," I said, watching the shoes sway, the laces intertwining, spinning the sneakers slowly around. "I can."

THE SKY WAS RED WHEN I WOKE UP, ONLY HOURS LATER. I was wide-awake at dawn, the way I used to be on weekend mornings in the dome. I tried to roll over and go back to sleep, but my body would not submit. So, before anyone else was awake, I showered and dressed in my old clothes, which I found in the Whitcombs' basement, folded in a tight stack on top of the dryer. The blue flannel felt warm and soft against my skin. My old blue jeans fit perfectly, and the cuffs reached all the way down to my shoes. I didn't put anything in my hair. I just let it flop down in its usual shag. I stared at my old face in the mirror. It was there. Unchanged.

My first real thought of the morning was to go outside, get on my bike, and ride off somewhere completely new. Just follow the highway and decamp from town altogether. Now would be the time to do it. No note. No good-byes. As far as I could remember, I had never journeyed out of North Branch. My parents might have taken me places when I was really young, but they were not around to ask anymore. So it was up to me to make some new memories. Maybe Meredith would even accompany me. She seemed just as weary of her life here as I was. The two of us could have adventures. Sid and Nancy. Sleeping in alleys, panhandling in the streets. We could forgo the heroin and the murder, but we would still live completely for ourselves.

I decided to make some scrambled eggs first. I went into the kitchen and began pulling ingredients from the fridge. Eggs. Tabasco. Butter. Cream. Then I located a tube of cinnamon rolls in a bottom drawer, some strips of meat that looked vaguely familiar. I started on the eggs first, and once I began breaking them into the deep metal bowl, I didn't cease until the whole carton was swimming in the bottom. Twelve orange eyes gaping at me. I added the other ingredients that Jared had showed me and poured the whole mixture into a skillet. I put all the meat in a wide frying pan and turned on another burner. I divided up the rolls with a butter knife and spaced them out on a tray like it instructed on the packaging. In ten minutes, I had everything cooking at once. It felt like a small miracle.

Janice was the first to come into the kitchen. Her hair was down and frizzing all over the place, and her eyes were only half open. She wore a long jersey nightgown that reached down to her knees. It took her a few seconds to even notice I was there.

"Sebastian," she said when she saw me. "Oh. What's going on?"

"Breakfast," I answered.

She wandered up behind me and squinted at the eggs, firming in the pan, and the meat, just starting to pop in its fat.

"It's okay," I said. "Sit down."

She didn't say anything else. She just walked over to the fridge, dispensed herself some orange juice and then took a seat at the dining room table. Soon the cinnamon rolls started to fill the kitchen with an oversweet fragrance. It mixed with the smell of the salty meat to make the best breakfast smell I had ever been in the presence of. *Bacon.* The word suddenly came back to me. I had eaten it once, before I lived with Nana. A distant memory of the taste came soon after, and I started to salivate. I flipped the strips with a fork, dodging the grease splatters. Janice watched me calmly from the table, taking satisfied sips of juice from a plastic tumbler.

Jared was the next to arrive. He walked into the room, his glasses on crooked, without a shirt. I hadn't seen his scar since the first time he showed me in his room. It wasn't quite as shocking this time. Just a line down his chest. Didn't everybody have one? I returned to the eggs. They were almost complete. Not yet brown. Nearly the perfect texture. Jared sat down next to his mother and removed the sleep from his eyes with his middle finger. He was totally silent.

Meredith emerged last, just as I was dividing up the eggs onto four plates. She was already dressed for school. Her hair was down like her mother's except over her eyes, where she'd clipped it back with a metal pin. She wore her full makeup and a skintight orange sweater and jeans. Her phone was to her ear. But when she came in and took stock of the quiet surroundings, she hung up. She sat down across from Jared just as I put the eggs and bacon on the table. The rolls were finished, too, but they needed to be iced. So I stayed at the stove while the Whitcombs gradually started to dine.

They ate quickly, which I interpreted as a compliment. I had mastered Jared's recipe after only one try. Or, at the very least, I had made a passable facsimile. I had yet to taste anything, but I could tell for certain that I had done a top-rate job with the rolls. Their scent was fantastic, and when I cut one in half, the consistency was perfect. Moist, but not too doughy. I iced each one with the back of a spoon and a large packet of frosting. Then I delivered them to the table and sat down in the one empty chair. We were all gathered now. I couldn't remember a time when we had eaten breakfast together.

Meredith spoke first. "Mom," she said, chewing a piece of roll. "Here's the deal."

Janice looked up from her plate.

"I think you should let them play at the talent show tonight," she said.

Janice made a noise.

"Now hear me out. Just listen," she said. "Jared is feeling better, okay. That's clear enough. He's taking his meds. And they've been practicing all week. Personally, I think they're terrible, but they seem determined. And if you know anything about your son, you should know that this is really the only thing that he enjoys. And he doesn't enjoy much of anything, so that's saying something."

When she was done speaking, Meredith instantly shoved half a piece of bacon in her mouth and looked down at the table. Jared watched his sister, his fork frozen in midair. Janice looked at both Jared and me, one at a time. Her eyes rested on Jared's scar.

"I don't know," she said. "You make a good argument, but you have to understand that I'm making the decisions of a nurse here, not just a mother. His health comes first, no matter what."

I waited for Jared to make a biting remark, but he stayed silent. Meredith looked at me. I wiped at my mouth spasmodically with a flowered napkin.

"Mrs. Whitcomb," I said. "I don't want anything to happen to

Jared. I really don't. But you can't make him live in fear all the time. He has to be able to . . . risk action. That's part of being human. Taking risks."

"There are degrees of risks," she said. "I don't want him risking his life."

I thought for sure Jared would say something in his own defense now, but instead he took a mouthful of eggs and spoke up with his mouth full.

"This is a great breakfast," he said. "I think we should just sit here and enjoy Sebastian's breakfast. I'm proud of the guy. I really am. Look what he did. He cooked a normal American breakfast. Like a pro. He's like thirty percent less of a freak today."

He raised a glass of orange juice to me then continued eating. No one said anything else. Aside from some extra rolls, the food was almost gone. It was nearly time to disband and go about our days. The last Whitcomb day I would be a part of. Jared was the only one who didn't know that now. I thought it might be a good time to tell him. But before I could reveal this information, Janice reached over and put her hands on his. He looked at her, puzzled. And when she broke down crying, he tried at first to remove his hand. The tears came out of nowhere. One moment, she was blank-faced, the next there were streams down her cheeks.

"I'm just trying to do the right thing," she sobbed. "Don't you see that?"

Jared tried to back up his chair, but Janice didn't let go. He looked at their hands.

"I know you are, Mom," he said. "I know."

She gripped his hand harder.

"I don't know what to do. I have to make all the decisions myself now, and it's not easy. It's not. No one tells you how to prepare for these things. No one can tell you how it works. I can't take it anymore."

Meredith scooted closer to her mother. She rested a hand on her wrist.

"It's okay, Mom," she said. "You're doing a great job. We love you."

Each had a hand on Janice now. She looked down at her plate of half-eaten eggs. She blinked out another tear.

"Your father's been calling for you, Jared," she said. "I didn't tell you because I thought it was going to hurt you. But you're old enough to make your own choices about it. He wants to talk, if you want to call him."

Jared took off his glasses and put them on the table. His expression was hard to read. His brow was knitted, but after a second or two, it relaxed.

"Okay," he said, looking at her. "Thanks for telling me, Mom."

I sat watching them from my spot at the table. And I felt at that moment like I was spying on their private lives. For the first time, I felt a great distance away, like I was looking in at them through their windows. It was an odd sense of displacement. I couldn't believe that they had ever taken me in at all. Maybe they had wanted me to live with them as a buffer, or a distraction. Or maybe they just wanted to appease Jared. But there was something between them that I couldn't share. I wasn't even sure I was in the room anymore.

And at the moment of my invisibility, that brief minute or two when they were together, I had a flash of metaphysical communication with Nana. At least I thought that's what it might be. I was sitting there, watching Mrs. Whitcomb being consoled by her children, then I went inside my own head. That blank white space opened up and in that feeling of nonexistence, I saw Nana lying in her bed, enclosed in the Geoscope. She was not facedown the way she was the night I saw her in the dome. This time, she was on her side. There was a pile of letters next to her on the bed, and she was reading one of them out loud. Just a whisper, but for at least ten seconds, I heard every word.

". . . and I can guarantee you that it is not my child. My wife and I have been unable to conceive for some time. So please think carefully before contacting me again . . ."

I caught a quick glimpse of the room around her. There were tea cups everywhere, with tea bags dangling from the side, or sitting in stained pools on her nightstand. Her hot water bottle was out on the carpet. She was still in her union suit, and her hair was not shaped into the round bouffant she favored. I was seeing her first from in the room, but as the scene began to fade back to white, I left the room through the ceiling, being sucked out of the dome and into the cosmos. I was both outside and inside. External and internal at the same time. Then everything was white again and I was sitting back in the Whitcombs' kitchen. Janice was still holding Jared's hand, and she was repeating herself.

"You can play," she was saying. "If you really feel up to it, you can play, Jared. Things are going to get back to normal around here. I swear they are. Just watch. You'll see."

30. Guitar Gods of North Branch

THE PHILOSOPHY OF BUCKMINSTER FULLER AND THE philosophy of punk rock are not as separate as they may seem at first. I considered this anew while I waited for Jared to finish a practice quiz in his geometry book that afternoon. Once, the two modes of thought seemed as contrasting to me as humanly possible; now I wasn't so sure. For example, both Fuller and the original practitioners of punk believed in the power of the individual over all else. Both had distrust for big corporations, big religions, and the government. Both had a do-it-yourself motto. If something wasn't out there in the world that needed to be, whether it was a new sound or a new form of housing, you were supposed to do it yourself. It is only those who dared to do something different who made real contributions to life and art. In this context, it is very possible that Bucky was a punk rocker in spirit.

And this was, perhaps, where Nana had gotten it wrong. Instead of allowing me to figure things out for myself, to explore life, she had kept me in a bubble filled only with her ideas. Ideas she had culled straight from Fuller. But Bucky didn't want his ideas to be taught this way. In the 1930s, when some of his inventions were starting to catch on, he noticed he was fast becoming something of a guru. He was being followed around by groups of people who took everything he said as doctrine. Thus, he made a resolution on New Year's, 1933, to discourage any blind followers by being as awful to them as possible. By cursing them and acting like a buffoon in their presence, Bucky believed he would ultimately be doing them a favor. No one should see another human being as having all the answers. Even if that person was Buckminster Fuller.

I felt, for the first time, like I might finally be ready to discuss some of these ideas with Nana. If we couldn't tell each other the truth, then there was no way we would be able to live together anymore. Seeing her in my head at the breakfast table that morning had made it clear to me that it was time to return home again. Whether it was clairvoyant communication or just another guilty visual floating around my brain, it was time to check back in and talk about my path once more. There was only one thing left to do before that could happen. And the moment of truth was fast approaching.

The afternoon was already half over and we needed to arrive at the church early to set up our gear. Nervous energy was beginning to build up in me in a severe way. My stomach was tight. My temples pounded. And I had caught myself holding my breath a couple of times for absolutely no reason. I could tell that Jared was starting to think ahead, too. He wasn't concentrating on his quiz. He was doodling in the margins, and skipping any question that gave him trouble. He'd only been working on the problems for twenty minutes or so, but the last ten had been completely silent. Finally he launched his pencil across the room. It bounced off the wall, leaving a gray mark on his D.Y.I. poster.

"Damn!" he said.

"What?"

"We need one last song," he said. "I've been thinking about it, and I know I'm right. I'm absolutely right about this."

"We need to practice the songs we have."

"Balls to that," he said. "What if we have to play an encore?"

"There's no time to write another song."

"We won't write one," he said.

He threw the geometry book from his lap and hopped off the bed. He moved over to a pile of discs, stacked in an unwieldy tower near his closet. He sat down cross-legged on the floor and started weeding through them. In a second, CDs were winging over his shoulder and landing behind him.

"Why are you throwing everything today?" I asked.

He kept sorting until he got to the case he wanted. I recognized the cover from a distance. He opened it up to make sure the actual disc was inside, then he tossed it to me. I managed to trap it against my chest.

"Track five," he said. "Play it."

I could hear the song in my head before it even commenced. But I did as I was told and inserted it into the disc player. The drumbeat exploded out of the stereo in seconds. The bass and guitar started in: *Bom, Bom, Bom-Bom. Da-Dah Dah Dah Dah!* Again and again and again. That menacing sound. "Teenagers from Mars." I looked at Jared with obvious anxiety. The song was fast. Much too fast. And it was also slightly profane. (*"Inhuman Reproduction. We're here for what we want!"*) But mostly, I didn't think I could make my fingers do what fingers seemed to be doing on that song, especially with just an hour or two of practice.

"Listen," he said. "It's the perfect cover for us. Now nut up!"

"I don't know."

"I'll show you," he said. "We'll make the bass part easier. We can cut a couple of notes. I don't have time to argue with you about this."

He picked up my bass and started tuning it. Suddenly, there was a wild look back in his eye, and I knew that I should do whatever he instructed. He was slipping back into character, getting ready to orchestrate this thing properly. I could already feel my muscles relaxing. And when he stood up and placed the bass guitar in my hands, I experienced a touch of that rush I'd first had running through the woodland around the dome. I draped the strap over my shoulder. It hung with a pleasing heft, straining my neck. I ran the palm of my right hand over the strings. I activated my amplifier. Jared grabbed his guitar.

"We know this song," he said. "We know it in our sleep. Just follow me for a while. Find the notes and play what sounds right. It's all on the E string."

Of course, Jared already knew it on guitar. But I was surprised how much his playing sounded like the track on the CD. He adjusted his distortion just right until it had that same crackle, that same power-tool roar. Then he just let loose with his vocals. He even tried for a deep resonant tone in his voice, and it almost worked. He pressed his lips right up to the cheap microphone in his room and belted it out. It wasn't until the second verse that he really started to find his footing.

"*We are the angel mutants!*" he yelled, "*the streets for us seduction.*"

I had trouble keeping up, but I hit the right note more often than not. And when we leaped into the chorus, it all came together. The room was buzzing with something almost musical. Jared was screaming the chorus. *And we don't caaaare Teenagers from Mars!*

And we don't . . . Teenagers from Mars! I jumped up and down, moving my finger from the third to the fifth fret. And for five minutes while we circled through another verse and yet another chorus, I was positive that we were going to conquer the Immanuel Methodist Talent Show. We were going to take the prize money. We were going to record a tape. And then we were going to spend the rest of our years doing exactly this. It was destined to happen.

THE CHURCH WAS EERILY QUIET WHEN WE ENTERED, pushing our amplifiers on their squeaky wheels, our instruments slung over our bony shoulders. I had presupposed that the place would be filled to capacity with milling spectators and performers, but we were one of the first acts to arrive. Janice withdrew from the church as soon as we had wheeled through the front doors (she would be coming back when the action commenced in about one hour; she had "errands" to run). So we were all alone in the hallway leading to the one large space that Immanuel had reserved for services. And when we opened the door to the rows of long empty pews, all I could see was a lone thin girl twirling a baton near the altar, and another larger girl holding a clipboard against her chest.

Above the makeshift stage was a banner that read, "And We Shall Sing His Praises! Winter Talent Contest." The banner was aslant and as Jared pointed out, "Totally fucking wonky." But here we were, making our entrance. I couldn't believe it was actually transpiring.

We guided our gear up the same red carpet (with plastic shoeguard) that the pastor used to enter the congregation on Sunday. Jared had explained the process of a church service to me once, and I had assumed that no one else would be allowed to walk where the pastor walked. But we rolled the heavy practice amplifiers over his path, plodding toward the zenith of the chapel. The stained-glass windows cast a blue light on the pews nearest the windows. I could see the dust floating in the rays of the setting sun. The girl with the clipboard looked up. I recognized her as Lindsey from Youth Group.

"Finally," she said, checking something on her board. "Somebody's frickin' here on time."

She smiled at us, showing two cavernous dimples.

"We should have showed up late," Jared whispered to me. "This is unspeakably lame."

All I could do was nod.

"Names?" she said.

"Lindsey," said Jared. "You know who I am. You spend half of every Youth Group meeting staring at me, waiting for me to do something awful. And this is Sebastian."

"Fine," she said. "Okay. Great."

She marked something on the paper in front of her.

"You guys are third," she said. "You should set everything up ahead of time so you can just come onstage and play your music. And not too loud, please. There's going to be children here, and people from the over-sixty bell choir."

"Don't worry," said Jared. "We're a family-friendly act."

Lindsey gave a hearty thumbs-up. Then she walked away to greet a kid wearing a magician's hat. Jared and I rolled our amps up onto the raised platform.

"Hey," said Jared when we stepped up there. "Look up."

I craned my neck. Hanging above us was an enormous gold cross with a halo over the top. It was suspended in the air with surprisingly thin cables.

"If God doesn't like us," he said, "he's probably going to drop that thing right on your head."

"Why mine?"

"I've been baptized," he said.

We immediately busied ourselves, wrangling some bright yellow extension cords from a supply closet and plugging in our equipment. There was an amplifier planted at each end of the small stage. We leaned our instruments against the amps. Our performance clothes were bundled in a white garbage bag that Jared carried in a big wad under his left arm. He also had his bottle of gel in the bag. We set off to the bathroom to change, but stopped in the hallway when we heard Meredith's voice behind us.

"Hold on, guys," she yelled. "Wait up."

I turned around and she was running toward us.

"What the hell do you want?" Jared said. "Sebastian's busy."

She didn't even glance at me. "I want to be your stylist," she said, huffing. "Please don't dress yourselves. I'm begging you not to."

Jared looked her up and down. She was panting.

"For Christ's sake," he said. "Did you run here?"

"To save you," she said.

"From what?"

"From your own disastrous hairstyles."

She glanced over at me for the first time and I thought I saw a wink. Jared turned to me and then back to her. He was grinding his teeth.

"She made the poster, Jared," I said. "Our poster. She designed it and drew it. I think she knows what she's doing."

He looked at me in disbelief. "You can't be serious," he said.

"When have you ever observed me drawing anything?" I asked.

He returned his gaze to Meredith. "Well, I'll be neutered."

He took off his glasses and rubbed his eyes.

"I just want to help," said Meredith. "I want to be part of it."

They stared at each other for an awkward few seconds. Then Jared thrust the white garbage bag of clothes in her direction.

"C'mon, then," he said. "I know you're no stranger to the boys' bathroom."

We reconvened by the urinals. Jared and I each stood in front of a mirror over a sink. The room reeked of lemon cleaning solution. Meredith dumped the contents of the plastic bag on the counter and frowned down at them. She was regaining her breath, and her face was flushed in the way that drove me completely crazy. She walked around us, examining us like poorly made sculptures.

"First of all," she said, "no Mohawks. I know it's part of the image, but you guys already look like you're ten years old, and that style isn't going to do you any favors."

"Just do what you're going to do, Meredith," said Jared. "And spare us the expert makeover analysis."

She set to work on Jared first, shaping his shock of ratty black hair into something more stylish. She combed it down over his ears and brought it up off of his glasses in front, pushing the bangs to the side. Next she went after his clothes. And because Jared dressed in approximately ten layers whenever he left the house in the winter, there was a motley array to choose from. She pulled his band T-shirt on over a long-underwear shirt, and put a zip-up hooded sweatshirt over that. When she concluded, the changes weren't drastic, but they were noticeable improvements.

She worked on me next, while Jared glumly puffed a cigarette in the handicapped stall. He was displeased, I think, because he had nothing bad to say about his appearance. I could hear him vocalizing our lyrics in a gruff whisper. Meredith actually made use of the gel with me, but she only applied a small dollop. She didn't speak as she worked, and it was all I could do not to reach out and put a clammy hand on her waist. But I knew it wasn't the time. She circled around me, pushing my hair up into a messy batch of spikes, adding bits of the pink stuff here and there. My scalp tingled each time she touched it. When she was done with my hair, she jerked my T-shirt on over my flannel the same way she had done with Jared's. She rolled up my long shirtsleeves and pulled my jeans down a little lower on my hips.

"All right, Jared," she said. "Get out here—I need to see the full effect."

I heard the sizzle as Jared extinguished his cigarette in the toilet bowl. He smacked open the metal door to the stall and stood reluctantly in front of the sink, looking in the mirror. His eyes moved over his reflection. I looked in my mirror next to him, and pushed up a wilting spike. We looked okay. Better, most likely, than either of us had thought possible.

Jared took something out of his pocket. It was his bottle of pills. He dumped out a large one and held it up to the light. I watched him swallow it dry. Then he ran cold water out of the tap and splashed three quick handfuls on his face.

"Be honest, Meredith," he said. "How big of a disaster is this going to be?"

He dried off with a stiff brown paper towel.

"A big one, I would imagine."

He looked over to me and clapped a hand down on my shoulder.

"Then we'll all go down in flames together!" he said.

He let out a high-pitched yelp and punched the paper towel dispenser. The sound echoed across the bathroom. I followed suit, smacking the dispenser and screaming. Jared laughed and slapped me on the back. Then the door behind us opened and the kid with the magician's hat peeked his head inside. He took one look at Jared and me and stayed where he was in the doorway.

"Who are you guys supposed to be?" he asked.

"We're the guys who are gonna beat your ass in the talent show," Jared said. "That's who."

"Oh," said the kid.

He delicately closed the door.

31. The Intervention

WITH FIFTEEN MINUTES LEFT UNTIL SHOWTIME, THE Youth Group volunteers finally fashioned some kind of real stage out of the altar space. They cleared away all of the accoutrements of Sunday service and hung a high black curtain behind the altar to form a backstage area. It wasn't a conventional performance space, but it wasn't a hopeless one, either. The dim lighting and the stained glass provided a mildly theatrical atmosphere. And the large pipe organ that sat off to the left added at least one token music-related object to the surroundings. Finally, the church was, above all else, an intimate venue. The first couple of rows of pews were directly in the action. In fact, we would almost be playing on top of the people sitting there.

They let the small gathering crowd into the place at five minutes until seven. Jared and I watched from the slit down the middle of the curtain. We didn't say anything as we saw our audience file in, laughing and confabbing with one another. As Lindsey had predicted, there was a host of older people. I could hear Jared's breathing steadily accelerate as we watched men with elastic-waisted dress pants enter with their wives who had shapely bouffants that could have rivaled Nana's. Next came a group of eight- or nine-year-olds who insisted on sitting up front, plopping down on their sneakered

THE HOUSE OF TOMORROW

feet only ten feet away from our amplifiers. Last came some mothers and fathers and a handful of people our age, dressed conservatively and entirely unsmiling.

"Where did they find these people?" I asked.

"These are the people who go to my church," said Jared.

"What about our posters?" I asked. "Where are all the music fans?"

Jared shrugged.

"Do we play the same set?"

"Hell yes, we play the same set," he said. "And we play to win."

His voice was a little hesitant, but I didn't question him again. The lights were dimming further, and we ducked out of the curtain opening and in among the other performers. There were a group of girls in matching tracksuits to the right of us. The magician was there, keeping his distance. And a couple of the other members of the Youth Group stood around in white shirts and bow ties, singing scales. Other performers were practicing in classrooms down the hall. We heard footsteps coming onto the stage in front of us, then a tap on the microphone. Lindsey's voice came next, so loud that it sounded like the microphone was lodged in her throat.

"HELLO, EVERYONE," she yelled. "Whoa. Ha! Okay. Welcome to the third annual Immanuel Methodist Youth Group Talent Contest. That's better. Thanks for coming out in the cold weather, and a very special thanks to those who provided snacks, which are out in the hall, by the way. I recommend the peanut butter cookies! It should be quite a show tonight. We have everything from a dance team to real live . . ."

The microphone sent a deafening squawk out over the crowd and Lindsey giggled. "Whoops! Ha! Well, I guess I don't have much else to say except that the winner gets two hundred dollars. And the contest will be judged by applause at the end. Okay. So let's get things started! Our first act tonight is by Holly Halverson, who is going to do her baton act to 'Love and Praise,' by the Modern Apostles. Let's have a round of applause for Holly. Yeah!"

The crowd clapped softly, and I went around to the side of the stage where I could observe the action. The thin girl I had seen twirling the baton earlier was now adorned in a leotard and matching skirt fringed with bright green sequins. She held a long-thin baton out toward the crowd, streamers flowing from the ends. She stood still as a statue until a rolling piano part came from the speakers on the walls of the chapel. Then she started to send the baton around and around in rhythm to the music. The streamers went windmilling with it in a green-and-white blur.

"I can praise and love him," began the song. *"I'll give my everything to him and he will seeeeeeee!"*

As the song picked up, she suddenly sent the baton flying into the air like a helicopter. The crowd gasped as a single thin streamer grazed the bottom of the hanging gold cross. But the metal end of the baton just missed and the whole thing came boomeranging back into her grip without incident. She leaped through the air, her sequined fringe catching the lights and sparkling like a row of emeralds.

"He seeeees me as I am. Beautiful like him. And together he will teach me how to flyyyyyy!"

Up went the baton again, whipping through the air. If you listened closely, you could hear the *whoop-whoop-whoop-whoop* over the swelling orchestration of the song. It spiraled out over the crowd this time. And the spindly girl was in the aisle now, leaping to catch it. For a moment, I thought it might batter an old woman in the second row, but again, the baton landed solidly in the girl's palm.

The crowd hailed her efforts again, louder this time. And when she danced her way back to the stage, the song reaching its crescendo, she was greeted with hoots and whistles throughout the auditorium. Lindsey counted to ten (audibly) and came sprinting back out to center stage.

"Okay," she said. "Yeah! How about that?"

I stopped listening and went back to search for Jared. He was sitting in the same spot with his eyes closed, humming. I squatted down across from him and he opened his eyes, magnified as always behind his glasses.

"Did you see that?" I asked.

He shook his head.

"It was really pretty accomplished. She was throwing this piece of metal around to the song. It seemed fairly popular with the crowd."

"I've seen it before," said Jared. "She does it every year."

On the other side of the curtain, the magician, whose name was Wayne something, was being called to the stage. The crowd clapped at his entrance.

"After this guy," I said, "it's us. Are you prepared? This is it."

Jared didn't answer. He produced his pack of cigarettes and lit one. He stood up and took a deep drag. It was only a moment or two before the performers backstage took notice and started looking over. Lindsey introduced Wayne, and as the crowd quieted, she jogged backstage and spotted Jared right away. She almost dropped her clipboard.

"What the heck do you think you're doing?" she whispered as loud as she could. "You can't smoke back here. This is a Methodist church."

Jared stared at Lindsey for a second and then turned his back on her.

"I know you're leaving," he said to me. "Janice told me today."

Onstage, Wayne was talking about a levitating piece of string. The audience laughed at a joke that I couldn't quite hear. But it ended with the line, "That's why I'm always hanging by a thread with this trick. Ha. Ha. Ha. Ha."

"There's nothing I can do," I said. "I don't have a choice in the matter. Nana has taken care of me my whole life. She's my legal guardian."

Lindsey stepped in front of us. "Hey," she said. "Did you hear me? I said you can't smoke in here. Now put out the cigarette or I'm going to have you disqualified."

People on the dance team were coughing and waving away the smoke. Someone else had appeared with two dogs in matching pink sweaters and one of them started to bark.

"I don't want you to go," said Jared. "This is a goddamn travesty."

"I know," I said. "I'm sorry."

"You're not sorry enough!" he said. "You're my best friend, man. It doesn't matter that I don't have any other friends. Okay? You're such . . . I don't know. You believe in my stupid ideas. You . . . what the hell am I supposed to do without you around?"

Lindsey walked over and tried to grab the cigarette from Jared's hand. Instead she knocked it to the ground. It landed by a dance team girl's foot and the girl screamed.

"Hey," said Wayne the magician from beyond the curtain. "Settle down back there or I might have to saw someone in half."

The audience laughed, and he went back to explaining a cup and ball trick.

"Dammit, Lindsey," said Jared. "Get your righteous ass out of the way. Can't you see I'm trying to have an important moment here with my friend?"

I grabbed Jared by the biceps to hold him back.

"We'll still spend time together," I said.

"Yeah right," he said. "It's going to be back to diddling myself in my bedroom. Endless days of diddling."

"Meredith will be around," I said. "And your mom. They care about you, Jared. You know they do."

"I know," he said. "But we're not friends. It's different. Don't try to make me feel better. It's not going to work. My life is a giant pile of dung now. I wish none of this would have happened at all."

"I'm having you disqualified," said Lindsey. "I made up my mind. I'm going to tell Pastor Ron right now. And you're going to be out of the show. I don't have to take this! I'm president of the Youth Group."

She started walking away, but Jared reached out a hand and grabbed her shoulder.

"Wait, Lindsey," he said. "Just hang on a second."

"Let go of me!" she said.

She tried to jerk away from him, and accidentally hit one of the guys in white shirts in the chest. The kid wheezed. Jared held on. I tried to pull his arm away.

And that's where we were when we heard the sound.

Jared had one hand on Lindsey. I was right behind him, and the dance team was watching in horror. But the sound made us all stop. It was like a thunderclap. Or two thunderclaps in short succession. In reality, it was the sound of the back chapel doors slamming against the wall. The whole crowd quieted at once. Then there was a moment of silence, followed by a shuffling of feet and the sound of the audience murmuring and shifting in their seats.

"Hey," shouted Wayne from the stage. "What's going on? I'm trying to finish my act."

Jared and I let go of Lindsey. And we all walked as if under a spell toward the slit in the curtain. When I got a view, I couldn't believe what I saw. It was a group of ten, maybe fifteen people led by the clerk from The Record Collector, guiding them forward. They were parading down the aisle, between the rows of pews, and they looked like a bunch of vagrants or mental-hospital patients. Some of them were dressed in leather. Others wore blue jeans that had more holes than fabric. There were spiked hairdos, a couple of Mohawks, and a lot of long greasy hair. Some of them were carrying cans of beer in brown paper bags. And even after they saw the look of the rest of the crowd around them, they moved all the way to the front and huddled around the stage.

"What is this?" asked Lindsey. "What's happening? Who are these awful people?"

"Holy mother of crap," said Jared.

Onstage now, Wayne looked like he'd been paralyzed. He held his top hat at his side, gripping the brim tight. He looked over the latest members of the audience. In front of him on the table were three cups, facedown. He took a reluctant step toward them and then tried to continue with his trick as if nothing unusual had transpired. He lifted one of the cups and underneath it was a cotton ball.

"Wait!" he said. "Oh! Hang on, you weren't supposed to see that. I just got a little . . ."

He laughed nervously and fumbled with the cups, accidentally knocking one off the table. It bounced off the carpet and rolled into the aisle.

"Shit," said Wayne, louder than he meant to. "Just let me get that cup back . . ."

He bent down to try to spot the cup, and that was what prompted the first round of boos. It began as just one voice, a random heckling from the new crowd. Then there was another lower and more sustained boo. In a couple of minutes, the whole renegade posse at the front was booing Wayne's magic act. He walked to the edge of the stage, but the crowd wouldn't part for him to get his cup.

"I need that cup back," he said.

"Your cup sucks!" yelled a wiry guy in front of him.

A middle-aged man stood up from the crowd in the back, his bald head shining under the lights. "What's going on here?" he said. "Why don't you leave my son alone?"

Someone from the group threw a bottle cap and it whizzed right over the man's head. Then the whole group started jumping up and down. Wayne had turned a bluish pale color, and he didn't even stop to pick up his cups before leaving the stage from the side. He walked right off the end of the altar and down a side row. He was saying something to himself under his breath the whole way out of the chapel.

Jared and I were completely silent. Our faces were locked in an expression of unabashed awe. I had never seen any of these people around town. I had no idea where they had come from. I was going to ask Jared about this, but before I could get the sentence out, I heard the name of our band uttered for the first time.

"Did you hear that?" I asked.

"Hear what?" he said.

"We want The Rash!" yelled the record clerk.

His crew whistled and shouted and then someone else said it.

"Yeah! Bring on The Rash!"

"Free beer!" someone else yelled.

"That," I said to Jared.

Then they commenced the feet stomping. Quietly at first, a series of muffled steps on the plastic carpet cover. But they got louder, putting all their weight into it. And they were clapping, too, making the wood of the pews vibrate noticeably. Stomp! Stomp! Clap. Stomp! Stomp! Clap. And in the midst of this racket, our name became a kind of chant. "We want The Rash." Stomp. "We want The Rash." Clap.

"Holy mother of all sacred crap," said Jared.

Lindsey had disappeared somewhere. Wayne had left the building. The dance team was long gone. Only the solitary baton girl was still there. She was watching us with her eyes wide. Jared and I turned around to look at her. The chanting grew louder.

"WE WANT THE RASH! WE WANT THE RASH!"

She peeked out of the slit in the curtains.

"Is that you guys?" she said. "Are you . . . The Rash?"

"Yeah," said Jared. "That's our band name."

She looked at the crowd again and then back to us. "Well, you better go out and play, then," she said. "Or these assholes are going to tear down our church."

She turned and walked away from us, her baton streamers trailing behind her. Jared looked at me. "That weird baton girl is right," said Jared. "I think we have to go out there."

"But they think we're a real band," I said.

An intense look was forming on Jared's face. A punk snarl combined with that unadulterated focus that came over him from time to time during our practices. He took long deep breaths. Then he put his hand over his chest, feeling his heartbeat.

"Then I guess we'll have to play like a real band," he said.

32. Spaceship Rock

AS BUCKMINSTER FULLER REACHED THE END OF HIS career, he became more and more unwavering in his beliefs about the metaphysical. Some questioned his sanity, yet he continued to claim he was capable of telepathic transmissions. His most oft-cited example of proof was the metaphysical connection he had with audience members during a speaking engagement. He believed, when he was onstage, that he could look out over a crowd and receive hundreds of shortwave messages from his admirers; the easiest method of transmission was to make eye contact. The eyes, said Bucky, provided the fastest and most efficient form of communication on earth.

On that stage, under the golden cross of Immanuel Methodist, I finally understood something of what he was talking about. The next five minutes under the lights came at me in a series of revelatory images. My head was reeling. I gazed around the crowd at the front of the stage and saw every pair of eyes flitting back and forth from me to Jared. I saw the record clerk's face contorted in a tight-lipped scowl. In his head I saw an image of myself, being booed off the stage while he laughed. I saw one of his friends slurping the foam off the lip of a beer, the white bubbles gathering in his beard. On the inside, this man was terrified for us, pulling for us to do something competent. And in the back row of the pews, there was a line of old ladies whose minds I didn't need to read. Their looks all said exactly the same thing: What in the name of all that is sacred is this?

The whole crowd had quieted when we walked out onstage and picked up our guitars, and that quiet was still around us. Now we were motionless. We stood on opposite ends of the stage. We were thin as rakes, and our boyish faces shone with perspiration. The crowd, I believed, was too stunned to boo.

Jared made the first move. With one shaky swoop, he leaned down and flipped on his amplifier. There was a loud click, then the red light came on and soft buzz filled the air. Jared slowly turned the distortion and the volume all the way up until his V-shaped guitar was producing nothing but feedback. But he didn't turn down the volume. He looked over and motioned for me to plug in.

In a stupor of nervous energy, I couldn't even feel my hand as I turned on my practice amp and slowly notched the volume up. The feedback from my amp was somehow worse than Jared's, more piercing. And I saw people all across the pews clap their palms to their ears. Jared inched his way to the front of the stage and calmly adjusted the microphone down to suit his diminutive posture. He hovered over it, sweat already dripping from the thick strands of his hair. I looked to him for a signal. He put a hand to his forehead and looked out over the crowd.

"Good evening, Methodists!" he said. "We are . . . The Rash!"

The only sound was the feedback, still screaming around him. He was taking pleasure in it, I could see. The noise dipped in register, already playing a deranged song of its own. *WeeeeeOOOHHHweeeeeeeAHHHHHHweee.* Jared looked at me and grinned. Then he put his lips to the mike and shouted, "One-two-three-four!"

He strummed one time, a quick jerk of his forearm, and the feed-back was instantly replaced by the opening note of "Stupid School." It came out unbelievably loud and raw, like the last note sung from a hoarse throat. But it was in tune. He let the riff coast a moment, just like he had with the feedback. Then he started playing his part, frantically sending those sharp little notes into the crowd in wave-lets of noise. My finger fumbled for the right fret, and I joined four beats too late. But we made our way through the opening somehow. Jared waited until we were on beat, then he took a deep breath and leaned into the microphone.

"Mom's taking me to stuuuupid school!"

His voice was unsteady. He sang as loud as he could, but his range wasn't there. I wondered if he could even hear himself over the guitar. We had not adjusted sound levels at all. He kept going and wandered in and out of tune on the next line. And when he screamed that long *"and I wanna dieeeeeee!"* his voice broke off because he was out of breath. I watched him cringe, but he didn't start over. He just barreled into the next part.

"Teacher, teacher, teacher, and I want to die! Teacher, teacher, teacher, and she teaches lies!"

Jared looked at me and I leaned into the mike. I felt the heat rising up my neck until my entire face was flushed. I opened my mouth but nothing came out. Jared glared at me. But then he just turned back to the mike and moved brazenly into the chorus, tap-ping out a rhythm with his foot as he sang.

"Everybody goes to stupid school, then the stupid rule the world. No. No. No!"

It was right after that third "No" when he broke a string on his guitar.

It made a loud pinging noise and flew back, barely missing his eye. He ducked out of the way, and his voice faltered, ending the song more like a question than a bold statement.

"Everybody goes to the stupid school, then the stupid rule the . . . world?"

The music tottered to a stop on an accidental extra note from my bass, followed directly by more feedback from our instruments. Then we stood facing the audience, doing absolutely nothing. The song had collapsed out from under us, and it felt like we had played it in about twenty seconds. It had caved in quickly and we'd been lucky to escape from it alive. I knew this. And Jared knew it, too. I could tell by his dazed stare. Without even looking at his guitar, he reached up and yanked off the remains of the broken string. It made a terrible noise. Like someone snipping a piano wire.

What we needed now was some kind of response from the audience. Any kind. It didn't matter if it was positive or negative, but I knew something had to happen before we could play our next song. I looked for a familiar face, but I couldn't locate Meredith or Janice. For an agonizing five or six seconds, we had nothing. Silence. Maybe it took that long for people to recover and try to assess what they had just heard. But it wasn't until those first agonizing seconds passed that we heard another noise coalescing with the feedback from our guitars. The sound of a small child.

More specifically, it was the sound of a small child shrieking. We had made a toddler weep. And not just one, actually. Soon after the first, two other children started in. This set off a shuffle of mothers scooping up keening babies and whisking them out of the chapel. They were all athletes suddenly, sprinting with their progeny. They filed out, one by one. I watched for Lindsey to come back out and toss us off the stage, to beg everyone to stay. But she was nowhere to be seen.

The renegade bunch in front watched the evacuation with curiosity. But after half the original crowd was gone, they turned back around and examined us. And just when we seemed destined to sink into quiet defeat, a bearded guy, who was twice as large as the record clerk, jumped up in the air. I watched him leap, rising surprisingly high in the air, and spilling a beer on the church carpet (and himself) in the process. When he reached the zenith of his jump, he yelled one triumphant, "Hellllllll yeaahhhh!"

A moment of silence passed, as his friends seemed to gauge his reaction. Jared and I watched him, too. But not too long after he yelled, his yell was returned by a volley of other loud yells. A rejoinder of YEAHs. A real rallying cry. And then the stomping and clapping began again. *Stomp! Stomp! Clap. Stomp! Stomp! Clap.*

Jared walked cautiously back up to the mike. He cleared his throat. "Um, okay," he said. "Thank you. Thanks. This next song is about naked girls, I guess."

"Yeaahhhhhh," yelled the big man again.

Jared looked at me and shrugged. He started to play again. At a higher volume this time, if that was possible. And I noticed a difference right away. He seemed more relaxed, and the sound was better. He didn't try to speed things up; he just left the song at its original tempo. This made it easier for me to find my place, and from the beginning this time, I felt locked in. A to the E string. Seventh to the eighth fret. Then down to the ninth and tenth. We were on beat and in tune.

"Saw you on the sidewalk . . . lookin' pretty cute."

He sang farther away from the mike this time and it made a world of difference. You could actually hear his voice.

"How I wish you were . . . in your birthday suit!"

This line, the most intelligible one yet, was greeted with a handful of chuckles and hoots from the front row. I watched as Jared absorbed the sounds like nutrients. He almost cracked a smile as he launched into the bridge. And I could tell even before he sang a word that he was going to nail it. He took a long breath before his first perverse tirade, and then he was screaming in the Immanuel Methodist chapel about zapping girls' clothes off. His eyes were closed and he strummed like a lunatic on the five strings he had left. And as he sang about the shirts and skirts he wanted to remove, he pointed to different women in the audience. Not girls. But grown women.

I still had to look at my fingers while I played, but out of the corner of my eye, I could see more people from the pews getting up to leave. Each additional second the song played, someone else stood up and walked to the exit. But it wasn't disappointing. The show had never been for that audience. They were completely expendable. Irrelevant. The show was for us. And we still had twenty-five people at the front of the stage. They were nodding their heads and pumping their fists. They were clearly all intoxicated, with the lowest of standards, but it didn't matter. And when Jared got to the end of the first chorus, I leaned into the mike to sing it with him. I yelled as loud as I could.

"*'Cause I'm going mad. I'm going madddd. I'm going madddd up in my room.*"

It was not in tune. But it felt amazing.

"Just keep playing those notes," Jared yelled when I was close to him.

I nodded, and as I played the bass part for the chorus, Jared embarked on a squealing discordant guitar solo. He knelt down right in front of the crowd. Then he lay down completely on the stage. He bent the highest notes he could play, looking up at the gold cross and picking the strings. He writhed around on the ground, shaking and seizing. I stood above him, keeping the bass line going. I moved to the mike, and Jared stopped playing.

"*He's going mad,*" I sang. "*He's going mad.*"

My bass rumbled through the chapel.

"*I'm going mad!*" Jared screamed from the floor. "*I'm going mad!*"

"*He's going mad!*"

"*I'm going mad!*"

"*He's going mad!*"

"*I'm so horny!*"

"*He can't take it!*"

"*I'm the horniest man alive!*"

"*He's disgusting!*"

"*I'm a chronic masturbator!*"

In the midst of our improv yelling, I let my eyes wander the crowd again. Aside from the front row of hopping drunkards, there were only a handful of people left in the crowd. I saw the baton girl, watching and smiling. The dance team was at the very back, two of them covering their eyes. One middle-aged couple was inexplicably dancing in the aisle. But at the very back, standing in the doorway, was Janice Whitcomb.

She was staring right at me.

I thought at first it was a look of mortification and shame, in response to our performance. She was hard to see clearly from so far away. And my powers were too weak to read her. But after a couple of seconds, it didn't appear to me that she was even listening to our song. She was just watching me. And it wasn't shock or embarrassment. Her mouth was tight, and her eyes were blank. She was rubbing the end of her scarf between two fingers. I saw no images from the depths of her soul, but I understood anyway. It was a look of fear.

My fingers were going around and around, bouncing over the frets. I wasn't watching myself play anymore, but the notes kept coming. Meredith walked up behind her mother, and I saw her face over Janice's shoulder. She looked equally concerned.

"What are you doing?" Jared yelled from the floor. "Don't stop. That was awesome!"

The crowd nearest to us was still clapping. Jared rose.

"Something has happened," I said.

"What are you talking about?"

"I have to leave," I said.

I didn't say any more. I stopped playing, and Jared immediately started again, picking up the slack. I lifted the bass off my shoulders and laid it on the ground. It moaned out feedback from the floor. I hopped down into the aisle and the noise seemed to follow me as I plunged into the crowd. My ears hummed with it. The crew parted for me when I made it into their midst. I looked up into drunken laughter, sweaty T-shirts, and crooked teeth. I felt claps on my back, but I kept walking past our new fan club and past the few people left in the pews. Jared continued playing onstage. I didn't turn around to see what he was doing. I just proceeded up the red carpet toward Janice and Meredith. When I got to them, Janice reached out her hand and I took it. Her grip was ice-cold.

"You've seen her," I said.

Meredith stepped forward and put a hand on my arm.

"Something's really wrong."

"She won't go to the hospital," Janice said. "You have to talk to her."

The noise from Jared's guitar echoed around the room. Then I heard it come to an abrupt stop. My bass was still braying from the ground. We all looked at the stage. Jared stood there alone, his thick lenses reflecting the makeshift stage lights.

"Wait!" he yelled. "Wait for me, you dickheads!"

He pulled the guitar over his head and set it down next to mine.

"Thank you very much!" he yelled. "We're The Rash!"

The two instruments began a loud shouting conversation with each other. The crowd by the stage cheered and screamed. Jared bounded down into the thick of them, and the cheering got louder. A beer can flew through the air and crashed onto the stage, erupting in foam. Janice looked on without a word. Meredith watched with mild astonishment. Jared walked slowly down the aisle, but before he made it to us, he stopped in front of Holly Halverson, the baton girl. She stared at him, her eyes wide. Suddenly Jared slung an arm around her and pulled her toward him. She didn't resist, and he planted a big kiss right on her lips. Their eyes met for a moment after, but then he was running to us, leaving a dazed Holly behind in the chaos. The crowd was now shoving one another, clapping and screaming. The guitars were possessed.

"Where are we going?" asked Jared, smiling.

"Home," I said.

"To our house?" he asked.

"No," I said. "Back to the dome."

We watched everything in the chapel for one last moment. It looked like the place was on the verge of collapsing. We left to the sounds of the record clerk and his gang howling like wild dogs.

Outside, the air was clear. No snow this time. The van was waiting, already running. We piled in like usual, Meredith in the front, Jared and me in back. Janice adjusted her scarf and put the van in drive. The tires skidded over the sand on the asphalt before they caught and found some traction. The van lurched forward out of the lot, and I watched the small church recede behind me. The dim light through the stained glass cast an array of pastel colors on the grass. Warm air poured from the vents under the dash as we passed one block after another. Jared blew into his hands for the first few moments, then put his arm around my neck. He held it there tight.

"Did you hear them?" he said. "Did you hear the crowd when we left?"

He was grinning like a fool.

"I heard," I said.

"I can't believe it," he said. "I absolutely can't believe it."

We headed out of town and toward the hill above the town. Only moments ago we had been onstage, now we were in a speeding vehicle. It had all happened so fast. I felt stuck in two different moments. The roads were a little slick from melting ice, but Janice drove fast. I closed my eyes when an oncoming car came by. But there wasn't an image to be found in my head this time. No Nana. Nothing at all. Just an empty space where there had formerly been pictures. I shivered thinking about what this might indicate. My ears were still ringing, and I listened for any waves of communication in the air. I listened for a voice in the static.

"Did you see me smooch the baton girl?" asked Jared.

I didn't answer.

"I totally smooched the baton girl," he said.

He kept his hand on my shoulder, and squeezed.

33. See You Forever

THE BRIGHT BEAMS OF THE VAN'S HEADLIGHTS CREPT
slowly over the countries of the Geoscope before coming to rest
somewhere in South America. In the days of old, the gleam would
have illuminated the rooms of the dome like the inside of a city
bus; now it was impossible to tell what was happening in there. All
you could see was a bright blotch of Surf Green or Lavender Mist
and only the vague impression of something beyond. So it was
only when the headlights had been switched off and the dome was
dark again that I could detect the single light in Nana's bedroom. It
shone weakly at the back, like candlelight.

"Do you have any idea what's wrong with her?" I asked.

My hand was already gripping the door handle.

"Another stroke maybe," Janice said. "I don't know for sure. But
she needs attention. I could see that. She's in bad shape."

Janice looked straight back at me, and I was glad she was there.

"And she wants to speak to me. Is that correct?"

Meredith turned around and nodded. She looked right into my
eyes. I had never seen her so serious.

"I'll go in alone," I said. "Then we can call the ambulance. Just
let me talk to her by myself, first."

I looked at Jared. He blinked twice. I yanked the van door open and stepped out into the clear evening. Aside from the soft huff of the van, all was quiet. I crunched over the stiff grass and up to the door of the dome. It was unlocked, and the glass door swung open with a light push. The last time I had been inside the dome with Jared, everything had been covered in paint-stained plastic, but now all of that was gone, and the place looked much the way it had the last ten years. It was neat, all arranged, and it appeared to me now like a kind of museum exhibit for a race of humans that had never actually lived. Here was the future that had never come to be. It was all planned like a party, but nobody had showed up.

I drifted through it like a ghost, passing the sleek white leather couch and the NordicTrack. I paused when I reached the door to Nana's bedroom and pressed my ear to the wood. She didn't make a sound inside. My throat was so dry I could barely swallow. I wanted to open the door, but I was having a hard time getting my hand to make a move. I eventually pushed it half open. And that was enough. I saw Nana right away, lying on top of her bedspread in a mismatched tracksuit. Green on the bottom, pink on the top. She looked like a wilted flower.

Her head was propped on three pillows. Her shoes were on, unlaced. And she had lost weight somehow, become an even smaller human. The room smelled musty and dank; the thick odor of unwashed clothing and an unbathed body met me at the door. She had tried to cover it up with lavender and spice candles, but I nearly choked when I slipped into the room. She had her eyes closed. I swallowed a breath and spoke her name.

"Nana."

Her eyes flipped open, and she looked directly at me. It took her time to focus. But once she had me in her gaze, it took her even longer to blink. She didn't cry, or scream, or ask me any questions straight off. She just looked me over. Her eyes were bloodshot, her lids heavy. Finally she readjusted her pillows and pointed vaguely at my head with a lumbering swing of an arm.

"Your hair is too long," she said. "You need to be shorn."

Her voice was husky. I wondered if she had spoken to anyone else besides Janice while I was gone. How much had she spoken in any given day at all?

"You were the last one who cut it," I said.

She sighed and rolled over onto her side. And even though she was in this weakened state, I was still afraid of her. I could see her standing up any minute and chasing me from the dome, brandishing the crowbar she used with those high schoolers once. I pictured her hollering at me, dashing through the woodland.

"Everyone outside is worried about you," I said quietly. "They think you need to go to the hospital."

She made a harsh breathing noise and shooed at me.

"They don't know anything," she said.

"This isn't an emergency?" I asked.

"Negative," she said.

"You're not . . . dying?"

"Negative," she said. "Not in the next few hours at least."

I took another few steps into the room.

"What's happened?" I asked.

"Don't be so dramatic," she said. "Things haven't been the same since my collapse, you know that. But we don't need to speak about that yet. It's not as important as some other things."

"Like what?" I asked.

She reached for a nearby glass of water, but it was too far away. I went instinctively to the side of her bed and edged the glass closer. With a touch of her old quickness, she grabbed my fingers right when they left the glass. She squeezed them hard. "Like how you left me."

She held on tight, her thin hand in a viselike grip.

"You instructed me to leave," I said, nearly in a whisper.

The bones of my fingers pinched against one another.

"Did I?"

"You did."

"I think you knew what I really meant. But we can quibble over technicalities if that's what you desire."

She released my fingers and they throbbed with pain. But I didn't show it. I was ready to hear anything she was willing to say to me.

"So," she said next. "Tell me. What did you think about when you were out in the world?"

"What did I think about?"

"You must have had time to ruminate when you were gone. Free to do whatever you wanted. I imagine you have some questions you want to ask me."

"I suppose," I said.

I tried to look thoughtful, but in reality my mind was empty of everything. She didn't rush me, though. She just lay there, taking small sips of her water, leaving cloudy lip smudges on the side of the glass. The first question came out on its own.

"Why didn't you ever talk to me about my parents, Nana?"

Nana didn't look surprised or upset at all by the question. She looked, in fact, like she may have been expecting it. She took a long sip of water.

"I didn't want to impede your growth," she said. And for a moment I thought that was all she was going to say. But she took a breath and started again.

"Just tell me how were you supposed to innovate if you were

constantly stuck in a past you didn't even remember? What was I supposed to do? Torture you every day with memories? Is that what a kind guardian does? Just tell me if you think that's true."

Already, her voice was growing sharper and more confident. I simply shook my head.

"You disagree with me. That's fine. I tried to do what was best. Now I guess you'll shake your head at all my ideas and everything will be erased."

"That's not true."

"But it is true. This is my punishment. I see that now."

"Your punishment for what?"

"Ask me another question," she said.

I looked around at the countries on Nana's side of the dome. From the inside they looked like colorful camouflage. I walked over to the glass and reached my hand out to touch it. "Was my father like me?" I asked. "Was he supposed to take over all of this?"

She thought a moment this time. Or at least she was surprised enough to take pause. "Yes," she said eventually. "He was like you."

"How?"

"Obstinate. That's how he was. Just like you. And always plotting. Also . . . he looked like you. His face was similar. Thin with those sad eyes."

"Nana . . ."

"And he broke my heart every day he was alive."

I turned around. She set down her water glass, and her arm was shaking.

"Just like you," she said. "He was supposed to lead the next stage. But he chose not to. He could have been brilliant."

She closed her eyes, and I walked back to the bed and sat down on the edge. She didn't touch me. "Ask me something else," she said in a quieter voice. "Just keep asking, please. For now. Can you do that?"

I tried to steel myself. I swallowed. Each breath was harder than the last.

"What happened with Bucky?"

She almost sat up, but lost a little strength on the way and readjusted herself on her pillows. Her eyes moved from my face down to her hands.

"You really want to know?"

I nodded.

"Listen," she said. "Listen to me closely."

She paused a second to look at the visible walls of her Geoscope, like she might find the story written there. I waited on the edge of the bed. Her eyes swept over the ceiling as she began to speak.

"You already know that I met him when he came to Edwardsville," she began. "And it was the single most exhilarating time of my life. It changed me entirely. He was an old man by that time, but he was still a whirlwind of energy. A spark plug of a man, glasses as thick as agate. When he spoke, he seemed like a bright impetuous child, and he loved explaining his ideas to young people, you see."

She was smiling now, already transported.

"I was a secretary in the department of Religious Education at the time. He came into the department office one day and simply introduced himself to me. He talked for over an hour about how young people like me were going to be the ones who solved all of humanity's problems. There was enough ingenuity and imagination to transform all of humanity into a prosperous race, he told me. All it was going to take was the right pressure from young people to make it happen. He ended our first meeting by asking me to help him and his assistants with the planning and organizing of his new architectural project. It would be a Geoscope prototype built onto the top of the new auditorium."

"A Geoscope?" I said. "I thought you said he never built it."

"He never built the one he wanted," she said. "But he built this first one. I was there for every step of the process, from the drafting to the construction. And during that time, I fell in love with him. I dreamed so many times that he would discover me, and fall in love with me, too. But he never did. He never even remembered my name."

"I don't understand, Nana," I said. "You were never . . . involved? I thought you said that you were going to move to New York. You were perfect for each other."

She closed her eyes. "I'm afraid these are just fantasies I've indulged over the years, Sebastian. I wish things had happened that way. But they didn't."

It took me a moment to digest this information, and all it explained. I could barely move. But I chose to speak again before I lost my nerve.

"I always wondered," I said, "if he was my grandfather."

She sat up the best she could. She looked weaker now. Just this brief conversation looked to have drained her energy. "I never told you that," she said.

"I thought you were waiting to tell me."

She smiled. "I wanted to give you hope," she said. "I wanted you to be great."

There were tears in her eyes now.

"Then who was my father's father?" I asked. "If it wasn't him."

"One of his assistants," she said. "One of Bucky's assistants on the SIU project. A man named Alden. He was intelligent, too, in his own way, but not dynamic like Bucky. He was more introspective, I suppose. Tall and thin with the saddest eyes imaginable. He taught architecture. After Bucky was gone, we had a brief affair. I was in shambles. But he inspired me to go back to college, to study architecture. I was going to show Bucky what he had missed. Alden helped me get into school, but he left soon after to return to his job. He never believed the baby was his."

I wanted to press her for more details, everything she knew about the man, but she was beginning to seem so frail again.

"Do you have a photograph?" I asked instead.

"Go to my closet," she said, "and find my book of clippings."

I did as I was told, rummaging through her files and the pieces of old models until I found the mahogany-colored book that housed newspaper scraps about a project of hers. I brought the book to her and she opened it up to the very first page. There was a black-and-white newsprint photo there that I had never seen. It was a picture of Bucky and his crew eating lunch in a park. Across the bench from Bucky was Nana, dressed in a flowing summer dress, her hair long and curly. Bucky was grinning at the camera, and Nana was shielding her eyes from the sun. But then, I noticed another man.

Seated next to Nana, nearly concealed by her outstretched hand, was a slim man with a hunched posture. His face was kind and bland all except for his eyes, which managed to convey ten emotions at once even in the blur of the dated picture. I couldn't believe I hadn't noticed him right away. He was so clearly related to me, so clearly my grandfather. He had a mustache and it was even groomed similarly to the way my father's was in the photo I'd nearly left in the Immanuel bathroom. They could have been brothers, not father and son. And if I had sat down next to them, I might have passed for the youngest.

"That's him," I said when this daze wore off.

"Yes," said Nana.

I looked at the caption: *Buckminster Fuller. Josephine Prendergast. Alden Hewitt.*

"I wanted you to save the world, Sebastian," she said. "That's why I lied. I'm not a horrible person. Am I?"

I lay back now, close to her, just the way we used to be when I was five. I ignored the smell of the sheets and pulled her light blanket up over me.

"No," I said. "But I'm not going to save the world, Nana. You must know that by now."

She didn't say anything for a while. We stayed next to each other. The bed had been cold when I first got in, but my body was warming it up.

"I might be saving a family, though," I said.

She took my hand, and didn't squeeze this time.

"I suppose that's something," she said.

She just rested her palm over mine. I gave her some of the blanket and she tucked it around herself. "It took everything I had left to finish the Geoscope," she said. "Every last bit. I haven't been feeling well for some time, Sebastian. Months really. The stroke was the last sign. I don't have much earthly time left."

I sat up. "But you haven't been diagnosed with anything," I said. "The doctors haven't told you anything."

She smiled. "Specialists," she said. "They can't see the forest for the trees."

I stared at her. I wrapped her in a tight hug, and I could feel her ribs. She was wasting away. Her skin felt cool and dry.

"I hung on as long as I could for you," she said.

"It's okay," I said. "I know. Just go to sleep, for tonight."

"I will," she said.

Then I heard a noise and we both looked up. In the doorway

stood the Whitcombs, all aligned. Janice stood in front, watching my grandmother and me. Jared and Meredith were behind her, looking around our dome, slightly mesmerized.

"Is everything okay?" asked Janice.

She stayed just outside the room.

"Yes," I said.

Jared and Meredith walked up to their mother's side. They looked more like children than they ever had before. I had never thought of either of them as shy, but both were speechless now, almost clinging to their mother.

"Nana," I said. "I'd like you to meet the Whitcomb family."

They all stayed frozen like mannequins on display. Nana looked at each one of them and nodded.

"That's my friend Jared," I said, pointing. "And my friend Meredith. And you know Mrs. Whitcomb."

I glanced at all of them. "Whitcombs," I said, "this is my Nana. Her real name is Josephine."

Everyone stared at one another for a quiet moment. Then Meredith spoke, shifting in place. "Nice to meet you, ma'am," she said.

"Yeah," said Jared. "Hi."

Nana smiled politely.

"I have to rest now," she said. "I'm sorry. But thank you for caring . . . for my boy."

The Whitcombs all looked at me. Janice, I could sense, was still waiting for a signal, waiting to call the hospital. All I needed to do was say the word. Meredith and Jared were, perhaps, waiting for me to beg to come back home with them.

"You're welcome," Janice said. "He's a terrific young man."

Nana nodded, half asleep.

"I can show you out now," I said. "I'll stay here tonight."

Nana tried a few times to blink her eyes open but they finally fell shut. Her breathing was loud and long. I left her bedside and guided the Whitcombs to the front door.

"Are you sure you don't need a doctor?" asked Janice.

"She's made the decision to stay home," I said. "And I'm going to stay with her. It's her choice."

She reached out and put a hand on my back. She held it there a few seconds, then she rushed forward and nearly strangled me with one last hug. She pressed me tight and I held my breath. "Please don't disappear," she said, speaking over my shoulder. "Please."

"I won't," I said.

She held me another moment and then let go. I stood just a foot or two away. I thought for sure she would start crying, but she looked very calm. Her face was still. She touched my arm. "If you need any help," she said, "I want you to call me. I want you to call and tell me about it. Anytime. Even if you just want to ask a simple question or talk about something from your day. Will you do that? Promise me you will."

"I will," I said.

"It's okay to ask people for help," she said. "That's how life works."

She smiled and put her hands into her pockets. She exhaled, and I watched her breath turn to fog in the air. She looked like she didn't know what to say next.

"I just want you to tell me one more time that you'll be okay," she said. "I need to hear it once more, then I promise I'll walk away."

Her eyes searched my face, resting on my eyes.

"I'll be okay, Janice," I said. "Really."

She pushed a strand of hair aside. Then, true to her promise, she turned around and commenced walking back to the van. Her arms swished against her wool coat as she walked. Her stride was perfectly steady across the lawn.

"Mrs. Whitcomb!" I shouted out. "Thank you for everything!"

She didn't turn around.

"She knows," said Jared.

"He's right," said Meredith. "She does."

Mrs. Whitcomb stepped into her van, and even through the tinting, I could see her adjusting the heat, and holding the wheel with gloved hands, waiting for her children. Jared and Meredith both looked up at my home, curving up into the dark sky.

"You're a crazy bastard, Sebastian," Jared said. "A real loony. I don't think I'll ever be allowed back in that church, and you helped make that happen."

"I guess I did," I said.

He adjusted his glasses and fumbled around in the pockets of his leather jacket. He pulled something from deep inside. It was his music player, the white headphones wrapped around it, the Buckminster Fuller sticker still affixed to the front. He held it out to me. "Take it," he said.

I just looked at it.

"Why?" I asked.

"Here's what we're going to do," he said. "I'm going to pass this to you, and we're not going to say good-bye or anything. This is just the last time I see you for a little while. So we don't need to say it. I'm just . . . I'll just sort of hand this to you, and if you take it that means good-bye for a little while, okay? It means that we'll see each other soon and record a tape and hang out and talk about what school is like. You get it, or do I have to write this all down?"

"I understand," I said.

He held it out again. I looked at him. He met my stare with a purely businesslike look. But he adjusted his glasses once and then a second time. I extended my hand and took the music player. Jared let go of it and then it was in my palm. Right after the transaction, he stepped out onto the lawn, looking over the dome again. He shook his head and then walked back to the van. He slid open the door and disappeared inside. As he moved to the back, I lost sight of him completely.

Which left Meredith standing in front of me. She looked at the ground in front of her and coughed. She smiled and then frowned immediately after.

"So are you really going to be all right in there?" she asked.

"Yeah," I said. "It's my home."

"Okay then," she said.

She stepped toward me. "I guess I don't have much else to say then."

"You don't?"

"Well," she said, "I did want to tell you that I thought your last song was pretty good. That's the only one I heard. And your hair looked great. That was probably the best part of all of it."

"Thanks," I said.

"And I guess I want to tell you that I'm going to keep an eye out for you," she said.

"Where?" I asked.

"Outside," she said. "To see if you're spying on me."

She smiled.

"What happens if I am?" I asked.

She shrugged. "Then, we'll just have to see what happens."

She gave me a hug then, a real one. There was no kiss at the end, but of course Janice was sitting right in the van. The hug was good enough. It was warm and not too short, and I realized that I had never actually hugged her before. I'd only kissed her and touched one of her breasts. Maybe it was finally time for an embrace of sorts. When she let me go, she turned away slowly and tromped over the yard. And before I could think of anything to yell after her, something perfectly romantic, she was in the van. I couldn't see her or Jared so I just held up my hand.

Janice was already pulling out of the driveway and back down Hillsboro Drive, the way she arrived the first day I met her. The van sprayed a little slush off to the sides, and made a noise like it was fording a shallow river. Its brake lights glowed cherry red when it slowed into the first turn. And I watched them fade in the distance. I shivered a little, and then stepped back inside. I took a deep gulp of warm air, and locked the front door behind me. Then I wandered through the dome. Above me the sky spread out over the North Pole. I could just barely make out a crescent moon above it all, and a couple of dim stars. The sky was bright the way it was when I first brought the bass guitar home.

Nana was asleep in her room. I checked to see if she was breathing okay. She was. I felt her forehead. She didn't have a temperature. I turned out the bedside light in her room. I heard her mumble something to me in the dark.

"You're back," she said "I sense you. You're back."

"I'm here," I said. "I'm back, Nana."

She quieted, and when I was sure she was done speaking, I left her room and closed the door. I stood there holding the handle, and then made myself let go. I walked to the foot of the stairs. And then I walked up them, growing tired myself now. There was still a faint buzz in my ears from the show. And I wondered who had eventually unplugged the instruments. The bass was back in its home, I guessed. If I wanted to play again, I would have to procure one of my own. There would be no more stealing. No more lying. If there was a Greater Intellect, at least he knew I'd kept my promise. I'd returned the bass when I was done with it.

I felt for Jared's music player in my pocket and gripped it tight. Then I walked into my classroom and turned on the light. I let out a small gasp. Sitting on the desk was the computer that Nana had discarded into the forest. It was sitting there, broken, the screen cracked. In front of it was a small piece of notebook paper with my e-mail address written on it. Nana had tried to contact me. She had tried to hook up the broken machine. I sat down at the desk and stared at my dark reflection in the shattered screen. I rested my fingers on the keys. I typed a message into nowhere. A message no one would read.

It said, "Hello, out there. My name is Sebastian. Things are fine for now on Spaceship Earth."

I flipped off the light and went back into my bedroom, where Nana had prepared everything for my return. My bed was made. My clothes were folded. She must have done it all before she fell ill again. I walked over to the northeast side of the dome where I peeked through the clear space of the Mediterranean Sea out at my view of the town. I looked at the few last lights on in the town. I searched, too, for the Whitcombs' van winding its way through the streets, but I couldn't see it in the darkness.

Tomorrow, I would scale the dome in the morning again if it wasn't too cold. I suddenly found myself missing that weightless feeling. That sense of wonder, hanging suspended in the sky. I'd experienced a version of it playing music, but it wasn't quite the same. Nothing was the same as seeing it all from a great height like that. It looked like an ideal world from up there. And before I had experienced it, I assumed it was. Now I could see why Nana created her own world entirely, as the paper said. But that didn't mean I had to do the same.

I got into my old bed and lay looking up at the night sky for a while until my eyes started to burn. I had no idea how much longer

Nana would be alive. Maybe days. Maybe weeks. The more I thought about her condition, the way she looked in that bed, the more I was inclined to take her at her word. A body was composed of energy, and when it stopped making energy, there wasn't much you could do. Even Buckminster Fuller eventually had to die. He did it just before his eighty-eighth birthday, on July 1, 1983. His wife was in a coma, and she never regained consciousness. She died thirty-six hours after he did. Was he sending her messages telling her to join him?

Among other things, he left behind a detailed autobiography and catalog of his ideas, though, called The Chronofile. When it was finished, it held over seven hundred volumes. And it weighed ninety thousand pounds. It mapped the progress of his entire life. From his first invention of a cone-tipped oar for his childhood rowboat, to the creation of pioneering spherical structures and new forms of geometry, The Chronofile pieced together every aspect of his life. It covered everything, every thought he ever had. But it never mentioned Nana.

Really, though, she didn't need anyone else to tell her story. She would leave behind her own legacy, the first Geoscope in the state of Iowa. I took one last look at it now before putting on Jared's headphones, nestling the small earbuds in tightly. I scrolled through all the songs, the glow of the screen on my face. I had no idea what I would leave behind when my time came. But it didn't matter. I was only on the first chapter of my Chronofile. I was barely out of the prologue. And now in the soft blue dark of my room at the top of the dome, I pressed the random key on the music player. I lay back. I closed my eyes. And I braced myself for the noise.

ACKNOWLEDGMENTS

Thank you first to my early writing teachers Wang Ping and Stuart McDougal, for telling me to give this a try. And to my later teachers Edward Carey, Elizabeth McCracken, Frank Conroy, Ethan Canin, Adam Haslett, Chris Offutt, James McPherson, and ZZ Packer, for your unbelievable breadth of knowledge and guidance. Thank you to everyone at the University of Iowa MFA program—especially Connie Brothers, Deb West, and Jan Zenisek.

A gigantic thank-you to Julie Barer, the best agent on earth (and a great editor, too). Another enormous one to Amy Einhorn, a dream editor and publisher. And to everyone at Amy Einhorn Books and Putnam.

Without the careful reading of Nick Dybek and Brad Liening, this book wouldn't be what it is. Tarik Karam was his usual bundle of energy and unwavering support. Thanks to Alex Albright, my earliest fan. And to Denis Hildreth, who let me write a play when I was eighteen. Thanks to Dick Cohn for getting me into a dome. And Blair Wolfram for building so many. And thanks to all my old bandmates, who helped me learn to play unlistenable songs on the guitar when I was young and angry.

Thank you to Macalester College, where I teach with wonderful colleagues and amazing students.

It's impossible to thank my family enough. Kathy Bognanni, thanks for bringing home half the collection of your library for me over the years. Sal Bognanni, thank you for your love of literature and your contagious sense of humor. Mark, thanks for reading my fiction when you were supposed to be studying. And thank you to the rest of my family, the Bognannis and the Rhynas clan, for all the love and encouragement from day one.

Finally, to Junita, I suspect you know by now that I write primarily to make you smile. Thank you for reading every draft, every change, every typo. Without you, this novel wouldn't exist. And neither would my confidence to write.

ABOUT THE AUTHOR

Peter Bognanni is a recent graduate of the Iowa Writers' Workshop, where he was awarded a teaching/writing fellowship for his work. His short fiction and humor pieces have appeared in *Gulf Coast*, *The Bellingham Review*, and McSweeney's Internet Tendency. He is a 2008 Pushcart nominee, and his short story "The Body Eternal" was chosen by Stephen King as one of the "100 Most Distinguished Stories of 2006" in *Best American Short Stories*. He is currently a visiting instructor of creative writing at Macalester College in Saint Paul, Minnesota. He once played in a terrible high-school punk band.